The Tethered World

The Tethered World Chronicles

The Tethered World

Book One of
The Tethered World Chronicles

Heather L.L. FitzGerald

The Tethered World
Published by Mountain Brook Ink
White Salmon, WA U.S.A.

The website addresses recommended throughout this book are offered as a resource. These websites are not intended in any way to be or imply an endorsement on the part of Mountain Brook Ink, nor do we vouch for their content.

This story is a work of fiction. All characters and events are the product of the author's imagination. Any resemblance to any person, living or dead, is coincidental.

Scripture quotations are taken from the King James Version of the Bible. Public domain.

ISBN 978-09960068-9-7
© 2016 Heather L. L. FitzGerald

The Team: Miralee Ferrell, Susan Marlow, Nikki Wright, Laura Heritage
Cover Design: Indie Cover Design, Lynnette Bonner Designer

Mountain Brook Ink is an inspirational publisher offering fiction you can believe in.

Map illustration by William Love@sevenoversix.com

Printed in the U.S.A. 2016

This book is dedicated to you, Dad. Thanks for passing along your creative imagination and love of story. If there's a library in heaven, I hope you can read my novel while you sip on the best cup of coffee in the universe. Miss you.

Then I heard every creature in heaven and on earth and **under the earth**... saying: "To him who sits on the throne and to the Lamb be praise and honor and glory and power, for ever and ever!"
Revelation 5:13

*This is a work of fiction from a Christian worldview. The ideas are strictly from the author's imagination, portraying what might be possible in places that Scripture is silent.

**A cast of characters' list with descriptions is provided at the end of this book for your convenience.

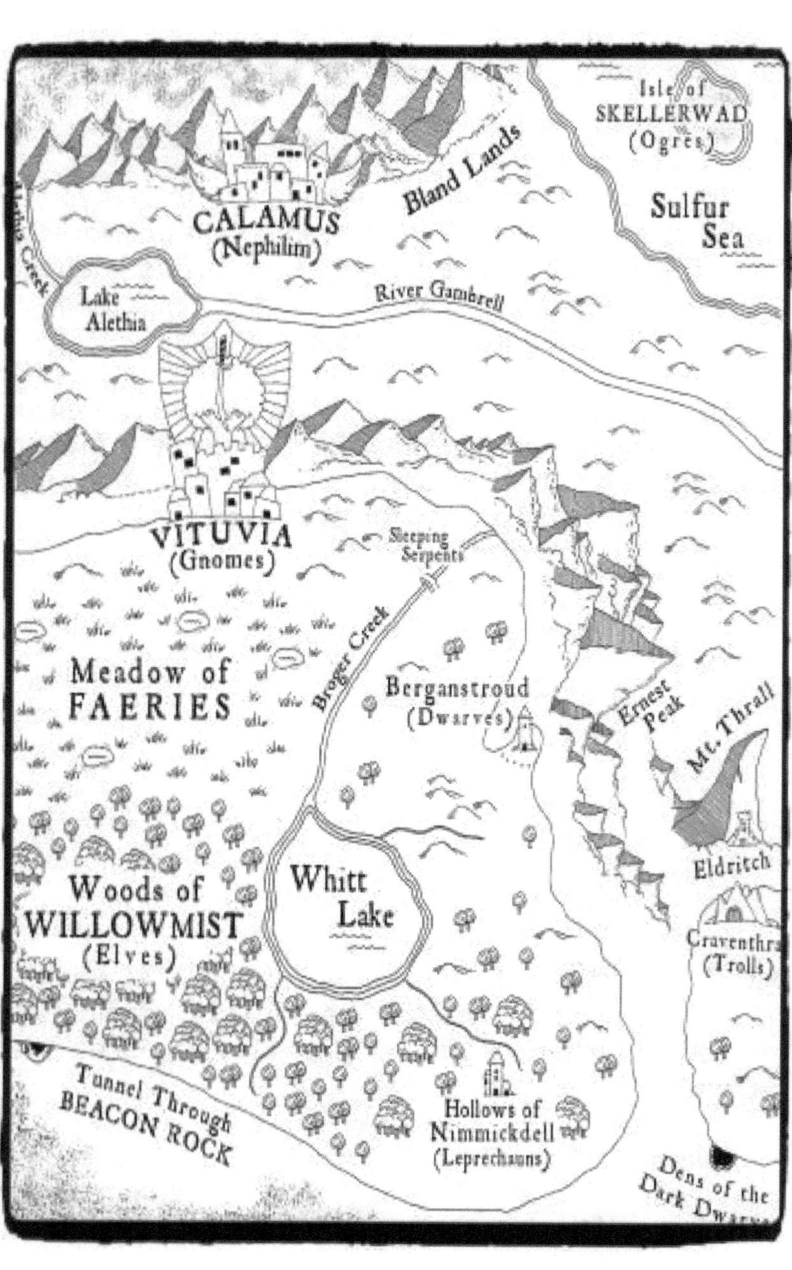

Isle of
SKELLERWAD
(Ogres)
Sulfur
Sea
Bland Lands
CALAMUS
(Nephilim)
Lake
Alethia
River Gambrell
VITUVIA
(Gnomes)
Sleeping
Serpents
Meadow of
FAERIES
Broger Creek
Berganstroud
(Dwarves)
Ernest
Peak
Mt. Thrall
Eldritch
Woods of
WILLOWMIST
(Elves)
Whitt
Lake
Craventhr
(Trolls)
Tunnel Through
BEACON ROCK
Hollows of
Nimmickdell
(Leprechauns)
Dens of the
Dark Dwarves

CHAPTER ONE

THE POUNDING WOULDN'T STOP. A PERSISTENT sound in my dream became an alarm that jolted me awake. I sat up, blinked against the darkness, and listened. Was that someone at the door or my pulse throbbing through my cranium?

The absurd time that glowed from the clock only added to my confusion. Friends don't swing by at three o'clock in the morning—if they want to remain my friends—and Santa doesn't make house calls in June. I couldn't come up with a good reason for anyone to be at the door, or why I'd want to answer it. But the silent house insisted that no one else heard a thing. *For real? I'm the one who has to miss my beauty sleep?*

"Ugh." I rolled out of bed, grabbed my robe, and made a beeline to my parents' bedroom. "Mom, Dad, someone's at the door."

Bam-bam-bam.

Banging loud enough to wake the dead. But not loud enough to wake the rest of the family. I guess it was up to me to find out what was going on.

The downside of being a light sleeper.

"Clark County Sheriff's Department. Anyone home?"

I popped my head into their dark room. "The police are here. Wake up!"

Adrenaline spiked. The police? I barreled down the stairs. My socks hit the tile and sent me skidding to the front door. I winked an eye at the peephole and flipped on the outside light. Brass and blue muddled in warped shapes, but I made out two officers blinking up at the overhead light.

"Just a minute." I turned and hoped to find my parents plodding down the stairs, half asleep. Instead, the bleak stairwell meant I better make a judgment call—and quick. Police officers seemed like a safe bet.

I unfastened all three deadbolts and the lock on the knob. With a jerk, the door opened as far as the chain allowed. Clearing my throat, I put on my best authoritative voice. "May I see some ID?" Hey, it worked for people on television.

A French-manicured hand slipped into the gap and flashed an official-looking badge inscribed with *Clark County Sheriff's Department, Dedicated to Serve and Protect*. An attractive blonde stared through the laminate. *Officer Pamela McKenzie*.

"Hang on." I worked the chain off its latch then opened the door enough to get a look at the early morning visitors.

"Is this the Larcen residence?" asked a burly man with a heavy mustache and eyebrows to match. Correction: just one eyebrow. The man had the biggest unibrow I'd ever seen.

"Yes, sir. I'm Sadie." I tried not to stare. Funny how your mind can make random observations, even in the midst of strange situations. I found myself comparing the man's unibrow to Bert's from *Sesame Street*. Bert's was definitely smaller.

"I'm Lieutenant James Garrett, and this is Deputy McKenzie." He waved calloused fingers between the two of them. "Do you own a white Honda Odyssey van?"

I nodded. "My parents do. What seems to be the problem?" I nabbed that line from TV too.

"We found an Odyssey abandoned in an empty lot next to Burgerville." The blonde had a cheerleader smile, complete with pink lip gloss and dimples. Not the stereotypical cop with skills for taking down felons. "The lights were on, the door wide open, which seemed odd since it's raining."

Drips from the overhang splatted behind the officers like sound effects on demand. I watched the water plop to the ground while my mind weighed their words. With a gazillion white Odysseys on the road, I felt sure they'd confused our van with one of the others. Pulling my robe tight against the damp air, I stepped across the cement to get a view of the driveway.

The *empty* driveway.

I turned to the officers. "Whoa! Our van *is* gone."

"Yes, miss, that's why we came by." Lt. Garrett offered a condescending grin. "McKenzie, here, looked around for signs of the driver while I ran the plates to see if it'd been reported stolen. Course, when a vehicle is jacked in the middle of the night, most people are fast asleep. We felt it best to come and check. Oh, and the deputy found this."

The man dug something out of his back pocket. He presented me with a plastic sandwich bag that held a filthy pocket knife. He plunked it in my palm.

I held it near the light for a better look. "That's my dad's pocket knife. Guess he left it in the van."

The blonde gave a curt nod. "I found it lying in the mud, blade exposed, near the driver's door. And the van looked suspicious, y'know? Way back towards the woods in the middle of a soggy night with the door open. Lots of red flags."

Dumbstruck, I ran a hand through my brunette tangles. Who would want our van? Why not the neighbor's Lexus? Besides, it looked like a pigsty. We could survive for a week on the stale food that garnished the inside.

"Miss, are your parents home?" The deputy peered into the silent house.

I nodded and stepped back into the foyer. "You can wait in here. I'll wake them. They must've stayed up late if they're sleeping through this noise."

The officers stepped inside.

"What's with all the deadbolts?" Officer Unibrow—aka Lt. Garrett—stared at our collection when the door closed.

"Uh, my brother. He sleepwalks. If you want, you can wait in the living room." I gestured towards the room on the right and took the steps two at a time.

Our van...stolen! I cringed to think of some creep slinking around our house while we slept. Maybe now Dad would allow our dogs to stay out of their kennels at night. I bet their barking would've scared the thief away.

"Hey, Mom! Dad!" I tapped the doorframe with my knuckle. "Wake up. The police are downstairs." I groped along to my mother's side of the bed. My hand sank down to the mattress when I reached to give her a shake.

"Wha...?" I straightened and switched on the bedside lamp.

The light didn't reveal what I expected. Dad and Mom were gone. Not sleeping as they should be. Not momentarily out of bed grabbing a midnight snack. The bed was made, throw pillows in place. An envelope with my name scrawled across it in blue marker lay front and center.

Confusion rummaged around my brain. I stepped back, trying to make sense of things. My foot caught the corner of the nightstand just right, and I toppled into the lamp with a yelp. Like a chain reaction, it tipped onto a framed photo and shattered the glass lamp base. The bulb blew as it tumbled off the nightstand, raining a stack of books on my feet.

I stared into the void, too dazed to move.

Footsteps bounded up the stairs. Both officers rushed through the door, guns drawn, flashlight beams sweeping the room. They targeted my face, blinding me. I squealed and backed into the wall, hands up. They do that on TV too, which I discovered is a natural reaction.

"Are you all right, miss?" The lieutenant shined the flashlight around the room. "We heard quite a commotion."

My insides were mush. My legs shook, and I sank to

my knees. "I'm okay. But I don't know what happened to my parents. They're gone."

They holstered their guns. The woman flipped on the light switch.

Lt. Garrett craned his neck and scrutinized the room. "I see no evidence of foul play."

Deputy McKenzie helped me up. "Sorry, didn't mean to scare you."

"I'm fine. Thanks." Fine as I can be with missing parents and police pointing guns in my face.

I walked to the bed and snatched the envelope. "Definitely not foul play. They left a note. I couldn't wake them, so I turned on the light. When I discovered they were gone—like, totally not here—I somehow tripped and knocked everything over. Sorry."

"Very understandable, Miss…Larcen?" Lt. Garrett continued to inspect the room.

"Yes, Larcen. Sadie Larcen."

The blonde took out her notepad and scribbled something. "Your last name is spelled L-A-R-C-E-N, like larceny, the crime, right?"

"Yes."

The officers looked at each other and shrugged.

"That's a new one." McKenzie pointed to the letter. "Why don't you read the note? It seems odd that, if they wanted to get away, they'd leave their car next to Burgerville with the lights on and door open."

My trembling fingers worked the flap open on the envelope.

Lt. Garrett studied our family picture on the wall. "Big family."

"Yes, sir."

"There're three, four, five, six—*six* of you kids? No wonder your parents wanted to escape in the middle of the night." He lifted his hat and scratched his head. "Good grief."

Although being the oldest of six made *me* want to run away sometimes, I didn't recall asking for his opinion. *Since you have a gun, I guess I'll let that slide.*

I unfolded the letter, aware of the officers waiting for

an explanation. My mother's voice filtered through her handwriting while I read the note to myself:

> *My Darling Sadie,*
> *Good morning! I know you're probably shocked to find Dad and I aren't home. I was called away on business and didn't want to wake you. Dad needed to come with me too. (Hey, there's a first time for everything!)*
> *I've contacted Great-aunt Jules to come and stay while we're away. She'll help you hold down the fort. Of course, she couldn't leave on such short notice so it may be a day or two before she arrives. You're in charge until she gets here.*
> *I can't say for certain when we'll be home. About a week, I'm guessing. In the meantime, keep everyone on a regular schedule, keep doing school, and don't forget about karate for the boys.*
> *Speaking of the boys, I really need you to keep a close eye on Brock. Closer than usual. Make sure those locks are in place on every door. I'd hate for there to be a sleepwalking incident while we're gone. Plus, keeping him on his schedule avoids needless frustration for everyone—as you know.*
> *I'll call when I can. Give Aunt Jules a hug from Dad and me. Of course, give all the kiddos a big snuggle and tell them we love them and we'll see them soon!*
> *Love you,*
> *Mom (and Dad)*

"Well?" Officer Unibrow pointed a thick finger at the paper. "Does the note clear things up?"

"I guess." I sat on the end of the bed. "My mom travels for work sometimes. But it's never happened in the middle of the night, and she's never taken my dad."

"What does she do?" The deputy tucked a loose tendril behind her ear.

Ah, the dreaded question. One that I tried to avoid. "My mother is a leading expert on Sasquatch. You know...Bigfoot."

Four eyebrows shot up—well, make that three—and four feet took a step back. The officers looked at me like I'd sprouted a set of antlers.

I shrugged. Though I tried to keep this odd, family fact from surfacing, there were times, like this, when it worked to my advantage. "Yep. That's what she does."

Then I decided to really freak them out. "She's also an expert on Faeries, Trolls, Leprechauns, Dwarves, and Elves. She has a blog."

Stunned silence.

"Although," I continued, "that doesn't explain why my dad would go along. He's a hairdresser. Okay— cosmetologist. Maybe he wanted to give Bigfoot some highlights or something. Who knows?" A combination of the late night and crazy circumstance made me a bit testy. *They can't arrest me for that, right?*

"A hairdresser." Lt. Garrett frowned.

"He owns the Camas School of Cosmetology. CSC for short. He hardly does hair anymore, though, except when he teaches a class." *Maybe he could wax that brow for you sometime. Soon.*

"I see."

"So, your parents' van." The blonde tapped her pen against her pouty, lower lip. "You think they got out and left it to hunt down Bigfoot?"

"Seems that way. Maybe that's why my dad decided to go along. Usually, my mom catches a flight somewhere, you know, more isolated. People call her or email with pictures and stories. If it sounds legit, then she hops a plane and goes to investigate."

"I'm curious." Lt. Garrett leaned towards me. "Has she ever seen one?"

"Oh yes. Several times."

"Really?" He looked doubtful.

"Really." It seemed likely the elusive, wooly Yetis

might be his distant relatives. Their whole body merely one, giant unibrow.

"May I read the note?" Deputy McKenzie extended her hand.

"Sure." While she scanned it, I couldn't help noting her resemblance to a life-size Barbie. The two officers were like Beauty and the Beast.

"It says 'keep doing school.' Do you guys homeschool?"

Oh, joy. A second awkward question in under five minutes. "Yes, ma'am."

She gave her partner *the look*. I've seen it a hundred times. It's the look that says, "Oh, you're one of *those.*" She made no attempt to be subtle.

"Well, I guess we're finished here." Deputy Barbie doll handed back the paper. "The van can't stay where it is, though. It's illegally parked."

They turned businesslike. You would think the plague had descended on the house, and the officers wanted to escape contamination.

I stood. "If you give me a minute to change, I can drive it home."

The deputy gave me a skeptical look. "Do you have a license?"

"Yes. I'm sixteen."

She looked at her partner. "Want me to keep an eye on things here until Miss Larcen returns?"

Unibrow nodded. "Probably a good idea with all the kids asleep."

"All right." McKenzie stuffed her pen into her pocket. "Bring your ID. I'll be waiting by the cruiser."

Throwing on sweats and flip-flops, I contemplated waking my brother Brady to explain the crisis. It didn't strike me that Beauty and the Beast would want to wait for that to happen. Since Brady slept through the commotion to this point, he'd surely snooze through the next ten minutes.

I locked the front door and jogged to the police car. The deputy held the door while I climbed inside. From the vantage point of a bulletproof backseat it was hard not to feel guilty of something. *I confess, I'm a homeschooler. Beware! I'm weird and unsocialized.*

At least my curious, late-night activity would go unnoticed by our neighbors. Hopefully. You never could tell with Mr. Marshall, World's Nosiest Neighbor. The man seemed to constantly peer from his blinds, cigar in hand, watching the world go by.

We pulled away from the curb, leaving Deputy McKenzie on the front porch. She clenched a flashlight between her pearly-whites and flipped open her notebook. If Mr. Marshall was awake, I hoped he enjoyed the show.

The tinted windows and concensation prevented me from seeing a thing, so I put a call through to my parents. Both numbers went straight to voicemail. I decided to leave a *safe* message—skipping over the cops coming by and hearing our life story. Without an explanation of how I knew where to find the van, I told them I would pick it up. They could call when they needed a ride home.

The water rivulets that ran across the glass reflected the maze of thoughts weaving through my brain. This whole scenario didn't sit right. Such an odd place for my parents to pursue this reclusive legend. Bigfoot spotted at the local fast-food joint? Really? And if so, what would make them leave the van like that?

I leaned my head against the cool, clouded window and closed my eyes. Too many questions—and not enough answers—meant things didn't quite add up.

CHAPTER TWO

Back at the house, I piddled around downstairs to keep myself distracted. Cleaned up. Washed dishes. Started a load of laundry. Tried to convince myself that chasing down Sasquatch *could* be a normal, midnight activity—for someone like my mom. And maybe sketchy guys that live in the woods and rarely bathe while they track the urban legend.

With a shake of my head, I attempted to keep my thoughts from veering into cynical territory. Minus my mother's strange hobby turned job, I would nominate her for Mother of the Year in a heartbeat. Let's just say that being homeschooled means I don't have to worry about Mom visiting my class on Career Day. Explaining her interest in mythical creatures always comes off like telling people my mom lives in her own little world. She plays pretend. All the time.

Not that my dad's profession falls into the *typical* category. But society at large has certainly heard of a career in cosmetology.

Apprehension dragged me back to our minivan. I poked around to see if anything stood out from the ordinary. It didn't take much effort to find napkins sporting the Burgerville logo, but who knew when those things had hitched a ride? Our family hit the drive-thru all the time.

Other than a damp seat, thanks to the rain, nothing alerted my attention. Nothing seemed out of place, though everything was a typical mess. If any clues lurked about, they were camouflaged in the chaos.

It felt creepy being outside in the dark. Alone. Mr. Marshall was no doubt up by now and had his eye on me. I found that comforting in a weird way. Perhaps nosy neighbors had their own special place in the world.

Still...I slid out of the Odyssey and zoomed inside, stopping to lock, lock, lock the front door. My heart thumped a spastic rhythm. I forced myself to take slow, deliberate breaths. *I'm overreacting. Shake it off.*

I decided to curb my paranoia by digging into something logical—math. I loaded my pre-cal CD into the disc drive and waited for the computer to wake. A little icon blinked that I had new emails. My pulse revved at the sight of an email from Dad's phone. Delivered *before* the police came to visit.

> *"Hey, hon,"* I read under my breath. *"I hope by now you've found the note Mom left in our room. If not, run up and get it. It'll explain everything. I wanted to add that when Aunt Jules comes, it's important you spend some time with her. She's getting up there in years, you know. There's a lot to be learned from her if you'll take the time. Remind her to tell you some stories—she's got a ton of them.*
>
> *"Mom and I may be away longer than expected. So sorry. Sometimes these things don't go as planned. I hope to be in touch soon. Remember to keep on schedule, unless Aunt Jules suggests otherwise. Love you bunches, Daddy."*

Great. Another vague note, which meant another dead-end. Why was Dad on this trip? Why did he and Mom leave in the middle of the night only to drive a whopping three miles down the road to abandon the van?

And what did he mean "as planned"? If this was planned, they both forgot to mention it to me.

Math was *not* happening—too many questions nudged out the numbers. Maybe Mom's blog would reveal a clue to their whereabouts. Perhaps someone left a comment or tip. Maybe she wrote an article that would disclose intentions to act on some insider knowledge.

I typed in Mom's blog address—www.landoflegend.net. Unfortunately, *The Land of Legend* got me nowhere. No secrets or implications to discover. I heard her talking about being leery of Leprechauns the other day, which appeared to be the hot topic for the month. The comments only revealed that there were other enthusiasts out in cyberspace with the same, offbeat interest as my mother.

Amazing how many people believed in this stuff.

My fingers froze on the keyboard. I had the unmistakable feeling of being watched. I listened. Chill bumps swept up my arms and tingled my scalp. Two round orbs—eyeballs—reflected in the computer monitor.

"You watchin' *Spy-bots*?"

I shuddered with relief to hear the voice of my fifteen-year-old brother Brock. *Man, I need to lighten up.* I spun to face him and forced a grin. "Hey, Brock, you scared me half to death."

"You watchin' *Spy-bots*?"

"Nope. I'm not watching *Spy-bots*. Just checking out Mom's blog. You having trouble sleeping?"

Silence.

Since Brock walked in his sleep, I needed to determine his mental state. It's an eerie experience to see someone up and about, eyes wide open, but realize their mind is completely disconnected. Right then—at half-past six—he may have woken up before his alarm. It happened on occasion.

My brother is more complex than being a hardcore sleepwalker, however. Brock is autistic. His world stays mostly silent. Mostly observant. But if we don't keep him on a regular schedule, all that changes. Disruptions carry the risk of a meltdown. A meltdown is similar to a human volcano: violent emotions spewing in all directions.

Something worth avoiding.

Because of this, we keep Brock and Brady—Brock's identical twin who isn't autistic—in karate year-round. Brock expects to do karate every Tuesday night, and life is easier on everyone when he knows what to expect.

I should have guessed that he stood behind me when I sensed someone near. We joke about Brock being the family stalker. He has an uncanny ability to walk into a room, quiet as air, and stand absurdly close, yet out of our line of sight. Half the time, when I turn to find him standing nearby—like eight inches from my face—I react with my own version of an eruption.

It wasn't something I could quite get used to.

One thing Brock loves, besides television in general, is *Spy-bots*. For a treat or to calm one of his meltdowns, we let him watch it on YouTube. Without fail, whenever someone's at the computer, he asks if we're watching his favorite show.

I could tell that Brock was alert and awake, so I made another judgment call. "Would you like to watch *Spy-bots*, Brock?" Silly question.

"Yes."

"Great. Have at it."

A few clicks of the mouse and Brock settled in, a grin stretched wide as he anticipated every line. He has a photographic memory according to his doctor. Images or sound bites are stored in a steel trap somewhere in his unique brain. He's brilliant in his own way.

Keeping Brock occupied gave me time to contemplate what I should tell everyone about Mom and Dad's "excursion." They'd be up soon to do chores and some school. In the summer, we continue our core subjects like math and English. It's another way to keep things scheduled for Brock.

It seemed best to wake Brady and tell him everything. He could handle it.

As I made my way upstairs, I decided my other siblings needed to view the news like a fun deviation from normal Larcen life. Once they heard Aunt Jules would be spending the week with us, details like Dad and Mom chasing down Bigfoot wouldn't matter.

There isn't anyone quite like our aunt.

Aunt Julie—or Jules to us—lives in the coastal town of Cannon Beach, Oregon. From her dining-room window, she has a view of this gargantuan monolith called Haystack Rock. It's a rock formation that looks like a massive mound of hay shooting up from the sand and water like a guardian over the coast. I always feel minuscule when I stand near it, like an insect looking to scale the wall of a very tall apartment building.

At less than five feet tall, most people tower over Aunt Jules as if she's a little bug too. She has a twin, Judith, whom we've never met because she lives abroad. Both are my late grandmother's sisters from Ireland. Our grandmother died before we were born, but Aunt Jules has been a stellar stand-in.

Not sure how I scored *two* family members with a love for mythical creatures, but Aunt Jules professionally sculpts garden Gnomes, of all things. Not the cheesy ones found in Walmart but intricate, bronze works of art that collectors buy from around the globe. Somehow, I find this more socially acceptable than my mother's line of work—maybe because she isn't my mother.

My younger sisters, eleven-year-old Sophie and seven-year-old Nicole, love to play pretend with the Gnomes scattered throughout Aunt Jules's garden. They've named at least thirty of them. We also adopted a few Gnomes for our own yard. Sometimes Mom uses their pictures on her blog.

The thought of a visit with Aunt Jules became a bright spot in my muddled morning. I looked forward to making a big deal about it over breakfast.

Ready to talk about the night, I opened the door to wake the dead—also known as my younger brother Brady. I anticipated dangling the night's drama in front of him as I poked at his ribs and weighed the outcome of sticking my finger in his ear—after I licked it, of course. I decided it wasn't worth the potential payback.

While he gained consciousness, I rambled through the

midnight events. He looked steamed that he'd slept through all the excitement. Especially when I got to the part about riding in the police car.

"No way! Why didn't you wake me?"

"It's not my fault you sleep like a brick. Besides, I'm the one with a driver's license. You would've been stuck here anyway. I did you a favor."

"Whatever."

"You can thank me later."

Right then I heard two-year-old Nate, our youngest sibling, give a squeal. I glanced at the clock and realized it was seven A.M. On cue, alarms buzzed from various bedrooms, including my own.

I stretched and stood. "It's been a long day already. I haven't any idea when Aunt Jules will arrive, so the plan is to stick to our schedule. I'll tell everyone the news during breakfast."

Brady shuffled to his closet, and I headed for the nursery. Nate sat on his toddler bed, a sheet over his head.

"Hmmm, where's Nate the Great?"

A giggle shook the lump on the bed.

"Guess I'll have to find him. Let's see... not behind the door. Um, he's not in the closet. Maybe... maybe he's under *here*."

With a flourish and "*a-ha!*" I yanked the sheet off his curly, dark hair. His chocolatey eyes met mine and he puckered his lips in a mischievous grin,

"Sadieee!"

"Nateyyy!"

I scooped him out of bed, polka-dotting his neck with kisses, and took him straight to the bathroom. He'd recently started staying dry all night.

I don't think God makes kids any sweeter than Nate. We all adore the little man. We adopted him from Ethiopia when he was five months old. He has brown eyes like the rest of us, but that's where the similarity ends—especially alongside my blonde brothers. We no longer notice the differences, though. He's as much our brother as Brady and Brock.

Heading down the hall with Nate in tow, I rapped on Sophie and Nicole's bedroom door. "You guys awake in there?"

"Yeppers."

"Remember to let Ollie and Mindy-loo out of their kennel, okay? I'm making breakfast this morning."

Downstairs I found Brock still absorbed with his cartoon. He'd probably skip a few meals if I let him sit there all day. Too much immediate gratification.

I clicked the mouse on the computer and stopped the show, breaking the spell. He gave me a glazed look, and his grin relaxed into a slacked mouth.

"Hey, dude, time to get on with the day." I smiled and waved my hand in front of his face. "I know you'd prefer a *Spy-bots* marathon, but *you* need to water the tomato plants, and *I* need to cook up some grub. C'mon."

Brock smiled. For him, that was like a hug and a "hi there, sis." I had learned to appreciate any sign of interaction.

The morning hummed along. I set plastic plates on the step stool for Nate to deliver to the dining room. He teetered on his toes, pushing each one onto the table.

No one asked where Mom and Dad were, much to my relief. Sometimes our parents skipped breakfast, so it didn't seem odd they weren't around first thing in the morning. Everything felt normal. I wanted to believe the events of the night were merely an absurd dream.

Brady said grace, and we chowed down. The long night had left me ravenous. I decided to get a couple of bites in my stomach before Twenty Questions began.

After a few impatient glances from Brady, I cleared my throat. "Hey, you guys..."

They looked up but continued to eat.

"You probably think Mom and Dad are still up in their room. Well, guess what? They're not even home. Turns out Mom had a Bigfoot lead to check out and Dad went with her."

"Really? In the middle of the night? With Dad?" Sophie is too smart for her own good. She's annoyingly bossy and big into pretending she lives in the medieval times.

"Yes, with Dad. But the real announcement is not that they left. It's who's coming to stay while they're gone."

"Who?" asked Nicole, our little pipsqueak. She scrunched the freckles on her nose as if expecting bad news.

I looked around the table, building suspense. Brady rolled his eyes when I passed by him.

"Aunt Jules."

"Aunt Jules?" Nicole bounced in her seat.

"Really?" Sophie looked pleased. "When?"

"That's part of the surprise." Brady smirked at her. "We don't know."

"You knew about this?" Sophie hated to be the last to know anything, and Brady was all too willing to egg her on.

"Of course."

"Yeah, he's known for a whole hour now." I shot Brady a warning look.

He shrugged.

"No school today, right?" Nicole's voice brightened. I noticed a bit of egg clinging to her tawny curls.

"You wish." Brady stuffed half a slice of toast into his mouth.

"So do *you*." I glared at him. "You just won't admit it." I handed Nicole her napkin. "Here. Your hair is holding a snack for later."

Nicole proceeded to mash the egg into her tangles with the napkin.

"Anyway...yes, we will go on with our day as usual. After school we'll clean up and get ready for company. Tonight, Brady and Brock go to karate like any other Tuesday. But I might be willing to get some ice cream on the way home *if* we get everything done."

"It's a deal!" Nicole bounced in her seat and clapped her hands.

"Deal!" Nate echoed.

Brock concentrated on eating everyone's leftovers, oblivious to what we discussed—or so it seemed. None of us know what he might recall and what becomes white noise. Dad thinks Brock hears and remembers everything. It doesn't come to the surface, though, without the right combination. We're always trying to figure out what that combination might be. He seems to change it every day.

I stood to clear the table. "Let's get moving, guys. No excuses that you're too excited to concentrate on school, either. I'm running on about four hours of sleep. If I can do it, you can too."

"Why didn't you sleep?" Sophie didn't miss a thing.

I kicked myself for letting on that I'd been up half the night. "Well, it was just one of those nights, ya know?" I hoped that would satisfy her.

"You didn't answer my question."

"Sometimes you wake up and can't go back to sleep." I walked off before Genius-Girl could give me the third degree.

The little sleuth followed.

"*What?*" I turned on my heels.

Smack! Sophie plowed into me. She stumbled back and glared. "Mom and Dad took off in the middle of the night. You haven't slept. What happened? Tell me."

"There's nothing to tell."

We held each other's gazes. I refused to divulge another ounce of info. I wouldn't back down first.

Sophie grimaced. The corner of her mouth twitched. So did mine. I huffed and turned away before she could have the satisfaction of seeing me laugh.

"Made ya laugh. You lose," she called after me.

The laughter managed to shake loose a subtle, sour thought lodged in the folds of my grey matter.

Something *had* happened. Would I be laughing if I knew exactly what?

CHAPTER THREE

With much effort, we kept our minds on schoolwork and finished after lunch. The rest of the day we cleaned and readied the house for company. I decided to bake some lemon-drop cookies, a favorite family recipe. Sophie and Nicole stared out the window, as if it would help Aunt Jules arrive faster, but to no avail.

After dinner we piled into the van and headed to karate. I planned to swing by Burgerville when Brock and Brady finished, under the guise of getting ice cream. I wanted to take a peek in the daylight at where the cops found the Odyssey.

Brock always sat shotgun when we rode to the studio. Mom usually played taxi, while I stayed home with the little ones. Thanks to three adult-size kids plus a car seat, we didn't all fit in the van—legally, anyway. I wondered if my driving today would make ripples with my ultra-scheduled brother.

I buckled Nate into his car seat, slid behind the wheel, and gave Brock a grin.

"Mom's gone." His face remained neutral.

I smiled again. I didn't know if he wanted to remind me or only realized it for himself. "Yes, Brock, she's gone. But she and Dad will be home soon."

"Maybe. But it might be hard."

The comment perplexed me. Turning onto the main road, I tried to understand how his mind processed things. Like always, I shrugged it off to the mystery of autism.

Brock punched the stereo button and rocked to the tune that played. He loved music and seemed to know every word once he heard a song. He tweaked the volume to level seventeen on the digital readout. His favorite number was seventeen. He collected precisely that amount of *whatever*—marbles, dice, Matchbox cars, even gum wrappers that he liked to roll into tight, little balls.

The van bumped the curb as I made the turn into the karate studio parking lot.

"Here we are." Brock parodied our mother's usual comment when we arrived at any given destination.

The twins dashed inside for forty-five minutes of jerky movements and guttural noises. Though I tried karate for a while, I didn't care for how it invaded my personal space. I'm not a touchy-feely person with my own family. Why would I want to throw myself at total strangers or defend myself from their flailing limbs?

I had brought an audio CD of *The Magician's Nephew* for the younger ones to enjoy. The warm breeze and low humidity made for a perfect Pacific Northwest evening. With the windows down and side door slid open, I tilted my seat back and texted my friend Deirdre while the others imagined themselves in the Wood Between the Worlds.

Someone poked my nose. "Hey! Sleeping Beauty. A little leg room would be nice."

"Huh?" I sat up, heart pumping. Brady hovered nearby. I slept through the whole lesson? My phone was full of texts from Deirdre, asking what happened with a bunch of *hello???* type of blurbs.

After a quick head count, I felt relieved to see everyone present and accounted for. No doubt Sophie had enjoyed my lapse and took advantage of overseeing the others while I snoozed. You could always count on her to be a substitute mother hen. Or just plain bossy.

At the Burgerville drive-thru, I bought a round of cones for all of us. Well, everyone except Nate, who confused food with finger paints. Sophie used a spoon to share a few bites with him.

I pulled into the empty lot beside Burgerville and put the van in park.

"What are we doing here?" Sophie craned her neck out the window.

"We're going to sit here, eat our ice cream, and enjoy the view and the weather." I caught Brady's eye in the rearview mirror.

"There's no *view*." Sophie's tone made me want to donate her body to science. "Why would we want to sit and gaze at Burgerville from a distance? This place looks abandoned. It might not be safe."

"Listen, Sophie, Mom left *me* in charge. I'm trying to treat everyone to ice cream. You can feed all of yours to Nate if you're going to complain about the way I do it."

Nate squealed and clapped his hands. "Yippee!"

"Sor-ry." She rolled her eyes. "Just wondering. We don't usually pull into vacant lots to eat, that's all."

"Well, tonight's your big night. Live it up." I shifted in my seat and looked back, hoping to sound casual. "Hey, guys, why don't we eat these messy cones outside? I'm tired of sitting."

Sophie crossed her arms with a huff.

"You can stay put and pout all you want. It'll be easier to keep track of the little man in here anyway." Before she could give a rebuttal, I hopped out with the rest of the crew. Not much of an excursion, but it gave Brady and me a chance to look around.

I tried to act indifferent when I walked to the muddy impressions left by our tires the night before. Other tracks crisscrossed through the hardened mud, but determining their age or purpose proved futile. The lot backed up to a grove of evergreens then dropped off into an embankment of woods and undergrowth.

What I hoped to discover, I couldn't say. My gaze roamed up and down, back and forth while I ambled along the tree line and licked my drippy cone. Brady scoured the opposite end of the wooded area and worked towards me.

He jogged over and whispered, "I think I found something."

I followed him back and tried to zero in on what he spotted. "I don't see it." I squinted into the branches.

"Right there, stuck to that twig." He pointed.

"I only see… wait! Is that hair?" I stood on my toes and reached for the branch, pulling it down for inspection. We stared at a large blob of brown fuzz.

Brady pulled it free. "Fur." He sounded awed by the prospect.

"Sure looks like it."

"Awesome! Bigfoot fur."

"Maybe. Maybe not."

Something glinted in the dirt beneath the branch. I plucked up the silvery item—a hoop earring—and held it in front of Brady's face. "Mom has the same earrings."

He gasped.

I shook my head. "I don't like the look of this."

"Me neither. But it only proves Mom and Dad *did* come to track down Sasquatch, right? Which is precisely what they told us."

"True." I nodded, my eyes riveted on the hoop. "It confirms things. I suppose that should make me feel better. But it doesn't."

"You're paranoid, Sadie. I think it's totally cool. Bigfoot, right here in little Orchards, Washington, hanging out at Burgerville. Sweet."

Footsteps thudded across the ground. Sophie must have been spying on us. "What are you looking at?"

"Aw, nothin'." Brady stuffed the fur into his pocket and shrugged.

"We found a piece of jewelry. Just a cheap, silver earring." I briefly dangled it between her eyes then clasped it in my hand. If Sophie assumed it to be one of many silver hoops worn by half the female population, it would make things less complicated.

"Lemme see it." She caught my wrist.

I should have known. I uncurled my fingers and

shoved my palm towards her. She examined the earring like it was a rare plant extracted from the heavens.

"Nothing but a plain ol' hoop." I gave a nonchalant shrug.

"Then why do you want to keep it?"

"I found it." The little lawyer ground on my last nerve. "I can keep it. What's the big deal?"

She studied my face, eyes narrowed, then turned to scrutinize Brady. "You guys are keeping something from me."

Brady laughed. "You're so dramatic."

"No, I'm not. I'm smart. And I can tel by the look on your faces that I'm right." She tucked a brunette lock behind her ear, crossed her arms, and gave us a smug smile.

"Get back in the van. We're done here." End of discussion. "It's getting dark and *someone* left Nate all by himself. Might not be safe."

Sophie looked ready to argue, but Brady cut her off. "Yo, Brock. Nicole. Let's go!"

We started to climb into the Odyssey when Nicole made another discovery. "What happened here?" She pointed to the post between the passenger and sliding doors.

Sophie jumped out and scrutinzed it. "There's a big scratch in the paint. Dad's not gonna be happy, Sadie. You'll probably get grounded."

"Well, *I* didn't put it there, so don't get your hopes up."

Brady inspected it next. He motioned for me to come around and check it out.

Can't anything be simple today? A deep scratch etched itself into the paint. Three scratches, really—like something swiped at the door handle. Something with claws.

Brady and I exchanged worried looks.

"Who knows? Let's go." I darted to the driver's side. "Now."

The tires were spitting gravel before everyone could buckle their seat belts.

"Maybe those scratches are from your crazy driving." Sophie wouldn't let up.

I no longer had the energy for her petty spats. My mind unraveled. If Sasquatch existed, I suddenly had bigger problems than bratty little sisters.

Though I'd heard Mom talk about the infamous creature in a matter-of-fact way for years, I categorized him as a myth. Now I had to face the fact that Bigfoot might be alive and well in small-town America. *My* small town. I could only pray my parents were also alive and well.

A thick fog engulfed our van on the way home. We crawled along, clinging to the white line that glowed in the headlights. Our five-minute drive stretched to fifteen. How bizarre that such a sparkling, clear evening could swiftly dissolve into a dense and dangerous situation.

I shivered. I couldn't shrug the feeling that "bizarre" might become the new normal for the Larcen household.

CHAPTER FOUR

I PULLED UP TO THE HOUSE and strained to see if Aunt Jules had arrived while we were gone. An empty driveway greeted us.

"Do we have to get ready for bed?" Sophie begged while everyone traipsed inside. "Can't we wait up for Aunt Jules?"

I wiped my feet on the entryway floor mat. "What if she doesn't come until tomorrow?"

Sophie shrugged and gave a dramatic sigh. She stomped up the stairs louder than necessary.

Drama queen! I shook my head and pushed the door closed, then reached for the first of the Brock-proof locks.

Tap-tap-tap.

I jumped. "Wha—?" How could someone be knocking on the door I just closed?

When I pressed my eye to the peephole, my heartbeat thumped against the wood. Only the distorted, vacant walkway stared back. Then a smidgen of red fuzz swayed in and out of sight in the lower portion of the circle.

Aunt Jules? I opened the door to a shock of red hair and twinkling green eyes.

"Hello, chipmunk!" Her petite arms reached for a hug.

"Aunt Jules! Wow, it's great to see you." I gave her a squeeze. "We walked in the door a minute ago and I didn't... how did... were you..."

"Yes, m'love, I've been waitin' fer ya to get home. I knew ya weren't expectin' me this soon, so I circled 'round, waitin'." She grabbed the handle of her suitcase and started to roll it into the foyer.

"Leave it there. I'll get it." I stepped around her luggage and padded down the walk to peer at the driveway. "Aunt Jules, I don't see your car."

"Oh, lovey, ya think me wants to drive two hours in the dark at my age? Heavens no." She shook her fiery curls. "I'm gettin' too old fer that. I got a ride."

"But I didn't see a taxi or anything when I opened the door. It was only shut for a second."

"Guess ya weren't lookin' fer one, eh?" She shrugged off her overcoat. "Don't be worryin' yer pretty brown head about it, pet. 'Twas a lovely night and the stars were glorious."

"The stars?" I grabbed her suitcase and stepped into the foyer. "The fog is as thick as a milkshake. You can't see any stars tonight."

"So it is, ladybug, so it is." She smiled. "Goes to show that I really don't need to be drivin', eh?"

I shut the door and took a breath. My blurry brain needed to refocus.

"Sure is quiet down here. Are all the critters asleep already?" Aunt Jules lobbed her coat onto the coat rack beside the stairs and headed for the kitchen.

"They're getting ready for bed. They didn't hear you knock or they'd be mobbing you already. Sophie and Nicole hovered near the window all day, hoping to be the first to see you drive up." I followed her into the kitchen where I pressed the button on the intercom. "Hey, guys, you'll never guess who's here."

Within seconds a stampede zoomed overhead and down the stairs, exploding into the kitchen.

"Aunt Jules!" Sophie hugged her first.

The rest of the throng surrounded and fussed over our Irish auntie. She hugged and kissed and bestowed her funny nicknames on everyone. I'm fairly certain Aunt Jules missed her calling as a cereal box model for Lucky

Charms. Her red hair and petite size make her very Leprechaun-like, even alongside my younger siblings.

Nate scrambled into her arms and ran his hands through her red curls. He patted her head with his pudgy fingers spread wide. "I pet you."

Even Brock became animated—for Brock, anyway. He stood nearby and studied her mouth while she spoke in her old-country brogue. Aunt Jules has a special way with Brock. Somehow his autistic veil becomes more transparent when she talks to him. They connect.

Sophie found the platter of lemon-drop cookies, and we enjoyed a late-night snack and good company. Aunt Jules brought out a box of seashells from her daily walks along the beach. We admired her collection and picked a few favorites to keep.

Brock held one of the larger shels to his ear and grinned.

"Did ya find the ocean in there, sugar?" Aunt Jules walked to where he stood.

Brock offered her the shell, and she pressed it to her ear. "Ya sure did! Loud 'n clear." She winked and handed it back.

He listened again, eyes closed, like he wanted to block out everything else.

The grandfather clock in the den tolled eleven-thirty. I remembered my mother's insistence to keep Brock on a schedule. Instead, he'd woken before his alarm and was now late to bed. Today could be chalked up as an epic fail, minus karate.

"Hey, guys!" I yelled over the din. "Time to say good night. It's way past bedtime, and Aunt Jules is probably tired from her trip."

"Aunt Jules is in charge now." Sophie jutted her chin at me. "*She* has to tell us when to go to bed."

Before I could react, Aunt Jules spoke. "Now listen, young'un. Before I can be in charge of this 'ere clan, I need to know exactly what ya little Larcens are expected to do. I will get *that* from yer big sister, Sadie, here."

"Yes, ma'am, but—"

"And furthermore, when Sadie *does* tell ya somethin',

whether I'm here or no, I expect ya to be obeyin'. She's perfectly capable of bein' in charge. No sassin' yer sister, is that clear?"

"Yes, ma'am." Sophie looked at the floor.

"And no poutin', no how. Ya can't control what happens to ya, only how ya choose to react." She put her arm around Sophie's shoulder. "Let me see that stunnin' smile now, kitten."

Sophie mustered a pitiful grin and gave a nod. Everyone wished Aunt Jules a good-night then made their way upstairs. Nate brought up the rear, hopping like a frog.

"I'll be there in a minute, Natey." I reached between the stair rails and tickled his toes.

"In a minute," he echoed.

Aunt Jules leaned towards me in a secretive way, though we were the only two in the kitchen. "I'll put the kettle on fer tea. You can tell me about yer day while sippin' on some herbal magic."

The relationship between older folks and hot tea has always perplexed me. It seems to be the tonic cure-all for everything from a stuffy nose to toe fungus. To me it tastes like heated water straight from a rain barrel. But I have learned to tolerate tea enough to down a cup when offered by well-meaning adults.

Upstairs I made the rounds to everyone's bedrooms. The girls looked wired, but at least they were in bed.

"Good night, you two." I reached for Sophie's foot and gave it a squeeze. "You. Me. Tomorrow. Fresh start. Right?"

She gave a sheepish grin. "Right. Good night, Sadie."

"Night."

I found Nate on his bed, *Green Eggs and Ham* on his lap.

"Sorry, little man." I placed the book on his dresser. "It's much too late for a story. Aunt Jules was your bedtime treat."

"I pet her." He stroked the air with his little hands.

"Yes, you did, silly."

"She's nice." He grinned and snuggled down onto his

green-plaid pillow.

I gave him a kiss then went by the boys' room.

"Brock's asleep, Sadie," Brady whispered. "Can't I hang out with you and Aunt Jules?"

I hesitated. It felt good to be in charge, and my first instinct was to tell him no—because I could. But since he knew about everything that had happened so far, what could it hurt? It would save me from repeating it later.

I shrugged. "Why not?"

He looked surprised to find me agreeable. He jumped up, grabbed my hand, then yanked me towards the stairs.

Back in the kitchen, the kettle began to whistle. Aunt Jules hummed "Amazing Grace."

"Better pull out another mug, Auntie. We have company." I grabbed the sugar bowl and placed it near the selection of teas.

"Oh! Brady's gettin' to be such a young man that he can stay up late too, eh? Well, come on, pick yer poison, and get it settled in yer cup. The water's a-hollerin'."

We doctored our brew and huddled around the table for a late-night powwow.

"So, pollywogs, tell me about yer day. And don't be leavin' an-y-thing out."

Had it really been *one* day—not even a full day—since I woke to the knocking at the door? It seemed like several with everything so out of sync. I felt this overwhelming urge to claim exhaustion and go to bed. Deal with it tomorrow.

Instead, I recounted the bizarre events, describing officers Unibrow and Barbie, and how I discovered my parents' empty bed. "Mom and Dad weren't there. They left me this." I pulled the dog-eared note from my pocket and slid it across the table. "Then I went to Burgerville with the police to retrieve the van."

"So they found the van at Burgerville." She sounded like Sherlock sizing up a new clue. Her eyes scanned the letter from Mom.

"Yes, ma'am."

"Remember, pet, it's important ya leave nothin' out."

Aunt Jules gave me an intense stare. "I must know *everything*."

Brady glanced at me, eyebrows raised. "Yeah, she left out leaving me asleep while she got to ride in a police car."

"No time for jokin', mister." Aunt Jules squeezed his forearm. "Let's stick to the story."

My turn to raise my brows. "When I got home, I couldn't go back to sleep. I tried to do some schoolwork, cleaned up a bit. Oh, I checked email and found one from Dad. He sent it from his phone before the police came."

Red hair scooched closer. "What did it say, love?"

"Uh…" I needed a second to clear the cobwebs. "It said he hoped I found the note from Mom. That they might be gone longer than they originally thought. Oh! He also told me to spend some time with you—as if I wouldn't—because you had lots of good stories to tell. In fact, he said to remind you to share your stories with me. Does that make sense?"

Aunt Jules grinned. "Oh, Liam Larcen, aren't you a subtle one?"

"What do you mean?" Why was she talking like that?

Curls quaked as Aunt Jules chuckled. "I'll get to it in a minute. Go on, finish yer story."

I ran down our day and finished with, "Tonight we went to karate as usual. Then we stopped by Burgerville, which is why we weren't home when you arrived."

"Yes, yes, and then?"

"I bought ice cream to distract everyone while Brady and I checked it out. And—"

"Wait!" Brady shot from his chair and clambered upstairs.

Aunt Jules and I blinked at each other across the table. "What's gotten in t'him?"

Though I had an idea, I only shrugged. "Let's hope he doesn't wake everyone up stomping around like that."

I cringed when I heard him come back down the stairs like Bigfoot himself.

He slid into his seat. "Look." He held up his hairy prize for Aunt Jules's inspection.

She studied it. Her tiny hand grasped the blob of fur, then she gave it a sniff.

Gross. "We found that fuzz caught on a branch."

"*I* found it!"

"Okay, *you* found it." I rolled my eyes. "*I* found an earring on the ground that looked like one of Mom's."

"My, my." Aunt Jules shook her head. "This is serious indeed."

Oh, that's comforting. "Serious? How?"

"Yeah." Brady slumped back in his chair. "Doesn't it prove they discovered Bigfoot? That's what they were after, right?"

"Oh, yes, m'dear, that's what they found. But there's somethin' ya probably don't know about Bigfoot."

Brady and I exchanged doubtful looks. We knew more about the big, hairy dude than most people—thanks to Mom.

"Bigfoot, Sasquatch, a Yeti..." Aunt Jules leaned in, her voice strained. "They're all names fer the same kind of creature, names people in different parts of *our* world have given to describe the same, elusive monster. However, in *another* world—in a world where legends are real and myths reside—they have another name."

My gaze traveled her face, wondering if this was a joke. She leveled her eyes on me, serious and unblinking. "What name?" I dared to ask.

Aunt Jules let out an unsteady breath. "Trolls."

CHAPTER FIVE

My brain went into disconnect mode. I didn't have a file for such information.

"Excuse me?" Brady stiffened his back.

Something heavy hovered in the air. Dread and disbelief slowly sank into my composure, a set of fangs that poisoned the atmosphere. Trolls were a different kind of threat. Though I couldn't recall Mom using that term for Bigfoot, mythology only had sinister things to say about such monsters.

A slow, deliberate nod from our aunt was the only motion in the room. Her gaze shifted to the tabletop. She looked numb.

Not a reassuring look.

"What do you mean, *Trolls*?" Brady tried again.

Aunt Jules gave a weighty sigh. Her eyes shifted back to us with a fresh glint of resolve. "Don't ask questions fer the moment. I need ya to get busy doin'. Double check the locks on every window and door. Shut yer blinds and drapes. We'll talk in a minute."

Silence stretched like a chasm.

"Go on, now, both of ya! Get after it." She shooed us with a wave of her hands.

"I'll take the upstairs." Brady dashed out of the kitchen.

With robotic movements, I probed the lower perimeter. The act of checking locks and closing blinds made me feel trapped in a horror movie.

I hate horror movies.

Fog smothered our house. Whatever we needed to conceal ourselves from couldn't get a peek inside without being smack up against a window. It took great focus to keep my mind in neutral when I glimpsed the blurred streetlights and shadows lurking outside. "Amazing Grace" wafted from the kitchen again. I tried to concentrate on the tune rather than the panic that crept into my imagination.

Back at the breakfast table, I sat closer than normal to my brother. I needed his courage to rub off on me. Instead, the ticking clock seemed to count down my emptying determination.

Aunt Jules looked from me to Brady. She twisted her wedding ring around her finger. If she didn't say something soon, I would explode or cry or banish her to a box of Lucky Charms. If Trolls exist, then anything's possible.

Finally, she spoke. "I figured to ease into our family history over the course of me stay here—which is exactly what yer father alluded to in his email. But with this…uh… turn of events, I'm afraid I'm needin' to drive to the point. I hope yer able to keep up with the amount of information I'm throwin' yer way. No time for beatin' 'round the bush."

This didn't sound like good tidings of great joy.

Apparently satisfied by our stunned silence, she cleared her throat and launched into our family's background. "As ya know, yer dear mum has done her share of research and writin' on the likes of Sasquatch, Elves, and whatnot. Ya may think she's spoutin' some ancient folklore and old wives' tales, and plenty of it's exactly that. But much of what she knows is less from research and more from yer family history."

She pointed her finger at us. "Ya see, through the ages—and I do mean the ages, doodlebugs. From the dawn of creation right up 'til this particular moment—

there've been families endowed with the secrets of"—she lowered her voice and leaned towards us— "*The Tethered World*."

It was so quiet I could hear myself blink. "The what?"

"The Tethered World, lovey." She patted my hand. "I know it's a foreign phrase to ya, but trust me, you'll be intimately acquainted with this place in a short time. The Tethered World is a realm that exists within the earth, in the depths of our world, so to speak. It's tethered—like a ball to a rope on a playground—connected to us, yet fully a world of its own."

After that statement, things officially stopped making sense in *my* world.

"The Bible explains that humans were created 'a little lower than the angels.' Those in the Tethered World were created a little lower than us humans."

Although my absurdity-alarm had sirens blaring, I dared not scoff at Aunt Jules. She looked serious.

"There are lands and peoples and creatures that are livin' and lovin', eatin' and sleepin', havin' wars and peace talks right under our feet. Families that've been granted special knowledge—even access—to this place, must do so with the utmost secrecy and care. Their identity unknown even to each other." Aunt Jules looked from me to Brady, eyes twinkling. "The history book tells an interestin' tale of how this land came into bein'."

"I've never read anything about that in *my* history books." Brady looked skeptical.

"No, and ya never will. But *the* history book, officially titled *The Inaugural Season and Perpetual Chronicles of New Eden and Thereabouts*, tells of the creation and foundin' of this land. I wasn't plannin' on diggin' this far back into things, but since ya asked…"

Brady shook his head like he had water in his ears. "The *what* season of New England?"

"Not England, lad. Eden. *The Inaugural Season and Perpetual Chronicles of New Eden and Thereabouts*. A long-winded title fer a very old book. If ya don't know what all that rhetoric means, consult with Mr. Webster. I've got more to explain than a bunch of voluminous words. Besides, no one calls it New Eden anymore. It's the Tethered World nowadays."

Aunt Jules lifted her teacup and sipped. The hot liquid sloshed out when she placed it back in its saucer with a quivering clink. It made me uneasy to see this rock of a woman wound so tight. It didn't bode well for my parents or the rest of us.

She reached across the table and gave our arms a squeeze when she spoke. "As ya know, when Adam and Eve were banished from Paradise, God had an angel stand guard at the entrance with a flamin' sword. No one could return to the garden after that...and nothin' could leave, either."

She released her grip and sat back.

"Well, when it came time for Noah and the Great Flood, the Creator gave special consideration to the creatures inhabitin' that particular patch o' land. Before the flood commenced, He relocated them below ground. Somewhere 'tween the earth's crust and the watery depths lies vast areas that are a safe dwellin' for those special bein's."

Brady cleared his throat, and I cut my gaze his way. We swapped looks of confusion.

"Now then, throughout history—be it from the earth a quakin' or whatnot—cracks and crevices and caves have provided a way for the creatures down there to come back to the earth's surface. In turn, humans and other animals have occasionally found their way down to the Tethered World. This interminglin' of our society and theirs has led to much of the lore ye've heard tell of over the years—tales of Elves or Faeries or Trolls and the like. Many a person has been called a liar or just a good storyteller whence it comes to talkin' about such oddities. But take note that all over the world such tales of sightin's and visitations are shared among cultures."

"I've never understood Mom's fascination with these things." I'd never admitted that to anyone. "I don't know if it's due to her Irish roots or because she finds this stuff interesting to research, but I used to beg her to tell me if she believed in their existence. Seemed like a big waste of time and energy if they weren't real."

"And how would she answer ya, m'dear?"

"Vaguely—usually with another question. Sometimes she asked if I could see God. When I said no, she reminded me that things can be real even if we don't see them. There's evidence if we look for it. Or she'd point out how creative God is and ask why I thought He would stop with our world. Her answers made me think that she, at least, believed them. Other times she asked how realistic it seemed to believe in such creatures, which made me think...maybe she didn't believe it, at least not deep down."

"Yer mum is a wise woman, Sadie. She wants ya to think fer yerself."

I nodded. "But *you're* telling me it's all true. Her blog and all of these sightings and legends and stories— they're completely true?"

"Goodness, child, is there a God? Yes. Does every religion of this world believe right and true things about Him? No. Wherever we find truth, we find someone distortin' it. Everyone loves a good tale, or some juicy gossip, or maybe a pile o' controversy. That's what causes the six-inch fish to become a foot-long catch, as the story is told. Likewise, some o' the accounts are true, and some aren't. Yer mum collects these tales so she can sift through the ones that are fluff and keep an eye on the accurate."

"I have no clue what that means." Brady stifled a yawn.

Aunt Jules took another swallow of tea and made a face. "Here, pet." She handed her cup to Brady. "I'd be obliged if you'd warm this for me. 'Bout impossible to reach that microwave above yer stove, and I cannot abide lukewarm tea."

Brady stood and stretched. "When do we get back to the Trolls? How weird is that? Bigfoot's really a Troll?" He grabbed her cup and crossed to the microwave.

"Yer jumpin' ahead. I'll get to it soon enough."

I studied Aunt Jules and tried to make sense of her story. Had the little lady finally snapped? Could a bronze sculptor get bronze poisoning, like a person who works with crystal can get lead poisoning? Was she crazy? If Mom believed this bizarre history, maybe *she* was crazy. The fact that I even asked such questions probably meant *I* was crazy. I'd been awake close to twenty-four hours, after all.

"Ouch!"

"Checkin' to see if yer still with us, chipmunk." While I'd been staring right at her—or through her—Aunt Jules reached across the table and gave me a fierce pinch.

"Yes, ma'am." I blinked and rubbed my arm. "Just… thinking."

Brady chuckled and handed Aunt Jules her cup. "I don't know, Sadie. You were so spaced-out I think you drooled. Need a napkin?"

"You're hilarious."

Aunt Jules took a lusty sip of tea and sighed. "Thanks, love. It's perfect."

"Is it magically delicious?" I gave my best imitation of the Lucky Charms Leprechaun. I grinned to myself thinking, *Ha! Pinched ya back!*

Brady buried his head in the crook of his arm and attempted to smother his laughter. I bit my lip and looked away, feeling vindicated. Even Aunt Jules grinned.

"Glad to see yer keepin' yer sense of humor." She offered a stiff smile. Then her fists clenched and her eyes flashed from Brady to me. The humor dissolved like water on a hot skillet. "But this 'ere is serious business, lovies, and we're long on story and short on time."

"Sorry." I put on my poker face. "I don't do sleep deprivation very well." I didn't dare look at Brady. It would have been like Mentos meeting up with diet Coke.

Aunt Jules leaned into us. "As I said, yer mum's a collector of tales. This isn't some job she picked from the newspaper, and ya can't go to the university fer a degree in Folktales and Folk Knowledge from Ancient to Present Times—at least, not that I'm aware. This job is yer mum's birthright. And let me tell ya, with the Internet and instant fooglin' on the worldwide spider web, she's done more with her callin' than most of the folks precedin' her."

My hand flew to my mouth in a poor attempt to smother more laughter. Brady appeared to fight the same battle across the table.

"Why are ya gigglin' *now*?" She gave us a steely gaze, but her remarks only added kindling to the fire.

Brady gasped. "Aunt Jules! It's *Googling* on the worldwide web, not *foogling* on a spider web."

"Oh, ya know what I'm talkin' about!" She smacked the table with her hand and jerked the fun right out from under us. "Let me finish."

With a dismissive wave, she pressed on. "The McGriffins—yer mum's side of the family—have been entrusted with the knowledge of the Tethered World. During a point in each of our lives, we talked with an elder of the family, exactly like this here talk I'm havin' now. We were told of our duty in keepin' these secrets concealed and made to understand the seriousness of our connection with a world we'd yet to see. Those in the Tethered World know who we are and what we do. Some aim to destroy us. Others may warn or even protect us."

"We're not McGriffins. We're Larcens. Is Dad one of these secret-keepers too?" I pinched the bridge of my nose.

"You're in the McGriffin bloodline thanks to yer mum. Yer father is plenty involved by virtue of marriage. We McGriffins must be careful about who we pledge our undyin' love to. They must be screened to be certain they're open to these deep yet concealed truths."

Great. I could see my chances of meeting Mr. Right bottoming out between *zero* and *dream on*. What a great first impression I'll give. *Nice to meet you. I'm Sadie Larcen, keeper of the underworld. I babysit Faeries and Leprechauns for a living.* That should scare off all the good guys and help me hook up with some barbaric creep.

"Me own love," continued Aunt Jules with a far off gaze, "dear Daniel, God bless him, believed the legends before we even met. 'Twas the most natural thing in the world to marry that man." She sighed. "I miss him every day."

"How did he...uh...die?" Brady asked.

Thoughts of Daniel must have soothed her late-night crankies. She looked at Brady. A sweet sadness clouded her face, and she grasped her wedding ring. "It's been thirty-eight years, lad. Thirty-eight years." She shook her frizzy head and came back to the present. "That's a story fer another time. Let's keep our focus on the story that involves yer parents and the rest of ya Larcens."

"So, Mom's been collecting these tales to learn which ones are true and which are fake." I contemplated the idea while staring at my untouched tea.

"More accurate to say she's been inspectin' them. There're plenty of counterfeits lookin' to get their fifteen minutes of fame. But some of what she learns is enough to keep track of the rumblin's down under. Ya see, yer family is to do more than keep an eye on things. There's a much bigger role for ye Larcens."

Something in her voice urged me to sit up and pay attention.

Aunt Jules folded her hands and looked straight ahead. "One of ya has been chosen to be ruler in the realm of Vituvia, a land that lies within the Tethered World. Yer parents were supposed to be makin' preparations for this while I spent the week with ya."

She shook her head. "But somethin's gone terribly wrong."

CHAPTER SIX

I PEELED MY CHEEK FROM THE pillowcase and looked at the plate-sized water spot where my mouth had sprung a leak. *Gross!*

Perky sunshine spilled through the blinds and reminded me that the world continued to turn despite the mind-blowing revelations from the previous night. I flipped my pillow over and buried my face in its coolness. How could my life—my family's life—have changed so drastically in two days? How could my parents keep our true identity a secret right in front of me? How did I miss it? Was I expected to fit in with the rest of... uh... *humankind...* knowing what I know?

My bedside clock revealed that I'd slept until lunchtime. Aunt Jules had insisted Brady and I sleep in— "Ya gotta rest up for what's t'come"—but noon seemed like overkill.

After all the freaky-family details had been exposed the night before, I filled Aunt Jules in on the daily grind then hurried to bed. It's often hard for me to sleep when new thoughts or ideas are swirling through my brain—but not last night. The things Auntie told Brady and me were flat-out inconceivable. There was no sorting things out. Instead, I wanted to shove everything far from my consciousness. Far from my life.

Now, the dreadful conversation blared back into my brain. How I longed to be sick and delusional rather than trapped in this family drama. The cold, hard facts were officially stranger than my craziest dreams. Wait. Could I have dreamt it?

Aunt Jules's animated voice floated up the stairs, placing the final nail in the coffin of my life as a typical teenager. Nope. Not a dream.

I yanked the quilt over my face and stifled a cynical laugh. "King Brock," my muffled voice announced. "Brock, High King of Vituvia." The irony left me shaking my head. Everything had turned upside down.

Fairytales freak me out. There's something about the cruel element of surprise, whether a curse or a coma, that I don't find amusing. Last night I learned I'm practically living in a bizarre fairytale tailored especially for my family.

My brother Brock—who can barely communicate with our household of eight—is to become ruler of some gargantuan kingdom. He's in line to be the king and protector of the Gnomes. Yes, *Gnomes.*

Aunt Jules had dropped the bomb on Brady and me last night. "Yer brother will begin his apprenticeship this summer," she told us, "with me own twin sister, Judith. All these years that you've heard talk of me sister livin' abroad has been the truth. We couldn't let on to her particular whereabouts, however. Judith is the current Queen of Vituvia, land of the Gnomes. She'll be retirin' when Brock becomes king."

"*King?*" Brady and I exclaimed.

"Yes, me darlin's. Brock shall rule the realm of Vituvia. Yer dad and mum were to rendezvous with Queen Judith this week, makin' preparations to bring yer brother there soon. It appears, however, that yer parents and me sister did not meet up as planned."

I grappled with that statement in silence.

"Yer brother is a savant. Brilliant and gifted in exceptional ways," Aunt Jules went on. "*Sui generis.* Unique. Like me sister. They don't fit in well with this world because part of 'em is meant to be in the other.

They'll be understood when they're in their rightful place. Savants of the ages have made perfect leaders for those in Vituvia."

Though I found it comforting to learn my brother had such a high calling, this was a bitter pill to swallow. I couldn't fathom what possessed my parents to keep these life-altering tidbits to themselves. Didn't they know I'd be traumatized by this information? Did the term "scarred for life" mean anything to them?

Though it all sounded phantasmagorical—I could think of no better word—I'd rather *read* about such adventures and continue to live my life as an average American girl, thank you very much. I should be thinking about grades and college and my future. How would my goals and dreams fit in with all this kooky stuff I now found myself tethered to?

Tethered? Ha! Like it or not, I was officially *tethered* to the Tethered World. What a dumb word.

To make matters worse, Aunt Jules believed our parents were in serious danger. Dad had asked Auntie to retrieve our van from Beacon Rock, a monolith on the banks of the Columbia River and less than an hour's drive from our home.

"When I couldn't find the Odyssey there, I knew somethin' must be askew and hurried over." Aunt Jules looked ready to cry. "Me thinks those nasty Trolls have been watchin' ye Larcens. They're the sworn enemies of the Gnomes, ya know. They must have a reason fer preventin' yer brother from comin' down to the Land of Legend."

"I thought the Gnomes ruled Vituvia." With fingers pressed against my temples, I willed my eyelids to stay open. Every part of me—especially my brain—wanted to shut down.

"Vituvia is the realm of the Gnomes, dovey. Vituvia is in the Land of Legend. The Land of Legend lies within the Tethered World. Make sense?"

I nodded, clueless.

"The Trolls nabbed yer parents at Burgerville, best I can tell. They must've followed them there fer a late-night snack."

"Are you serious?"

"No, no. Your *parents* were havin' a late night snack. Not the Trolls, pet. And if they're spyin' on yer parents it makes me wonder what may be happenin' to my dear sister, Judith. Is she even alive? Heavers! I can't bear to give it another thought."

Poor Aunt Jules had eventually given in to her emotions. By that time, it was pretty late. Brady and I put our arms around her while she sobbed into a napkin. She blew her nose and assured us she believed our parents were fine.

Fine as in...not dead?

"Likely bein' held as bait so they can lure ya below and capture Brock."

On that happy note, we'd gone to bed.

But now the morning brought the nightmare back to haunt me. I couldn't call the police or file a Missing Person Report. What would Unibrow and Barbie say if I reported my parents vanished on account of Bigfoot? Or crazier yet, kidnapped by Trolls? They'd probably split us into foster families and say good riddance to Amy and Liam Larcen.

The only way to handle this—the only way to get my parents home—would be for us to go and get them. Our wimpy, average family, taking on Trolls and coming up heroes? Al-righty then.

Don't get me wrong. I wanted my parents back ASAP, but I felt utterly inept to manage it. Of course, this wouldn't be a singlehanded feat. Oh, no. According to Aunt Jules, I'd get to bring Brady, possibly Brock, and Sophie. That's a winning combination right there. *Babysitting and Troll slaying. It's what I do.*

If not for my parents' predicament, there's no way I'd trek into Sci-fi Land—populated with creatures smart enough to stalk and kidnap. The idea of meeting cutesy Gnomes stressed me out, let alone ginormous Yetis. I couldn't muster any excitement about tackling in *real* life what most people only read about... because it's fiction.

Was living happily ever after too much to ask? Did my

parents expect me to embrace this burden of ancestry and walk away from college and a brilliant literary career? Apparently.

I needed to get my mind off things.

Sitting up, I caught a glimpse of myself in the mirror. Long hair snarled around my pale face. Puffy eyes tattled on my late night.

Great. I've morphed into Sasquatch.

My tired eyes burned and resented the sunlight. A thought struck me. Did they have a light source in this underground world? Would we need to bring a truckload of flashlights and batteries? Were there inventions like electricity and fluorescent lighting? Or giant fireflies?

What else might be giant? Cockroaches? Earthworms?

"Yecch!" I grabbed a T-shirt and jeans and tugged them on. If I stayed alone with my thoughts another moment, I'd morph myself into an insane asylum.

WHEN I JOINED THE buzz of controlled chaos downstairs, I grew more suspicious of Aunt Jules's connection to Leprechauns. Somehow, she'd managed to get everyone to complete their schoolwork while she washed two loads of laundry and baked bread. From scratch.

She had also shared our family secret with Sophie. The kid smiled so wide it made *my* cheeks hurt.

"I'm *sooo* excited, Sadie! Aren't you?" Sophie grabbed my shoulders and shook them with each word.

"Of course you are." I brushed her off and headed to the kitchen. Maybe it was rude to crush her enthusiasm, but if things went haywire, *I'd* be the one left to play Miss Fixit.

The smell of freshly baked bread lured me to the table. Slathering butter on a slice, I lost myself in yumminess, content to wallow in denial once again. I would live in the state of Washington and in a state of denial simultaneously. My hidden talent.

After a second slice of bread and a cup of coffee, I

asked Aunt Jules if I could fetch the mail. Mail sounded normal. I liked normal.

"As long as ya don't dawdle." She wagged her finger at me. "Trolls have an aversion to sunlight so it's unlikely they'd be lurkin' about. But we're all Troll bait, y'know."

Wow, I felt *so* assured. "Brady, I need to borrow you for a minute." I figured there was strength in numbers.

Brady opened the door.

I squinted at the sunlight, realizing that our blinds were still closed to the outside world. I noticed a new garden Gnome—a donation from Aunt Jules, no doubt—shouldered up against the brick wall along the walkway. This one was a freckled female with a shy grin.

"Great." Brady looked at the statue then at me. "Another statue. Can't have enough of those." He stepped outside, and I followed.

"Weird." I shook my head. How had Aunt Jules managed to lug that thing around and deposit it on the walkway before knocking on the door the night before? And...I didn't recall seeing it when I checked the driveway for her car. Maybe the fog hid it?

Though I felt an urge to sprint to the mailbox, I walked. Mr. Marshall didn't need a reason to watch our house more than he already did. Sometimes I wondered if he'd moved to our neighborhood simply to gawk at our family. Real, live homeschoolers on display. Step right up! See if you can catch the kids doing school in their pajamas.

Back inside, I found Aunt Jules in the kitchen tidying a mess only she seemed to notice.

"Looks like you brought us another Gnome," I said.

"My support hose!" Aunt Jules's hands flew to her face. She whizzed out the front door and hefted the statue inside. Brady scrambled to snatch it from her.

"Goodness, what was I thinkin'? Well, obviously I wasn't." She bustled back to the kitchen and pointed to the middle of the breakfast table. Brady placed it there with a thud.

"Thanks fer yer help, guppy. Now, go find Brock and Sophie and have 'em come join us."

Brady headed upstairs, and I turned to Aunt Jules. "So...Brock *will* be going?"

"I believe he shall." She grabbed a napkin and proceeded to give the Gnome a spit-shine. I cringed, remembering the horror of saliva baths from childhood.

"Won't that be dangerous, especially for Brock?" *How will I keep him on a schedule in another world?*

"Of course it'll be dangerous, ladybug. It'll be dangerous whether he goes or stays. I'm certain the Trolls are watchin' us, hopin' to find a way to nab him. If Brock stays, we risk endangerin' little Nicole and Nate. They may not recover from an encounter with a Troll, m'dear. Ya need to face those Yetis head on—let 'em know ya won't be bullied. Besides, Brock needs to begin his internship. Makes sense for him to make the trip now, while yer headed that way."

She made it sound like a trip to the grocery store.

Brady returned with the others, so I dropped the subject. Brock stepped up to the statue and ran his fingers over the intricate lines of expression. He appeared to read the surface, much like a blind person would read braille. His hand traveled up the pointy hat that stood at attention like a cone-shaped antenna.

"I see ya approve of the newest member of me Gnome family." Aunt Jules beamed at Brock. She gave us a wink and studied him while he studied the bronzed creature.

"She's grand." Brock smiled.

"Oh, yes, quite grand, my pet. This is Revonika. I've sculpted her 'specially fer yer family. She's the Gnome that yer folks were goin' to Vituvia to meet. I've had tea with her several times, and she's most anxious to get acquainted with ya."

"She's *so* cute." Sophie looked like she might burst with excitement. "I knew these statues were real. Nicole and I always said they looked too life-like to be pretend."

Brock hammered the statue with his fist. "She's real?"

"Not exactly. But ye shall meet the *real* Revonika soon. I brought her to show the family what she looks like, so ya can recognize her."

"Awesome!" Brady picked Auntie up in a big bear hug.

"I can't believe how cool my family is now."

Aunt Jules laughed. "We've always been *cool*, teddy bear. Maybe ya just weren't willin' to see it."

"Yeah, I guess." He set her down.

"So, when do we leave?" I wanted to put it off as long as possible.

"It depends on the weather. Yer way into the Tethered World must be under the cover of fog. The weatherman said we should have a repeat of last night's thick, heavy fog rollin' in. Therefore, we'll proceed as if yer leavin' tonight. I've arranged for ya to travel to the Tethered World the same way I traveled here."

"You've got a magic carpet or something, don't you?" Twenty-four hours earlier, I would've been joking. Now it was a legitimate question.

Aunt Jules grinned in a way that revealed I hovered close to the truth. "Better than a magic carpet, lollipop. I have an Odyssey."

"No way." I narrowed my eyes suspiciously. "*We* have an Odyssey. You're hiding something more exciting than a minivan."

"Yes and no." Her voice held a mischievous air. "I *do* have an Odyssey. Odyssey happens to be the name of me dragon."

CHAPTER SEVEN

We bustled about, emptying junk from backpacks and stuffing them with supplies. Bottled water, flashlights, batteries, snacks, and other items made a heavy load for each of us.

I dreaded the thought of what would arrive in the weatherman's predicted fog. The steady swirl in my gut forced me to invent things to stay busy. Dragons only come and go within a shroud of haze, I learned. The fact that I now possessed such knowledge about the habits of dragons disturbed me. The truth that they really existed terrified me.

Aunt Jules explained that her dragon, Odyssey, would deliver us to Beacon Rock—the same place my parents were headed the night before. Who needs a minivan or a magic carpet when you have a trained, flying dragon?

"Course, no one really *owns* a dragon," Aunt Jules told us. "I only get to ride him for *official* business."

We learned that large monoliths such as Haystack Rock near Aunt Jules and Beacon Rock near our home are portholes into the Tethered World. Back in the day of dragons galore, monoliths were a favorite place for these flying lizards to keep their lairs. The present-day beasts use the empty lairs of their deceased relatives to camp out where they're needed.

It's a sad fact—according to Aunt Jules—that there are precious few dragons left. "Slain in the days of King Arthur by a bunch of no-good trophy hunters. Lucky fer us, the beautiful creatures live fantastically long lives. The few that remain will be around fer some time."

Tonight we planned to take an express flight on the back of Odyssey to the ancient lair within Beacon Rock. Once inside, he would direct us to the passage that leads to the underworld.

Cue the scary music.

Through all the preparations, I kept a close eye on Brock, being that we ditched any sort of schedule after karate the night before. This was not the time for a meltdown. So far, so good, but I still didn't feel comfortable bringing him with us—High King in training or not.

I watched him attempt to stuff seventeen pairs of socks into his backpack. Thankfully, Brady talked him into removing ten pairs for the sake of batteries and bottled water. He knew how to handle Brock better than any of us, a perk of being twins.

Brady plopped into a chair at the kitchen table beside Aunt Jules and her steaming cup of tea. "So, how do we know where to find this place once we get below ground? Should we ask for directions to where the Trolls live? What did you call it—Craverfall?

"It's Cravenmall." Sophie looked proud of her superior knowledge. "And no, we won't be able to ask directions. We're supposed to sneak up on the place, not announce our arrival."

"It's Craven*thrall*," Aunt Jules corrected. "And you best lose yer attitude, little chickadee. It won't help things a bit for ya to act like a know-it-all. You're all on the same team and of the same blood. Ya stick together no matter what, ya hear? There may be times when ya only have each other to trust." One tiny finger jabbed in our direction as she peered at the four of us. She seemed to grow a foot when she preached like that.

"How ya find yer way around the Tethered World," she continued, "remains to be seen. There isn't a handbook for these here situations. This mission is in God's great hands, not yer own. He initiated it. He will accomplish it."

Sophie mumbled, "Yes, ma'am," and zipped her pack.

"Bye-bye?" Nate's coffee-colored eyes looked up at me.

"I'm going bye-bye, but not you, little man." I hefted him to my hip. "Natey and Nicole get to stay and play with Auntie Jules."

"Sadie, bye-bye." He took my face in his hands, planted a noisy kiss on my lips, and wiggled down.

I peeked through an opening in the curtains to inspect the night air. The sky was clear. "No fog." *Chalk another one up to the weatherman.* "Guess we'll have to wait another day to catch a ride to the underworld." *Boohoo.*

Aunt Jules stepped beside me and pulled the curtains a little wider. "Right on schedule."

I blinked. What? Fog smothered the house, the yard, and the sky like gravy. A small squeal escaped Aunt Jules's lips as she stared into the gloomy mist.

She paced back and forth, peering out every few minutes. I didn't know what she hoped to find.

We double-checked our packs then huddled around the table. I felt weary already, nerves stretched and stressed. Lack of sleep only made it worse.

Nicole wandered in, a doll under her arm, and slipped onto my lap. "How long will you be gone?"

"I don't know." I smoothed her bangs and adjusted her headband. "We'll meet up with Mom and Dad first. Then Brock will stay with Aunt Jules' sister for a visit." There. I'd managed to skip the scary stuff and give her a nugget of truth.

"Why does Mom need all of you to help her work? Why doesn't she need me?"

"She *does* need you," I assured her. "But we all have different jobs. Mom needs you to stay and help Aunt Jules take care of the dogs and Nate. Auntie's not used to watching a busy guy like him. You can be her assistant. You're perfect for that job."

Nicole seemed to consider this. "I guess that's a good plan. But I still don't get why she needs all of you—and

Dad—to help her find Bigfoot."

I shrugged. "I've wondered that too. I think we'll understand once we're all together."

"Yeah, I bet." She traced the shape of my hand on the table, apparently satisfied.

Nate came back, pushing a plastic dump truck. He plopped on the floor beside Brady and scooted it between his plump, toddler legs. I relished the cozy moment and took a mental picture of the last bit of normal I might see for some time. God only knew how long it would be before we were all together again. And together would only count if Mom and Dad were back.

After a few minutes, Auntie whisked the younger ones to bed. She returned in a hurry to a silent, tense kitchen. Even Sophie acted uptight. Aunt Jules crossed to the window, where she stood on tiptoes and craned her neck.

"Is there some signal you're looking for?" Sophie studied the window.

"Nope. Merely checkin' the weather. Sort of willin' the fog to stay thick and sticky. If the fog stays, Odyssey can safely come, and ye kids can safely go. Once the Trolls figure out yer no longer here, they'll be lookin' at huntin' ya down."

"Uh, that may not be the best way to put it in front of Sophie." I drummed a warning on the table with my fingers.

"Oh, puh-lease." Sophie rolled her eyes. "We're headed underground to rescue our kidnapped parents. What else could she say to freak me out?"

"Good point, sweet pea." Aunt Jules winked. "I'm really hopin' to send ya off tonight and fool 'em into thinkin' yer still 'ere. It'll give ya a head start."

I looked at Sophie and shook my head. We all needed courage, but she seemed to have more than her share.

A resonating thud made me grip the table. More felt than heard. *Something* had invaded our space.

Brock stood and faced the door. "I'm here," he said, as if he'd heard someone call his name.

Aunt Jules shifted into full animation mode. She bounded up and crossed to the window in one fluid motion. "Get yer things, lovies. It's time!" Her nimble movement defied her age. She turned and shoved us in various directions.

My fingers fumbled to pick up my pack and slip it on in hurried silence. Dinner churned in my stomach. My brain floated off into third-person mode—my standard coping mechanism—detached and observant.

Brady stood at the back door and bounced anxiously in place. He looked at Aunt Jules for approval, hand hovering over the knob.

"You may do the honors, doodlebug." Aunt Jules swept her arm in his direction.

Brady eased the door open and stepped into the mist. Sophie and Brock filed out behind, like a tentative game of follow the leader. I hung back.

Aunt Jules motioned me to hurry. "C'mon, pumpkin." She stepped into the backyard and was enveloped by fog.

My heart bungee-jumped to my feet, but I willed myself out the door. Despite the cool air, perspiration pricked my forehead and upper lip. It felt like everything unfolded in slow motion.

The fog billowed, sheer and secretive, like a cocoon that kept the creature from view. My eyes probed the shifting shroud, unable to focus. It was as if a black hole took up residence there and devoured my perception of space. Prevented me from making sense of things. Or maybe my brain flat out refused to believe it.

From their kennel, Ollie and Mindy-Loo barked a frenzied warning that was picked up by neighboring dogs. I discerned movement. A mist rolled around a shadowy shape in the center of our yard. At last the fog parted enough to expose something moist and glistening and alive. Gold, reptilian eyes the size of headlights found a break in the mist. And then, with a twitch of its head, the eyes found *me.*

"*GORRRNT!*"

I jumped and toppled into the shrubbery. The dogs clammed up. I scrambled to catch my breath and remove myself from the bushes.

"Shush now, Odyssey!" Aunt Jules pointed a scolding

finger at the mass. "Yer scarin' the children. Ignore those pups and be quiet, ya hear? The neighbors might wake, which would be a disaster." I could barely make out her fuzzy hair, halo-like in the moonlit haze, bobbing in anticipation. "This is it, dumplin's. Time to go." Her voice sounded young, like Nicole's when she knows it's Christmas morning.

I watched my siblings move towards Odyssey, devoured by mist. My feet were rooted, and my legs trembled. I was reduced to a quivering blob of uselessness while Auntie gave hasty directions. Her words made no sense. Everything remained surreal.

"Hey, lassie." Aunt Jules emerged in front of me. "I know ya have a lot on yer shoulders. This isn't an easy task that you've been chosen fer. But ready or not, it's time to go."

"I'm not ready. I'll never be ready."

She slipped her arm around my waist and gave me a squeeze. "I need ya to be strong and calm. Yer Mum and Dad and siblin's need ya to be strong and calm. We all have faith in ya, Sadie. Ye can do this, with the help of the good Lord."

Aunt Jules tried to propel me towards the dragon, but I resisted. Panic sprang up behind my eyes, and I felt the humiliating sting of unshed tears. I crumpled into her arms and cried awkwardly over the top of her shoulder. "What do I do if Brock has a meltdown in this underworld place?" I sobbed. "I don't think he should go. I don't know if I can protect him."

Her comforting hand ran through my hair. "I know, I know, me pet. There're many questions I can't answer. But Brock needs to go. I feel strongly about it. He's only endangerin' sweet Nicole and wee-little Nate by bein' here. Ya must go below, and ya must take Brock."

She pulled away and looked me in the eyes. "It's time, dear Sadie. Time to go and get on the back of me dragon and rescue dear Liam and Amy. The four of ya—with God Himself—are their only hope. That's a load to carry, but it's the truth. Pray a lot. We'll be prayin' here at home. I know it's hard to process. But yer gonna need to do yer processin'—and yer prayin'—on the way to Beacon Rock. Time's meltin' away along with the fog. We can't risk dawdlin' any longer. Ya must begin to be brave right now."

I nodded, wiped my tears, and swallowed the ones waiting their turn. *Right now.*

Walking through the haze, I kept my eyes on the ground. I'd face this creature the way I faced ski lifts and roller coasters—with very little courage but a lot of resolve. I refused to notice anything specific, not the size nor shape nor feel of this... *thing*.

Somehow I climbed on its back. A long ridge of humps ran across the Dragon's spine and provided each of us a secure seat in between. I was vaguely aware of Aunt Jules sending us off with love and good wishes. The mist wrapped me in a cloudy curtain and made it easy to avoid the reality of where I sat. My mind remained blissfully disengaged until I was off the ground and headed into the starry night.

Tendrils of fog tumbled down and away as the ancient reptile propelled itself forward and up with little effort. My heart thudded a drumroll, and my lungs heaved with ragged, short gasps. We rose above the murky ground, broke through the layer of fog, and into a brilliant, sparkling sky.

The nervous laughter and squeals of excitement from the others became a distant, muted sound.

Blacking out was a relief.

CHAPTER EIGHT

SOMEONE CALLED MY NAME. I FELT myself being yanked from behind. Repeatedly. In a rush, the night's adventure coursed back to my consciousness like a splash of cold water.

I sprang up then recoiled. The wind sliced into my eyes and pressed moisture out of the corners even as it whistled in my ears. I gasped and swallowed lungfuls of air, unable to catch my breath.

"Sadie!" Sophie sat behind me, screaming into the wind. Her arms encircled my waist. "Are you okay?" She sounded terrified. I must have scared the spit out of her.

"Yes!" I yelled with what little strength remained, my energy sapped. I nodded for emphasis and gave her arms a reassuring squeeze. Her grip relaxed, but she continued to hug my middle. If I didn't get myself together, no one would follow me anywhere. I certainly didn't trust myself to lead.

I sent up a silent plea for help. Maybe gliding above the clouds would allow me to be heard—and answered—faster. I willed my pulse to slow a few notches and added a prayer for my parents, wherever they might be.

The stars would have taken my breath away if the wind hadn't already. Far above the lights of the city, I saw more stars than I dreamed existed. It looked like

God had poured piles of sugar-crystals across a black, velvet blanket. Though I felt very small in the expanse of the sky, I also felt significant. Despite my overwhelming circumstances, I wanted to accept the unique place my family occupied in history.

My gaze drifted lower. I forced myself to recognize the situation at hand. I was zipping through the air on the back of an Odyssey. *And this ain't no minivan!*

Though it disturbed me to touch the creature, I ran my hand up and over the large, leathery hump that rose in front of me. It looked like an overgrown saddle horn. I felt another one swelled up against my back. Twisting around, I saw Sophie, Brock, and Brady behind me, single file.

It amazed me to watch the expanse of wings that stretched with grace from the ancient beast. They danced across the sky, tasting the currents and making adjustments as we roamed the heavens. Odyssey's neck looked like a sturdy tree trunk. It shot straight ahead, purposeful and aerodynamic. His skin shimmered like chiseled granite. Power radiated from his scaly armor. I relaxed and forced a grin. What an inconceivable place to be.

Goosebumps stood at attention, and my teeth clacked together. If only I'd known how cold it would be up here! I needed my jacket. Or a parka. My hair lashed against my face and neck in frenzied waves. Though the air chilled me, it smelled so pristine, so *alive*, I hoped to never forget it. With a frozen attempt at a smile, I permitted myself to be a part of the infinite, evening sky.

We started our descent into the mist. I must have been unconscious for quite a while if we were already nearing Beacon Rock. It bummed me out to miss so much of the trek. I was actually enjoying myself. Better late than never, I guess.

We spiraled down. Large circles became tighter, and Odyssey plunged into the fog. I white-knuckled the hump in front of me and hoped the dragon had a built-in radar that prevented him from crashing into trees or—worse yet—overgrown rocks.

He leveled out. Breaks in the haze offered a glimpse of headlights and taillights snaking along the highway that followed the liquid course of the Columbia River. Boats speckled the water. Their lights reflected off the inky swells and winked at me like they would keep our presence a secret. Then the clouds whited everything out again.

"Close your eyes." A voice, mellow and deep, resounded. It sounded like it came from everywhere and from inside myself, all at once.

"Did you say something?" Sophie screamed in my ear.

She heard the voice too. I shook my head and pointed at the dragon.

"Close your eyes, Larcens." Like a bow being drawn across a large, double bass, the voice sang with bold authority.

I closed my eyes.

With swift and precise motion, Odyssey careened into a dive. My legs gripped the beast as my body lurched backwards. The rise of his hump behind me pressed my backpack up against my head.

In unison, we screamed.

My life flashed before me. Three times. We continued to fall like a rock from the Grand Canyon. Then the dragon made a one-hundred-eighty-degree turn. My body whipped forward, arms clinging to the large hump like a drowning victim flung against a log.

"Duck!" the voice boomed.

I pressed my face into his armored ridge, inhaling Odyssey's metallic scent.

In an instant, the whistle of wind became hollow. It felt like we'd flown into a giant seashell. The swirling air made ocean sounds. It smelled musty and contained. Damp.

Somehow we were inside Beacon Rock. Though this had been the plan from the start, I couldn't fathom how Odyssey made it happen. *Magic* didn't fit into my world... yet in all the times I'd climbed this hunk of rock, I never knew there to be a cave or tunnel in sight.

"You are safe now." The voice offered comfort and

assurance as if he understood we were young and frightened.

My heart attempted a normal tempo.

"Wow!"

"Cool!"

The others expressed their amazement. I sat speechless and let my eyes adjust to the light.

Wait. There wasn't any light.

Shimmery flecks that peppered Odyssey's skin began to glow. His violet light penetrated the dark cave and tinted us purple. It made me smile.

"You may dismount, Larcens."

We climbed down like astronauts leaving the safety of their spaceship. Slow and stiff, we made our way to the ground. I rubbed my hands and huffed hot air across them, trying to get some feeling back.

"We thank thee, oh Odyssey. Thy strength and beauty are resplendent." Sophie, first to break the spell, praised the dragon with her medieval enthusiasm. She walked towards the head of the gentle giant.

"The pleasure and honor are mine. Did you enjoy your ride?"

"Unbelievable!" Brady's face split with a smile. "Better than *anything* at Disneyland."

The purple-blue glow around the dragon's face blushed pink.

We gathered near his enormous head and inspected our legendary friend up close. Though his flared nostrils and snake-slit eyes looked fierce, his face reflected kindness and wisdom. Rather human—for a reptile.

"You must make haste to the Land of Legend, my friends. Sorry that we cannot visit or linger together. My orders were to send you off upon your arrival."

"We need to get Mom and Dad." Brock looked pensive.

Wow! Brock understood why we were here. This motivated me to get things underway.

"Yep. Sure do." I removed my backpack and stretched. "Thank you, Odyssey, for delivering us safely. We would hate for you to get into trouble with Aunt Jules. She may be small, but she's intimidating. We'll head out as soon as we get situated."

My siblings dug into their packs. I opened mine and pulled out a flashlight and my much-missed jacket, which I slipped on then zipped to my chin. My hair was a snarled mass of hopelessness, but I ran my fingers through it anyway.

"I'm hungry." Brock paced in a circle. That's another side of Brock—his perpetually hungry side. Which meant we didn't entrust the food supply to his pack.

"Here." I tossed him a granola bar. "Just one. We've got to stretch out the supplies. No telling how long it needs to last."

Brock inhaled the snack then held up the empty wrapper.

"Place it in the corner." Odyssey bobbed his head in the direction he wanted Brock to follow. Brock complied and added the wrapper to a small collection of unidentifiable stuff in the shadows.

Like a jumbo flame thrower, fire shot from Odyssey's nostrils. We jumped. Brady screamed like a girl. The trash became a heap of embers in a split-second. Heat rolled off of the cave's ceiling and washed over us.

Odyssey's luminescent skin surged a few watts. He appeared to enjoy surprising us. *"And that's how a dragon recycles."*

Laughter rippled through the cavern. Dragon humor—who knew?

The beam from my flashlight revealed several tunnels yawning at the back of the cave, eager to swallow us down. I wondered which one would take us to our parents and where the others might lead. Brock, Brady, and Sophie were now shouldered next to me. The guys wore headlamps, while Sophie and I held flashlights.

I felt their courage and sense of adventure seep into me as we huddled close and stared into the unknown. It helped to have a lizard the size of a small bus watching our backs.

"The second tunnel from the left will take you to your destination." The reverberating voice brought focus to my brain.

I squared my shoulders and cleared my throat. "Thank you, Odyssey. We look forward to meeting you again—with our parents."

"God speed. God guide. God protect." Odyssey spoke his blessing on our little group.

"We need to get Mom and Dad." Though Brock often repeated himself, this sounded like an urgent reminder.

"Yeah, bro." Brady placed his hand on Brock's shoulder. "That's like our mission statement, isn't it?"

"Yes." Brock nodded. "Our mission."

"Let's roll!" Brady looked at me. "I'll lead the way. Sadie, why don't you play caboose?"

Sounded good to me. Brady could be first to meet spider webs and who-knew-what head on. "Gotta love chivalry." I curtsied.

We turned to face the living, breathing Stealth Bomber and called out our sentiments and good-byes. With flashlights slicing into the veiled hollows of the cavern, we pointed ourselves to the mouth of the tunnel. Second from the left.

I held my breath when we crossed the threshold into a rough, silent cylinder. The floor began to slope down and to the right within moments. It led us away from any trace of Odyssey's effervescent glow. My flashlight trembled in my grasp and revealed my anxiety to the rest, much to my embarrassment.

The narrow, slate shaft looked cold and uninviting. Rust-colored veins ran helter-skelter through the rock. The ground was slick and looked worn from use. It made me wonder who—or what—had been using this tunnel so frequently. Water trickled from small fissures in the wall. I heard the occasional drip echo through the passageway. The air grew cooler. If not for the exertion of the hike, I'd have been miserably chilled.

We marched in silence through the monotonous channel of stone. Although the weight of the earth above increased with each step, it couldn't compete with the burden of thoughts that pressed on me from within. The reality of trudging into unknown dangers must've bothered the others as well. Everyone seemed wrapped in their own musings. Or perhaps I oozed enough distress for all of us.

"Great." Brady came to an abrupt stop. The light from his headlamp revealed a fork in the path. "Which way, Sis?"

"To the left," Sophie piped. "It looks more worn out and used."

"I was asking Sadie." Brady aimed his headlamp at the two choices. "But yeah, it does show more wear."

"Fine with me." I shrugged. "I just know if I stop for long I'm gonna freeze. Pick one."

We went left.

The tunnel sloped at uncomfortable angles. I hoped we wouldn't run into a dead end. Backtracking on these inclines seemed impossible. There were times when we hung on to the walls or clung to rocks that jutted out. One precarious spot sent me sliding into the others like a bowling ball knocking over pins.

"Ouch!" A chorus of yelps bounced around the passage.

"I'm so sorry. Is everyone all right?"

We untangled our limbs and stood, inspecting each other for damage. My jeans and flashlight got the worst of it. Ripped jeans were always in style, so I could live with the tear across the knee. The flashlight, on the other hand, died a violent, shattered death. This tweaked my mood from anxious to angry. In less than an hour I'd managed to lose one of the most important items I brought.

"I think everyone's okay," Sophie declared for the group. "We better take it slow on these inclines, though."

Your wish is our command, Captain Obvious.

My frustration over ruining a much-needed flashlight veiled my true resentment. My little brothers and sister seemed way more equipped for this escapade than me. I felt like a cat tossed into a mud puddle. *I want out!*

To be honest, I was fine if everyone else made the decisions. Then no one could blame me when things went crazy. Yet, I knew—deep down in the tunnels of my soul—I would need to step up and make some tough choices. For now, I would act the part of confident big sis for their sakes. Maybe I'd also come across as being a considerate sister if I included their input with my decisions.

I unzipped my pack and pulled out an extra flashlight. We forged ahead with renewed energy, thanks to the adrenaline-rush of being toppled over. Brock started to whistle, a sound which carried well throughout the tunnel, though a bit piercing in the constricted space. I didn't want him to announce our arrival to the underworld. But I also didn't want to add *paranoid* to my list of under-qualifications. I wrestled with how to handle it.

"Whoa!" Once again, Brady pulled up short.

"What's wrong?" I asked. "Looks okay from here."

"Yeah, for about ten more feet. Then we'll need to stay smack against the wall or take a little trip off the side of a cliff." He highlighted his discovery with a sweep of his headlamp.

Words like chasm and gulf sprang to my mind.

"We'll need to use extreme caution," Sophie informed us.

"No kidding, Einstein." I'd had enough of her self-assurance. "Cartwheels might be our other option."

"Chill, Sis." Brady nudged Einstein. "Sophie's only trying to help."

"Yeah." Sophie put her hands on her hips.

"Whatever," I said through clenched teeth. I knew I should back off but couldn't make myself care. It seemed too soon to face danger. I wasn't ready. I don't prefer to do my own stunts.

Brady approached the narrow ledge. We followed his example and pressed against the wall, face first, creeping along sideways. I fought the image of my backpack tilting me off balance and into the dark pit below. Once past the narrowest part, I remembered to breathe. It probably only took a minute to cross, but it felt like an eternity.

The overhang widened and looked like a great spot to regain my composure. I paced the patch of rock that jutted into the open chamber. The high ceiling and sweeping space below echoed the sounds of our anxious breathing. Brady offered a round of high-fives. I resisted the urge to kneel and kiss the ground.

"Time for a water break, captain?" Brady pulled his bottle from his pack.

"Definitely." It felt terrific to slip off my backpack, and the water helped to drown the fiery thoughts I battled.

We sat along the edge of the broad slab of rock. The others let their feet dangle over the side. I kept mine safely tucked beneath me, the precipice too vast for my comfort. Our flashlights revealed two-story stalactites that dangled overhead, ready to impale intruders. Below us, stalagmites posed like enormous, silent statues.

No, not statues. Teeth. A mouthful of overgrown fangs, and we sat on the bottom lip of a starving rock giant.

This place might've made an awesome field trip for school, but it was a horrifying hole in the ground under the circumstances. I shivered and scolded my imagination. If I didn't get my thoughts under control, I might show Brock what a meltdown really looked like.

"How long have we been traveling?" I tried to sound casual.

"Ninety-six minutes," Brock stated, his face lit by his watch. He probably didn't need a timepiece to make an exact guess.

"No wonder we're tired and thirsty." Brady yawned. "But we better keep moving. I'm guessing we've got a long way to go."

"Hey, what does everyone chant at the end of *The Last Battle* in the Narnia series?" Sophie asked. "Further in..."

"Further up and further in!" Brock recited the words with dramatic flair, exactly the way Dad always read them.

"Yes." Sophie smiled. "Except we can say, 'further down and further in,' right?"

"Ha! Good one." I gave her a fist bump. "We should look at this as—"

"*Oh no!*" Brady screeched and clawed after his pack.

Too late.

As it plummeted over the edge, Sophie snatched at it and lurched off balance. She shrieked and grappled for Brady. He steadied her, but not before she tried to counterbalance and brace her foot against the closest object—two more backpacks. The motion launched both bags into the abyss.

"*Noooooo!*" I watched our supplies—along with two flashlights perched on top—take a nosedive into the mouth of the giant.

CHAPTER NINE

THE SOUND OF OUR BACKPACKS RICOCHETING off the rocks punctuated the silence like stinging slaps across my face. I winced with each blow. My optimism shattered, falling fast with our things. The light from the twins' headlamps exposed dark blobs of fabric wedged between the rocks, mocking our incompetence.

"You've *got* to be kidding." I shook my head, refusing to accept what happened. "What were you guys thinking? Why would you set your packs so close to the edge? Brilliant! Just brilliant."

"Uh-oh. My socks." Brock wrung his hands and rocked back and forth.

"I'm s-sorry." Sophie sniffed and wiped her eyes. "I was only trying to help."

Brady cleared his throat. "What are we going to—"

"We're going to get ourselves down to this stupid place, with its stupid Trolls, and rescue Mom and Dad. That's what!" If I didn't bark out the obvious, I would cave into despair.

I stood and swung my bag—the only surviving backpack—onto my shoulders. Then I snatched Brady's headlamp and jammed it on my head. Though it pricked my conscience, I ignored the realization that I'd placed my own flashlight on top of the packs that went overboard. My strides were heavy and spiteful, an attempt to stomp out the hopelessness that threatened to strangle me.

The others scrambled to get up and follow me. Sophie's sniffles spanned the gaps between footsteps and made me feel like a tyrant. I wished Brock would whistle again. Instead, I heard him mumble repeatedly, "I need my socks."

The darkness stayed barely out of reach. It threatened to gobble us down, with only two headlamps to fight it off. When I came to another fork in the passage, I chose the one that looked well-traveled in hopes it meant we would get to the Tethered World soon. The cold air fingered itself through my clothing. I picked up the pace to fight the chill.

Tedium slowly edged out anger. Fighting off the monotony of so much sameness became harder to battle than the cold. The rock surroundings looked more or less unchanging everywhere we went. I hoped we weren't looping around and back again.

The word "lost" kept asserting itself in my brain, and I kept shoving it back into the shadows. I also tried not to dwell on the batteries that had plunged away with our supplies. If our headlamps ran out of juice, we'd be trapped in a granite-encased black tomb. There would be no finding our way out of this mountainous catacomb. We would starve to death if we didn't freeze first.

"Do you think we're lost?" Sophie sounded weary.

"No," I said a little too forcefully. I couldn't verbalize my thoughts and didn't want to admit them, even to myself.

The passageway closed in around us. Everyone except Sophie needed to stoop. My thighs quivered from walking downhill for so long. Now my back complained from the awkward hunch. *Oh, for a steamy bubble bath and hot chocolate!*

"Hang on." The tunnel took a sudden downward turn—straight down. My headlamp caught sight of a dirt floor waiting at the bottom, but I couldn't judge the distance through the small opening. "Looks like we have to slide on our backsides at close to a ninety-degree angle. Or we can return to the last fork in the tunnel and try another passage."

Neither option sounded appealing. It would be quite a hike to turn back.

Brady leaned against the wall. He looked exhausted in the beam of light I aimed his way. "Let's keep going. We must be getting close. I feel like we've walked so far we oughta be in China."

"Let me go first." Sophie peered into the hole. "I'm the smallest. We don't know how narrow that rock gets the farther down it goes."

"Sure." I stepped aside to let her pass. It seemed a fitting payback for the supplies she shoved into Never Never Land. I handed her my headlamp.

Sophie wasted no time. She scooted to the edge and plugged her nose—like she was jumping into the water—and disappeared down the hole. In the fleeting time between her launch and landing, I wondered what we'd do if she got stuck, or if she fit through but the rest of us could not. Another big-sister fail.

"It's all good! Pretty soft landing." Sophie's voice drifted up in time to ease my panicked afterthought. "You probably want to toss the backpack to me rather than wear it, just to be safe."

"Okay, here it comes." I tossed it down then slid in after it, glad to find the whole thing non-eventful.

Brock landed with a *plop*. He usually fights against any enclosed, constricted space. He hates to be confined in any way. But I saw no hint of that anxiety today. The fact that he'd handled all of this upheaval so well seemed nothing short of miraculous. That realization cheered me a bit.

Brady yelled, "Geronimo!" and joined us.

Sophie handed me the headlamp. I stuck it on and looked around. We were in an enormous cavern. This place was stadium-sized but desolate and oppressive. It swallowed up our two measly beams of light and made me feel small and lost, with no sense of direction.

"Ugh." I gave the backpack a frustrated kick.

"Look!" Sophie pointed to the walls and ceiling.

"What?" I stared into the void.

"Shut your lights off." Her voice echoed off the rock. "Let your eyes adjust."

Brock turned his off, and I followed suit. For a moment, I felt like Jonah inside the belly of the whale. Soon, I made out the others' silhouettes. Like Odyssey, the rocks were flecked with phosphorous material. Unlike Odyssey, they glowed a sickening greenish-yellow. We looked like a bunch of nauseous zombies and made scary faces at each other in the gleaming light.

Laughter slightly shifted my mood. It helped to be out of the tunnels with more space to move about. Once our eyes adapted, we decided to conserve the batteries on the two remaining lights.

Brady grabbed the backpack. We wandered aimlessly, trying to find where the tunnels picked up again. The soft, flat ground was a welcome change from the steep, rocky tunnels. Pools of water refracted the pinprick light, especially when a hefty drip splatted the liquid and made the colors dance. Crystals jutted out of the ground here and there, glowing gold and looking like magical diamonds fit for a giant.

I noticed numerous treelike shapes clustered up ahead. "What are those?" They struck me as odd, maybe because there hadn't been anything to look at so far besides dirt and rocks.

Sophie studied the shapes. "I think they're mushrooms. Giant mushrooms!"

Sure enough, the towering blobs appeared to be part of the fungi family. But these things must've been on steroids. They stretched taller than Brock and Brady. Their umbrella-shaped caps covered half their stems and were as wide as they were tall. A sphere of amber light pooled around their base.

"Maybe this *is* the Tethered World." Sophie stretched out her arms with a shrug.

I sighed. "Maybe."

"I'm hungry." Brock tugged my sleeve.

"Okay. Quick break."

We sat on the mossy ground beneath one of the mushrooms. Its faint, filtered light lit our little picnic. Most of our food went belly up inside our backpacks. One bottle of water and one package of beef jerky offered little satisfaction. I rationed our water to two swallows each. One piece of beef jerky per person left three pieces for later. *Yippee.*

Brock ate his piece so fast he probably didn't taste it. "I want more."

"Sorry, but we lost most of our food." I spread my empty fingers and shrugged. "We need to save some for later."

"I'm hungry," he insisted.

"Yo, Brock, we have to wait." Brady used his chummy, twin-brother voice.

"I'm *hungry*." Brock jumped up.

Oh no! Meltdown City straight ahead. I braced myself for weeping and gnashing of teeth.

Brady looked at his half-eaten strip of jerky. Like a peace offering, he handed it to his twin. Brock snatched it up and scarfed it down.

It did the trick.

Brady's sacrifice made me feel ashamed for not thinking of it myself. I offered Brady what was left of my piece. "Thanks. I know you're Starvin' Marvin like the rest of us."

Brady waved me off and stood. "No, thanks. We better keep moving or I'm going to curl up on this moss and sleep. I think we've been up most of the night." He slipped the backpack on his shoulders.

I got up and looked around. There seemed no indication of which way to go. "I wish we knew if this was the Tethered World, or Vituvia, or what. If there's life anywhere around here, it must be hiding."

"This isn't the Tethered World. Not even close." It sounded like Sophie had been sucking helium.

We all laughed.

"What's wrong with your voice, Soph?" I tried to see her better in the dim light.

She giggled. "*I* didn't say that!"

"She didn't say that. Skoon said that." The same quirky voice interrupted our laughter. We spun towards the sound.

A miniature man stood in the glow of a nearby mushroom. The light revealed a slouchy hat, bearded face, and well-proportioned body. He sported a burgundy jacket with shiny, brass buttons.

"Who are you?" Sophie sidled up to the shrunken man and crouched for a better look. "You're so *cute*."

He reached up and tweaked her nose. "Don't call me cute."

"Ouch!" She swatted at him and jumped back.

"Hey!" Brady stepped between them.

"Hay is for houses." The man drew himself up. "She can't talk to me like that. I'm not gonna take it." He rammed his fist at the air.

"Okay, calm down." Brady pressed an authoritative hand in the air.

Sophie rubbed her nose and shot the man a glare. "Hay isn't for houses. It's for *horses*."

He glowered back and stuck his tongue in her direction.

Protective-sister mode sprang to life. "What's your problem?"

Brady looked at me and shook his head. "My name's Brady." His voice was sweet and syrupy. "This is my sister Sadie, my brother Brock, and...I believe you've already gotten acquainted with my other sister, Sophie."

The little man swiped the crumpled hat from his head and gave a theatrical bow. "My apologies for the rough start to our relationship." He grinned, replaced his hat, then drew himself up and puffed out his chest. "My name is Skoon. I couldn't help overhearing your conversation. You're looking for Vituvia, yes?"

"Yes." I nodded. "Are you from there?"

"Bah!" He spit on the ground. "I'm not a Gnome. Why, if I could reach your nose I'd squeeze it so hard—"

"Dude!" Brady stepped towards him. "Where I come from, guys don't beat up on girls."

"Where I come from, we don't take kindly to insults."

The little man—Skoon—grew red in the face.

"Look." I raised my hands in surrender. "We don't mean to insult you. We're new here. We're trying to find our way into the Tethered World. To Vituvia."

"Obviously you're new if you can't tell a Leprechaun from a Gnome." Skoon stuck his chin in the air and crossed his arms.

"A *Leprechaun*?" Sophie seemed impressed to have been tweaked by such a creature.

Skoon took a step away from her. "I don't know what you've heard about Leprechauns, but I'm sure it's false information."

Sophie smirked. "My mom's a Leprechaun *expert*. She knows what you're really like."

"Oh, she does, does she? Well, she must've kept it a secret from the likes of you. You thought I was a *Gnome*. A sappy, happy Gnome. Ugh!" He spit again.

Great. Our first contact in the underworld was a bearded, infantile man that threw temper tantrums. It didn't exactly stir my confidence. We needed this guy on our side, and Sophie needed to zip it before he refused to help.

"You're right." Brady was ever the diplomat. "We don't know much about Leprechauns. Is it true you guys are super great with directions? Smart guy like you probably knows exactly where we need to go."

Skoon visibly swelled. Brady must have hit the bull's-eye. "I suppose I could take you there. For a small fee."

Brady and I looked at each other. We didn't bring money.

"What'd you have in mind?" Sophie asked.

Skoon scrubbed his beard with his finger and thumb. "A few gold coins would be lovely."

"So, Leprechauns *do* hoard gold." Sophie jabbed a finger his way. "Let's label that little rumor as *fact.*"

Skoon balled his fists, his body stiff with anger.

"*Sophie.*" I snapped my fingers then made a slicing motion across my throat. Turning to Skoon, I pretended to be calm and controlled. "We're fresh out of gold coins, Mr. Skoon. But we need to find Vituvia and would be grateful if you'd help us do so."

Skoon looked us up and down. "Your travel pouch for my services."

"Our what?" I scratched my head.

"Travel pouch." He pointed at Brady's backpack.

"No, no, no." I shook my head. "Those are our supplies. There's nothing valuable in there."

"Of course there isn't. Why else would you lug that big thing from topside all the way down here?" Skoon narrowed his eyes. "This is my last offer. Your travel pouch for my services. I'll not waste another moment arguing about it. I'll return to harvesting mushrooms and moss, while you fumble around trying to find your way to the fancy-shmancy Gnome home."

I looked at Brady and tried to guess his thoughts. He shrugged.

Our one surviving pack of supplies wouldn't last long. With other options non-existent, I agreed. "Fine. You drive a hard bargain, Mr. Skoon, but we'll take it."

His eyes glinted. He stuck out a greedy hand. "Gimme."

Brady crossed his arms. "Nope. You'll get the pouch when we get to Vituvia."

Skoon spit and stomped.

"Oh, real mature." Sophie scowled.

I stared her down. "Can we play nice and get to where we need to go? Is that too much to ask?"

Skoon apparently thought I was taking up for him and tipped his hat my way. He motioned for us to follow and began to wind his way through towering mushrooms and shimmering, moss-covered stones.

I fell into step beside Brock, behind everyone else, and placed my hand on his shoulder. My heart swelled a bit, thinking of how well he was doing despite the craziness and lack of schedule.

"Mom says you can never trust a Leprechaun."

"I remember that." I gave him a squeeze. "But I don't think we've much choice. We can't find Mom and Dad if we're lost."

Brock shrugged off my hand and retreated into his

silent world. He barely tolerates physical touch. My parents had an awful time with him as a toddler. He hated to be placed in a car seat or shopping cart and refused to be held. Thankfully, things have improved with time and persistence.

Skoon walked with a vengeance. His legs were a blur as they scrambled over the terrain. While he forged ahead, he repeated a strange little chant:

"Griff, graff, groan,
Oh, those sappy, happy Gnomes!
But the grace that fell in Nimmickdell
Shivers far from home."

I found the tune tedious, but it beat dealing with his cranky disposition.

After a while, we entered a narrow passageway. Our shoulders brushed the walls in places. It had the feel of a hallway instead of a tunnel. Maybe because the ceiling stood a good bit higher than the earlier passages. The rock continued to illuminate our trek just enough to avoid the use of flashlights.

The close quarters became an amplifier for Skoon's rhyme. Sophie placed her hands over her ears. I found myself walking in cadence with his chant, much to my annoyance.

We marched single file, and I brought up the rear. Brock walked in front of me, shaking his head. Over the repetitive, nasally voice of the little man, Brock muttered to himself. "Mom says you can never trust a Leprechaun. Never, never, never, *never*."

CHAPTER TEN

The temperature took an upward turn for the better. I peeled off my jacket and tied it around my waist. No sense stuffing it into the backpack as a donation to our greedy tour guide, Grumpy the Gremlin.

Though we tried to deter him from the irritating rhyme with different questions, he wasn't much for conversation. He would snap an answer and pick up his chant where he left off.

The passage became less claustrophobic and offered more space to shift about. I pilfered what I could from the backpack before it became payment for Skoon's services.

Unzipping the pack while Brady walked, I felt for the beef jerky. "Don't mind me," I whispered. "I'm pocketing a few items for safe keeping." I pulled out the package and stuck it in my back pocket beneath my jacket.

"Good idea."

Next, I groped for the water bottle and snagged a small first aid kit. I slid the water into the deep, side pocket of Brady's carpenter jeans, and the kit into his back pocket. The Leprechaun wouldn't score much loot. Only a blanket, a notebook, a pencil, and a roll of toilet paper—which I hated to part with but couldn't disguise.

A faint glow illuminated the tunnel ahead. We rounded

a curve and found ourselves blinking in bright, glorious light. I squinted and stumbled. After hours of semi-darkness, I didn't mind being blinded. *Let there be light!*

The mouth of the tunnel opened wide and spit us onto a flat, rock ledge that offered a panoramic view of the countryside. We appeared to be halfway up the face of a mountain or cliff. From my vantage point, I could see down a sloping hillside and over the top of a forest. Beyond that, a valley stretched to the horizon, dotted with something indiscernible—maybe a town or village— and a few glistening bodies of water. In the distance, more hills and mountains ran along the horizon. It looked so *normal*. Perhaps this wouldn't be the freaky adventure I'd conjured up and feared.

I glanced skyward, half expecting to see clouds suspended in the heavens. Instead, a vast, dome-like structure arched overhead. The closest portion came low enough to reveal solid quartz, then soared up to where I lost focus. The crystalline sky emanated golden-yellow light, a toned-down version of our sunshine. By all appearances, we stood inside a massive, glowing geode.

It lit the broad, wild world that lay before us and made it—almost—inviting. The mellow luster and warmth reminded me of a perfect autumn day. The kind that begs me to ditch school so I can lounge outside with a book or take the dogs on a long, pointless walk.

"Here we are. Now, hand over your payment." Skoon's puny voice brought me back to reality.

"Is this Vituvia?" I scanned the scenery.

Skoon mumbled something unintelligible.

"Pardon me?" I narrowed my gaze, daring him to try something sneaky.

"Not exactly." He scrambled up a boulder, which gave him some height. "Vituvia is across that valley, straight ahead." He pointed. "At the base of the smaller range of mountains in the foreground."

"That won't do." I crossed my arms. "You need to get us closer to our target or you can forget about the travel pouch."

Skoon jumped to the ground, pounced up and down,

and threw a genuine hissy fit.

If this is how grown Leprechauns behave, I'd hate to babysit their children. "Are you finished?" I tried to keep my cool.

Skoon vanished, lickety-split.

"*What?*" We gasped together and jumped. One moment he was stomping and spitting, the next—gone.

"What on earth?" Brady turned in circles. "What's going on?"

I caught sight of a green blur latched onto the backpack Brady wore. Skoon had somehow materialized on top of it. He yanked at the straps.

"He's riding piggyback," Sophie squealed and pointed.

Brady stopped spinning. He reached over his head and tried to grasp the little parasite. Skoon ducked and continued to jerk the pack.

"Hey!" Brady looked livid. If he got his hands on the twerp, Skoon would be history.

Brock walked over to Brady, clamped his large hands around the nimble creature, and pried him from his brother's back.

I stood there with my mouth open, too stunned to help. Brock never took charge. Meltdowns aside, he was always a go-with-the-flow kind of guy. Sophie and I shared a quick look of amazement.

Skoon writhed and twisted. He reached for Brock's nose, but Brock held him at arm's length like a smelly sock.

"You need to control your emotions." Brock's advice was a perfect imitation of Dad coaching Brock in the midst of a meltdown. "Acting like that will never result in getting what you want."

Skoon calmed to some degree and studied the giant that held him at bay. "You aren't so tough, ya know." He spit. "I can disappear again."

"Not if you want your ugly hat back." Sophie reached a lightning-fast hand towards Skoon and swiped his hat. I admired her swift thinking.

"Why, *you...*" Skoon morphed into another fit of fury. If things weren't so tense, it would've been laughable to see this pint-sized man convulse with rage in the grip of my tall, sturdy brother.

"You may have your precious hat back," I said, "along with *our* precious pouch, when you lead us to Vituvia. You're making this simple agreement very difficult."

Sophie stuffed the hat into the backpack and flicked Skoon a satisfied smirk.

I raised my eyebrows and jutted my chin in her direction. Her abrasive attitude did not serve the greater good. We needed Skoon's cooperation.

Skoon glared at each of us, his fists in little knots, his legs stiff. Then—obviously out-sized and outsmarted—the imp went limp.

"Are you going to help us or not?" Brady stared him down.

Skoon nodded. "I'll take you within sight of Vituvia, but that's it. Now, put me down."

"Do you agree to stay visible at all times?" I stepped closer, hoping to intimidate him.

He nodded again.

I signaled to Brock to lower the pitiful creature to the ground. Skoon smoothed his suit, squared his shoulders, and appeared resigned to his job. Without looking our way, he tramped down the path to the left of the cave. We fell into step behind him.

He wasted no time launching into the annoying limerick. "Griff, graff—"

"And no chanting!" I could not tolerate that broken record a minute longer.

"Yeah," Brady agreed. "What on earth—or should I say 'under' the earth—is a nimmickdell?"

Skoon stopped and turned, hands on hips. "It isn't a *thing*. It's a place. It's where I live—the Hollows of Nimmickdell."

"Obviously." Brady rolled his eyes. "Is it near Vituvia?"

"Nope. It's a two-day journey from Nimmickdell to Vituvia. That's why I'm not taking you all the way." Skoon continued his trek. "Besides, if I'm not home soon, my father will be spittin' daggers."

"Your *father*?" I said. "You still live with your parents?"

"Of course I do. I'm only a kid."

I tried to wrap my head around this revelation. His wrinkled, bearded face placed him as a middle-aged man in human terms. If ever someone could've benefitted from Botox and laser hair removal...

"So, how long have you had that beard?" Brady rubbed his jaw, apparently searching for his own contribution to facial hair. "That's pretty impressive for a kid."

Skoon shot Brady a perplexed look. "All male Leprechauns have a beard. You ought to know that since your mother's such an *expert.*"

"Eew. Even babies?" Sophie made a face.

"Of course." Skoon stopped and turned to us. "How else do you tell the boys from the girls?"

Now *there* was a mental picture I didn't need. I had a feeling this bit of Leprechaun trivia would even surprise my mother.

"Um... how long is the journey from *here* to Vituvia?" I wasn't sure I wanted to know.

"One day, if your walk is brisk." He spun and headed back down the trail.

It would go down as the longest day of my life after putting up with this infantile shrimp.

"Tell me something, Skoon." Brady caught up to him. "How did you know we were from the *topside* of the earth? Have you met other humans before?"

Skoon shrugged. "We see Adam's kin down here every now and again. I could tell you weren't Nephilim. You're too ordinary. So you must be a Topsider."

Nephilim? They still existed? Adrenaline blazed a trail through my body as reality continued to shift in my brain.

"What?" Brady stopped in his tracks. "You mean actual half-human, half-angelic, super-people kind of Nephilim?"

"Do you know of another kind?" Skoon hurried ahead. We scrambled to keep up. "They tend to keep to themselves, but they travel on occasion. They're a lot bigger than the likes of you, though."

"So they *live* down here?" My mouth fell open again.

Skoon nodded. "They live on the other side of the

Berganstroud Mountains. Vituvia is on one side, and the Nephilim live on the other, in Calamus."

This stretched my brain in unwelcome ways, like bubble gum stuck to my favorite shoe.

"Are they nice?" Sophie, ever the inquisitor, trotted beside him.

Skoon stopped and looked Sophie up and down. "Nicer than *you.* Although I wouldn't want to get on their bad side. They're powerful. And huge."

"Well, it wouldn't take you long to get on someone's bad side." Sophie glared down at the little man. "And anyone's *huge* compared to you."

"Sophie." The word hissed through my teeth.

Too late. Skoon vaulted, clamping onto Sophie's nose. He hung from her face like an over-grown lobster. She screamed.

"Skoon!" Brady and I shouted. Before either of us could intervene, Brock reached over and plucked the vermin by his ear.

Skoon released his grip on Sophie's nose and swatted at Brock's hand. Brock flung him down the path like a lit stick of dynamite. He careened through the air with a bitter snarl and—*poof*—the little monster vanished again.

"You can find your own way to Vituvia!" We could hear his high-pitched voice but saw nothing. "And you can keep your travel pouch and my hat. It shall remind you of the day you met Skoon the Leprechaun. A day you'll live to regret, if you live long at all."

CHAPTER ELEVEN

My eyes refused to focus, and my brain felt socked in a fog. *Where am I?* Sophie came into view. She lay on her stomach, her cheek pressed against the dirt. *Why is she on the ground?*

I sat up with a start. My siblings were zonked, sprawled about the leafy floor like they expected someone to make chalk outlines of their bodies.

After trudging down the mountainside trail and into the woods below—minus one irritable Leprechaun—we'd stopped for a rest and a snack. Brock recognized some edible mushrooms, and we feasted on fungus, small shreds of jerky, and a few swallows of water. Then we drifted off from exhaustion.

I decided to let them sleep while I cleared my head.

The trees shrouding our resting spot reminded me of weeping willows. They looked tired. Like us. Their curly branches hung disappointedly, as if they realized the sun would never shine down here.

Woods of Willowmist was etched into an ancient-looking sign that greeted us when we descended the cliff. The woods looked more like thinning hair on an aging giant than a lush forest. A few evergreens shot up tall and proud between the droopy trees, boulders, and a variety of low-growing brush. Some plants looked familiar, like ferns and ivy, but most seemed unique to the Tethered World.

I rehearsed what I knew of this place from Aunt Jules and marveled that it did, indeed, exist. Unfortunately, I could never share this adventure with anyone outside my family. Who would believe me?

But the Tethered World was *real*, and against all logic, I was in it. I'd flown on the back of a Dragon and met a Leprechaun in under twenty-four hours. This meant all the other crazy things Mom blogged about were on the guest list too.

Terrifying!

My brain clicked into movie mode. All manner of outcomes—most of them horrific—played on the screen of my mind, leaving me anxious and dizzy. I dropped to my knees and fought to overcome my panic. The way God made me didn't fit with what He expected me to do. Maybe that's why my parents had so many other kids. They could tell I wasn't cut out for the family business.

I decided then and there that if I made it out alive I'd resign from being tangled up with this secret society. I would *not* follow in my mother's footsteps. I wasn't equipped for it.

With effort, I focused on counting the pebbles sprinkled in the dirt about my knees. My overactive imagination calmed, and my emotions leveled off. I stared at the ground until I felt nothing—one way or the other.

Guilt crept in. This wasn't about *me*, but about saving my parents. *They* needed to be my motivation to face the unknown. They were the ones in the clutches of some monster. To move forward meant I had to make a truce with myself: stop panicking and have faith. Faith that I could manage this mission because I wasn't alone. I murmured a desperate prayer, thankful that God heard me no matter how far below ground I might be.

Feeling somewhat better, I returned to the sleeping masses. "Brady, Brock, Sophie, time to wake up." I tried to sound perky and ready to face the day.

Groggy heads lolled around the mossy, leaf-strewn

ground. One by one they jerked upright. Sophie blinked, Brady hopped up, and Brock looked at his watch.

"What time is it?" I waited, but no response.

Brock looked at me, puzzled. Was he having a fake-awake moment? I waved my hand in front of his face, but he stared through me.

Brady shook his brother's shoulder. "Brock, wake up, man."

Brock's head bobbed down and up. "What?"

"You awake?" Brady patted him on the back.

Brock nodded and stood to stretch.

"Why that little..." Brady weaved around the landscape, hands on hips.

"What?" My eyes followed his movements.

"The backpack. It's gone."

"You think that little twerp took it?" Sophie trekked behind Brady.

"Yeah, I do. He probably followed us the entire time—invisible—and waited 'til we dozed off."

I shrugged. "At this point it doesn't matter. There wasn't much inside we can't live without. We're here. That's what counts."

"Well, I'm still steamed." Brady kicked a rock. "What an annoying little thief!"

"Mom said you can never trust a Leprechaun," Brock spouted.

"And now we know why." Brady swiped a leaf from Brock's hair. "Let's cut our losses and get moving. How long were we asleep?"

Brock checked his watch. "It's ten thirty-three A.M."

I smacked myself in the forehead. "Seriously? We slept over three hours? Let's scoot."

When we'd stopped for a break earlier, we agreed it was important to keep track of the days and hours spent in this place. Based on how lousy I felt, I never would've guessed I'd slept that long.

"We should never trust Leprechauns." Brock shook his head. "Mom warned us." When something made an impression on Brock, he had a hard time changing the subject.

I walked over to him and smiled. "Mom knows her stuff. So do you. Do you know how proud Mom and Dad will be when I tell them you protected Brady and Sophie from that nasty little man? You took care of us."

I gave Brock's arm a soft squeeze. He didn't pull away, which made me melt a little.

He grinned. "Yeah, I know my stuff."

That made the rest of us chuckle. We fell into step and trekked through the woods, headed for the grassy prairie that peeked through the scrubby trees.

Sophie giggled. "I have this urge to chant 'lions and tigers and bears, oh my!'" She linked her arms with Brady and me, and we made a clumsy, brief attempt at a *Wizard of Oz* style skip.

"I think our life has become stranger than any story, don't you?" Brady dropped my arm. "Think about it. We're *inside* the earth meeting Leprechauns and Gnomes. Creatures no one believes in—unless they're kids."

I nodded. "Yep. I was thinking about that earlier. We're experiencing this life-altering adventure, and no one's gonna believe it. People will think we're crazy." My thoughts spun. *Which may be why our parents never mentioned it.*

"But we have to keep it a secret, right?" Sophie looked from Brady to me.

"True," I said. "But it's the principle. Everyone would think we were nuts even if we *could* talk about it."

We crossed the imaginary line from woods to open prairie. My stomach marked the occasion with a loud grumble. I wished we'd remembered to pick some mushrooms for a snack. Foresight and planning didn't seem to be among my strengths. I wasn't sure I had anything even *resembling* a strength. Being the oldest meant I was in charge by default.

I didn't count birth order as a natural talent.

The terrain spread before us. Lush plains stretched across gentle, rolling hills. Clumps of trees and steamy bodies of water flecked the landscape. Mountains rimmed the horizon with stately peaks. Before us lay an entire world swallowed by our own. A world that held mysteries, dangers, and...our parents.

The lack of direction left me frustrated. We didn't have time to lose our way. I looked back at the mountainside. Skoon had pointed towards Vituvia from the mouth of the cave on the cliff. He said it lay straight ahead against the distant foothills. Best I could tell, we were heading the right way.

"Gross. What's that smell?" Sophie held her nose.

Brady clamped his hand over his mouth and mumbled, "Sulfur."

The smell of rotten eggs engulfed me. I tried not to gag.

Brock, our walking encyclopedia, pointed to an overgrown pond. "Thermal spring."

Delicate tendrils of steam danced off the water's surface. We strolled to the edge and looked into the pure, mineral-laden water. It reminded me of a liquefied, glass marble.

"We could drink it, but I think I'd rather hold out for something cooler and less fragrant." Brady shuddered.

We skirted the pond and walked into the weedy growth that sprouted in this area. It consisted of tall, thick stems with fuzzy tops, like enormous dandelions gone to seed. Other than trees clustered here and there, the lime-green vegetation blanketed everything. When our legs brushed the plants, the seed heads scattered, wafting free of their stalks. Feathery, cotton tufts floated up and drifted around us.

The more fluff we stirred up, the more I smiled. It felt magical to be engulfed by this slow-motion confetti—our very own special effects. I tried to catch the wisps, but they stayed barely out of reach, propelled by the air currents I produced.

A subtle, tinkling sound caught my attention. It reminded me of chimes or distant sleigh bells. I stopped and tilted my head, straining to make it out. The others must have heard it too because we all stood with the same curious expression.

"Welcome, King Brock! Welcome, King Brock!" It was a

cheer. Or maybe the lack of sleep made me hear voices.

"Do you hear that?" Sophie whispered to me.

"Yes. Where's it coming from?"

The fuzzy, floaty things no longer swirled in random patterns but encircled us. We stood in the eye of an opaque cyclone. The chant grew in volume as the cloud picked up speed and density. Other fluff balls joined the ones we'd disturbed. We exchanged puzzled looks, and I worried Brock might panic at the high-pitched noise.

Though I guessed I could huff and puff and blow the stuff away, it made me nervous. The chorusing voices most likely came from this shroud of fuzz. Something wasn't right. Overgrown lint balls shouldn't have vocal chords. Or coordination. Or momentum.

I clutched a hand on each side, not sure who I grabbed. We backed ourselves into a tight circle. The spiraling swarm continued to thicken until we were in a whiteout condition. The motion created a strong current that whipped through my hair, messed with my equilibrium, and made me dizzy.

The volume of voices swelled to an earsplitting frequency. I dropped the hands I held and covered my ears, wishing I could disappear.

And then...I did.

CHAPTER TWELVE

Since disappearing was not my usual *modus operandi,* I didn't know what to make of the curious sensation that buzzed in my bones, or the sudden shift in scenery. At least I wasn't dead.

The white fluff shot overhead and formed our own, personal cumulus cloud. Before us stretched a long, wooden table surrounded by short, rotund people in pointy hats. Compared to us, everything except the room itself was miniature. *Alice in Wonderland: true story.*

Startled expressions from around the table reflected the same wonder and surprise I felt. Their small but sturdy bodies anchored them to the low, rustic table like a collection of Aunt Jules's masterpieces come to life. Torches stationed around the perimeter flicked their glow onto the marbled walls and floor. It didn't take a geography whiz to figure out we'd been transported to Vituvia.

"Excellent, Sprighten Fey! You found our new friends. Job well done." A smile radiated from the oldest-looking of the little folk sitting at the table. His crinkled face looked kind and wise. My pulse wandered back to normal.

"Welcome, Larcens. Welcome." The aged Gnome stood to his feet, removed his conical hat, and bowed. Though thicker in build, he stood shorter than Skoon. "I hope you'll forgive us for utilizing our meadow Faeries to transport you to Vituvia. You needed to arrive swiftly and safely, and the Sprighten Fey are our best and brightest for the task."

Brady shot his palm into the white mass overhead. "High-five, little faery people. That was super cool!"

Sophie clapped her hands. "Yes. Awesome!"

The fuzzy things surged with laughter that ricocheted through the room and reminded me of wind chimes.

The little people around the table stared at our group with expectant, grinning faces. I recognized one in particular.

"Are you Revonika?" I nodded at a freckled young lady. "Our Aunt Jules showed us a statue she made of you."

She gave a shy smile, stood, and bowed.

"How rude of us not to introduce ourselves." The elder Gnome looked embarrassed. "What kind of hosts are we to allow you stand there so? Come join us at the council table."

He motioned us over. The white wisps shifted, levitating above our movements. Other Gnomes appeared from the shadows with chairs. Very small chairs.

I perched on one, but only half my backside fit. "Mind if we sit on the floor?"

"Not at all. Sorry we weren't better prepared. We didn't expect you this soon. Why, only this morning we sent a message to the meadow Faeries of your anticipated visit."

He gestured to the servants then plucked something from the table. A mallet. He absentmindedly twirled it while the extra chairs were removed. The four of us arranged ourselves in the space provided, legs folded beneath us. Seated on the ground, we sat eye to eye with our hosts.

The Gnome looked up at the fluff and cleared his throat. "Sprighten Fey, we thank you for the crucial service you have performed on behalf of the Land of Legend. The peace of our realm is advanced by your kind assistance. Please bid our guests farewell."

The cloud descended, and gossamer bodies danced around us. I tried to focus on one individual Fey that hovered nearby, rather than the mass of motion. Shimmery wings fluttered from an intricate body—so small it seemed an impossible creation. Part butterfly, part human-like, the tiny form waved its appendages at me while singing a good-bye with the others.

"Farewell, Larcens. Long live King Brock!" the chorus called as they flitted to each of us. The chant grew louder, and their motion intensified. The billow of Faeries churned into a tight cylinder overhead and disappeared, leaving an odd, hollow silence.

The grandfatherly Gnome became serious. "This meeting is highly secretive. It is best that the Fey be spared the details of our council. They're delicate beings. We wouldn't want to frighten them without cause. Now, shall we commence with our gathering?"

"There's cause for all of us to be frightened, is there not?" a middle-aged gentleman spoke from across the table.

"So it would seem, Smarlow, so it would seem." The leader laced his fingers together. "But we needn't get the Faeries involved. Their magic is most effective within the bounds of a healthy constitution." Taking his seat, he sighed and gave a weak smile. Up close, worry lines etched his face despite his energetic attitude.

"My apologies again, Larcen children." He nodded in our direction. "We are no doubt alarming you with our ominous talk on the heels of your arrival. Let me introduce our assembly with all proper courtesies. We shall cover business soon enough."

He patted his chest. "I am Sir Noblin, Premier Advisor to her Majesty, Queen Judith. I work closely with her highness and keep affairs in order—both inside and outside the palace. To my right sits Tritter, our scribe, who will take meticulous notes of our meeting today for posterity's sake. Next we come to Revonika, my personal assistant, as well as the palace liaison for public relations. Your Aunt Julie has captured Revonika's likeness in her sculpture, based on your quick recognition. Beside Revonika sits her assistant, Izzy. When one must tend to an entire castle and realm, one cannot have enough assistants."

Sir Noblin chuckled, indicating an attempted joke in his long-winded introduction. No one else laughed.

He cleared his throat. "Yes, well, to my left sits Chancellor of the Court, Sir Kittrick. Followed by our military advisor, the distinguished General Muggleridge. Next to him, we have Colonel Smarlow, Chief of Covert Reconnaissance. And finally, Commander Reiko, head of our Special Forces unit: Stealth Gnomish Warfare and Clandestine Operations, or SGWCO, for short."

I hoped there wouldn't be a test. I found it disturbing to hear such intimidating titles given to Gnomes. Covert Reconnaissance? Special Forces? Good-bye, cute little garden statue. Hello, lethal undercover agent!

With each introduction, a Gnome gave a polite nod and lifted his or her hat. They were a multi-cultural bunch. Tritter looked like he came from India, while Reiko possessed the almond eyes and glossy, black hair of East Asia.

Based on their polite stares, I guessed it was my turn to speak. "Um... it's our pleasure and honor to meet you." I groped for my tongue and brain to make a coordinated effort at speaking. "Disappearing was an exciting and...uh...*unusual* experience. But we do thank you for— you know—speeding up the process of arriving in Vituvia." *Smooth.* I wished I could ask for a do-over.

Sophie rolled her eyes. "What my sister is *trying* to say is that we're glad to have your help, and we're going to need it to find our parents."

"Ah, yes. That is one of the matters we're here to discuss...in due time." Sir Noblin looked amused by Sophie's enthusiasm. "It would be most appreciated if you'd introduce yourselves. I see there are two young men who look alike. One of them, no doubt, is our future king."

Some instinctive cue must have prompted Brock to rise and offer a stiff bow. "I am Brock."

Chairs screeched away from the table. The Gnomes stood with reverence, removed their hats, and offered low, solemn bows.

Brock seemed unaffected, although a faint smile settled on his lips. He sat down. The Gnomes replaced their hats and did the same.

Sophie sat between her brothers and drummed her fingers on the table. "*Okay.*" She flitted her hands in the air. "I guess I'll go next. I'm Sophie, I'm eleven, and I'll fight all manner of evil to find my mother and father."

Although she whacked the table with her fist for emphasis, the Gnomes merely nodded and turned their attention to the next in line, Brady. How would he feel about introducing himself, knowing he wasn't the Chosen One?

"I'm Brady." He waved. "You can tell me apart from Brock by my hair. It's longer."

The Gnomes looked like they expected more. Brady merely grinned.

Then all eyes turned to me.

Though I wanted to say something like, *Hi, I'm the inept older sister*, I kept to protocol. "I'm Sadie, the oldest."

Sophie explained, "We're anxious to find our parents. We appreciate any help you may be able to offer."

"Excellent! Truly a pleasure." Sir Noblin clapped his stubby hands and smiled. "We've been looking forward to this day for many years. Though I dare say, we expected it to transpire under more pleasant circumstances. This is a sad time on many levels."

"Meaning what?" I leaned towards him. "Do you have information about our parents?"

Sir Noblin's brow furrowed. "Yes, yes, there's news about your parents." He glanced at Reiko, head of the SGW-something or other. "Reiko will give you a full report in a moment. There's other news particularly distressing to Vituvia—not to imply that your parents' abduction is any less horrific—but, you see, this is...this involves..."

The torchlight threw restless shadows that made it

hard to read Noblin's face. His voice caught, as if he struggled to keep tears in check. Some of the other Gnomes sniffed or wiped their eyes.

Revonika leaned behind Tritter and whispered something in Noblin's ear. He nodded, and she stood to speak. "Dear friends, please forgive the queen's council while we wrestle with our emotions. The last few days have been difficult. You see, our fair queen has been queen-napped. The Leprechauns turned a peaceful visit from her highness into an unspeakable travesty. They abducted her from our caravan during her annual visit to the Hollows of Nimmickdell. They...they charmed the guards and...took our sweet Queen Judith."

Revonika lost her composure and collapsed into her chair, sobbing. Sir Noblin and Izzy reached over and patted her back, sniffling in harmony.

Brock mumbled and rocked back and forth. He often reverted to such behavior when distressed, repeating something for eons as he swayed. The experts called it *perseverating*. It often preceded a meltdown. I watched, ready to intervene if things got out of hand.

His volume increased, and the words grew distinct. "The grace that fell in Nimmickdell shivers far from home. The grace that fell in Nimmickdell. ."

Brady, Sophie, and I gasped and looked at each other. Skoon hadn't recited a bunch of nonsense while he marched along the tunnels. He taunted us with every step!

"Sir Noblin, uh, sir." Brady raised his finger to get Noblin's attention. "We met Skoon, a Leprechaun, while we were in the tunnels. He chanted an annoying rhyme most of the time. I think what sounded like gibberish to us was actually a riddle."

"What exactly did he say?" Tritter sat poised with his quill.

Brady turned to his twin. "Brock, would you mind reciting the rhyme?"

Brock stopped rocking and looked at the Gnomes. He cleared his throat and picked up the cadence from our journey underground.

"Griff, graff, groan,
Oh, those sappy, happy Gnomes!
But the grace that fell in Nimmickdell
Shivers far from home."

Smarlow pounded one fist into the palm of the other hand. "Precisely like a fickle Leprechaun to wallow in his deed and dangle it in front of us. How dare that little imp mock our queen, our 'Grace,' and rub our noses in it!"

"What did you say his name was?" Revonika asked.

"Skoon." I pronounced his name like it tasted bitter. "Do you know him?"

"Can't say that we do." Revonika glanced at the others. "Leprechauns make up rhymes about everything. It's their way of spreading news or preserving history. The fact that this Skoon knew about her majesty doesn't mean he was responsible for her kidnapping."

"Guilt by association, I say," Colonel Smarlow yelled. "If we lacked definitive proof to declare war on Nimmickdell, we have it now."

"Order, Councilman, order." Sir Noblin whacked his mallet several times. "We will look at our options according to protocol. We mustn't act in haste and jeopardize Vituvia any further."

"Excuse me." I rapped my knuckles on the table. "Does this have anything to do with our parents' disappearance?"

The Gnomes looked at each other, then back at us. Several squirmed.

"Well?" It came out with more tenacity than I felt. "What's the connection?"

Sir Noblin nodded at Reiko. She sighed and leaned onto her elbows.

"Technically, the connection would be Brock." She nodded towards my brother. "I was part of the caravan that escorted Queen Judith to the Hallows of Nimmickdell. We arrived in the evening, too late to take care of any official business. We set up camp on the outskirts of their village, as usual. The next morning a few of us planned to travel to the Heights of Willowmist—where the tunnel would bring your parents into the Land of Legend—and the same place you came into our province, I assume. Meanwhile, the queen would hold her annual meeting with the Chancellor of Nimmickdell. My company was to wait for the arrival of your parents then take them to meet with the queen's caravan when it headed back to Vituvia."

"But...?" I looked around the table, trying to read the faces.

Reiko grimaced. "When morning broke, we found our dear queen had been taken hostage in the night. A note lay in her stead."

From the shadows, a steward appeared with a tray that held a piece of paper. He crossed to Revonika. She picked it up with trembling hands and read:

> *"The Flaming Sword of Cherubythe*
> *For Queen Judith's life we trade,*
> *Seven days to deliver it,*
> *Or Vituvia we raid.*
> *And if you try to rescue her,*
> *There's more that you should know,*
> *The parents of your future king*
> *To death will also go.*
> *Save them all, or all shall die,*
> *It's hinged on your compliance.*
> *The Sword is ours, even if by force,*
> *If you try to deny us.*
> *Submit, we say, if you are wise*
> *And simple this shall be.*
> *Resist us? Many shall be killed*
> *Beginning with these three.*
> *Signed,*
> *Worshipful Master Nekronok of Craventhrall,*
> *Land of the Trolls."*

CHAPTER THIRTEEN

I BLINKED. REPEATEDLY. AS IF RAPIDLY beating my eyelids might help my comprehension.

"I thought the Leprechauns took the queen," Brady said when Revonika finished reading.

"The Trolls take credit." Smarlow jabbed his finger in the air. "But the Leprechauns had to pull it off, even though the little minions deny it."

"The guards would've heard the clumsy oafs if they'd been prowling around." Reiko gazed at her comrades. Several nodded their agreement. "And it's not as if Trolls possess any magical powers. They had to use the Leprechauns to do their dirty work. Leprechauns are famous for trying to appease everyone, while their greatest interest lies in how *they* will benefit."

"Mom says you can never trust a Leprechaun," Brock reminded the group.

"Your mother is a wise woman." Sir Noblin tipped his hat. "We've always been wary of Leprechauns. Our Treaty of Trust with them has been tenuous at best. It's a complex relationship, but so far it's been in their favor to remain at peace with Vituvia. The Trolls must have promised the Leprechauns something they find more appealing than the safety and light Vituvia offers the realm."

"Light?"

Sir Noblin nodded at me. "Light. You may have wondered how our land has been granted light when we haven't any sun. It is a gift from the Creator—the Flaming Sword of Cherubythe."

Brady nodded. "The Sword the Trolls demanded in their letter."

"Yes." Sir Noblin stood and leaned onto the table. "The Sword gives us light. And protection. It is the Sword mentioned in the book of Genesis. The very one held by the angel that guarded the entrance to Eden after humans were banished for their disobedience—though unique creatures in the Garden were permitted to stay.

"Later, when the Maker moved us into *this* safe abode—before the flood of Noah—He placed the Sword into our care. Here in what would become Vituvia. He decreed that it would provide light and safekeeping to the Land of Legend. We cannot for *any* reason allow its power to fall into the hands of the Trolls. We must protect the Sword at all costs. Even at the cost of those we love if it comes to that."

"What do you mean?" Sophie scowled. "Do you expect us to help you protect the Sword and forget about our parents?"

"No, no, my dear girl." General Muggleridge spoke for the first time. His voice reminded me of gravel. "We shan't sit by and let our loved ones suffer. Nor shall we toss aside the peace of our realm and allow the Trolls to have the Sword. We shall fight, but fight smart." His finger poked the side of his greying temple for emphasis.

"A rescue is in order." Smarlow gripped the edge of the table as if he could hardly wait. "Which is the reason you've traveled here, no doubt. We're here to assist you in finding your parents. In return, we hope you shall assist us in retrieving our queen. And if we're lucky, maybe take out a few Leprechauns and Trolls."

"Of course." Sophie crossed her arms and lifted her chin. "Even if the queen wasn't our great aunt, and our parents were safe at home, we'd help you rescue her. It's only right."

Speak for yourself, little sister.

Sir Noblin clasped his hands together in an impromptu prayer. "Thank you, kind Creator. And thank you, Larcens. I feel like a load has been lifted. We must chew on our options and design the best plan of action."

"Speaking of chewing." Brady gave a mischievous grin. "If I don't get something to eat soon, I may start gnawing on this table. Could we possibly—"

"Of course, of course!" Sir Noblin smacked his palm against his forehead. "How rude of us not to consider your welfare."

Revonika escorted us to a wing of the palace that looked outfitted for humans. The simple furnishings were an enlarged version of the Gnomes' things throughout the palace. Though they towered over the Gnome they proved an ideal fit for the four of us.

At least *someone* had thought of our welfare. A sumptuous feast greeted us. The food choices weren't entirely recognizable, but everything tasted delicious. Brady and Brock ate like camels would drink water— storing up extra in case they encountered a food shortage in the future. We demolished the meal with lightning speed then stretched out on luxurious, silken pallets.

"We figured the Trolls had our parents all along." Sophie's eyes brimmed with tears. "But that note Revonika read makes me think Mom and Dad are way worse off than we thought."

She cried herself to sleep. I hugged her from behind, trying to be as mother-like as I knew how. Sophie was a tough kid, but this evening's events had taken their toll. I listened to her breathing change from ragged to relaxed as she drifted off.

Exhausted and petrified—and still angry that my parents had kept this side of our life in the dark—I couldn't sleep. The more I learned, the less I wanted any part of it.

We had three days to rescue Mom and Dad. And Queen Judith. And save Vituvia.

We were tired.

We were scared.

We were mere mortals.

I was glad when my eyelids finally began to feel heavy. Sleep was vital. Tomorrow would be a tough day.

EARLY THE NEXT MORNING we prepared for battle. Because the Gnomes feared losing two monarchs to the Trolls, they insisted Brock remain at the palace. The implication of this safety feature meant, of course, that our mission might fail.

I gave my brother a fierce hug, which he resisted. I did not want to leave Brock behind. How could I possibly protect him? But I saw the wisdom of the Gnomes' decision. It was the safest route and one my parents would approve.

Outfitted with chain mail and a sword overtop my jeans and t-shirt, I looked like an escapee from King Arthur's court. The Gnomes had a well-stocked selection of human-size battle attire—hoarded leftovers from the Dark Ages, I'm sure. Under different circumstances, it might have been interesting to hear tales of others who'd worn these items.

I tried to get used to the stiff feel of wearing a chain-link fence around my middle. I felt as graceful and coordinated as the Tin Man and hoped I wouldn't slow everyone down. If Brady and Sophie experienced the same burden in their armor, it didn't show.

The metal getup transformed my brother into a strutting peacock. He waved and worked the crowd. "Thanks for coming out," he called. "It's a pleasure to be here."

Sophie's breastplate hung past her hips. Everything she had tried on swallowed her up, but she was too big for Gnome-wear. With her hand on the hilt of her sword, she grinned and waved, every bit the medieval princess she was, no doubt, pretending to be.

We traveled with Colonel Snarlow, General

Muggleridge, Reiko, and three of their best warriors—two brothers and a sister. Mighty, Muscle, and Zest. Clad in full body armor, they came off like small, adorable robots—probably not the look they were going for. Their stern gaze and serious manner reminded me that this was a grave situation.

A thin veil of mist swirled about and lent a mystical air to the sea of itty-bitty people in pointy hats. They surrounded Brady, Sophie, and me while we traipsed through the cobbled streets of Vituvia. More locals poured out of their shops and homes to cheer for us, and to plead tearfully that we rescue their beloved queen. They received us as heroes, though we'd yet to do anything but show up for work.

Sir Noblin and an entourage of officials escorted us, led by a soldier proudly bearing the Vituvian flag. The banner's royal purple fabric boasted a green silhouette of a tree, whose trunk morphed into a silver sword. Golden beams of light radiated from behind the silhouette. I understood the Sword and rays of light, but wondered about the tree.

"For you, miss." A cherub-faced child dashed in front of our group and interrupted my thoughts. He extended a fistful of flowers my way and sprinted back to his mother before I could thank him. Although humans did make an occasional appearance in Vituvia, it seemed we were still a curiosity to be touched and gawked at.

Celebrity status for certain.

Though I was a reluctant tourist, the town charmed me. Quaint shops bordered the cobblestone road. Most sported thatched or slate-shingled roofs that extended past the buildings to offer covered porches stuffed with onlookers. Though Gnomes could comfortably live in a structure the size of Ollie's doghouse, it appeared they built their town to host a variety of visitors.

With businesses from shoe stores to the neighborhood saloon, Gnomes seemed to have most of the comforts of humans—except for a place to buy paint. The buildings were constructed with wood and rock. Like the clothing worn by the residents, the town displayed a neutral color scheme.

The crowd pressed in and jostled us down the road. The haze dissipated, replaced by grit that churned beneath our feet and irritated my throat. The Gnomes' short stature made walking difficult. I feared kicking them or tripping if I didn't pay attention. The awkward armor added to the clumsy feeling. Between the dusty obstacle course of Gnomes, the clanking chain mail, and all the fanfare, it was sensory overload.

We came to a wall that encircled Vituvia and offered protection like an old-fashioned, fortified city. Sir Noblin climbed onto a platform clearly erected for such occasions.

He lifted his hands towards the crowd. "Vituvians!" The throng grew quiet, which helped mellow my jitters. "We set out this day to extract our queen and her family from the hands of the enemy. We send but a few, accompanied by the hopes and support of all."

Cheers and applause swelled from the sea of Gnomes.

"May they go with the blessing of our Maker and the faithful prayers of each of you." He steepled his fingers. "We must pray for peace yet prepare for war. Let us put our houses in order and ready our soldiers."

This brought more celebration from the crowd and a fresh bout of anxiety from my fear factory.

"Raise the gate! Make way for our brave friends as they set out on their noble journey."

I looked around. Which brave friends? *Not me.*

The mass of little folks parted to open a pathway leading to an enormous, wooden gate. Stout sentries grunted and struggled with a series of ropes and pulleys. As if commiserating with the guards, the lumbering gate expelled a groan. We followed our petite commandos out of the city and through the outskirts of town. Fanfare and good wishes propelled us on our way.

Vast farmland soon blanketed either side of the thoroughfare. Colorful, patchwork gardens stretched before miniature cottages and log cabins. Gnomes wielded hoes between tidy rows of greens. Others held baskets of freshly picked produce.

Workers dropped their tools and ran to greet us and root for our mission. One young girl eyed the flowers I carried, so I handed her the bouquet. The Gnomes stared at my siblings and me with fascination. I had a Dorothy-on-the-yellow-brick-road experience—Munchkins and all.

"Look." Brady nudged me out of the land of Oz. "A chicken."

Sure enough, a hen bobbed and weaved her way around a nearby ditch.

I stepped beside Smarlow and pointed. "Is that a *chicken* chicken, like where we come from?"

Smooth. It had to be one of the dumbest things I'd ever asked. *Next I will impress you with my amazing ability to sing the entire alphabet—all by myself!*

Smarlow gave a crooked grin. His cone-shaped, metal helmet extended onto his cheeks and made his smile squeeze together like an accordion. "Yes, that's a chicken. You may also recognize dogs, cats, and a few other animals known to man."

"I don't know, Sadie." Brady smirked. "If you're not sure about an average chicken when you see one, there's little hope of recognizing when you're face-to-face with exotic animals like dogs and cats."

Sophie laughed. I gave them my best glare.

"I'm sure Sadie wasn't expecting to find the same animals below ground as you have topside." General Muggleridge smiled at me in a fatherly way. "And I bet you two didn't either."

"Exactly." I stuck my chin in the air.

"Yes, yes, the Tethered World boasts many of the same animals and several unique ones." Smarlow came alongside me. "Some were brought here. Others found their way through caves and cracks, in the same manner as humans. Still others have lived here since the Creator moved Eden below ground. Part of His provision for us."

"I see." Time to save face and change the subject. "When can I take this chain mail stuff off? I feel trapped and uncoordinated."

"It's best to leave it on, Miss Larcen." The general lowered his voice. "You may need the protection before the day's through. We're heading into untamed land."

Oh good. My favorite.

"I think the armor is cool." Sophie slid her sword from its sheath. She hopped to the side with a *ha*—which changed to a *haaah* as she struggled to keep it extended. The weapon won and nosedived into the dirt with a *twang*.

It was my turn to laugh.

"Hey, Sophie, you need me to carry that for ya?" Brady flexed his muscles.

Sophie pursed her lips and yanked. With ungainly grace, she slid the sword back into its sheath. "I'm good." She laughed along with us.

"Everything is so heavy." I used my thumbs to heft the chain mail off of my shoulders then rolled my neck back and forth. "Brady and I took fencing classes, but we wore modern clothing. The sabers we used were nothing like these."

General Muggleridge looked amused. "Perhaps some sword-fighting practice is in order. Tonight when we make camp, Muscle, Mighty, and Zest can work with you." The three warriors nodded and nudged each other.

"Actually, I've been fencing most of my life." Brady inflated his chest. "Sadie dropped out after a couple of years, but I've been at it since I was nine. Fencing and karate. Seems my parents were secretly preparing me for hand-to-hand combat." He laced his fingers together and cracked his knuckles.

I rolled my eyes.

"Then I'll pit you against myself, young man. It shall also include a lesson on humility." Muggleridge chuckled then cleared his throat. "Let's stop dawdling and pick up the pace. We've a long trek to reach those foothills."

To spare Brady's ego, I resisted the urge to gloat. Instead, I focused on the hills ahead of us. From my vantage point, the slopes looked like violet caterpillars slinking across the horizon. Behind the hills rose a mass of charred, thorny peaks. They towered above like jagged teeth lurking behind purple lips. Everything seemed to recede into bleak shadows.

"Do those hills have a name?" It didn't hurt to learn the layout.

"Those are the Hills of Berganstroud, home to our friends the Dwarves," Colonel Smarlow said. "We hope to make it there tonight—if we hike a lot and rest a little. Over the ridge and into those dark mountains is where we think your family and our queen are being held. We hope to persuade a few of our Dwarf friends to set out with us first thing tomorrow."

"Those tall, spiky mountains?" I pointed.

Smarlow nodded. "The Trolls live in Craventhrall at the base of Mount Thrall. It's the tallest, most pointed peak you can see."

Oh, I could see it all right. It eclipsed the other razor-sharp teeth and loomed above them with a menacing swagger.

It looked like a fang.

CHAPTER FOURTEEN

We trudged along in silence. The narrow road turned into little more than a rut. Evergreen trees darkened the distant hills, standing solemn and watchful while we passed. Birds flitted by, a few rabbits scurried across our path, and I sank further into fear of the unknown. A menagerie of questions pummeled my brain. They loomed larger than the threatening mountains. I anguished over my parents and resented every ounce of the situation they'd put me in. I missed Nicole and Nate.

"Larcens, fall back!" The general's command yanked me back to reality. I jumped to avoid squashing Reiko as she came to a halt.

The Gnomes shifted into combat mode, hands on their weapons, waiting for the general's order. Brady and I sandwiched Sophie behind the soldiers. My heart took a flying leap though I didn't know why we were in such an uproar.

Someone approached on a horse. Dust formed a small cloud that hovered around the legs of the powerful animal and made it appear to float our way.

Sophie nudged me. "What is that?"

"A horse." I felt redeemed from my earlier stupidity with the chicken.

"No, what's that *on* the horse?"

So much for redemption. I squinted. Before I could make sense of the lump on the back of the beast, General Muggleridge shouted, "Friend or foe? State your intention!"

"Friend! Friend!" the rider shouted. "I come with word of the queen."

The Gnomes relaxed as horse and rider thudded to a stop. A squat man, bigger and broader than a Gnome or Leprechaun, dismounted before the grey equine pulled up short. He had quite a drop from the height of the horse but alighted with ease.

He was a burly block of a man, though half my size. Clad in leather boots, he wore a long tunic and sported a gnarled beard that hung past his barreled chest. Hazel eyes blazed with intensity beneath wiry brows. A worn, leather hat slouched on his head, and a cloak made from layers of animal skins and fabric encircled his shoulders. He swept it around his body as he stepped forward and bowed.

Due to the process of elimination—rather than my cleverness—I decided he must be a Dwarf. After all, I'd met the likes of Gnomes and Leprechauns so far.

"Captain Wogsnop at your service, my fair people," his scratchy voice boomed. "I'm on my way to Vituvia to bring word of the queen. Are you fine soldiers on rescue detail for Queen Judith?"

The general nodded. "Affirmative, my good man." He raised his sword, and the Dwarf removed a dagger from his belt. The two touched tips in greeting. "General Muggleridge. I believe our paths crossed many years ago in the Battle of Three Wives. It's most fortuitous that we've met, and it will expedite our journey to have your information. Speak on."

Wogsnop cleared his throat and fingered his beard. He looked from me to Sophie, then to Brady. "Where did you find these young ones? They're not Nephilim from what I can see. Topsiders?"

The general shifted his weight and tapped his foot. "Yes, yes, they're relatives of our queen, if you must know. Now on with it, please. We mustn't waste precious time."

"Very well." The Dwarf continued to eye us. "The Trolls have your queen."

"We know *that.*" Smarlow's face grew red. "Why do you think we're headed this way?" He spat in the dirt.

The captain leveled his gaze on Smarlow. "Your queen is ill."

"Expound," Muggleridge urged. "What's her condition?"

Wogsnop clearly enjoyed having the upper hand. He crossed his stocky arms and gave a long, mournful sigh.

Great. Dwarf drama.

"It isn't good, my friends. Our spies sent word that the queen is lethargic, in and out of consciousness, and mumbling incoherently."

"Why didn't your spies think to rescue her while she was in their sights?" Smarlow glowered. "Or at least glean where the beastly Trolls were taking her?"

Wogsnop shook his head. "They did not have an opportunity. Our men watched as the Trolls, with the help of the Leprechauns, crept out of Nimmickdell."

"I knew those Leprechauns were scheming little—"

"Smarlow! Let the man speak," the general barked.

The Dwarf grinned. "I share your frustration, my friend. Leprechauns are treacherous troublemakers. As I was saying, our spies followed a band of Trolls and Leprechauns out of Nimmickdell. They did not witness the travesty of her Grace being abducted but heard the Trolls bragging about what they'd pulled off. Some of the big apes commented to the others that she was ill and described her symptoms. They hoped that whatever ailed the human queen was not something Trolls could contract. I'm sorry to bring you this news."

General Muggleridge held up his hand. "You needn't apologize for circumstances beyond your control. We're grateful for your faithful service on behalf of the queen and the peace of Legend. This affront by the Trolls and Leprechauns will have far-reaching effects on your people as well as ours if it isn't resolved with haste."

"Agreed." Wogsnop placed his hand over his heart.

"Her safe return is vital, and being ill makes her rescue critically urgent. I shall ride back to Berganstroud and fetch men and mounts. They'll return with me to deliver your clan to our village by suppertime. We'll dine and devise a plan of rescue. Does this suit you?"

"Aye." Muggleridge saluted. "We'll continue to travel in your direction and shorten the distance your men must ride."

Wogsnop walked to his steed. It was then I noticed the unusual stirrup configuration. It made sense considering the difference in height between horse and rider. There were several stirrups strung together like rungs on a ladder, which enabled the Dwarf to climb up.

Sophie broke away and ran to the horse. "Mr. Wogsnop! Have you heard anything about our parents? They've been kidnapped by the Trolls too."

The Dwarf looked at her, brows furrowed. "Sorry, young maiden, I've no knowledge of them. I'll ask around, but such information would be hard to suppress."

Sophie nodded and shuffled back, head down.

"Good day, and may the Creator's celerity be with you." The general gave a salute, and Wogsnop turned his horse around.

I watched him ride off a few paces, then he turned and came back. "I almost forgot." He trotted around us, swirling up dust. "There are hundreds of Sleeping Serpents ahead. Too vast to avoid on foot. Proceed with caution when you near Brodger Creek."

Smarlow spat again. "I wondered about that. It's almost serpent season, though they are a bit early."

"A sign of the times, soldier. Everything seems out of sorts right now."

"Indeed. Thanks for the alert." Muggleridge saluted.

The Dwarf returned the salute and spurred his horse back the way he came.

"It's peculiar." Reiko rubbed her chin. "I had guard detail the night Queen Judith was taken. She appeared in good spirits when she retired. Didn't complain about feeling ill. Perhaps the Leprechauns or Trolls did something to her. There's no doubt they charmed the rest of us before they smuggled her out from under our noses."

Smarlow kicked a rock. "Those lousy, devious Leprechauns. Why, I'd like to get my hands—"

"We press on." Muggleridge held up a silencing hand. "What we need to understand, the Maker shall reveal. Wrongs done shall be righted in due time. To Berganstroud."

"*Hello?*" With my arms crossed, I stared at the Gnomes. "Would anyone care to elaborate on the Sleeping Serpent things?"

Muggleridge shrugged. "Not a big worry for Gnomes. Dwarves are unable to interface with animals like we can. They rightfully fear the venomous vipers." He began walking. "Since you're with us, there is little to fear."

Although my anxiety eased in the glow of his convictions, I secretly hoped to get whisked away by Faeries and skip the snakes altogether. The whole idea of how one might interface with animals left me puzzled, especially since I knew exactly what venomous meant.

I mused to myself and plodded along dutifully. *Plod* is the best way to describe a grueling expedition in metal clothing. Even Brady-the-Brave slumped and looked weary. I welcomed the idea of speeding our journey along under four hooves instead of my own two, tired feet. My only consolation was the steady temperature bestowed by the fake daylight. It didn't beat down like the sun. Its warmth remained comfortable.

Rocks sprouted from the ground in odd formations. Twisted trees speckled the landscape. During the course of the journey, I spotted occasional farms, cows and all, and noticed various wildlife. Still, I had the impression that there was less life here than topside.

After miles of silent, steady trudging, the road took a downward turn and dipped towards a murky swath of water that rippled through the yellow dirt. Large stones and tree limbs littered the banks like discarded bones from a buffet meant for giants. An ancient-looking, wooden bridge spanned the water from shore to shore.

Muggleridge stopped and gave us a serious look.

"We're approaching Brodger Creek. There's nothing to fear, Larcens, as long as you remain silent"—he raised a cautioning finger—"and are careful to follow my precise path."

"Well, good luck with that." Sophie shifted, hands on hips. "It looks like an obstacle course of rocks and branches."

"Those aren't branches." Muggleridge raised an eyebrow. "Those are the Sleeping Serpents."

CHAPTER FIFTEEN

"THOSE ARE *SNAKES*?" NAUSEA PLAYED ITS game in my gut. "How are we going to avoid stepping on them, let alone waking them?"

"Do as he says"—Smarlow jerked his thumb at Muggleridge—"and no one gets bitten. It's that simple."

Brady squeezed my shoulder, and we headed downhill to meet the serpents. Resigned, I glued my gaze to the back of our fearless leader and followed him as precisely as possible. The other Gnomes inserted themselves into our line, and we approached in single file.

As we neared the first few snakes, the Gnomes emitted a low hum. My ears barely perceived it, though my chest reverberated with the depth of the note. It was so penetrating that I wanted to curl up against a rock and snooze. The humming numbed my internal rage against the logic of what we were doing.

The snakes' unblinking eyes watched us like beady cameras tracking our movement. Concentrating on every nuance of Muggleridge's actions, I stayed close. There was no matching my foot strides to a Gnome's, but I kept to his path as he zigzagged between the loathsome creatures.

Even up close, the serpents resembled tree boughs. Their scales, a few shades darker than the dingy yellow soil, were specked with white—similar to lichen growing on tree bark. A few snakes coiled in typical fashion, but the majority lay straight as sticks. Some looked as long as I was tall.

The bridge loomed closer, and relief dared to make an appearance. Never mind that more serpents waited on the other side. The ground dropped sharply right where the bridge was secured to the bank. The rickety structure didn't cultivate much confidence. It lacked a railing and was less than two feet wide. Missing slats offered holes that could swallow any one of us and spit us into the murky water below. Several serpents floated in the creek like poisonous driftwood.

I shuddered. These things were everywhere!

But no snakes lounged across the bridge. One by one, surrounded by continuous thrumming from the Gnomes, we began to make our way onto the wooden strip of safety.

A gasp and scuttling noise made me whirl in time to see Brady scraping his way down the embankment on his backside. He landed with a grunt on the end of the bridge. Rocks and dirt rained down on him. Reiko stood a few feet away, shaking her head at the human avalanche.

In that mysterious marriage of panic and slow motion, I saw the ground behind my brother come to life. The "branches" began to writhe in our direction.

Reiko clamored down the incline. "Run!" she urged a staggering Brady. "All of you, *run.*"

She didn't need to tell me twice. I shoved Sophie ahead of me. We sprinted across the bridge, jumping over missing slats and struggling to stay upright on the shaky platform. Sophie leaped across a gaping hole and landed on a plank which busted beneath her weight. She screamed and the bridge swallowed her right in front of me.

"Sophie!" I skidded to avoid tumbling in behind her.

She managed to catch the wood that supported the slats with one hand. "Help me!"

"I'll grab your wrist." I stretched out on the bridge and

clasped her forearm with my hand.

"Hold tight!" Muggleridge trotted back and peered into the hole.

Sophie looked at me with terror. Her legs dangled inches from the water.

"That's right, eyes on me. Can you get your other hand up here?"

Sophie swayed her body enough to latch her other hand on mine.

"Okay, but the snakes are crossing the bridge." Brady stood near my feet.

"Then do something about it." My sweaty hand struggled to maintain its grip. I couldn't deal with any distractions. Reiko shouted orders at Brady. The clash of swords on the bridge made the structure shake.

"Do you think you can pull her up?" Muggleridge lay on the other side of the opening. "It's either that or she drops to the water and we scoop her out as fast as possible."

Sophie whimpered. "I'm slipping." She curled her legs as a snake floated beneath her.

"We can't let her drop. No way." I felt her fingers slip a little more and gasped. "But I'm losing—no!"

Sophie plunged into the murky creek, screaming all the way.

My heart dropped with her. I scrambled to my feet. Muggleridge bolted to the other end and down the bank where Smarlow and the warrior siblings already stood. I sprinted behind, praying the bridge would hold. Brady clambered at my heels.

By the time I made it to the water's edge, Sophie clung to a rock and the Gnomes were humming with deep intensity.

"Find a branch." Brady searched the bank but all possible branches appeared to be sleeping serpents. And they were beginning to stir.

A snake writhed towards Sophie but the current carried it swiftly downstream. That didn't stop her from flailing her legs in its general direction.

"Remain still, my girl." Muggleridge paced in front of

me. "I know it's difficult but the serpents won't be alerted to your presence as easily."

Sophie nodded her tear streaked face. I looked for some idea to present itself. Anything. The vipers on the bank moved lethargically. I hoped the Gnomes' interfacing-thing would do its job.

A twisting snake plopped into the water from the same hole that Sophie fell through. And then another. My sister stared wide eyed and shaking. Her legs curled instinctively but she kept from thrashing in fear and they floated past.

The water turned glassy and calm. I blinked, trying to make sense of it. Three more snakes floated beneath the bridge, heading for Sophie. Inexplicably, the first one turned aside and the others followed. As if guided by something unseen, they followed a path across the smooth surface, avoiding my sister.

Sophie screamed and I jerked my attention back to her. A silvery set of hands, webbed between its fingers, wrapped themselves around Sophie's quivering body. A wave of water swelled beside her. A liquid face emerged from the creek and belonged to the translucent hands.

"Shh. Shh." The creature soothed my sister's cries with a bubbling voice I wasn't entirely sure I heard. Perhaps the water lapping against the shore had fooled me.

"I've got you." The voice assured, more distinct. It sounded female.

Sophie gasped and threw her arms around the entity. The water woman rose up, bearing my sister in lithe, liquid limbs. Below the waist her body was merely a gathering of water. Like a wave rolling to shore, the creature moved with fluid grace towards our awestruck group.

I gaped up at the shimmering face. Though her features were obscure they reflected kindness. Ever so gently, she placed Sophie in Brady's arms.

And then, she melded back into the current.

Sophie, Brady, and I exchanged looks of disbelief. He lowered Sophie to her feet. I crossed to them and we embraced and cried with relief.

My sister morphed from crying to laughing and it percolated around the group. The Gnomes clapped each other on their backs. I had the impression they were equally stunned.

"Who or what was that?" Enchantment lingered on Sophie's face.

"That, my dear, was a very rare sighting. One none of us have ever witnessed." Muggleridge beamed up at Sophie. "You were saved by a Water Nymph."

Before we could ponder his revelation, Reiko cleared her throat. "Larcens, we must move. Soldiers, return to your interfacing."

Sure enough, the serpents squirmed with more vigor. Several plunged into the water off the bridge and the other shore then nosed towards us. The Gnomes struck a deep chord and scrambled up the gritty embankment.

The three of us groped our way behind the warriors while dodging the serpentine speed bumps. By the time we reached the top, the Gnomes stood shoulder to shoulder between the advancing vipers and the three of us. They amped up their droning which soothed the reptiles like anesthesia. Within seconds, some of the snakes froze, as if paralyzed, while others turned back.

"You can let go now, Sadie."

I looked at Sophie. She tugged her hand out of my death-grip. "Oh, sorry." I shook my stiff fingers and assessed my little sister. She looked relieved but energized. "You okay?"

She wrapped her arms around my middle, her wet clothes soaking my own. "I am now. I hate snakes—but I'd totally do that again to be saved by another Water Nymph."

I looked at her captivated face. "I still can't believe it, and I watched it happen. Incredible."

Muggleridge turned while the other Gnomes continued to hum. "Yep. Once in a lifetime occurrence, right there. Nymphs are private, shy creatures. It's unlikely one would come to the aid of the likes of us. Count your blessings, Topsiders." He dusted off his hands. "Now then. Let's put some space between us and those serpents, shall we?"

All business, he marched ahead.

The silence that followed us, as we followed him, made it seem like we were still walking among the snakes. Huffing breaths and trudging footfalls ticked away the time. My adrenaline nosedived, and I fought the urge to request a pit stop.

The closer we trekked to the distant hills, the more rugged the terrain became. After the creek, our path had stretched for miles at a slight incline, and my thighs were killing me. Imagining the disdain on Reiko's face was enough to keep my complaints in solitary confinement.

We finally stopped to rest on an outcropping of large, flat stones. I wasn't the only one glad for a break. Everyone gulped from their canteens with gusto.

"Does it ever get dark?" Brady asked between gulps. "Without the sun to mark time, I can't tell how long we've been traveling."

"You arrived in Vituvia late yesterday according to our time." Muggleridge took another drink and went on. "We don't have night in the sense you're used to. The light provided by the Sword of Cherubythe dims for a period of time each day. We call it dusktime or dusk. Those of us in the Tethered World do not require as much sleep as Topsiders. We are not subjected to many of the stresses you encounter, so our bodies need less time to recover. Daylight lasts about eighteen of your hours. Dusktime about six. There are presently four hours left before dusk."

"Maybe it's because you're short." Sophie swung her legs from the ledge of the rock.

"Maybe *what* is because we're short?" The general had an edge to his voice.

"The fact that you don't need much sleep or time to recover."

Muggleridge scowled in a way that suggested he'd not considered that possibility. "Our height has nothing to do with it. We're strong, hardy people. Not subject to weakness and sickness like humans. We get more done on less sleep than you. Simple as that."

I leaned over to Sophie and whispered, "Guess that's a touchy subject."

"Like they might consider themselves tall if I don't point out the obvious?" She giggled and hopped off the rock. "I want to learn how to use this thing." Sophie pulled the sword from her hip—with both hands this time—and jabbed at a rock.

"These swords are way different from the sabers we use in fencing." Brady unsheathed his weapon and stabbed at the air. "I'm not entirely comfortable with them."

General Muggleridge stood and stretched. "I'm sure you'll be quick to learn when you have a chance to train this evening, Miss Sophie. For now, our respite comes to a close. We soldier on."

He removed his helmet long enough to run stubby fingers through his coarse, silver hair. "I do hope the Dwarves return soon, or we shan't have time to plan anything, let alone practice dueling. Now, higher up and further in!"

"Hey!" I gasped. "Have you read—"

"Of *course* I have." Muggleridge waved me off and took brisk steps ahead of the group. "We enjoy good literature as much as the next person." He shoved his helmet back on his head.

Smarlow stepped up beside me. "Although books are hard to come by down here. We have to use underground connections. *Really* underground."

Laughing, I fell into step with Brady.

"You know why most homeschoolers don't approve of chain mail?" He thumped his armor for effect.

"No, why?" *Corny joke, straight ahead.*

"Because it's *heavy metal*, get it?"

I rolled my eyes.

Brady elbowed me and pointed. "Here comes your knight in shining armor."

A hazy wall of dust was approaching. The clamor of hoofs resonated in my middle, then grit inundated my oxygen supply. I coughed and twisted away until the dirt subsided.

The receding cloud revealed a crew of crusty Dwarves, as thick as they were wide, sitting astride four horses. Their long, snarled hair and cascading beards sprawled over their shoulders and onto billowing capes. They looked like four small mountains in their own right.

Wogsnop nudged his horse a few paces ahead of his comrades and saluted. The other three Dwarves held thick, lengthy ropes. Lion-like forms emerged from the settling dust. They were tethered to the ropes and paced beneath the horses.

I gasped.

These creatures were not lions, nor did they look like topside animals that might have wandered below. In fact, they weren't recognizable from myths or legends or my mother's blog.

Leathery, grey skin stretched taut over their lithe, muscular bodies. Built low and long, they patrolled with a menacing swagger, their whip of a tail swaying behind, ridged and dragon-like.

When I focused on their faces, my pulse surged as if given an electrical shock. These beasts were unlike anything I'd ever dared to imagine—and seemed straight from the pages of the apocalypse.

CHAPTER SIXTEEN

Dreadlocks.

I'm sure it was some sort of wooly mane, but by all appearances these creatures had wild shocks of charcoal hair that framed their faces like thick tentacles. Faces that turned our way and watched us approach with eerie, amber eyes.

Pewter horns sprouted and curved through masses of hair. Warty nodules covered their muzzles, which otherwise reminded me of a mountain goat. Four-inch fangs protruded from a fierce under bite that skimmed either side of their snouts.

Creeped out took on a whole new meaning.

The Gnomes talked between themselves and strolled towards the beasts.

I grabbed my brother and sister and anchored them to where we stood. "You're nuts if you plan on waltzing up to those things." My grip tightened. "Dad warned us about petting strange dogs for a reason."

"They're not dogs." Sophie pointed out the obvious.

Brady yanked his arm free. "Yeah, they're way cooler."

"You guys mind listening to me for once? Wait and see what we're supposed to do, okay?"

The Dwarves watched our exchange. They looked at

each other and chuckled. The Gnomes glanced back at us.

"Larcens, there's nothing to fear from the Toboggans." General Muggleridge waved us over. "They won't harm you unless you're a Troll."

That was all the assurance Brady and Sophie needed. They hurried over.

I didn't budge, convinced I was trapped in an excruciatingly long dream. I stared, unmoving, and willed my subconscious to pull me back to reality in the safety of my bedroom.

Nothing happened.

"Really, it's fine. They're fierce-looking creatures but friendly." To prove his point, Smarlow stretched his hand towards one of them. It nuzzled his palm like a kitten. "You see?"

I saw, all right. I simply didn't believe it.

He stroked its back. The Gnome would've made a tasty mouthful for the beast if they weren't on good terms. "Toboggans are similar to your guard dogs topside. They protect us from Trolls, and they can see a Leprechaun that's turned himself invisible."

I took tentative steps their way.

Brady and Sophie stroked the animals' manes with gasps of excitement. The Toboggans responded playfully. Their cloven feet pawed the dirt as they rubbed against my siblings' outstretched hands.

Here goes nothing. Resigning myself to this alternate reality, I joined our group but kept my distance. I was in no hurry to get acquainted with these house pets from the pit.

Wogsnop removed items from the pack behind his saddle and tossed them to Smarlow. He passed one to Reiko and one to Muscle. Or was it Mighty?

Each Gnome strapped the object to the back of a Toboggan in saddle-like fashion. It appeared to be a stiff blanket molded into two seats. The creatures became prehistoric, tandem bikes.

"Each of you humans—up—onto a horse and into a saddle behind one of my men." Wogsnop snapped his fingers for emphasis.

Brady helped Sophie mount an Appaloosa then strode over to a large black stallion. I made a wide girth around the creepy Toboggan things and approached a black-and-white Paint horse. The Dwarf straddling the horse shifted forward and reached a calloused hand my way. I strained against the stirrup to mount.

"Glavashian at your service, m'lady," his gruff but jolly voice greeted. "But please call me Lava. Everyone does."

"Nice to meet you." I squirmed to situate myself, unsure of where to place my hands. I settled for bracing them behind my backside. Seemed too weird to strap my arms around a total stranger.

He nudged the horse in a roundabout turn.

"Thank you for coming to get us. I'm not used to walking around in armored clothing."

Lava wheezed out a raspy laugh. "Yes, m'lady, times've changed topside. Smart bombs and camouflage uniforms have replaced the need for hand-forged weapons and clothing. Practically put us Dwarves out of business, ya did." He clicked his tongue and dug in his heels. The horse lurched.

My feet flew up, and I careened backward, squealing, through the air. With a *thunk*, I crashed to the ground head first. Everything hurt, but not as badly as my pride. My vision swam. I tried to force myself upright, determined to downplay my inept ability to stay on a horse.

A kaleidoscope of Gnomes and Dwarves surrounded me, peppered with the floating faces of Sophie and Brady. I found it hard to focus on any one person. My head felt like a ripe melon ready to burst open.

Pain won out. My pride—and my body—lay in the dirt while one of the out-of-focus faces inspected me.

"How many fingers am I holdin' up, m'lady?" a gruff voice asked.

I squinted at a fleshy blob hovering over my face. "I don't... wanna wake up yet... Dad." Why did my words come out so slowly?

Somebody snickered.

I willed the voices away and rolled over to snuggle into my pillow. My fingers dug into something that felt suspiciously like the gravel walkway in our backyard. "What's wrong with this pillow?" I pushed myself up to look at it.

"Be still, miss." Strong hands cradled my head. "Looks like you've a nasty gash."

"Are you okay?" Sophie's face came into focus above me.

"What happened?" I studied her expression. "My head hurts."

She brushed the hair from my eyes. "You fell off the horse and hit your head. Scared me half to death."

I reached a shaky hand for my little sister and gave her a pat on the leg. "Sorry about that."

"Well, *this* is a dandy delay."

I recognized the voice—and rousing optimism—of Smarlow. Clarity returned on the heels of his dismal statement. So did the motivation I felt a few moments before. I needed to get off the ground and past this whole, unfortunate incident.

"Be still now," my impromptu doctor ordered. "Gonna wash the grit out of your wound with my canteen. Grab your sister's hand, 'cause this will hurt."

I did as Lava suggested. My nails dug into Sophie's palm. Her eyes grew round in response.

"Good girl." The Dwarf gave my shoulder a squeeze. "Didn't make a sound. Almost done. I'm pressin' the cut together to stop the bleedin'. Wogsnop, I need a strip of cloth."

I heard a shredding sound. Within moments, a headband accentuated my throbbing headache and, no doubt, my new rough-and-tumble fashion sense.

Slowly, Brady and Lava helped me up. Sparks of light pricked my vision. I stumbled, and a host of hands shot forward to steady me. A deep breath or two later, I pronounced myself fit for travel.

"We'll have Doc Keswick take a look at you when we get to Berganstroud." Wogsnop pointed to the animals. "Let's mount up and get moving."

Brady squeezed my shoulder. "You up for this, sis? I could have someone take you back to Vituvia, or even take you myself."

I started to shake my head—a movement that gave me a good reason to speak instead. "No, I want to go. Just say a little prayer. My head hurts, and a bumpy ride on a horse won't be the cure."

"You bet. C'mon, I'll help you up."

The sturdy Dwarf offered me his forearm. Brady helped displace some of the weight and coordination of my undignified climb onto the horse. I settled into place, aware of new pains in my back and hips as I sat astride the broad beast. The chain mail did nothing for my predicament.

"Brady Larcen." My brother extended his hand to the Dwarf. "Thanks for doctoring up my sister."

The Dwarf shook hands with enthusiasm. "Call me Lava, son. All part of life in these parts. Bumps and bruises are the price of adventure, at least that's how I explain it to my wife when I walk in with a knot on my head." He chuckled. "Your sister has officially paid her dues. I promise to get her situated so she doesn't have to relive this particular adventure today."

Brady gave a thumbs-up sign. "Sounds good." He turned to me. "Hang on tight."

I shot him my best *duh* smirk, and he walked to his horse.

"Now, m'lady, wrap your arms around my middle and hang on as tight as ya need to. Relax your legs and move with the horse. That's all there is to it. I should've told ya the first time. I feel responsible for what happened, and I do apologize."

After such a disgraceful dismount, I lost my inhibition about wrapping my arms around someone I'd recently met. Lava felt like a sure anchor on a stormy, four-legged ocean. "No apology needed. I'm not new to riding horses, believe it or not. I chose to be shy rather than safe. It's my own dumb fault."

"Let's move." Wogsnop pulled ahead of the group, and the other animals followed.

My head protested every hoof fall, but I dared not complain. I'd caused enough delay already.

"Do ya have a name, m'lady, or do ya want me to call ya 'm'lady'?"

"Yes." I winced. "I mean no. No, don't call me m'lady. Yes, I have a name. It's Sadie. Sadie Larcen."

"It's a pleasure, Miss Sadie. Haven't been in the company of humans for at least eighty years. Maybe closer to a hundred."

"What? How old are you?" My words came out muffled when I buried my throbbing head against the cushion of his thick, snarled hair. The rest of his hair, along with his cape, whipped around my arms and face. He smelled of dirt and leather and pipe tobacco. I found it a comforting concoction.

His chest rumbled with laughter. "Let's just say I'm ancient compared to any of Adam's kinfolk. It's nothin' to live a few hundred years down here."

Something else to wrap my brain around—later, when it hurt less.

"What do you mean by us humans putting you out of business?" By now our horse had settled into a steady canter, and I found the rhythm in my lower body. This relieved the jarring motion on my head.

"Who do ya think made the finest armor in the world during the reign of King Arthur? How 'bout the Romans? Ya think Caesar built his own chariots? And the Egyptians? Well, the number of things we manufactured for those tyrants is as big as the pyramids we built for them."

"Dwarves built the pyramids? You're kidding."

"No joke. Some of our finest work. Course, no one wants to give us proper credit, but truth is truth."

I stopped asking questions so I wouldn't have to contemplate the answers. My brain felt like it might blow a fuse. I turned my head and spit the grit from my mouth. We rode behind Sophie and her Appaloosa, eating their dust. I tried to peek at our posse without getting dirt in my eyes.

To my left, Reiko and Zest kept stride on the back of

their shared Toboggan. They looked completely at ease while the slinky creature sprinted around rocks and sprang over dips and ruts. I realized it would be undignified to expect a Gnome to ride a huge horse, needing to be held like a doll or puppet. For their stature, Toboggans were a perfect fit.

I, however, maintained zero interest in getting acquainted with the creatures.

WITH A PAINFUL GROAN, I dismounted the steed that now munched grass in a paddock. My legs ached with early signs of being saddle sore.

Lava bounded down after me and extended his hand. "You're good company, Sadie. It was a privilege to carry the sister of our future king on my horse, Pike." He patted the animal on its flank.

I reached down and shook Lava's hand, getting a good look at his smiling, cobalt eyes and crinkled face. "The pleasure and privilege were mine. Thank you for the history lesson and for fast-forwarding our journey to Berganstroud."

"Fast-forwarding?"

He was obviously unfamiliar with the slang, but before I could explain he said, "Ah! I think I understand. That's a new Topsider term I can use on my comrades." He chuckled.

I giggled and scratched the horse's muzzle. "Thank you, Mr. Pike, sir. It was a fine jaunt, minus the rough start." From the corner of my eye, I saw Lava smirking at me. "What?"

"He's not a talking horse, m'lady. This isn't Narnia." He winked.

I burst out laughing. "I didn't expect him to talk back, silly. I spoke to him like I would any animal. But you've no idea how Narnian this whole experience has been. *No idea.*"

I joined the others in front of the barn. We all shared

the same stiff-legged walk. If we were already this sore, I hated to think about tomorrow. On the upside, my head no longer felt like a pulsating orb.

"How's the battle wound, Miss Larcen?" Muggleridge asked as we filtered through a gate and onto a stony path.

"Much better." I touched the bandage. "Maybe I can take it off."

"Leave your pretty little head wrapped up till we get ya to the doc." Lava wagged his finger.

"You're the boss."

"Actually, *I'm* the boss." Wogsnop brushed passed us.

No point explaining the slang. I let it go.

Wogsnop led us into the streets of Berganstroud. Well, the street—singular—as it turned out. The town had one rugged, furrowed lane running along the curve of the hillside.

The pasture and stable sat at one end of the road. A few free-standing buildings shared the same side of the street. I was too far away from the other structures to identify them. Based on the fences that separated the pastures from acres of garden land, I guessed the buildings were agricultural. In the distance, a glossy smudge hinted at a large body of water. A veil of mist bloomed on its surface like a blanket unfurling in slow motion.

The other side of the lane looked altogether different. It displayed the Dwarves' craftsmanship, in all of its glory, throughout the edifices that towered above us.

My mind flashed to the cliff dwellers of Utah I'd studied in American history. The Dwarves had the same idea but on a grander scale. The scope and depth of the town seemed to traverse deep into the granite hillside. With dusktime falling on Berganstroud, exterior torches winked to life. Gilded light warmed the elaborately carved openings, four and five stories tall, making the stone façade recede in its glow.

"Wow." I didn't expect such a welcoming sight.

Dwarves peeked from windows and doorways then crowded into the street to welcome our crew. They stared, taking in our height, while whispers of "Topsider" and "upper earth" swirled roundabout. I was instantly self-conscious about my beat-up appearance and cringed at giving these folks such a lousy first impression.

We walked several minutes, following the curve of the towering cliff. It jutted in front of us and formed a protective wall around the town in the way it curved back towards itself. Once we rounded the tip, the bluff returned to join the mass of hills.

A formidable wall layered with chiseled slabs of stone extended from the bluff and came towards us, then rejoined the cliffs about a hundred yards away. An iron gate stood in the center of the barrier and offered an intimidating entrance. I guessed that behind it lay the Dwarves' fortress. It looked impenetrable.

Along the top of the cliff a fence made from spear-like shafts formed barbed sentinels. Here and there, guards stood posted like stout, hairy boulders. The dusktime sky had stopped its dimming and gave the feel of subdued lighting used in fancy restaurants.

Ambience for the Tethered World.

Wogsnop made a throaty noise, and the gate opened at our approach. We walked into a courtyard outfitted with cannons and other antiquated weapons. Leftover weaponry from earth or original to the fortress? Either way, Lava had made it clear the Dwarves made the stuff.

Surly-looking soldiers saluted our group. We walked the cobbled path to a tunnel sculpted into the granite and flanked with torches and more warriors. I looked at my siblings. Awe and enchantment were written plainly on their faces.

I wished I could share their enthusiasm. Instead, I felt tense and short of breath walking into the stone citadel. The weight of being responsible for my siblings' safety, along with the angst of our mission, loomed large and unyielding as the rock. It was as if a fearful parasite had hitched a ride on me about the time I hitched one myself—on the back of a dragon. I couldn't go five minutes without an anxious thought. The fresh spike of fear revived my headache.

We followed Wogsnop through a labyrinth of torch-lit halls reminiscent of the tunnels in Beacon Rock and into a spacious, rustic room. A massive wooden table staked its claim in the center. Regal flags perched along the far wall like sentries. A layer of musky smoke hovered over the room, evidence that the Dwarves had a penchant for pipes.

The room hummed with activity. Male and female Dwarves dashed in and out of the shadowy torchlight. Others clustered together in deep discussions. Four came over to Wogsnop and Lava and spoke in hushed voices.

I gazed about, taking in the gruff looks on the weathered, chiseled faces—a physical reflection of the stone room in which I stood. The ceiling soared overhead. From the pinnacle, a colossal chandelier held a dozen more torches that flickered like giant birthday candles.

"Pinch me, Sadie," Brady whispered. "I think maybe we've time traveled."

"Definitely."

Sophie frowned. "Too bad Aunt Jules wouldn't allow us to bring a camera."

I nodded and turned to view the rest of the room behind us.

"Ahhh!" I screamed and jumped out of my skin. Shaking—and instantly nauseous—my vision locked onto what loomed several feet away.

Brady and Sophie gasped. "No!"

My worst fears stared me in the face. *We've walked into a trap!*

CHAPTER SEVENTEEN

Three Yetis towered over us.

My knees wilted, and I grabbed Brady and Sophie. They trembled in my grip. We were helpless to do more than stare back at the beasts.

Their scowling brows gave way to ferocious lips curled into a snarl. Yellowed fangs glinted in the torchlight. Neanderthal heads sloped to linebacker shoulders, their hulking bodies clad only in a leather loin cloth. They were covered in matted fur. Their arms reached for us, ready to pounce.

None of them moved.

It took a moment to comprehend that these behemoths were missing something—life.

They're dead.

Stuffed. Taxidermic.

I let out a ragged breath.

Reiko and Smarlow rushed to our aid and offered pats of comfort on our legs. Brady, Sophie, and I panted like a pack of hunted prey and tried to regain our composure.

"Oh, Larcens! My apologies, my friends." Wogsnop trotted over with Lava on his heels.

"They're not alive. If they were, I'd slay them myself." Smarlow shook a fist at the creatures.

"I... noticed." My voice felt as unsteady as my legs.

"Whew, close call." Brady shook his head. "I was about to take them down."

I'd remember that comment later when I needed a good laugh.

"The one in the middle is Chorazin. Chief of the Trolls in the Battle of Berganstroud." Wogsnop pointed. "That's the last time the overgrown apes were foolish enough to start something with us—about twenty years ago."

"Trolls are not the cleverest mice in the maze." Lava jerked his thumb at the beasts. "They're minus any organization or strategy."

"They make up for it in strength and size," Smarlow said.

Lava nodded. "True, my friend. But once we killed Chorazin in the heat of the battle, the other Trolls retreated. They lacked a secondary commander or backup plan."

Wogsnop stroked his beard. "They've been restless of late. Threats and skirmishes are becoming more frequent. Chorazin's son, Nekronok, vows to avenge his father's death. He seems to have some extra-clever DNA. Our spies report that he's divided his men into ranks, and they're getting expert help in combat training. Not sure who the expert might be, however."

"Probably those measly Leprechauns." Smarlow crossed his arms with a *humph*.

Wogsnop shook his head. "Doubtful. The Leprechauns don't possess battle smarts. They're all about foolery."

"Someone had enough smarts to track down and kidnap our parents and"—Sophie snapped her fingers—"abduct the queen."

"Indeed, young Larcen." Captain Wogsnop gave her a lopsided grin. "Which is why I'd like to proceed with supper and discussion. We want to reunite you with your family as soon as possible." He turned and gave me a questioning look. "I also want Doc Keswick to take a look at your head. Would you like to eat first or go to the clinic straightaway?"

I touched the bandage and battled a fresh round of self-conscious thoughts. The swelling had lessened, however, and I had weathered the worst of it. "Food first. Definitely." I patted my stomach. "I don't think there's need for a doctor. Only a shower."

Brady's stomach rumbled loud enough for the others to hear. "My stomach's trained to do that whenever someone mentions food."

The Dwarves chuckled, and Lava slapped Brady on the back. Wogsnop waved for us to follow. He led us away from the overgrown, stuffed animals. A smorgasbord of delicacies welcomed us at a long, wooden table hemmed with chairs of varying heights. The smell of smoked meat tugged me into the nearest seat.

Today's adventure had left me famished. I easily kept up with Brady's ambitious appetite. Once we ate our fill, the three of us were good for nothing. The Dwarves and Gnomes wanted us to join their war party, but we took turns nodding off.

General Muggleridge saved the day by asking the Dwarves to excuse us from the meeting. A young, clean-shaven Dwarf escorted us to a set of guest bedrooms connected in the middle by a smaller room that contained a bathing area and a closet.

"Miss Larcen," the Dwarf called from the doorway, "Wogsnop insists your contusion be examined. I'll be waiting in the hall to fetch a nurse once you get cleaned up. Please let me know when you're ready."

I agreed, though I'd forgotten about the injury yet again. Our escort shut the door, and I carefully peeled the bandage away from the gash. Dried blood adhered a sizable wad of hair to the cloth and made me yelp with each twang on my scalp. Once freed, I scratched my head like a flea-bitten cat—avoiding the wound itself and relieved to have the bandage removed.

Brady beat me to the bathroom and pumped water into the large stone basin. "You guys stay on your side. I'll be out before you know it." He slid the wooden pocket door closed.

Sophie and I stood and looked at each other, blinking. Things suddenly felt *normal*.

"Well..." I looked around, dumbstruck.

"Well…what?"

I shook my head. "I don't know. I'm too tired to have a coherent thought. How 'bout you?"

Sophie flashed a grin. In that instant, I knew she had savored every twist and turn of this real-life novel. She was also the character with the biggest heart and bravest soul. I envied her enjoyment.

All of a sudden, she ran to me and started sobbing. "I feel so awful, Sadie. I'm so selfish."

"Selfish? What are you talking about?" I wrapped my arms around her, confused.

"I'm selfish, Sadie. There's no other word for it." A fresh round of tears gushed. I stroked the top of her head.

We stayed like that a few moments, then I pulled back and lifted her chin. "What's going on, Soph?"

Sophie struggled to catch her breath. "I'm having too much fun." She wiped her eyes with her sleeve. "Dad and Mom are in danger. Their lives are at stake. Yet, I'm so excited to be in this place, meeting people who belong in…in Middle Earth or Oz. It's not right to be enjoying this, Sadie. It's just not."

"I don't think you're selfish."

She looked up, wide-eyed. "You don't?"

"No. Your attitude makes you better equipped for whatever happens."

"Really?"

"Definitely. What does Mom always tell us—whether we're writing a report or taking a class?" I cocked my head.

"She says you need to squeeze all you can out of every opportunity."

"Because?" I raised my eyebrows.

"Because there are some things you'll hope to only study once. Learn them well, and you won't have to repeat them."

"And?"

Sophie grinned. "There are other experiences you may never get to have twice, so make the most of each one."

"I think you've taken her advice to heart. Mom would

be proud." I smiled and hugged her again.

"Thank you, Sadie."

A muffled yell from the bathroom signaled Brady's exit.

"I call the bathroom next." I poked Sophie's ribs, forcing her to release me, and ran to the door.

"Sadie."

I turned. "What?"

"I might be having fun, but I'm still really, really scared." Her eyes revealed a quiet terror.

I didn't know what to say to quell that kind of fear. It ran in my veins just as deeply. I nodded. "Me too, Soph. Me too."

MUFFLED NOISES ROUSED ME from a dreamless sleep. Someone stirred the fire. Golden hues spilled across the hearth like liquid light. It cascaded to the floor and brushed my side of the bed.

I watched a small, stout figure stoke the logs. For one rare moment, I felt safe. The stone walls offered a protective vault against the chaos my life now encompassed. The bed cocooned me in layers of earth-tone cloth and animal skins. Though I wanted to close my eyes and relish the comfort, I feared it might be snatched away if I wasn't watchful.

It was all too perfect. Fragile. Like a mirage.

The attending Dwarf hummed a soulful tune. The notes further quenched my thirst for tranquility. *Peace.* Something I missed so acutely that I felt the burn of salty tears. I swallowed and sniffed them back. If I breached the dam and let them flow, it might take longer to repair than I could afford.

The Dwarf turned a smiling face my way. "Good mornin', lovey." The whispered greeting was cheery and distinctly female. Her accent reminded me of Aunt Jules.

"Good morning." I sighed. "Thank you for keeping us warm with the fire."

"My pleasure, m'lady." She stepped beside me, her crinkled face glowing from the fire. "I've brought hot tea and fresh biscuits to warm yer insides as well. How does that sound?"

I stretched, unsure I wanted to give up the cozy featherbed. Food was the only competition for such comfort—and a good distraction for my emotions. "Couldn't sound better." I turned to find Sophie burrowed under the blankets beside me. She slept so hard I couldn't bear to wake her.

Sliding out of the covers and onto a tapestry rug, I stood with a snap to my knees and a throb in my head. It reminded me that I'd failed to call for a nurse after my shower and instead nestled into the covers, asleep before Sophie finished her bath. I touched the sore spot. The knot was nearly gone, though still tender. Stiff-legged and saddle sore, I shuffled to a small table adorned with steaming biscuits and a silver tea set. The petite woman poured scalding water into my cup and plopped a pouch of tea leaves, tied with string, into the liquid.

"I heard about yer accident, yesterday. Mind if I have a look? I think everyone would be happier if I could give yer head a good once-over."

I nodded. "I didn't mean to ignore the captain's request. I was so tired I forgot."

"Of course ya were." She stood behind me. "Here now, tilt yer head down a bit. Yer such a tall one." Her fingers worked through my hair, gently parting it. "Oh yes, lookin' good. Nasty bump, wasn't it? Healin' nicely, though."

"Are you the doctor?"

She giggled. "Goodness, no! I'm a bit of everything around here. Nurse on call for today. You've slept good, yer eatin' good, so I'm goin' to pronounce ya good as new. Need anything else, m'lady?"

"One thing." I grinned. "Your name."

She seemed bashful but pleased by my request. "Name's Joanie. I've been workin' in the citadel for as long as me brain can fathom. Me mum worked here before me."

I patted the table. "Would you join me for breakfast, Joanie? I'd love to chat if you have time."

With another giggle, she hopped onto the human-sized chair. "Dwarves never turn down an invitation to dine. Though I dare say this is one of the most special invitations I've yet to receive. To dine with the sister of our future king—oh me!—I'm honored." She covered her mouth with her hand, eyes wide.

It was my turn to laugh. "It's not like that at all. We're ordinary people. I hardly know who you're talking about when you say things like that. I only learned about this place and our part in it a couple of days ago."

"Aye, but yer very special to us down here."

"Thank you. That's kind of you to say." I bit into the fluffy biscuit and rolled my eyes when the warm pastry melted like cotton candy. "Delicious! Did you make these?"

Her eyes twinkled. "No, dear. Me sweet husband made them. Gwix is head cook here at the fortress."

"Give him my compliments." I buttered a second helping of heaven. "Maybe you can explain something. His name is Gwix, yours is Joanie. His name is unusual to me, but yours is common. You and I are speaking English. Yet, the Tethered World has its origins in the Garden of Eden. I know they didn't speak English back then." I shook my head, confused. "Help me make sense of it."

She gave an understanding nod. "We've changed with the times, like y'have topside, m'lady. At one time, the universal language was Babylonian. Then Hebrew. Later it became Latin, then Greek. Now 'tis English. Since those of us here don't always remain down here, we bring things back from our travels Topside. English is one such thing."

"Makes sense." I took a sip of tea. "I figured there would be a Dwarf language, and a Gnome language, and so forth. Still, I've heard some rather unique names around here. Are those native?"

Joanie nodded and sipped her tea. Her wrinkled face would not be considered beautiful by human standards, but I had a feeling that in her youth, Joanie must have been a real looker among the Dwarves. Deep-green eyes beamed with inner enthusiasm. Her grey hair, neatly braided, hung past her chair. She was gracefully plump.

"Since most of the creatures moved from the Garden at the same time, they were used to sharin' a common tongue." She dunked her biscuit in her tea. "There *are* some inner languages and slang unique to each creature group. Many of the unusual names stem from those origins."

"I see."

"Then there are names that I don't think are meant to be names. One of me great-granddaughter's playmates is called Bungee because her papa went bungee jumpin' several years ago. That's plain silly if ya ask me."

I had to agree. "Bungee? Yes, that's awful. I suppose that's how Toboggans got their name?"

She nodded. "It's their nickname. Clovenboar is their given name. We don't get to enjoy snow in the Tethered World, but they say that ridin' one of those creatures is as close to slidin' down a mountain of snow on a toboggan as we shall ever get. My grandfather used to raise Clovenboars. He let me ride 'em when I was a tot."

An image of Gnomes slinking across the landscape on the back of the garish animals played in my brain. "I'd say that's a good comparison."

"A comparison of what, Sadie?" Sophie's voice wafted our way.

"Hey, sis. Come eat breakfast with our new friend Joanie."

I heard a tremendous yawn. "Sure."

Joanie slid off her chair and crossed to Sophie's bedside. "Good mornin', lass." She patted Sophie's arm. "Did ya sleep up an appetite?"

The dimly lit room couldn't conceal Sophie's eagerness. She sat up and grinned at her surroundings. The adventure was *on* once again. She gave the Dwarf an impulsive hug. "You're real. It's all real."

Joanie seemed confused. "'Course I'm real, young'un. Whatever do ya mean?"

Sophie plunked to the floor and straightened her twisted clothes. "I dreamt we were home. I told Mom and Dad about a crazy dream about being here. About the Gnomes and the Water Nymph. As if all this wasn't real. It made me sad." She held up a finger. "But happy my parents were safe."

"Sorry to say, I'm not yer mum, love." Joanie led Sophie to the table. "I'm here to fix ya up with some vittles so you can be strong enough to get to yer mum and yer papa and bring 'em home."

"Thank you." Sophie stuffed an oversized bite of biscuit into her mouth.

Joanie stood near the table and looked from Sophie to me. Her sunny disposition clouded. She bit her lip, blinking back tears.

"What is it?" I placed a hand on her shoulder.

Sophie stopped chewing and looked at Joanie.

"You two are very special." Joanie's voice was husky. "And very brave. Those of us here will be prayin' to the Ancient One for all of ya to be safe. I fear you'll need to be braver than either of ya think possible. I hope yer both the prayin' sort, as well."

"We are," I said.

"Good, good." She sighed. "If the Creator sends ya, He will give ya the guts and the gear. It's just..."

"Just what?" Sophie bit her lip.

Joanie took a deep breath. "The Trolls. They're very dangerous."

"We know. We think they kidnapped our parents."

"Oh!" Joanie shuddered. "I do hope that's not the case. My papa was taken captive by the brutes. They snatched him away when I was a wee girl, and—"

Bam! Bam! Bam! "Larcens! Make haste!"

We looked at each other, dazed. The banging on our door continued. "Wake up, Larcens. Make haste!"

Joanie bustled to the door and tugged on the knob. Lava toppled into the room as he reached to strike the door.

"Lava!" Joanie stood, hands on hips. "What's all this fuss about?"

Lava grimaced and regained his composure. "There's been an attack on our guards near Ernest Peak. We're rerouting our rescue plan. We must mobilize immediately." He looked from Joanie to me. "We fear they know you're here. We need to get ya out now in case others are coming."

"Oh, heavens! Let's get ya dressed." Joanie shooed us towards the bathroom.

"I've already alerted Brady," Lava said. "We're to meet in the Near-Deep Tunnel Chamber straightaway."

In the closet, Joanie sifted through an assortment of human-size clothing and withdrew two tunics and genie-style pants. "Let's get ya out of those rumpled clothes. You'll find our handmade attire very comfortable, especially under the likes of armor."

Rare visits from humans didn't keep Dwarves unprepared for company. Several stocked shelves stood waiting for use. My heart pounded a frantic beat while I pulled on the loose-fitting layers and strapped supple, leather boots around my ankles. The tranquil morning shriveled up, allowing anxious thoughts to crowd in again.

'Cause it'd be a shame to go an hour without freaking out about something.

"You didn't finish telling us about your father." Sophie wrestled with the drawstring of her pants.

Joanie heard Sophie but clearly pretended not to. She pressed her lips together and plucked our pajamas from the floor with more force than necessary.

"Your dad," Sophie urged. "What happened to your dad?"

Joanie slowed long enough to look from me to Sophie, her eyes somber. "I can't rightly say."

"He's okay, isn't he?" Sophie's eyes searched the woman's face.

"Not likely, young'un. He never came back."

CHAPTER EIGHTEEN

ANOTHER ROUND OF TUNNELS. *BLAST IT!* Not my favorite scenery.

Inside the stone arteries of the Hills of Berganstroud, I followed the Dwarves through a web of secret passages. Dwarf-size passages, I might add. Those of us with taller statures stooped in a most uncomfortable way.

Bad for us, but great for keeping Trolls out.

Sometimes the shaft dipped so low even the Dwarves had to crouch. My siblings and I crawled on all fours—a relief to my back but murder on my knees. Of course the Gnomes marched along with ease. The torch smoke burned my eyes and made breathing difficult no matter what position I took.

Because of the way we needed to hunch over, we were unable to wear our protective gear. I'd loathed traveling with armor the previous day, but now I felt reluctant to leave it behind. The danger level was rising. We still carried our swords, which offered little comfort to me. Thanks to fatigue, our sword-fighting lessons never transpired.

Wogsnop and three of his men led the brigade. Lava brought up the rear. Each wore a dagger at his side. Wogsnop and one of the others sported a quiver of arrows on their backs and bows slung across their shoulders.

General Muggleridge assigned Mighty, Zest, and Muscle as personal bodyguards to Brady, Sophie, and me. Reiko and the general rounded out our group, while Smarlow remained at the fortress to watch what might develop—ready to sprint back and warn Vituvia if more Trolls turned up.

"Only a bit further and we'll be in one of the supply chambers," Wogsnop called to our trailing group.

We rounded a bend that fed into a decent-sized room. The ceilings hung low enough to touch but high enough to stand upright. *Marvelous!*

Lava lit torches along the walls. The flickering light revealed wooden crates and latched trunks stacked against the back wall. The room smelled damp. It reminded me of the unfinished basement at my friend Deirdre's house. When we were kids we'd dare each other to go down there in the dark. This rock chamber was more inviting, thanks to the torches and well-armed friends.

We found spots to sit and stretch and rub various body parts. Brady, Sophie, and I sat on the crates. Lava leaned against a nearby chest secured with leather straps. Wogsnop and the rest of the Dwarves sat along an adjacent wall. They took out their beloved pipes and passed them among each other.

The Gnomes were nervous wads of energy with legs. They paced in a tight circle near the door, taking turns looking into the passageway and occasionally sniffing the air. Flasks of water and something similar to beef jerky made the rounds.

This is not the time or place for germ-a-phobes. I smiled and took my share.

The jerky reminded me of the supplies we lost, which reminded me of my lost parents, which reminded me that more of this bizarre journey stretched ahead through tunnels, up mountains, and who knew where else and what else.

Brady leaned towards me. "Did you guys eat breakfast?"

"Yuck." Sophie waved her hand. "You've got nasty breath."

"*Sorry*." Brady moved away. "I didn't exactly have a toothbrush."

"Yeah, Sophie." I smacked her shoulder. "We all have the same problem."

"Boy-breath is the worst. Especially Brady's."

Brady rolled his eyes. "You want to answer my question?"

I nodded. "We had tea and biscuits."

"Seriously?" Brady's jaw dropped. "That's *so* not fair. I got nothing."

"*Had* nothing," I corrected, sounding like Mom. "Here, eat my snack. You need to feed your bottomless beast."

Brady snatched the meat. "Thanks."

I looked at Sophie, expecting her to do the same.

She ripped her piece in half and stretched a reluctant hand his way. "I'd only eaten half a biscuit when Lava pounded on our door."

Having eaten three helpings myself, I let that slide.

General Muggleridge strolled over. In his armor he looked like a toy-sized R2D2 from *Star Wars*.

"Sorry for the discomfort in the tunnels. Being short has its advantages." He glanced at Sophie, no doubt offering a rebuttal to Sophie's "short" comment the day before.

"We're good." I waved the notion off. "Safety first, right? Besides, we're partial to avoiding danger."

"Speak for yourself." Brady puffed his chest. "I like to live on the edge."

"Me too!" Sophie laced her arm through Brady's elbow.

"Looks like you're outnumbered, Sacie." Muggleridge chuckled. "At any rate, this is the best way to get in and out of Craventhrall."

"Then why wasn't this the original plan? Weren't we supposed to head *over* the hills, not through them?" I took a swig of water.

The general cleared his throat. "Well...you see...there're dangers in many places in this part of the Tethered World. If we head over the hills of Berganstroud we risk running into the Trolls. Until this morning, we didn't see this as much of a risk. Dwarves know many alternate and seldom-traveled routes. But the attack on Ernest Peak indicates the Trolls are mobilizing. They could be a greater threat compared to the risk inside the tunnels."

Oh, great. I crossed my arms. "*Inside* the tunnels? And what might be inside the tunnels?" *Please let it be as simple as small, aggressive rodents.*

"Dark Dwarves known as Stygians."

Dwarves are larger than rodents.

"Dark? What makes them dark?" Brady asked.

"They're dark because they're on the side of darkness. The side of the Trolls. The side of evil."

"They sound charming," I said.

He didn't grasp my sarcasm. "No, no, my dear, they aren't charming. They're dreadful. They've chosen to serve themselves, to reject the light, to join with evil and its dark deeds. They live in the valley, in the shadows of Ernest Peak and Mount Thrall. They've been known to frequent these tunnels."

"Um...*how* frequently?"

Do I really want to know?

"According to the captain and his men, the Stygs have ransacked supplies in chambers such as this one. Skirmishes break out here and there when the Dwarves of 'Stroud meet up with the Stygians. The Stygs always get the worst of it and run off—proving they're smarter than they are greedy. But there *is* a risk in traversing the tunnels. That's the reality. Today, however, the tunnels are the lesser of two dangers."

Muggleridge took out his dagger and stabbed the air. "As much as I'd like to take down a few Trolls, they've quite the advantage in size and strength. And they rarely take prisoners. I've seen Vituvians and Dwarves torn limb from limb on the battlefield."

I tried to block out *that* mental image.

"Why, I remember once finding a fellow's foot lyin' by a rock—"

"Okay! We get the picture." I held my hands up.

"Thanks."

Wogsnop slipped his quiver and bow around his shoulders. "Time to get moving, folks. This isn't Disneyland."

We gathered our things and fell into line with the others.

"Did he say Disneyland?" Sophie looked from me to Lava.

Lava nodded. "His son worked at the theme park as Sneezy. He followed Snow White around, letting Topsiders take pictures of him with bratty kids. He throws it out to try and impress us." He snorted. "As if it's news."

Back in the shafts, I resumed my much-loved, bent-over position. The threat of Dark Dwarves loomed in the back of my brain like a dull headache. The list of strange and dangerous creatures continued to grow: Trolls and Leprechauns, snakes and Toboggans, and now certain sorts of Dwarves. I hoped these Stygs completed the list and remained head knowledge only.

Will I be able to tell a good Dwarf from a bad one, simply by looking?

The maze of tunnels was a spider web of confusion. Wogsnop's torch flicked light on endless, pewter stone and irritated my lungs and eyes with smoke. Dwarves and Gnomes fared much better than us Topsiders. I crouched low to avoid the hovering smog, but my back and legs wouldn't cooperate for long.

Please let it be time for another pit stop!

Without warning, Wogsnop pulled up short. I plowed into Sophie. She slammed into Zest. Down we went like a row of dominoes.

Everyone grumbled as we righted ourselves.

"Shhh!" Wogsnop held a finger to his lips.

I leaned against the wall on all fours. My heart smacking against my chest.

Distant chatter floated our way, alerting us that we were not alone.

"Back, back!" Wogsnop waved his hands and pointed. We banged into each other, struggling to turn around.

Finally, the tail became the head, and we backtracked with Lava in the lead.

"Take them to one of the sealed rooms. The Styggies heard us. They're coming," Wogsnop called from the rear.

Lava diverted into a smaller tunnel, one I hadn't seen earlier. The circumference was tight—tighter than anything we'd climbed through yet. Even Lava stooped low. Brady, Sophie, and I crawled. I tried to rein in my imagination and think only about what was being asked of me here and now. A futile task. My mind kicked into worse-case-scenario mode. As usual.

Scrunched, and shaking in fear, I didn't see how Lava pulled it off, but suddenly we were scrambling through a small, hidden opening in the rock. Mercifully, we found ourselves in a large space. Lava lit two stationary torches.

"I must help the others," Lava said. "You three stay put and keep quiet. I'll be back. Muscle, Mighty, Zest, come with me. I may need your help."

I hadn't realized the Gnome warriors followed us inside. They were stealthily quiet and unobtrusive as shadows. They climbed back through the opening behind Lava. The doorway sealed, leaving us alone in a bare, granite room that wasn't much bigger than my walk-in closet.

"Whew! That was scary." I flopped to the ground and rubbed my knees.

Sophie stretched her arms up, arching backward. "Yeah, it's impossible to run fast in these tunnels if you're human. It's like being in a dream where you're racing as hard as you can but not getting anywhere."

"No kidding." Brady popped his knuckles. "When we heard those voices and couldn't turn around, I thought for sure those dudes would catch up. Almost had a panic attack."

"Hmmm, I thought you liked living on the edge, little brother." I raised an eyebrow.

Brady shrugged. "Well, it caught me off guard."

"Hey!" Sophie held up her hand. "Listen."

The faint sound of voices and clinking metal propelled me to the concealed door to listen closer. Brady and Sophie crowded beside me. Muffled shouts and grunts grew in volume. The distant clang of swords hinted that a full-out fight was taking place. My pulse echoed the pounding blows in my ears.

I hoped our side was winning. "Maybe we should pray," I whispered.

"I've *been* praying," Brady said.

"I know, but I mean right now, together."

Thump! Thump! Banging outside the wall jolted me upright. I clutched Brady's arm. Sophie grabbed my other hand. She nearly drew blood with her fingernails. We bowed our heads and prayed in fervent whispers.

"Hellooo..." A nasal voice called from the other side. "Isss someone or sssomething hiding in there?"

The three of us shared wild stares and clenched our hands tighter.

Bang, bang, bang.

"I know there are secrets somewhere around here. I dislike secretsss."

Brady shifted closer to the doorway and motioned us to get behind him. With a grip on Sophie, I jockeyed into position. Brady slid his sword from its sheath. I followed suit. My hand trembled so terribly that I hoped the clatter of weapon and scabbard didn't carry through the wall.

An awful scratching noise made me shudder. *Give me nails on the chalkboard any day!*

"I think I see sssomething in the stone. Sssomething secret. I dislike secretsss."

The anticipation of the unknown stabbed like an invisible knife.

"Wahhh!"

A loud scream. A snarl of voices and metal collided outside. Thuds and scrapes carried through the stone.

The door slid open. We jumped back, weapons at the ready.

Lava stumbled inside displaying a mess of cuts and abrasions, his cape slashed and torn. He couldn't have looked better to me—considering the alternative. "It's all right, Larcens. Stand down. Ya did well. Look at ya—ready to fight. You kids have guts." He nodded his approval. "You're gonna need plenty."

I lowered my sword, panting hard. Going from panic-stricken fear to a rush of relief turned me into a quivering blob.

"What happened out there?" Brady put away his weapon.

Lava stepped aside. Our bodyguards hurried in to take their places among us. "Wretched Stygs. Murderous thieves. Pilferin' our supplies and lookin' for trouble. They must've been feelin' cheeky today. One of many clashes of late."

"Do you think they saw us?" I pressed my eyes closed as if to shut out the possibility.

"No, m'lady, I don't. The nasty bloke outside this chamber knew he was on to *somethin'*, but I daresay that's all he knew." Lava waved us towards the tunnel. "In any case, we're safe. Let's join the others."

Lava, torch in hand, helped us squeeze through the opening. It was all I could do to avoid squishing the slain Stygian Lava had taken down. I shuddered when I brushed up against him on my way out.

Once we emerged from the narrow passage, Lava led us back down the path we'd taken before all the hoopla. The tunnel held a half dozen slain Stygs, sprawled about like terrifying land mines. I averted my gaze and stepped over mangled, bleeding bodies.

Walking hunched over made it difficult to look anywhere but down at the carnage. Dark Dwarves appeared to be paler than the Dwarves from Berganstroud, but loss of blood may have been to blame. The torches didn't provide much light and made the dead, creepy faces flicker to life. Shadows played tricks on my eyes.

A faint groan came from a body that lay in a heap on its side. A mop of hair covered the Styg's face and muffled his moan. I held my breath and crept past, hoping his wounds were serious enough to keep him down.

"Argh!"

An iron claw grasped my ankle. I fell flat. My hands scraped against the gritty floor. I screamed and thrashed, desperate to free myself. Another hand gripped my calf. Despite my writhing, the Dwarf drew me in with animal strength. I twisted and kicked with my free leg. The Stygian fended it off and pulled me closer, hand over hand. I heard shouts and saw movement in my peripheral vision.

The miscreant clamped my wrist like a vice and continued to work his way up. Clammy fingers grazed my neck then yanked my hair, forcing me to look at his wild, dilated pupils. The Styg's crooked, bulbous nose trickled with blood.

I screwed my eyes shut and spit in his face. His heavy hands wrapped around my throat like a python. I clawed at his pasty flesh. *I need air!*

Sophie's screams mingled with my choked shrieks. I was dimly aware of Brady pulling on the monster. Where was Muscle, my bodyguard?

Lava shouted orders, but reality became hazy. I heard a guttural yell. My captor gave a jolt and tightened his grip, strangling my airway. Nothing mattered except oxygen.

My vision swam. My heart sputtered frantically.

The Dwarf expelled a slow, sulfurous breath into my face, and everything went dark.

CHAPTER NINETEEN

Being slapped is an effective but unpleasant way to wake up after passing out. I should know. After several stinging whacks I thought were part of a brutal dream, I woke to find Reiko standing over me, hand raised and ready to strike again.

"Whoa! Th-that's enough." I swatted at her hand.

"You must wake up, Larcen. We've no time to waste." Reiko scowled down at me.

"What happened? Why am I—" Coughing overcame my question. I remembered being choked.

"You all right, sis?" Brady rushed over with Sophie on his heels. They smothered me in hugs—the good kind of smother.

"She's fine." Reiko crossed her stubby arms. "We need to keep moving. This is an unsecured place."

I shook off the remnants of brain fuzz and gave her an incredulous stare. "Are you for real? I almost had the living daylights choked out of me. Give me a second."

"We don't have a second. I don't mean to sound harsh, but it's for everyone's safety that we move on."

Brady placed a protective hand on my shoulder. "I think she needs a minute."

Reiko stalked to where the rest of the group sat huddled in discussion near several boulders.

It finally registered that I'd made it out of the tunnels, but not under my own power. "Thanks, Brady." Gratefulness washed over me. "You guys okay?"

Sophie nodded. "You gave me such a scare. I thought that dirt bag was going to kill you." She started crying. "Brady saved you."

I hugged Sophie close and looked at Brady.

He gave a shy, awkward shrug.

"You wanna tell me about it?"

"Maybe later. I'm still... processing. I did what I had to do."

I noticed crimson smudges mingled with grime splattered all over his arms.

Blood.

His gaze followed mine. He jerked his arms behind his back and stepped away.

"It's okay. You don't have to rehearse it. But thank you for saving me."

Lava ambled up before Brady could reply. Sophie wiped her eyes and pulled away from me.

"How are the brave Larcen ladies?" Lava's eyes held warm affection.

"We'll survive." I glanced at Brady, now rubbing the blood from his arms with his shirt. "Thanks to my brother."

"Yes, indeed, Brady was valiant. Each of you rose to the occasion. This has become quite an initiation. Wish I could tell ya that there's nothin' more to worry about, but I'd be lyin'."

"I understand. But that doesn't mean I have to like it."

"Like what?" Reiko returned.

Even though I was on my backside, I still looked down at her. Small but irritating. Like a splinter. "I don't like being choked." My irritation with Reiko increased. "And maybe I don't like tunnels, either."

She shrugged. "It was the safest way."

"Oh, really? Safe for whom?" Something inside snapped, and my frustration spewed everywhere. "Funny, but being choked in the tunnels didn't leave me with the most secure feeling, no thanks to the shrimpy bodyguard that left my side. In fact, something about this whole place leaves me pretty creeped out."

I took a deep breath. "I didn't ask to come here, and I can't wait to leave. I'll be happy to go back to leading a normal life and never set eyes on this world—or you— again. At the moment, that's not an option. A little sympathy might be nice."

"You want *sympathy*?" Reiko didn't flinch at the giant teenager who deftly told her off. "Last time I checked it was your *parents* being held by Trolls, not you. Your *elderly aunt* has been kidnapped, not you. Each of us has come alongside you, risking our lives to retrieve your family and our queen."

She huffed. "This isn't about *you*, little girl. You need to stop whining and get things in perspective. All of this serves a greater purpose than the whims of one person. Many things are at stake. Many lives are at risk. It's too bad about your mishap in the tunnels, but it probably won't be your last. Get over it. Get up. Let's find your parents and protect this realm as the Creator expects. There's no time for pity parties."

An uncomfortable silence settled over the group.

Mishap, huh? Who was she calling a little girl? Reiko's words smarted, but I didn't want to give her the satisfaction of seeing it. By now, everyone had stopped what they were doing and encircled the two of us. Muscle—formerly referred to as a shrimp—gave me an icy glare, but I wasn't about to apologize.

"I guess we better be on our way." I stood and avoided looking anyone in the eye.

With stilted effort and obvious tension, our group assembled and followed Wogsnop.

Silent and dutiful.

MOUNT THRALL LOOMED AHEAD like a menacing shard of broken glass, as if it could shred the domed sky into slivers of muted gold. Being so close to the mountains meant much of the light emanating from the quartz remained trapped behind the towering peaks. Shadows cloaked the ground—the perfect place for evil to lurk, even if it sounded cliché.

We wound our way along the back side of the hills of Berganstroud. A valley dipped below us then meandered between the erupting peaks of Thrall and its neighbors. Though traversing the valley would offer a more direct route, it exposed us to Stygians and wandering Trolls.

"We'll stick to the foothills, where we can use the trees for camouflage." Wogsnop pointed at the lay of the land. "We can work our way near Mount Thrall."

The shriveled trees looked like overgrown tumbleweeds and offered little more than a thin veil of twigs to disguise us. The lack of light, or maybe the presence of evil, seemed to have stunted the greenery. We dashed from one clump of trees to another, or crouched behind fallen boulders from the nearby cliffs. Thick dust coated the ground, the rocks and, of course, each of us.

This isn't about you, little girl! Reiko's speech rang in my ears. She had a point, but she also had some nerve to accuse me of being whiny. I'd like to see how fast she could snap back from a good choking. Hmmm... tempting.

"Back, back against the rocks." Wogsnop waved emphatically. He readied his bow and arrow as fast as Lava drew his sword. They squared off to the path we had recently traveled, bodies tense. Wogsnop narrowed his gaze at the cliff above, his eyes scanning back and forth. Lava sniffed the air.

The rest of us dashed to an outcropping of boulders and sandwiched ourselves between them and the cliff. Fear seized me. Wogsnop and General Muggleridge conferred and signaled us to stay put.

The two comrades sheathed their weapons and crept up a small hill that extended away from the cliff where we huddled. They used another large rock partway up the hill to shield their lookout.

I steadied my breathing and watched the Dwarves from over the top of the closest boulder. Wogsnop pulled out a retractable scope and aimed it at the ledge that loomed above us. Time crept by at the speed of a slug.

He closed the scope with a snap. Lava broke away and scrambled up the remaining length of the hill, staying low, then lay on his belly to peer over the edge. He turned and motioned our group to join him. Wogsnop added hand signals urging us to stay low to the ground.

The military crawl revealed that my knees were painful and tender, thanks to my fall in the tunnel. I rolled over and squirmed up on my backside, careful to avoid too much pressure on my scraped palms. I cringed at the sight of my filthy, torn pants. They were the second pair of trousers I'd ruined in this place, and they didn't even belong to me.

"False alarm, thank the Maker," Wogsnop said when we assembled. "Sometimes a large rock can look an awful lot like a lumpy, pudgy Styg, especially from a distance. Can't be too cautious. This is a good spot to scope out the enemy, nonetheless."

I squirmed to the very edge and peered down at the valley below. What greeted me wasn't exactly the scenic overlook one might encounter on vacation. A sprawling, desolate plain, spotted with crude huts, gave way to a filthy-looking town. The mounds of rock and mud reminded me of giant igloos made from dirt. It looked like the Trolls had stumbled on a pile of rubble—remnants from an avalanche courtesy of Mount Thrall—and said, "Hey, let's move in!"

"This is it," Muggleridge whispered. "Craventhrall."

"Quaint." I shuddered. "If you're into primitive decor."

"Why would anyone, even Trolls, want to live there?" Sophie asked.

"The big brutes can sling stones around but not in an orderly manner." Wogsnop spat over the ledge. "They tend to make do with shelter and hunting for food. Very primitive." He pointed further up the base of the mountain. "That is...until Nekronok came to power."

Like a skull with gaping eye sockets, the lower portion of the mountain exposed cavernous openings, less elaborate but similar to the Dwarves' dwellings in

Berganstroud. The portals evolved from simple to sophisticated as they were hollowed from the mountainside. At the pinnacle stood a Gothic-style, grotesque building carved from the mountain itself. It perched in ominous dominion over the town.

"Is that a castle or a cathedral?" I asked.

"From what we know, a little of both." Lava glared at the spectacle. "The upper portion is new, built in the last ten years or so; the topmost portion within the last five. We nicknamed it the Eldritch—a word that means "sinister" and is quite fitting. Nekronok has proved to be a clever and resourceful leader. He has established himself as head of the military, head of their religion, and head of state. He is a tyrant with the blessing of his people."

"Does he live up there?" Sophie squinted at the distant building.

"Yes, our spies have confirmed this. Seems the average Troll makes an occasional visit to pay homage and perform rituals or ceremonies, like a place of worship." Wogsnop turned and looked at us. "It's definitely the seat of power."

"So that's where our parents are being held? And the queen?" I glanced from Wogsnop to Lava.

Lava raised a bristly brow and caught Wogsnop's eye. Wogsnop gave a faint nod. "That's our best guess."

"*Guess?*" I rolled onto my side and leveled my gaze at the two Dwarves. "As dangerous as this is, why are we guessing?"

"Wish I could give you a better answer, m'lady." Lava grimaced. "We didn't know about your parents' situation until yesterday. We know the Trolls have our queen. *You* know the Trolls have your parents. This is the logical place to look."

Denial and defeat waged war against my threadbare hope. What if they weren't here? I couldn't bear to consider the possibility.

We observed the town in silence. Torches flickered in the gloom. Shadowy, hulking figures came and went in a semblance of normality. They were indistinct from where

I watched, but I had no problem discerning their immense size.

Meanwhile, back on the Planet of the Apes.

It was a surreal moment for me—the daughter of a Bigfoot expert watching an entire community of the rare, normally reclusive animals going about their business. An intermingling of the barbaric and the human on display.

It must be a bittersweet captivity for Mom, seeing them up close in their natural habitat. I cringed. Probably more bitter than sweet.

I wished I'd listened to more of Mom's ramblings about Bigfoot—or Trolls—when I had the chance. Any extra information on the beasts seemed like a good idea if we were going into their territory. As a child I'd been curious about Bigfoot, but after my recurring nightmares Mom stopped discussing the creatures in front of us.

"Back to the cliff." Wogsnop jerked his thumb towards our earlier spot behind the boulders. We skidded our way back down the incline. In the rocky shadows, we enjoyed handfuls of nuts and dried berries. The Dwarves and Gnomes put their heads together, mumbled back and forth, and drew in the dirt with their fingers or daggers.

I hugged my knees and laid my head against them. *So tired.*

When I looked up, Reiko was staring at me. She probably thought I felt sorry for myself. I toyed with giving her a good reason to stare. *Too bad I can't turn her into a garden statue. Then she can stare all day long.*

Muggleridge waved Brady, Sophie, and me to where he and Wogsnop were sitting. Reiko kept her eyes on me. I had the urge to stick out my tongue just to see her reaction.

Wogsnop cleared his throat. "We've decided to scout Craventhrall and see if we can learn anything more precise. Reiko and her warriors are trained to make themselves invisible. They'll sneak into town and try to glean useful information."

"Cool! We saw a Leprechaun do that too." Sophie's eyes sparked to life.

Muggleridge chuckled. "Not *literally* invisible, Miss

Larcen. They're trained to spy. They have amazing stealth and, when necessary, deadly force."

Note to self: Reiko has skills. Deadly skills.

"We'll send them to listen and investigate," Wogsnop said. "In the meantime, we shall explore the terrain up here and see if we can find a back way into *that*." He jabbed a calloused finger towards the haunted-looking spectacle. "That devil's den."

"Sounds like a start." I wanted to change Reiko's opinion of me—from wimpy to capable. "Hopefully we'll find some answers."

"Yeah." Brady stood and offered Sophie and me a hand. "Let's giddy-up."

Wogsnop grinned and raised one wiry brow. "Hi-ho, Silver."

CHAPTER TWENTY

After hours of trying this trail and that path, we called our side of the expedition a failure. All possible routes from the backside of the mountain to gain entry to the Eldritch seemed a dead end. If we had mountain-goat hooves, or perhaps a helicopter, we might have met with some success. I hoped Reiko and her Three Musketeers had fared better.

Back at the boulders, we scarfed down cold meat pies—they taste better than they sound—and dried apples. Then we waited.

And waited.

General Muggleridge marked time by pacing back and forth and grumbling to himself, which only added to the tension. Lava, Wogsnop, and their men sat apart from the rest of us and passed a pipe between themselves. The earthy smell reminded me of Thanksgivings spent with my Great-grandpa Gary. He used to smoke his pipe out on the porch and reminisce about his army days. He passed away when I was four, so I mostly remember the comforting whiff of his pipe.

I smiled. He'd fit right in with these rough, gnarly Dwarves, swapping stories in a cloud of smoke.

"I can't stand sitting here doing nothing." Brady threw a handful of pebbles against the nearest boulder.

"Me neither." Sophie chucked a big stone at the same target.

I sighed, as much from nostalgia as frustration. "If they don't show up soon, I think we should go look for them."

"You do?" Sophie sounded as shocked as Brady looked.

"Yes, I do." Was it really that surprising? "I may not be as eager to learn about the family business as you two are, but I want to find Mom and Dad ASAP. Every delay is a dangerous risk—for them and for us."

"Definitely." Brady drew up his knees and stared at the horizon. "I'm also worried about Brock being on his own. It's weird to be away from him this long. What are a bunch of minuscule Gnomes going to do if he has a meltdown?"

"Maybe they'll change their minds about having him for their king." Sophie looked as if a lightbulb had switched on over her head. "That could be a blessing in disguise. He'd get to stay with us."

Now there's an idea. Before I could contemplate it in more detail, however, the long-awaited search party clamored over the hill. "Finally!" We hurried over to hear their report.

Reiko and her crew were filthy yet unruffled—as always. They seemed impervious to stress and danger. Lack of personality must make one highly qualified for Special Ops.

After a round of water and nuts, Reiko cleared her throat. "Here's the plan..."

"Ugh! That's creepy." Sophie scrunched her face when Wogsnop and his soldiers walked to where we stood. They had disguised themselves as Dark Dwarves with ashen-colored body paste they'd brought along "just in case".

"Cool. Didn't know we'd get to hang out with zombies too." Brady inspected the Dwarves.

Wogsnop grimaced. "No time for foolish banter. Let's move out." He looked at Lava, the only Dwarf without camouflage. "Ready?"

Lava double checked his gear. "Believe so. I'll let Reiko and her warriors lead the way, since they know the lay of things. The Larcens and I will follow them into the servants' entrance to gain access. Correct?"

Zest had overheard talk about a meeting—or conclave as she called it—taking place between the Trolls and the Stygians at dusktime. This translated into a perfect distraction for our mission and an ideal cover for sneaking inside.

"Aye." The captain cinched his belt a notch. "The rest of us shall hide among the rocks in the valley. We'll wait for an opportunity to slip into the crowd alongside the Stygs when they meet at the Eldritch. Once inside, one Dwarf will attend the meeting and spy on the Trolls' plans. The rest of us will break away and search for the queen." He glanced my way. "And your parents. Coming at it in two groups, from two directions, will help us cover more ground."

"Excellent." Lava clapped his hands together. "If we don't cross paths inside, we'll meet back here."

We traveled with Wogsnop and his crew part way, then Reiko split off and headed towards the Eldritch. Three Gnomes, three Topsiders, and one Dwarf followed her. My less-than-optimistic side had a hard time imagining this going off without a hitch. How could a medley of humans, Gnomes, and a Dwarf go unnoticed?

Still, I felt better attempting it with Lava at my side. He served as a physical mediator between the petite Gnomes and our towering, human bodies. Whenever I walked beside a Gnome, I turned into an awkward buffoon, self-conscious and klutzy, afraid I might trip and impale myself on their pointy helmets.

Our group approached Craventhrall from the side that seemed less occupied. The gathering with the Stygians provided a buzz of activity around the main entrance. We skirted behind a ridge of rock that fringed the town as an apparent boundary marker. Once near the Eldritch, we came to a thick, granite wall. Four Trolls patrolled along the top, but closer to the hubbub. They monitored the crowds, making it easy for us to clamor over the barrier and into the back courtyard.

I crouched next to Lava behind a statue of a winged Troll. His flying appendages stretched taut and bat-like, giving the carving a fallen-angel resemblance.

"Do some Trolls have wings?" I asked Lava.

"Not that I've ever seen. Likely a heap of wishful thinkin', glorifying themselves or Nekronok." He pressed his spyglass to his eye and peered around the base of the statue to scope things out.

"The service entrance is the door below the balcony." Reiko pointed to a certain portion of the façade. I risked a glance towards the building. A singular, arched door stood beneath a second-story terrace that included another, identical door on top.

Lava grunted. "I see torchlight coming through the windows in the door that opens onto the balcony. I don't like the thought of someone stepping out right above us while we're breaking in."

"I climbed the vines growing on the side of the balcony earlier," Reiko said. "There isn't a room of any sort behind the door. Only a long hallway."

"Climbed the vines? How do you Gnomes get away with such brazen actions?" Lava shook his head. "Never mind. I don't want to know."

"That's *awesome.*" Brady offered her a fist bump.

Reiko cracked the first hint of a smile I'd seen since we met. She touched her knuckles to Brady's. "It's what we're trained to do."

Lava put a finger to his lips and pointed at the second story again. An odd flicker of shadow and light pulsated from behind the window for several moments.

"Is it a signal?" Sophie studied the scene like she might break the code.

Lava put his finger to his lips again.

Sophie recoiled.

We melded into statue mode. No one moved. I held my breath and stared at the door. *What now?*

When the light steadied, Lava turned to us. "It wasn't a signal. That was a line of Trolls—or perhaps Stygs—walking down the passageway. They were either holding torches or walking in front of one mounted on the wall. They're headed somewhere besides the balcony, thank the Maker. Now, on my count we'll sprint to the door on the first floor."

I latched onto Brady's and Sophie's hands, willing some of their bravado to rub off on me. It was time to steel myself and forge into the unknown.

Lava held up calloused fingers and counted down. Three...two...one... We dashed across the courtyard. I felt about as subtle as a marching band in a library. Although the door was maybe two hundred feet away, running across scrubby ground in plain sight had a nightmarish quality, like a slow-motion sprint.

Beneath the balcony, we clustered together, huffing silently.

In a moment, Lava tried the handle. It wasn't locked. He inched open the massive wooden door while my overactive imagination cranked up the theme song to *Jaws*.

We filed inside a long hall that came to a T at the opposite end. A single torch lit the intersection of the two hallways. Lava gestured for Reiko to take the lead. With my back against the wall, I held my breath and watched her peek around one corner then the other. It seemed a good plan to have a Gnome play point man. She'd be inconspicuous standing ankle level to a Troll.

Reiko went left, and we followed. The hall then curved to the right and prevented us from seeing what might be coming our way. We slipped past several closed doors. This part of the palace felt deserted, though burning torches indicated the possibility of traffic.

We rounded another curve. A mixture of light and shadows spilled across our path from a wide opening ahead. Reiko pulled up short and gave a careful glance around the edge of the doorway. She jerked back and pressed herself against the wall.

Voices drifted our way, but I couldn't decipher the

words. The severe pounding in my chest may have caused some interference.

Reiko signaled Mighty to join her. Lava put out a protective arm and indicated we Larcens needed to stay with him. Reiko and her partner tiptoed around the corner.

The voices intensified.

I glanced at Brady. He winked, which calmed my ballooning tension. He no longer seemed like my awkward, puberty-stricken brother. He'd become a man before my eyes in the last few days. He'd saved my life. He had risen to every occasion.

My vision clouded, and I looked away. *Have I?*

A ghastly, gargling sound interrupted my thoughts. Adrenaline surged. Sophie grabbed my hand.

"It's safe!" Reiko called.

I followed Lava around the corner on unsteady legs. My mind replayed the vile sound I'd heard. How in the world can Reiko declare things safe?

I stopped short at the top of a set of stairs. A huge, grey creature lay sprawled across the bottom steps, legs askew, torso twisted, and eyes void of life. Blood trickled from his ear, down along his jaw.

Mighty stood next to the Troll, wiping his needle-like dagger on its furry bicep. The Gnome remained calm and nonchalant as ever.

I found this disturbing.

At the foot of the stairs stood a towering, amber Troll wearing a leather vest and linen pants. He stared at his slain counterpart, his face a mixture of disbelief and alarm. It appeared he froze mid-stride, body stiff, afraid to breathe.

Even more incredulous—to me anyway—was the sight of Reiko straddling the thick neck of this Yeti. She clenched the honey-brown fur on top of his head and pulled it forcefully to the side with one hand. With the other, she held her slim sword. The tip of it rested just inside the Troll's ear.

CHAPTER TWENTY-ONE

REIKO LEANED TOWARDS THE TROLL'S OTHER ear. The one without the point of her sword playing Q-tip. "Do I have your attention?"

The Troll gave a careful nod.

"You have our queen," Reiko continued.

Another nod. His beady, black eyes scanned our group.

"And you have the other Topsiders—a man and a woman—correct?"

The Troll's gaze rested on me in an unnerving way. "Incorrect."

"You lie!" Ever so slightly, Reiko pressed her slim sword into his ear canal.

The Troll winced. With a raspy whisper he said, "They've been moved."

"I don't believe you," Reiko spit.

"It's true," the Yeti insisted. "The Leprechaun Skoon brought word that the Topsiders' family had gone to Vituvia." His gaze drifted to Brady and Sophie then returned to me. "That would be you three."

"That weasely, measly, little...ugh!" Brady seethed. "I should've stuffed him into my backpack and—"

"Where have you taken our parents?" Sophie cut into Brady's rant.

"Skellerwad," the Troll replied.

Lava and the Gnomes exchanged looks.

"Where's that?" My voice was a lame whisper.

No one answered.

"Where's Skellerwad?" Sophie asked.

"Not here." Lava waved the question off. "We'll explain later. Let's find Queen Judith. Then we'll figure out how to help your parents."

"I'll take you to the queen," the Troll offered, "*if* you'll let me leave with you."

"*What?*" Reiko demanded.

"Take me with you," he repeated. "I hate it here. My father's a tyrant, and I hate him too. I want to be free from him."

"You're tellin' us your father is Nekronok?" Lava glanced up at Reiko.

The Troll swallowed and gave another faint nod. "My name's Chebar. I'm the sixth of Nekronok's eleven sons. I know where your queen is. I'll take you to her if you promise to take me with you."

"We promise no such thing. You'll take us to the queen or forfeit your life. Pick one." Reiko didn't sound willing to negotiate.

"Kill me if you want." Chebar's calm demeanor defied Reiko's wrath. "I would prefer death over a life beneath the iron fist of my maniacal father. Won't you allow me to earn your confidence?"

"Never." Reiko's glare could have melted ice. "Take us to her *now*."

Lava stepped forward. "Take us, and I'll consider your request."

"Are you *crazy*?" Reiko's look shot darts at the Dwarf. "We can't bring a *Troll* back with us. We can't trust him. I will never trust a Troll."

"I'll prove you can trust *me*," Chebar insisted. "Head back up the stairs, and I'll take you to her. If I get you in and out—all the way out—without a problem, will you allow me to join you?"

Reiko's face showed the idea made her sick.

"I say it's a worthwhile offer, friend." Lava gave Reiko

a pleading look.

"We'll see how this plays out." Reiko hissed the words into Chebar's ear. "If you lead us into a trap or take us on a wild-goose chase, you'll get your *other* wish—death. I guarantee it."

"Fair enough." Chebar seemed amused. "If you'd kindly move your sword to a different vulnerable spot— the nape of my neck, for instance—I shall find it easier to move without bumping your sword into my eardrum. If I do make it out of here, I'd like to have my hearing intact."

Reiko looked bewildered by the Troll's words. She appeared to ponder his logic then with a nimble flick, she withdrew her sword and repositioned it across his throat.

Chebar grinned. "Equally effective. You're well trained. Back up the stairs and to the left. You picked the perfect night for a rescue. Everyone's at the big meeting."

We shuffled around, allowing Chebar—with Reiko—to migrate to the front and lead us to the queen. *Or maybe to our deaths.*

Caught up in the silent but swift posse, I kept my focus on the immediate issue at hand—Aunt Judith—and not on the ache that gnawed my insides. *My parents are not here.*

We took so many turns, it would have been impossible to find the queen without inside help. Our arrival at the Eldritch during the Trolls' meeting—along with encountering this disgruntled Bigfoot—could not be coincidence. This revelation quelled my grief and offered a flash of hope.

"Shh." Chebar turned to our group, a leathery finger to his lips. He motioned us against the wall. I watched him lean into Lava. He whispered and pointed. Reiko slid off his neck and leapt to the ground, quiet as a cat.

We stopped near the intersection of another hallway. I heard a fitful sound. *Snoring?*

Chebar strode around the corner and out of sight. Reiko kept a watchful eye on him from the edge. Lava stood close behind, ready to pounce.

"Sleeping on the job, are we, Minchess?" Chebar

barked.

"S-sorry, commander," a muffled, sleepy voice answered.

"Think you can doze because you're stuck here with the old woman while everyone else plots to take over the world?"

"N-no, sir."

"You're nothing but a big, lazy orangutan in disguise. I've no use for a lump of fur like you."

"I apologize. I've been—"

"I don't want your excuses." Chebar raised his voice another octave. "Lucky for you we're shorthanded. Any troops with sense between their ears were called to the meeting. Ol' queenie here is too important for the likes of your sleeping skills, however. I'll take over Judith duty. You can take a message to Gwendolyn."

Silence. Then, "Yes, sir. Thank you, sir."

"You think you can remember what I'm about to tell you? Do I need to write it down?"

"I'll remember, sir."

"Tell my crazy stepmother that Father is in an important meeting and cannot spare the time to read to her tonight. She'll have to do her own reading and sing herself to sleep." Chebar chuckled. "Oh wait, she can't read. Well then, you better duck before she starts lambasting you with various objects."

I heard Sleeping Beastly clear his throat and sigh. He didn't sound enthused about his new assignment. Gwendolyn must be a real charmer.

"His highness cannot read to her tonight. Got it."

"Don't forget to duck," Chebar said.

"Um...yes...duck."

Footsteps faded. Chebar peeked his head around the corner and waved us on.

This big ape seems legit.

Chebar took a ring of keys off a nearby hook and fumbled for the correct fit.

"Ooooh!" A groan slipped from under the cell door and into the hallway.

"It's all right, Your Highness. It's me, Chebar." The

Yeti slowly opened the door.

"Chebar," a thin voice rasped. "Did you bring tea?"

Chebar filled the doorway with his furry bulk. Reiko stood between his feet and strained to see inside.

"No, Your Majesty. I brought something better." He heaved the door wide and swept his hand our way. "Friends!"

Reiko and Zest rushed inside and exchanged frantic greetings.

The dim room prevented me from seeing my great-aunt, queen of Vituvia, from where I stood. I bit my lip, nervous and hesitant. It felt strange to meet a close relative who seemed more like an ancient ancestor—a figure on the fringe of our family, talked about in fond stories but never seen.

Chebar stepped aside.

Lava waved us inside then stood guard. He drew his sword and glanced around the passage and over his shoulder at Chebar.

The Dwarf's apprehension did nothing to ease my strung-out nerves. What a trophy catch for Chebar to simply slam the door on the lot of us. *Cha-ching!*

Brady hung back, opposite the doorframe from Lava. I took a tentative step inside.

On a cot in the corner of the cool, stone chamber sat a small woman who looked *very* familiar. Aunt Judith seemed smaller than Aunt Jules—if that were possible. Her fiery curls gave her smiling face a halo effect. She radiated joy, exactly like her twin.

Sophie took over the introductions. "This is my older sister, Sadie," she yelled and pointed a finger my way.

"Why are ya yelling, m'dear? I'm not deaf." Aunt Judith's voice had the same Irish lilt as her sister's.

I crossed the room and gave a clumsy bow. How should one behave in the presence of royalty and family combined? "It's a pleasure to meet you, Aunt...uh...Your Highness."

"Aunt Judith to you, m'dear." She hugged me. "And that strappin' boy better come give me a hug as well."

Brady smiled and left his post by the door.

Thirty years underground had been good to Aunt Judith. Her skin looked smooth and clear. She had very few wrinkles and no signs of sun damage or age spots. She seemed more like Aunt Jules' younger sister than her twin.

Chebar cleared his throat. "We need to scramble if we're to slip out unnoticed before the meeting ends."

Lava remained at the door but stepped inside. "Your Majesty, I know y're ill. It'd be my honor to assist you, along with my new friend Brady."

"Who's ill?" Aunt Judith bolted to her feet. "Nothin' wrong with this 'ere triathlete! Unless, of course, y're a Troll—then I'm as sick as an aardvark on evil ants. Chebar's been takin' good care of me, and he knows the truth. He wants to help me escape."

Not ill? Triathlete? Evil ants?

"This is your chance, Your Highness." Chebar offered her a curt bow. "I assured your faithful followers that I wish to escape from here as well." He turned to Reiko. "Have I convinced you of my allegiance, deadly warrior friend?"

Reiko studied the ape man. "We're by no means safe. Get us all out—alive—and we shall talk."

"Fair enough. Follow me."

Aunt Judith—dressed in a tunic, harem pants, and cape—adjusted her gold-gilded clothing and bounded after Chebar. I fell in line near the back, my thoughts in disarray.

With clandestine movements, our group wound through one flight of stairs after another, detouring down various hallways as Chebar determined the safest route. We made it to a passage that looked familiar. I felt certain the balcony wasn't far off.

"Wait here." Chebar came to an abrupt stop. Obediently, we backed against a wall. A rustle of clothing and footsteps reached our ears.

The sound came from behind us. *Someone is on our tail!*

Chebar signaled us to stay put. W th swift strides, he moved from the front of the line to the back. He crept to the end of the hall, near the corner we'd rounded a moment before.

The sound closed in.

A figure turned the corner. With deft movements, Chebar had the creature in a headlock, ready to snap his neck like a twig.

"Wogsnop!" Lava cried. The rest of the undercover Dwarves rounded the corner and found their leader in the grasp of a Troll.

Swords rang out, unsheathed. I didn't know who was in a worse position—Wogsnop with his neck about to break, or Chebar staring down the tips of several sabers.

"At ease!" Lava stepped forward. "This Troll is trustworthy. Chebar, release that Dwarf. He's my captain."

Looking skeptical, the Dwarves slowly lowered their weapons. Chebar released Wogsnop and raised his hands in a show of surrender.

Wogsnop shrugged, huffed, and composed himself. "This Troll is *trustworthy?* Have you been bewitched?"

"I'm in my right mind, Captain." Lava saluted. "I'll explain later. We must make haste."

The Dwarves glared at Chebar, sizing him up. He looked back with level-headed calm.

I like this guy.

Wogsnop gave our group a dubious look. "I hope you speak the truth. The Dark Dwarves are on to us. They're coming, and we must—Your Highness!"

The Dwarves gave a swift bow, acknowledging Queen Judith. Then Wogsnop continued, "We must leave at once. Each time we lose the brutes they find us again." He gave a sidelong glance at Chebar. "They're bringing their big, hairy friends with them."

"Lead the way, Chebar." Lava stepped aside.

"Thank you for your trust. I shall not disappoint. Follow me."

A clamor of snarls and growls echoed in the distance.

"Chop, chop!" Queen Judith ordered. "Follow Chebar or get out of my way."

CHAPTER TWENTY-TWO

Footsteps and a pounding pulse beat a muddled rhythm inside my head.

Our footsteps.

Their footsteps.

The sound of Stygians and Trolls swelled from behind.

Probably swelling in number too.

Stone corridors, torches, and doorways blurred in my peripheral while capes, swords, and fur demanded my immediate attention. I hoped Chebar understood the Eldritch's complex maze like Brock knew *Spy-bots*.

A screeching halt from Chebar resulted in an uncomfortable pileup. We had hit a dead end. *Not good.*

I reached for Sophie's trembling hand. Stuck in the dim light, I couldn't tell what Chebar was doing at the front of the pack. *We need to turn around!*

Suddenly, the floor beneath my feet shifted.

"*Ahhh!*" A collective scream rose as the ground opened up and swallowed us in one, swift gulp. Debris rained down on our piled-up bodies. A hazy light shone from above, where we'd stood a moment before.

The ground shifted again.

"Ouch! Get off me."

"If you please..."

"Careful, that's my shoulder."

"You're on my beard."

Wogsnop went through rollcall while we untangled our limbs and found our footing.

"My apologies, friends," Chebar called over the din. He lit a torch and handed it to me. The light revealed yet another stone passage. A crude one.

"We're not your friends." Wogsnop dusted himself off. I caught his glare even in the low light.

"Whatever," Chebar said. "This is no time to feud. We need to move away from the hole above us. *Quickly*. Or the others will catch us."

With uncoordinated effort, we shifted away from under the sinkhole. The chamber extended beyond the reach of the torchlight and smelled like stagnant water. We pressed into the shadows, distancing ourselves from the opening.

Chebar pressed his weight against one particular rock that jutted from the adjacent wall. He grunted then signaled Wogsnop and Lava for help. The Dwarves were too short to offer much in the way of leverage.

Brady stepped forward. With a fierce grunt, he and Chebar shifted the rock. It didn't move far, but it moved.

"Down there! In the bowels of the palace!" Footsteps echoed in the passage above us. Shouts of "hurry" and "we can't let them seal it" carried through the opening.

"We have to make this rock press into the wall," Chebar told Brady.

"Try this." Brady took out his sword and ran the tip around the rim of the rock, like a butter knife loosening a muffin from a pan. Pebbles and grit sprinkled the ground. They tried again.

"They're down below," a raspy voice called from overhead. "I see movement."

I shoved the torch at Sophie and scrambled to help Brady and Chebar muscle a desperate push against the rock.

"Ugh!" A final shove, and it sank into the wall.

"Run!" Chebar yelled.

We dashed across the room and flung ourselves headlong in the direction of the others. Floodgates opened somewhere overhead and released a dump-truck load of sand through the hole in the far corner of the room. It was like being trapped at the bottom of the world's biggest hourglass. A deluge of sand poured onto the floor. It piled higher and higher, filling the hole and sealing us into the area below.

Fascinated, I watched with shielded eyes, coughing at the inescapable grit. We had set off a booby trap—Indiana Jones style. *Epic!*

The torch didn't emit much light in the dusty space. My mind flashed back to our study of ancient Egypt, where catacombs and secret passageways abounded in the pyramids—which were nothing more than glorified tombs.

I sure hope this place doesn't become my burial chamber.

"We're safe." Chebar's long fingers swiped at his gritty face. "The sand is piled clear to the ceiling in the corridor above us. It will be a long time before they can dig through that load of dirt. My father designed several escape features for himself when he had the palace constructed. Each feature connects to secret tunnels in Mount Thrall. Nice to know this one works. Let's head out and get you back to Berganstroud."

He led us into a damp passageway tucked into the dark recesses of the chamber. To see a way out of this death trap settled my anxiety and—for the moment—left my fear buried in the sand pile at my back.

In the granite cylinder, we fought to catch our breath. The sound of lungs expanding, punctuated by coughing, made for a ragged symphony. But another sound caught my attention, one that caused me to latch onto Lava's shoulder.

"What's that?" My ears strained to hear it again.

"I didn't—"

The thud of footsteps from behind made all of us flinch and turn.

A bulky shape lurched into view, as dark as the shadows but coated in sand. A Troll.

"Infidels!" He snarled the word and swiped at the

closest person.

Brady!

The Troll slammed my brother against the wall then took an uncoordinated swing at Wogsnop. The Dwarf had already drawn his sword but missed his target when he ducked to avoid the big ape's fist.

"Bad idea, Spargo." Chebar pushed me aside, making for the other Troll.

Spargo stepped towards Chebar but Brady lunged at the Troll's ankle, causing him to fall forward. The Yeti roared and rolled onto his back. In one swift movement he had Brady plucked from his leg and pressed against the floor. His leathery hand encompassed my brother's neck.

Sophie screamed.

Queen Judith shouted, "Maker help us."

Chebar closed the space and landed his heel in the neck of his fellow Troll. "Release the boy."

The black Troll gurgled, spittle flying in rage but he couldn't shake Chebar from his neck. Chebar pressed his heel further into the black fur.

Brady gasped, eyes bulging, clearly choked harder than before. His fingers dug into the hairy hand, drawing blood.

I yanked the torch from Sophie and swerved around Wogsnop who now pressed his sword tip between the eyes of the beast. A desperate cry escaped my lips as I crouched and plunged the flaming end of the torch against the creature's head.

"*Ah!*" Spargo released my brother and swiped at his flaming fur.

I jumped back, as if I'd been burned as well. What had I done?

Brady scrambled away coughing and rasping for air. Spargo's large hands smothered the fire and he writhed into the wall with a savage scream. Wogsnop thrust his sword between the Troll's shoulder blades. The beast stiffened, his arms flailed in the shadowy light, then dropped limp.

The Dwarf braced his foot against the Troll's back and

jerked his sword free.

My mind reconnected with the scene. I shuddered and looked away from the carnage and blinked at the torch in my hand. Had I really set the brute on fire?

Sophie ran to Brady's side.

Chebar leaned over, hands on legs, his backside propped against the wall. He appeared distressed.

"One less problem." Wogsnop wiped his sword against the dead Troll's trousers. The Dwarf turned a raised brow to Chebar. "What did you think I was going to do? Send him off with a warning."

Chebar shook his head. "No. You did the right thing." He straightened. "Spargo and I grew up together." His gaze traveled our ragtag group. "I'm committed to the good of the Tethered World. Even if it costs my friends and family."

He extended his hand to Wogsnop. "Good work." They shook, then Chebar offered his hand to me. "Quick thinking, my Topsider friend."

I shoved the torch into his palm. "Take this." I stepped away, and he chuckled.

Wogsnop crossed to Brady. "How are you?"

Brady rubbed his neck and nodded. "I'm good." He glanced at the crumpled pile of fur ther at me. "Guess we're even."

I forced a grin to hide the fact I'd rather vomit.

"Let's move out." Chebar strode to the front and we fell in behind. The stretch of silence gave me time to compartmentalize what happened and pack it in a box marked 'do not disturb.'

"Tell me, how's me sweet sister, Jules?" Queen Judith asked while we trooped along. "It's been much too long since we've had the pleasure of a visit."

"She's terrific." Sophie kept pace with our spry aunt. "She's staying at our house with Nicole and Nate while we rescue our parents."

"Your parents? Rescue them from what?"

Long story.

"The Yetis kidnapped them," Sophie hissed.

"Shhh!" I hissed back. "Let's discuss it later when

we're not in the middle of Yeti-ville."

"I had no idea!" Queen Judith sounded distraught. "Maybe Chebar can help ya find 'em. He's loyal to the crown. The Vituvian crown, that is. You can trust him."

I hope you're right.

I wondered if the years spent in the Land of Legend had eroded what made Aunt Judith different—like Brock. I didn't detect any quirkiness in her. Would I want Brock to become more "normal"? It seemed like a no-brainer on the surface, yet would he still be Brock if he lost his idiosyncrasies?

Hmmm. Something to think about.

Plodding through the corridors of Mount Thrall offered plenty of time to mull and muse. The stone shafts looked the same step after dreary step. Without Chebar, I doubted this rescue would have succeeded, despite Reiko's prowess.

Like Reiko, I didn't entirely buy what Chebar hoped to sell. So far, so good, but...

We were still in the heart of his father's palace.

CHAPTER TWENTY-THREE

THE AROMA OF ROASTING NUTS LURED me from sleep and back to a reality stranger than any dream. Hours earlier we'd staggered out from the belly of the mountain and into a cove of rocks, which encircled us like a small fortress. One moment I watched while Chebar disguised our exit from the tunnel. The next—I'd fallen asleep.

I cracked my eyelids. Brady's blurred shape lay sprawled on the ground next to me, snoring softly. He needed a shave. Shaving wasn't an everyday occurrence for him. He saved up facial hair until he had enough to count as whiskers. It looked like he'd mustered up enough for a razor these past few days.

A pungent, burnt odor assaulted me. The nuts smelled beyond roasted. I rolled over to see what had happened to breakfast and found Lava bound to a tree. He struggled and grunted while wrestling against a rag stuffed in his mouth. I froze.

Who would do this? Chebar!

With a subtle sweep, I took inventory of our group. The Gnomes were tied up back to back, unconscious. Thankfully, they were breathing. Wogsnop was either dead asleep... or dead. Grass obscured my view of his chest.

I gasped. Aunt Judith and Chebar were missing. He

brought everyone out to make us his prisoners! Why, oh why, did we ever trust him?

At the sight of Sophie asleep on Brady's other side, I felt a tinge of relief. At least we were still together. I reached out a hand to wake my brother. Movement from above caught my eye.

The large boulder that shielded us had grown a lump of brown fur. Chebar.

He looked down.

I quickly faked sleep. *What to do?*

Maybe he didn't want prisoners. Maybe he would kill us and stuff us like the Trolls back at the Dwarves' citadel. The ultimate revenge.

"Ugh!"

My eyes flew open at the guttural sound. Chebar sailed from the rock, headed straight for me.

I screamed and rolled away.

"Nooo!" Another voice joined mine. Then *whack!* Chebar landed on…something.

I scrambled upright, grasping to make sense of the blur of motion and noise. Brady woke and shot to his feet. He pulled out his sword.

Chebar and a pale-skinned lowlife with sunken eyes and a slicing dagger were entangled. A Stygian. With one swift movement, Chebar put the cretin in a chokehold. The Dark Dwarf went limp.

Sophie woke and clambered over to me, wild-eyed. I wrapped a quivering arm around her shoulder and held her close, needing the comfort myself. Everything had unfolded in seconds.

"Whoa! What happened?" Brady shook his head like he couldn't see straight.

Chebar released the Styg, letting him crumple to the ground. He snatched the dagger the Dwarf had been carrying. "Looks like we had more than one tunnel rat following us."

"What do you mean?" One look at the pasty-faced creep left me shaking off memories of being choked the day before. I tasted bile. *You got what you deserved, tunnel rat.*

"Hang on." Chebar cut Lava free with a slice of the dagger.

Lava yanked the gag from his mouth and spit. He fumbled to his feet and pounced up and down. "That no good...what does he....who does he...*argh!*"

He tramped to where the Stygian lay and gave him a solid kick in the gut. Snarling, he balled one fist and grabbed the Dwarf's collar with his other hand.

"Hang on!" Chebar pried the unconscious lump from Lava's grip. "We don't want him dead."

Lava grasped at the Dwarf. "Yes, we do. *I* do. I'll kill 'im. I'll kill 'im!"

"He's worth more to us alive, my good man." Chebar pushed Lava away from the Dark Dwarf. "He's our prisoner. We can make him talk."

Lava stood there, obviously weighing Chebar's words.

"Someone tell me what happened," Brady demanded.

Chebar stood over the Stygian and lifted an eyebrow towards Lava. "Can you control your temper and allow us to get on with saving the kingdom? *Your* kingdom, I might add, not mine."

Lava relaxed. Slightly.

"It seems Spargo wasn't the only one to go sand diving when we sealed our escape. Upon waking this morning, I noticed that the disguise in front of the tunnel had been breached." He pointed at our exit hole. Sure enough, the bottom portion gaped open.

"The queen was nowhere to be found, but—"

"Oh *no*," Sophie burst out.

"She's safe. I discovered her tied to a tree on the other side of the rocks. The Styg left her there to make more mischief here—no doubt wanting to finish what he began while everyone slept." He looked at Lava. "Guess you woke in the middle of it."

Lava rubbed the back of his head. "Came at me from behind."

"He must have done the same to Re ko." He nodded towards the slumped Gnome. "She volunteered for guard duty, and I get the impression she isn't one to sleep on the job. Anyway, I came back to track cown the traitor.

When I returned, I found all the warriors incapacitated, and the villain about to overtake you." He nodded in my direction. "I pounced on him and... well... here we are."

"Wow. Thanks." *Looks like I misjudged this guy.*

Lava kicked dirt on the fire and muttered something about perfectly good food going to waste.

Chebar chuckled at the griping Dwarf and cut the Gnomes free from their bonds. Brady bent over Wogsnop and worked on rousing him from his stupor.

I felt numb, disconnected from the others. I continued to hold Sophie. She didn't seem to mind.

"Why didn't he just kill everyone?" Brady asked Chebar. He shook Wogsnop to no avail.

"To kill an enemy isn't nearly as fun as taunting him—if you're a Dwarf." Chebar shot a sidelong glance in Lava's direction. "It's a matter of pride. Dwarves enjoy rubbing a victory in your face more than a total conquest. They want the enemy to wallow in their failure."

"Interesting tactic." Brady slapped Wogsnop's cheeks. "I can't get this guy to budge."

Lava, who'd been nosing around the scrubby brush, came back with a handful of weedy-looking plants. "Here." He shoved one into Brady's hand. "Snap the flower from the top and wave the stem under his nose. That'll wake 'im." He turned and offered some to Chebar.

Brady yanked the flower free and sniffed. He reeled back, choking and coughing. The plant dropped to the ground.

"Try not to breathe in the fumes, lad." Lava snorted his amusement. "They don't call 'em Fiendish Flowers without reason."

Sophie and I couldn't keep from laughing. I was glad to see I hadn't forgotten how.

WE REGAINED OUR COMPOSURE, extracted the queen from hiding, and made it back to the Dwarves' fortress without any more life-threatening incidents.

Lava and Wogsnop had hogtied the Styg to a branch and carried him like a rotisserie chicken. When he awoke and realized his predicament, he flew into a rage. He shrieked and cursed until Chebar thumped him across the head and knocked him out again.

The Dwarves and Gnomes at Berganstroud greeted Queen Judith with enthusiastic fanfare. Instead of royalty, she seemed more like everyone's long-lost grandmother. She passed out hugs and high-fives to her ardent, adoring subjects.

Chebar, on the other hand, did not receive a warm welcome. The Dwarves jeered him and refused to listen to Wogsnop's explanation of why he accompanied us. They escorted the giant Yeti to an isolation room, along with our unconscious prisoner.

Those in charge sorted out their differences. "Why would you allow this beast to gain your confidence?" General Muggleridge drilled Reiko.

"This beast earned our confidence, sir. We wouldn't have made it out alive without his guidance. No one was more skeptical than I."

"It's true," Wogsnop agreed. "I kept a wary eye on the bloke, certain he would turn on us at any moment. We were out of options. Chebar claims he wants nothing to do with his father's empire. After everything that's transpired, I tend to believe him."

"Has anyone noticed the lack of *parents* around here?" Sophie gave the group a hard stare.

"Oh, my, yes." Muggleridge shook his head. "I mean no, my dear. Forgive us for not asking."

"That's our next order of business," Lava said. "According to Chebar, the Larcens have been moved to the Isle of Skellerwad. The Ogres have 'em now."

Ogres?

"Blast it!" Wogsnop smacked his fists together. "We need to figure out our marching orders on the double. Nekronok and his reprobates are probably on their way as we speak. There's no time to waste."

"Are we *finally* going to rescue my parents?" Sophie gestured dramatically.

"Yes, little lady." Muggleridge gave her a curt bow. "And protect Vituvia. *And* figure out what to do with that big ape you guys brought back." He sighed. "So much to do. We must lay out a plan at once. Where's Smarlow? Has anyone seen Smarlow?"

Reiko shook her head. "He's probably with her majesty. I'll check."

Lava and Wogsnop conferred in hushed tones. Then Wogsnop clapped in a Morse-code-type rhythm. The activity level shifted into beehive mode.

Dwarves swarmed to set tables, stoke fires, and deliver mounds of food. The heavenly aroma reminded me of how long it had been since I'd eaten much of anything. I staggered over to a tray full of steaming, buttery rolls, hoping I wouldn't salivate on myself.

Brady beat me to it. He reached a paw towards the luscious-looking loaves.

Smack! A small hand swatted him. "Yer not touchin' my bread without a good washin'," Joanie said. "Let's get you kiddos properly cleaned up."

"Joanie!" I hugged her, comforted by her mother-like demeanor.

"Sorry to hear about yer parents, Larcens." She shook her head. "Simply means the Maker has a detour for ya. Now, come along with me. I'll track down some help to make everyone presentable."

CLEANING UP THE OUTSIDE rivaled filling up the inside. What a nasty mess I'd become. I hadn't given any thought to my ragtag appearance after crawling through the bowels of mountains and sleeping in the dirt.

Quite the beauty regime I've stumbled on. Very organic.

The amount of muck that washed from my body would have made a pig proud. When I slipped on a clean tunic and pants, I couldn't prevent an *ah* from escaping my throat.

"Nothin' like a good scrubbing, is there?" Joanie returned and nudged me into a chair. "Here now, allow me."

The little woman brushed through my hair, working on the snags and snarls with gentle fingers. "All that adventure is hard on long, wavy locks like yers."

"Yes, ma'am. Thank you for pampering me. I feel like a new person."

Joanie giggled. "It's my pleasure, love. Taking care of the family of our future king is a special privilege. Now, sit still. I'll get ya fixed up in a jiffy, I know yer starvin'."

I had no energy to argue about being special. Her deft fingers worked through my hair and cultivated magic on my disposition too. Hope flourished for the first time in days. If we can rescue Queen Judith from the Trolls, we can rescue Dad and Mom from the Ogres.

From the rhythm of Joanie's hands, she was braiding my hair. Good idea. I needed to keep it pulled back if I had more *adventures* to muddle through.

"Finished." Joanie produced a hand mirror for me.

"It's lovely." I touched my braids. They twisted together in an elaborate way on the back of my head. "Thank you so much. It's a work of art."

I turned to catch a blush on her plump cheeks. She pushed me to arm's length and admired her handiwork. "Are you hungry?"

"I've been hungry since"—I had to think—"since the last meal you gave me. I've no clue when that was. I can't keep track of time without night and day. Drives me crazy."

"You ate biscuits yesterday mornin', lass. Too long to go without food. C'mon."

I followed Joanie back to the Great Hall, where Brady and Sophie waited. They looked fresh and revived. I slid into a chair between them. "Never underestimate the power of a good bath."

"I love your hair." Sophie pushed my chin away so she could see the back of my head.

"Yours too." Her two braids came together down her back.

"What about mine?" Brady flipped his head from side to side and fluttered his lashes. "I feel so pretty!"

A trumpet blast interrupted our laughter. Everyone stood. Queen Judith made a regal entrance. If I didn't know better, I would have taken her for Aunt Jules in a heartbeat. Aunt Jules playing dress up, that is.

An emerald cape set off her burnished hair. The velvet material glinted in the warmth of candles and torches. A band of gold seemed to levitate, halo-like, over her head. In reality, her curls kept the crown from sitting low. The feisty woman from our trek through the mountains had vanished. Before us stood a resplendent queen.

Queen Judith glided to the head of our table. Attendants pulled out her chair, and she sat with a billowing *plop*. The rest of us followed suit. Dwarves uncovered dishes and served us edibles in mass quantities.

The silence revealed everyone's voracious appetites. The clatter of utensils harmonized with the sizzle of food and the sputter of torches. Seemed the Dwarves worked a little magic of their own, throwing this meal together as fast as they did.

After my third helping of spicy, sautéed mushrooms, I had a needling thought—a Brady-brainwave vibe. *What if this is my last helping of food for another twenty-four hours?*

I kept eating.

At length, the scarfing slowed, and we slipped into easy conversation. No one broached the subjects of Trolls and Ogres when dessert showed up. No one asked about rescues and invasions when a small quartet began to strum melodic, intoxicating tunes that made us sway in our seats.

The tempo swelled. Hands clapped—some smacked the tabletop—creating a mass metronome.

"Shall we dance, young man?" Queen Judith stood and extended her hand to Brady. He grinned and clasped her fingertips, following her towards the musicians. A handful of others made their way to the floor.

"M'lady?" Lava bowed low, inviting me to join the

festivities.

I bit my tongue to avoid giggling my way through the movements. I twirled *him* around. The alternative was impossible.

I searched the crowd for Sophie. To my horror, I discovered her climbing on top of a table. She stepped around dishes and goblets, weaving her way to the end of the table near the dance floor.

I froze in the middle of a promenade. Lava stumbled. *No, Sophie. No!*

Sophie's face glowered. She pulled herself erect, eyes bulging and fists squeezed tight.

I broke away from the merrymakers and sprinted in her direction. I had to put a stop to the impending eruption.

I didn't make it.

Sophie's head tilted back. Her mouth opened.

And, boy, did she scream!

CHAPTER TWENTY-FOUR

"*Hey!* Stop the music! What about my mom and dad?" Sophie demanded. "What about rescuing my parents?"

The festivities ground down. Everyone turned to gawk at the distraught little girl.

Sophie scowled. If looks could annihilate, the crowd would have incinerated on the spot. "Well?" She spoke through clenched teeth. "Are we going to save my parents from the Ogres and protect the kingdom from Trolls, or are we going to dance the night away and hope everything works out for the best?"

I skidded to a stop beside her and found my voice. "Sophie, get down. *Now.*"

"Oh, oh, oh." A wail rose from the crowd. "The music. Where's the music?" Hands wringing and eyes wild, Queen Judith rocked back and forth on her heels.

Great. Aunt Judith's own version of a meltdown.

"Where's the music?" Her voice was shrill.

"Where are my parents?" Sophie stomped her foot.

"Sophie, you're being disrespectful." I reached for her. "Get *down* and we'll discuss it."

Queen Judith grew more animated. She shook her head with quick jerks. "We didn't finish the song. No meetin' until we finish the song."

"You heard her highness," Wogsnop barked at the

band. "Resume the music!"

Sophie evaded my attempts to yank her off the table. She dodged my grasp and spilled someone's drink. *What is the matter with her?* Sophie had seen Brock in a meltdown. She knew the drill. The only solution was to appease the queen and wait for the outburst to pass.

The music revved again. Brady came to the table, encircled Sophie's legs, and shouldered her like a sack of potatoes.

She writhed and hollered in protest. "Put me down, Brady. Put me down!"

"Depends. Are you going to behave?"

"I'm the only one doing what needs to be done." She pounded his back. "Everyone else is prancing around like everything is dandy."

"We're in a different land with different customs." I grabbed her wrists and held on tight. "We need to go with the flow. When in Berganstroud...do as the Berganstroudians. Got it?"

Sophie shot me a bitter look from her awkward perch on Brady's shoulder. She nodded.

"Brady can't hear you nod. Got it?"

"Got it," she mumbled.

Brady slid Sophie to her feet. She shot up, marched back to her seat, and flopped down in a huff.

I looked at Brady. "Crazy kid, but smart. She's right. How can they hit the dance floor when Trolls could attack at any moment and our parents are—"

"Friends, come with me." Lava stood beside us, Sophie in hand. He led us out of the Great Hall and into a small room with a well-worn, elongated table.

Chebar eclipsed the far end with his bulk, towering over a plate mounded with food. He looked up, his mouth busy chewing.

"Chebar!" Sophie ran to his side and gave him something short of a hug.

He swallowed his food and winked. "Hello, young lady. Ready for more adventure?"

Wogsnop, Smarlow, Muggleridge and Reiko—along with the Three Musketeers—shuffled into the room and shut the door.

"Take a seat." Lava stretched his hand towards the table.

We filed in and sat down.

Smarlow gave Chebar a dubious stare. "What's going on?" He glared from Chebar to Lava. "Shouldn't the queen join us? Why is this barbarian meeting here and not her majesty?"

Wogsnop cleared his throat. "As we've all witnessed, it's difficult to extract Queen Judith when there's music to be had. She made a few requests, and our musicians are obliged to honor her. She'll join us shortly."

Wogsnop raked his stubby fingers through the snarls in his beard. "As far as the *barbarian* is concerned"—he indicated Chebar—"let me assure you that we've thoroughly investigated the events of this past week. Our queen has heartily endorsed his character throughout her imprisonment. Her majesty—and her rescue party—would not be present in this room without Chebar's assistance."

Wogsnop stood and faced Chebar. "We all owe a debt of gratitude to our new friend." He bowed.

"Here, here!" Lava stood and did the same, followed by the rest of us, even a reluctant Smarlow.

Chebar placed a hand over his heart. "Glad to be of service. It's good to be part of what's best for our entire realm, not merely what would benefit my father's selfish ambitions."

"Those are dangerous words in the wrong company." Smarlow jutted his chin towards Chebar. "You're willing to risk your life for the benefit of those that have consistently been your enemy?"

"I haven't come this far for any other reason."

Smarlow nodded but appeared unconvinced.

Wogsnop cleared his throat. "Let's proceed, shall we? Miss Sophie is correct. We need to get on with our strategy for rescuing the Larcens and securing the peace of the Land of Legend."

"Lava, would you ask the Creator's favor on our plans?"

Lava slipped off his hat. We closed our eyes. "Give us

wisdom, oh Creator of heaven, and earth, and under the earth. Show us what we need to do and give us strength to obey. So be it."

"So be it."

My eyes opened with a start when the others repeated the last phrase in unison. In the flash of a second before everyone finished, I noticed Chebar hadn't been in a prayer posture. He merely observed.

Someone rapped on the door. A Dwarf entered and announced: "Her Majesty, Queen Judith."

We stood.

Our sweaty, tousled aunt walked into the room cooling herself with a brocade fan. "Whew, that was fun." Her eyes glinted playfully as she crossed to her seat. "Great stress relief, all that dancin'. Really clears me head."

She stopped and looked at Brady, Sophie, and me as if seeing us for the first time. "Where's me sister, Jules? Is she well?"

"Yes, very well." I grinned politely. "Still taking care of our little brother and sister while we rescue our parents."

"Your parents? Rescue them from what?"

I groaned inwardly. *Deja vu.*

"That's why we're having this meeting, Your Highness. Remember?" Smarlow's voice lost its edge.

"It is?" she asked. "It is!"

Okay, this must be part of her quirkiness.

Wogsnop offered his hand to the queen, and she slipped into the chair beside him. The rest of us found our places. Lava spread out a map of the region.

It took a while to orient myself to the map. My eyes opened wide. We'd only explored a small smidgen of the realm. Massive amounts of land, dotted with bodies of water and mountain ranges, spread beyond the Land of Legend.

Although it might be helpful to see a directory—like in the mall—and find the spot marked YOU ARE HERE, I couldn't muster much curiosity about this bizarre place. Quite the opposite, in fact. An ardent desire to be done with the whole mess and not get sucked in further engulfed me. The possibility of locating other creepy, lethal life forms held zero appeal.

What if Mom and Dad aren't even at this Skellerwad place? *How long can I keep trying…and failing…and fighting for my life along the way?*

Brady and Sophie were plenty capable without me. And way more enthusiastic. I only wanted to go home. Yet, there wouldn't be any semblance of home without Mom and Dad.

Therein lies the rub.

I could do this. I *had* to. For their sake. Get parents. Get home. Get on with life above ground.

My wish wouldn't be granted any time soon. After much discussion and juggling logistics, which flew right over my head, we were shuffled from the meeting room to a supply chamber. Once laden with fresh foodstuffs and weaponry, we split into groups.

Smarlow and General Muggleridge planned to escort Queen Judith back to Vituvia. The army would then prepare for battle, ready to defend their queen, Brock, and the Flaming Sword of Cherubythe. Wogsnop would remain in Berganstroud to muster the troops for the Trolls' inevitable onslaught. Chebar offered to stay with him in the role of strategist.

Lava, Reiko, and a crew of Dwarves—along with our faithful bodyguards—would accompany us Larcens to Calamus, the city of the Nephilim, located on the way to Skellerwad. Our stop there would be twofold. Ask for help rescuing our parents, and request soldiers to come fight for the crown. I admit… the thought of meeting angel-people triggered a little thrill inside me.

Everyone followed Lava through town and back to the paddocks.

"The Toboggans are watered, fed, and rested." Lava patted one of the slinky creatures on its dreadlocks and motioned the Gnomes to mount up.

He turned to Queen Judith. "I've arranged for several of my men to accompany you and yer associates back to Vituvia, Yer Majesty. Would you prefer to ride with one of them or have yer own mount?"

"I can handle me own horse." She stood with regal

posture. "Give me yer best, fire-bellied stallion."

Wogsnop snorted. "Exactly what we figured." He led a snowy mare to our group. I'd never seen such a white, pristine horse. It practically glowed.

The Dwarf reached up and scratched the horse's muzzle. "A stallion? Nope. Fire-bellied? Yes." He positioned the mare alongside our group. "Your Highness, I believe you've met Sonnet, our resident Pegasus."

Brady, Sophie, and I gasped.

"Come, Larcens. See the most beautiful creature within the Land of Legend." Wogsnop waved us over. Queen Judith climbed the ladder-style stirrup and mounted with youthful ease.

"Unbelievable."

"Fantastic!"

"Are you serious?"

The leggy creature performed an impatient prance. I gasped again at the sight of her silken, silvery wings. They furled at the horse's withers and curved below the custom-fitted saddle. Seeing this gorgeous creature almost made me glad I came.

Almost.

Sophie clasped her hands together. "Can we watch her fly?"

"Not now, m'lady," Wogsnop said. "Sonnet will fly when faced with danger, or when there's a reason to travel a great distance in a hurry. A Pegasus tends to need an adrenaline rush to resort to flying. Otherwise, they're more like a glorified horse. Maybe a horse with limited superpowers."

I was sure Sonnet understood—and disapproved. She pawed the ground, reared up, and unfurled her wings.

Sonnet didn't fly. Just showed off. All the while, my great-aunt giggled and let out a whoop, maneuvering with grace. She looked quite comfortable on the back of a horse.

Lava laughed. "Looks like ya insulted her, ol' chap. She's smart, that one. She understands exactly what yer sayin'."

Wogsnop looked chagrined by the horse's retort. He

put his hands up in surrender. "I stand corrected, oh Sonnet, my dove. If you wish to fly, by golly, you shall."

Sonnet trotted in a proud circle then calmed down enough for Queen Judith to nudge the horse to where we stood.

"Thank ya fer all yer help, children. Please give love and hugs to me sister and yer parents when ya get home. Be safe, and return fer a visit soon."

"Your Grace." Wogsnop appeared to search for the right phrasing. "If you'll recall... the Larcen parents are still being held by the Ogres. The children are headed to Skellerwad—not topside."

"They are?" She looked from Wogsnop to us. "They are!"

Hmmm. Dementia seemed like a good reason to retire.

The queen smiled. "May the Ancient of Days give ya favor, young'uns. And I promise to take care of yer brother, High King Brock, upon my return to Vituvia."

At least she hadn't forgotten about Brock. "Thank you, Aunt Judith. Tell him we miss him." I reached for the Pegasus and stroked her wispy mane. My fingers couldn't resist straying across the feathered, silken wings. *I'll never wash my hand again*.

"Farewell." Judith blew us a kiss then trotted to where her traveling companions waited. I mounted my own four-legged ride—sans the ability to fly.

Smarlow and Muggleridge rode tandem on the back of a Toboggan. They led the queen and two accompanying Dwarves out of the paddock.

Wogsnop strolled between the other two Toboggans, where Reiko sat with Zest, and Muscle sat with Mighty. We didn't have to ride double with the Dwarves this time. Each of us had our own set of hooves. Lava and another soldier, Bennett, rounded out our group.

A couple of stable hands and Wogsnop were all that stood between me and the road to Calamus—wherever that was. Chebar hadn't come to the stables. He'd stayed at the citadel to "persuade" the Stygian POW to divulge information.

Wogsnop opened the pasture gate. "Bennett, lead the way. Reiko, bring up the rear. Lava, you make sure everything goes as planned, which means you get these guys from point A to point B and on to point C without a hiccup."

Lava saluted. "Aye, aye, Captain Crunch."

Wogsnop laughed and returned the salute when we trotted past.

Sophie cracked up. "Captain Crunch? How do you know about Captain Crunch?"

Lava chuckled. "Dumpster diving. Dwarves invented the sport. Nothin' beats free food, and no one wastes food like Americans."

"Dumpster diving? No way." Brady grinned.

I couldn't suppress a laugh. What a picture! Stubby legs poking out the top of a metal dumpster. Could their squat bodies really climb inside a big, metal box, let alone hop out clutching plundered food?

With Bennett in front, we followed the curve of the hill away from Berganstroud then veered onto a gently sloping path. Many switchbacks later, we found ourselves at the crest of the hill overlooking the Dwarves' town. The protective peninsula of rock jutted to our left, and pastureland stretched lazily before us. Rectangular swaths of scrubby earth that butted against a shimmering spread of water.

"Is that a lake?" I pointed.

"Whitt Lake. Brodger creek feeds into it." Lava indicated a ribbon of water that curved towards the distant lake. "Ya crossed the creek on yer way to Berganstroud."

"Oh, yes." I shuddered away visions of snakes. "Sure did."

A worn trail stretched away from town to the right and faded into the horizon. Moving specks along the route, one of them bright white, showed the progress Aunt Judith and her companions had made. Vituvia lay somewhere in the distant crook of mountains that stretched out of sight.

"That's Ernest Peak." Lava pointed to a chunk of rock

that shot up in the distance opposite Vituvia. "Mount Thrall looms behind it, the base on which sits Craventhrall."

It wasn't hard to see the spiky summit of Thrall. Ernest Peak looked like a termite mound in comparison. I'd rather face the snakes again than return to Craventhrall. *Maybe.*

Bennett turned his horse and grunted, "This way."

Relieved to put the menacing mountain behind me, I followed on my buckskin Cruz. "Ends with a *Z*," Lava explained when he had introduced us.

The path continued to climb, and we fell into a comfortable silence. Being alone with my thoughts for very long never turned out well. My mind wandered from Aunt Jules fighting off Trolls topside to Ogres doing who knew what to my parents. I felt myself slipping into emotional quicksand, and I didn't have a rope or a remedy.

What did an Ogre look like, anyway? Scarier, or hairier, than Trolls? I couldn't recall Mom describing such a creature. Since I didn't keep up with her blog that didn't mean much. Still...one more living, breathing legend I'd get to meet. The *idea* of fantasy had *become* a fantasy.

We slowed at the top of another bluff. Lava suggested we take a drink and let the horses graze. Without Brock as our ever-vigilant time-keeper, I felt inept to guess at how much time had passed. An hour? Two?

After a welcomed gulp of water, I sat and stared at nothing in particular. We hadn't traveled too far away from anything, mostly above it. We rested on a high ridge that overlooked the hill where we'd stopped earlier. From here, Whitt Lake was only a puddle. To my left, Berganstroud and its one-lane road looked miniature, like the towns created for a train set.

Movement caught my eye. I zeroed in on the cliff top that loomed right above the town. Giant ants appeared to be swarming the pinnacle. I nudged Lava and pointed. "What are those things moving around on the hill above Berganstroud?"

The Dwarf looked up from fiddling with the clasp on his saddlebag. "Huh?" He leaned forward and squinted in the direction I indicated. "Blast it."

"What? What do you—"

Lava bounded past me and started yelling at everyone to follow. "Maker help us! Let's move."

We scrambled onto our horses and hurried to follow. Bennett galloped after Lava. "What in the name of Beacon Rock are ya doing?" he hollered. "Wogsnop ordered *me* to lead."

Lava charged out of sight. The Toboggans took on speed, which urged our horses into a gallop. The path curved around the hill, out of view from Berganstroud. It took several minutes to catch up with the wild-eyed Dwarf.

"Ya mind telling me what *that* was all about?" Bennett demanded.

The horses snorted and huffed from their exertion. I was every bit as breathless. Fear has a way of doing that.

"We needed to get out of the line-of-sight from Berganstroud. If we can see *them*, they can see *us*." Lava's horse stamped the ground, as if sensing the urgency.

"See who?" Bennett asked.

"The Trolls. Trolls are invadin' Berganstroud, Bennett. The war we've dreaded for so long begins today. Begins *now!* We must press on to Calamus...and do our share of prayin'."

CHAPTER TWENTY-FIVE

It was a grueling ride. We pushed our horses hard through the mountainous terrain. Crossing valleys and fast-flowing streams, we forged ahead to our destination, trekking through the day and on into dusktime.

I dozed off and on in my saddle—a feat I hadn't thought possible. My head drooped and jerked up so many times that I strained my neck. Sore knees, sore hands, aching legs and backside. Why not top it off with a headache?

My sure-footed steed rounded yet another bluff. The scenery changed in one breathtaking instant. Across a wide, turquoise river in the dale below, a city sprawled like a pile of jewels washed up on the riverbank. Domed buildings and spires towered over smaller structures and a plethora of roads. It glowed in the ever-increasing light of a new day. A gilded wall embraced the city, wrapping around and out of view.

"This is it, folks," Lava announced, sounding revived. "Calamus, land of the Nephilim. Thank the Creator we made it. I half expected an ambush along the way."

"Wow, it's the most beautiful place I've seen." Sophie sounded breathless.

Lava bristled. "Not nearly as sturdy and functional as *our* dwellings in the muscle of the mountain, but it has its own kind of comeliness."

"Comeli...what?" She gave him a confused look.

"Never mind. Let's stop yackin' and get down there." Lava nosed his horse onto the path then pulled up short. "Bennett! Lead on, soldier. I seem to remember somethin' about ya bein' ahead of the pack."

"Oh, *now* you remember," he mumbled and trotted to the front.

My horse plodded behind Bennett and his palomino. Feeling like a pro, I leaned back in my saddle to counterbalance the downhill plunge. Every muscle in my body had been screaming for hours. This crazy position brought groans and grunts with every hoof fall. I noticed Brady was "singing" the same tune.

"Once we cross the River Gambrell," Lava shouted while we bumped along, "we'll no longer be in the Land of Legend. This part of the Tethered World lies in the Land of Ancients. One and the same, if ya ask me, but the Nephilim fancy themselves above the likes of legends. They think they're better than us 'cause they're mentioned in the book of Genesis."

"That's true," Brady said.

"Humph. Not any truer than the rest of us. Fact is, the Creator placed us here below ground *before* the Nephilim realized they best get movin' along or become extinct. Long story. Suffice it to say, they isolate themselves from others in hopes to imitate the life they miss topside. When they came into the Tethered World, they went right to work buildin' Calamus."

It took the better part of an hour to reach the river. When we arrived, my horse was so parched that he nearly jumped in headfirst. The Toboggans *did* plunge in, once the Gnomes dismounted. I climbed down on stiff, wobbly legs and wondered if I'd ever find the strength to remount. Seemed unlikely. Maybe I could swim across?

The crystal water swirled over smooth, colorful stones. The sound danced around me like an intoxicating melody. I knelt and drank greedy mouthfuls. The sweet liquid tempted me inside and out. I didn't want to stop with one drink. I wanted to immerse myself in its brilliance and let the water wash away my anxiety. I splashed water onto my face and most of my extremities then stared at my rippling reflection. I flinched at who looked back—my mother.

Not really. But with my hair pulled away from my face, as my mother often wore hers, I couldn't miss the resemblance. The same wide-set, brown eyes and sprinkle of freckles. *How long has it been since Mom had clean water to drink? Or food?*

I shook my head. *Can't go there.* I stood and turned my back on the painful reminder of who was missing in my life. Silly, since she and Dad were the whole reason we were in this crazy place. With so many distractions, I could push the questions away... most of the time.

"Let's get movin'." Lava screwed the top onto his canteen. "If ya didn't fill up your water bucket, do so now—and make it snappy."

I grabbed my canteen and squatted beside Reiko, who did the same. She'd yet to speak to anyone on this leg of our journey. How could she live in such isolation, even in a crowd?

Better not throw her a curveball by offering polite chitchat.

I turned and heaved my aching body into the saddle. Cruz probably dreaded it as much as I did.

We followed the river's path towards the bustle of the city. The terrain was a welcome change from our journey through the mountains. The horses tossed their manes and stamped the ground. The Toboggans frolicked like puppies. My beat-up behind appreciated the flat ground we now traveled.

People worked along the river's edge. Other than their incredible height—obvious even from a distance—they looked like regular folks. Well, regular folks in the days of Caesar. Togas appeared to be the fashion of the day. Two sizable children splashed near a woman, probably their mother, who stooped to fill a large pot. Further away, men cast nets to catch fish in a deeper part of the river, where the water turned navy blue.

We led the animals into the water and approached the

woman. She stood up and appeared to grow even taller as she straightened. Holy cow! She must have been married to the Jolly Green Giant.

She topped out around seven feet tall. At least. And not the lanky, overgrown, beanpole-sort of tall. Well-proportioned and muscular.

"State your business, creatures." She did not sound pleased to see us.

Her disdainful gaze traveled from the Gnomes to the Dwarves. But when it fell on my brother, sister, and me, she brightened and turned into the Welcome Wagon. "What have we here? Welcome, Topsiders."

Her children gawked and squealed. The next moment they waded into the water and approached Sophie, who giggled and chatted while they stroked her horse.

"Are you here to make contact with an ancestor?" The woman looked from Brady to me.

I stared back, dumbfounded.

"Madam," Lava interjected, "we are here on official business from Queen Judith of Vituvia. Forgive us *creatures* for our lack of conversation. We need to move on to your fine city." Lava clicked his tongue in a way that sent the horses lurching forward, out of the water.

The woman gave a thin-lipped smile to Lava and Bennett, while altogether ignoring the Gnomes. Her face softened when I rode by. Our eyes shared a moment of mutual fascination, yet I sensed she felt superior.

I kept my eyes straight ahead when we entered the city. Many more inquisitive stares greeted us as we rode through the arched gateway. We were an odd assortment, no doubt.

Life in Calamus appeared similar to life in any city topside. I could nearly convince myself we were back where we belonged. There were no cars or electricity, but I felt like I'd stepped into the Rome or Jerusalem of a thousand years ago. Or the land of giants from *Gulliver's Travels*.

I couldn't suppress a smile. It was inconceivable that I was *here*, in a place as extraordinary as the fantasy books Sophie loved. Maybe...just maybe those stories are based on a measure of truth. Maybe one day I'd write our story.

A sea of people parted ahead of our group. Pummeling hoof beats jolted my attention. I jerked on the reins. My horse reared in protest. Landing with a thud, I found myself muzzle to muzzle with a massive steed straddled by an equally massive young man. His skin matched the color of my little brother Nate's, and his raven braids flew about his chiseled features. He grinned at me.

Four men in uniform flanked him. I got the impression he was in charge, though he looked only a few years older than me, despite his towering height.

"Welcome Topsiders, Gnomes, and Dwarves." He did not take his eyes from mine. I felt my face grow warm. "Welcome to Calamus, my beautiful city. I am Prince Alexander." He winked, which startled me.

He laughed at my reaction and added in a low voice, "My friends call me Xander."

Lava cleared his throat. "Thank you, Your Majesty. We are *all* pleased to make your acquaintance." He sounded annoyed and protective. "We come on urgent business in the name of her highness, Queen Judith."

Finally, the stranger tore his gaze from mine and acknowledged the rest of our party. "Certainly. Queen Judith is our respected ally and friend. Follow me."

The prince rounded his horse and gave a staccato command to the soldiers. Two of the men galloped ahead. The other two, along with the prince, led our group through town. People stepped aside, gawked, and waved.

To my dismay, Prince Alexander circled back, cape whipping, and trotted beside me. "How do you like my city, Princess?" He winked again.

The nerve! Something in your eye, mister? I hadn't expected to meet up with a cheesy, flirtatious boy in this neck of the...uh...planet. I stared at the backend of the horse in front of me. He pulled into my line of sight.

"I'm sorry." He dipped his head apologetically. "This is starting off wrong. Forgive me for acting like an imbecile, will you?"

Not what I expected to hear. I risked a quick glance and found sincerity in his smiling, blue eyes. "Forgiven."

"Thank you, Miss...?"

"Sadie. Not Miss Sadie or Princess Sadie. Just Sadie."

"It's a pleasure to have you and your friends here in Calamus, Sadie. I hope—"

"I hope we can have an audience with King Aviel and Queen Estancia." Lava nosed his horse between ours. "There are pressing matters to discuss."

Lava's bold intrusion made me smile. I would bet he's a great dad. I wondered why Brady hadn't stepped up to play defense and found him waving at young maidens two feet taller than himself.

These girls are out of your league, little brother.

The vibrancy and enormity of Calamus swept me away. Towering people on foot, on horseback, in wagons, and even driving chariots made me feel like I'd stumbled onto a Hollywood set, with convincing giants in costume. But these sky-high individuals were the real deal. Fascinating, but freaky.

At length we came to the heart of the city, the palace. Gleaming and iridescent, it appeared carved from one enormous, polished pearl. We rode in silence past fierce-looking sentries guarding elaborate gates. We followed manicured pathways through a courtyard so lush and fragrant with blossoms that it made me lightheaded. The soldiers riding ahead of the prince arranged for stable hands to take our horses and Toboggans, while servants led us inside.

Standing next to the Nephilim gave me an awkward, intimidated feeling. I had a fresh appreciation for Gnomes and Dwarves—my bold, confident companions. Getting around without getting squished must be a full-time job.

The prince and another soldier led us into a marbled hallway. A colorful, peacock tapestry hung on one wall, opposite a bench that came up to my waist. A set of ornate doors stood at the end of the passage with armed guards on either side.

"If you'll excuse me." Prince Alexander offered a bow. "I shall speak with my parents and hope to receive you shortly." He nodded towards his companion. "Typhel will wait with you."

I watched Alexander's powerful frame disappear down the hall and found myself praying the Nephilim kingdom would come to our aid. A verse from a Bible story came to mind. Moses sent twelve spies to check out the Promised Land—a land of giants. Most of the spies returned with bad news. "We seemed like grasshoppers in our own eyes, and we looked the same to them."

I hoped the Nephilim had an affinity for grasshoppers.

CHAPTER TWENTY-SIX

The opulence of the palace hall could not overshadow the two imposing figures sitting on the thrones before me. I stood surrounded by all things giant, yet the king and queen seemed even more formidable.

The set of their chins and their condescending stares made me feel like a loathsome pest that had slunk inside. Prince Alexander paced nearby, which heightened my uneasiness.

I didn't have the energy to sort through these strange vibes. When presented to their Highnesses, I kneeled with my companions.

"Rise, Legends and Topsiders. State your business."

I chanced a closer look at the royal couple. Shocking-white hair set off King Aviel's dark skin and crystalline-blue eyes—a trait shared with his son, the prince. Queen Estancia reminded me of a warrior rather than a queen. A frown unfurled across her face as she scrutinized our group with penetrating, chocolate eyes. Disdain oozed from her expression. Long, ebony braids twisted together and cascaded over her shoulders like an African princess. She and her husband wore simple, elegant crowns—golden rings that rose and fell in a wave pattern around their heads.

"Your Majesties," Lava began, "we come as

representatives of Queen Judith of Vituvia, your ally in peace. We bring news of war and humbly request your assistance."

"War?" the king demanded in a rich, resonant voice. "With whom? And why have these humans been permitted to explore the realms of the Tethered World?" He paused then snapped, "Explain yourselves."

I flinched. For allies in peace, these guys sure didn't radiate friendliness.

Lava cleared his throat. "Yer Highness, the Trolls and Leprechauns conspired together and kidnapped Queen Judith, who is also the great-aunt of the three humans before ya."

When Lava explained the events from the past few days, the royal couple's countenances softened. Prince Alexander stopped pacing, clearly riveted to the explanation. He glanced up and caught me watching him, much to my horror. I looked away and mentally kicked myself.

"...and so our first request is for assistance in rescuin' the Larcen parents from the Ogres," Lava said. "The second for reinforcements to be sent to Vituvia and Berganstroud. Even now the Trolls may be attemptin' to capture the Flaming Sword of Cherubythe." Lava finished and gave a curt bow.

The queen curved one long, elegant finger towards her son. "Xander, come."

He ascended to where his mother sat and dipped his head to confer. When he straightened, he looked pleased.

"Prince Alexander will show you to your quarters." The queen's voice carried an icy edge. "You may refresh yourselves while we meet with our advisors. Someone will bring you to our council chamber when we have reached a decision."

We accompanied the prince in silence down several long corridors. I caught Alexander's troubled gaze more than once. Even so, hope stirred that his parents—once in council—would take our needs to heart. Surely they understood the danger of the Sword falling into the wrong hands. Its safety was in their best interest as well as Vituvia's.

Whether they cared about the lives of my parents remained to be seen.

I stared at the prince's broad frame and leaned closer. Was that a hump on his back, under his cape? Not a *Hunchback of Notre Dame* hump, but something bulky that his cape rested on. I had mistaken it for billowing fabric. Strange.

We approached a guarded door. The sentry caught sight of the prince, bowed, then held open the door.

Goblets of drinks mingled with trays overflowing with fruit and nuts throughout the room. They sat on tables among chaise lounges of varying sizes. Exotic flowers tumbled out of vases. Cages displayed birds with breathtaking plumage. The room contained floor-to-ceiling eye candy.

Prince Alexander did not linger. "Someone will fetch you when all is ready." He left the room with my gaze fixed on his back, trying to make sense of the lump I'd discovered.

"Ah, the young maiden is smitten with the handsome prince, yes?" Lava nudged me.

"What? No! Not at all." I felt my face redden.

"Come now. I saw ya starin' after him."

"True, but—"

"Ha! I know what I saw." He gave me a friendly punch in the arm.

"No, you *don't* know. I was looking, that's true, but at his back. At the hump."

"Oh, *that*." He shrugged. "If ya say so."

I eyed him. "So, what's the deal with the hump?"

Lava raised one bushy brow. "Ya don't know?"

"Uh, no. Hence, my question." I noticed that everyone was listening.

Lava smirked. "The hump, m'dear, is from his wings."

"Wings? What, like an angel?"

Lava closed his eyes and recited, "'The Nephilim were on the earth in those days—and also afterward—when the sons of God went to the daughters of humans and had children by them. They were the heroes of old, men of renown.'"

He opened his eyes. They twinkled. "That's the Nephilim's claim to fame from Genesis, y'know. At the beginnin' of humankind, angels came to earth and propagated the race of the Nephilim. Half angelic, half human—the first superheroes, see? Those born with wings were thought to have a superior bloodline. They became royalty."

"Whoa. Amazing."

"Not to say that in the scheme of the genetic pool you don't find things turned on their head," he continued. "Once in a while the royal bloodline births a non-winged Nephilim. Likewise, common Nephilim see the occasional wings develop on their toddlin' children. When that happens, the commoner may be allowed to marry into the royal family. At the very least they're offered a prestigious position at the palace."

"Very cool." Sophie wandered over, eyes wide. "I've always wanted to fly. Riding on the dragon was awesome, but it would be *really* awesome to have my own wings."

"Keep dreaming, sis." Brady elbowed her. "You're definitely *not* half angel."

"Well, wings or no wings, I hope they can help us get our parents back. *Soon.*" I plucked a grape from a nearby fruit bowl. "I can't believe we're still searching for them after however many days we've been here. It's time to go home."

"Yep." Sophie grabbed my hand. "Once we rescue Mom and Dad, we can enjoy the Tethered World and all the cool stuff. Until then, we need to stay focused."

"You're not listening, Sophie. I said we rescue them and go *home.*"

"I say it's up to Mom and Dad." She dropped my hand and crossed her arms. "Do you think *Mom*—the expert on all these magical, mythical creatures—will simply run home without investigating things? No way! She'll want to stay, and you know it."

Harsh thoughts spewed inside my brain. *I know I've had enough of your smug attitude. I know I'm sick of traipsing all over this place, meeting people of abnormal size. I know I'd rather have a bath and a pedicure and read a good book for a taste of adventure. And I know I can't relate to you or Mom.*

I chucked the grape back in the bowl and stalked to a leather couch and flopped down. I wouldn't spout my thoughts to the underworld, but I also wouldn't pretend to be pleased with the situation. Sophie's words about Mom hit the bull's-eye—and struck me in the gut. I had no wish to stay in this giant cave one minute longer than necessary.

Maybe Mom would reconsider her affiliation with this place. Surely she could refuse to associate with something that put her family in danger. Aren't we more important than a world no one knows exists?

Shutting my eyes against this new and undesirable reality, I dreamed of Nate and Nicole, Ollie and Mindy-Loo.

CHAPTER TWENTY-SEVEN

My eyes opened feeling puffy and sticky. I glanced around at the unfamiliar assortment of couches, tables, and chairs. Where am I? I sat up, confused, but found clarity when I caught sight of Lava and Bennett. They were stringing along my brother and sister with some animated tale. Reiko and the "Gnomes of deadly force" rested in another area, enjoying their characteristic, anti-social behavior.

I rubbed my eyes, wondering how long I'd been out on the sofa. Had the royal family ditched us?

As if on cue, the door opened and in walked our earlier escort, Typhel. "The king is ready to receive you in his council chamber. Follow me."

The hulking soldier escorted us into a room lined with bookshelves built into dark-paneled walls. An enormous table anchored the stately space. Maps and books peppered the surface. Everyone stood behind their chairs, apparently waiting for the king to seat himself. I came in last, dismayed that the only available spot was beside Prince Alexander.

The king peered down his nose, waiting for *me*.

I hurried to my spot, careful to avoid eye contact with the prince. The size difference did a number on my nerves, and I didn't want him to notice.

Once the meeting convened, it didn't take long for my mind to start drifting. Most of what they discussed dealt with places I'd barely heard of and strategies that meant little to me.

The hump on Alexander's back lured me with its secret. I longed for a glimpse of his concealed wings. His father, the king, sat a few seats away, but I couldn't see his wings either. For some reason, the queen had chosen not to join the discussion.

Xander grew animated about details of the invasion and shifted in his seat. He flicked back his cape for emphasis. At that moment, the fringe of his silver feathers brushed my arm. The velvety touch and glossy exquisiteness made me gasp. I was thankful the hubbub drowned me out.

Amazing. Angelic blood ran in his veins!

"Does that sound like a good plan, Sadie?"

"Uh, sorry?" I snapped back to the discussion.

"I said, does that sound like a good plan?" Lava repeated. "Haven't ya been listenin', lass?"

"Sure." My blushing face said otherwise. "It's hard to follow all this"—I swirled my hand towards the maps—"since we're unfamiliar with the area. Whatever you locals decide would surely be best."

"I'm following it fine." Sophie gave me a superior smirk.

"Me too," Brady said.

I fired off my best close-your-mouths-pronto look. "Well, I'm not. Forgive me, but I have a lot on my mind and many responsibilities to consider." The guilt of my lie deepened the heat of my blush.

"We all have things hanging in the balance." Reiko broke her silent streak with a sermon I knew was aimed at me. "Perhaps Sadie prefers to stay here and nap while the rest of us stick our necks out for the good of the realm—and for the sake of her parents."

Brady jumped to my defense before I could respond to the verbal slap. "Back off, Reiko. We're all on the same team. Sadie's been hanging in here as fine as you or anyone else. She's not a quitter. This hasn't been easy for any of us."

"Thanks, Brady." I gave him a smile then shot Reiko a sneer. "I apologize for not staying focused. I also trust that Lava and his Royal Highness know their business and can strategize without *my* help. We're behind you, Lava and King Aviel. We'll do what you deem best."

"Very well." The king stood. "Let's divide up into our various factions and do whatever it takes for the peace of the realm. May the Creator grant success."

As we filed out of the room, one questioned lingered. Divide up?

WE STOOD TOGETHER IN the palace portico and waited for the king's men to bring our horses and Toboggans around. The original valet parking.

I made my way to Brady and put distance between us and the group. From Reiko in particular.

"Tell me exactly what's going on." I shifted close so our voices wouldn't carry.

"The king and the bulk of his army will head to Vituvia from two different directions. They plan to meet the Trolls head on and then surround them by bringing up the rear. Since the Sword is in Vituvia, it's assumed to be the main focus of the enemy. Another battalion is being sent to Berganstroud."

"What about Mom and Dad?"

"Prince Alexander and another soldier will help us sneak into Skellerwad."

"He's bringing one lousy soldier to pull this off?"

"You really missed the discussion, didn't you?" He gave me his you're-a-doofus look.

"Apparently so. Explain."

He shrugged. "Well, if we're sneaking onto the island, it stands to reason we should be inconspicuous. Reiko and her crew will be coming. Lava too. Keeping all of us plus two Nephilim under the radar will be challenge enough."

"Okay, and...?"

"Since we're gaining the prince and his soldier, two from our group will go back to Vituvia, accompanied by some of the king's men."

"Which two?"

He winced. "Bennett and Sophie."

"What? Nuh-uh. We are *not* splitting up." I crossed my arms. "It's bad enough we had to leave Brock. There's no way I'm going to let Sophie trot off into the sunset without us. She's my responsibility."

"Listen! It's too dangerous. The king said so."

"She's braver than half the soldiers in his overgrown army."

"That's not the point. King Aviel said he'd only agree to assist us if Sophie went back to Vituvia. Ogres have a reputation for taking prisoners and keeping them on display like a freak show. They're brutal, and torture others for sport. Children are a prize catch for the brutes. It's for Sophie's safety."

My mind imagined what Brady described. I shuddered. "That's creepy." I paced a tight circle, feeling trapped. "All right, if it's the only way. It looks like the decision has been made for us."

I turned to look for Sophie. My protective instincts wanted to smother her with hugs, prayers, and words of wisdom. A window into my mother's heart opened in a way I'd never before experienced. How anxious Mom must feel right now! How could she function from the confines of a dungeon while wondering about our well-being?

I can't let her down.

Instead of smothering my sister, I encircled her shoulders from behind. "You okay?"

She nodded. "I wish I could go with you, but this is best. Brock's probably confused and lonely. I need to be with him."

"You're right." Her levelheadedness impressed me. "Give him a hug for me. Tell him we'll all be together soon."

"I'll do that." She chuckled. "If he'll et me. You do the

same from me to Mom and Dad."

"Deal."

The footmen brought the horses and Toboggans to where we waited. King Aviel mounted an enormous draft horse and barked, "You, Dwarf, and you, human, find your horses and mount up. Four of my best men will lead you by way of Lake Alethia to Vituvia. It's the safest route."

Bennett and Sophie followed orders. Four imposing soldiers and their steeds clustered around them.

Sophie looked back and blew us a kiss. I put on a brave face and waved back. It didn't take long for tears to blur my vision. By then she was too far away to notice.

"Next group," ordered the king. "Mount up and move out."

I found my buckskin, and the prince found *me*. He held the reins. I swallowed my protest and swung into the saddle. *Chivalry lives on. Lose the pride, girl.*

He scratched my horse's muzzle and crossed to his own.

Brady trotted up beside me. "Do you need me to set the royal dude in his place? I could beat him up and tell him to back off *or else*."

I chuckled. "That I'd like to see."

"Hey, I work out."

"Yeah, whatever. If you haven't noticed, his bicep is the size of your head."

"Ah, c'mon, have a little faith."

"I have a lot of faith." I waved him off. "In God. Not you."

He laughed. "Guess I can't argue with that."

"In all fairness, you *have* been pretty amazing," I said. "You saved my life more than once. You've shown awesome maturity and bravery. Your attitude has been *way* better than mine. I can't wait to brag about you to Dad and Mom. Welcome to manhood, little brother."

He puffed out his chest and beat it, Tarzan-style. "Me brave. Me *man*."

"Follow me," Alexander called.

We nudged our horses in his direction. One of the

mounted soldiers peeled away from the king's group and joined ours.

The king nodded at me when I passed. "Tell your parents we look forward to meeting them in Vituvia. We shall be together in battle within a couple of days."

"Thank you, Your Highness." I bowed from my saddle but cringed internally. *Battle? Is that his idea of a pep talk?*

Prince Alexander spurred his horse and galloped away in the opposite direction from Sophie's group. Our horses and the Toboggans shifted into high gear and gave chase across the pasture. Lava let out a whoop.

Everyone slowed when we entered the streets of Calamus and wound our way to the deserted outskirts of town. A bored-looking soldier stood beside an iron gate in the far reaches of the wall—a gate apparently reserved for private use.

Freed from the confines of the city, the deserted stretch of land beckoned our horses to run. I gripped the reins, nervous at first. I'd never ridden with flat-out abandon.

My tension melted away as the rhythmic movement turned the horse into an extension of my body. I gave way to his pounding hooves and leaned forward to give Cruz his head. For the first time since I'd entered the Tethered World, I felt like we weren't shooting in the dark. We had a plan. We had purpose.

I had hope.

I will embrace the moment and anticipate the adventure.

CHAPTER TWENTY-EIGHT

"This has got to be the ugliest place I've ever seen." I tramped through putty-colored dust dotted with putty-colored rocks. "This makes the Texas panhandle look like paradise."

"Welcome to the Bland Lands. The desolation is due to the Sulfur Sea," explained Prince Alexander. "Noxious fumes kill everything. It won't be long before you smell it. Only harmful to plants, however." He slowed down and allowed me to catch up. "So, you've been to Texas?" He looked impressed.

"Yes, I have cousins who live there. How do you know about Texas?"

"Geography class. We study the topside *and* the underside of the world." He tilted his head and narrowed his eyes. "Word gets around these parts, *pilgrim*," he drawled.

I nearly fell out of my saddle, laughing. "John Wayne? How do you know about John Wayne? Most kids my age haven't heard of him."

He seemed taken back by my amusement. "I know much about Topsider life. My father hires Dwarves to present plays about things they've learned from mingling with humans. It's entertainment. Like your boxes with moving pictures."

"You mean television?" I suppressed a giggle.

"Yes, exactly. Cowboy pictures are my favorite."

I bit my lip. Hard. The visual image of a Dwarf playing John Wayne was wildly funny.

"So, who is this *Jonween*?" he asked.

More lip biting. "Um, it's John. Wayne. Two separate names. He's famous."

"I see." Xander tossed me a crooked grin. "I'm famous."

I chuckled. "Do you even know what that means?"

"Certainly. It means well-known. He's the well-known cowboy. I'm the well-known prince of Calamus."

"Ah! I see." I smiled. "The famous Alexander the Great."

He shook his head. "We read plenty of books down here. I know all about *that* Alexander. Don't confuse me with some old, dead guy."

"Certainly not."

"And call me Xander. All my friends do."

Before I could argue about our status as "friends," he trotted ahead, leaving me with an unsteady rhythm in my heart.

A putrid smell assaulted my nose. Through the gritty haze, a shimmering ribbon stood out on the horizon. The Sulfur Sea awaited in all of its rotten-scented glory. By the time I reached its shore, my tunic covered my face in an effort to breathe without gagging. If a Water Nymph dwelled in Brodger Creek, a Water Demon probably lived here.

"This is so wrong." Brady cringed. "Nothing can smell this bad."

"I don't think it's a figment of our collective imaginations," I said.

The water was deceptively beautiful. Like the sulfur ponds we'd first encountered after arriving in the Tethered World, the mineral content made the water pure and transparent. The size of this sea blew my mind. I wondered yet again how a place this extensive could be tucked away undiscovered inside Middle-earth.

"We'll follow the shoreline." Xander pointed to the

glinting boundary. "A sand bridge appears when the tide is low."

"The tide?" Brady scoffed. "You have high tide and low tide here?"

The prince looked annoyed. "The moon's gravity has pull on *all* sources of water. Even ours."

"Cool," Brady said.

"No, it's quite warm."

"Uh, that's only an expression." Brady caught my eye, and we chuckled. "A way of saying 'that's great.'"

Prince Xander looked perplexed. "Interesting use of the word."

The Toboggans acted oblivious to the smell and temperature of the water. They stooped to lap up the stinking liquid. As hideous as these creatures were, I wasn't surprised they could drink the noxious stuff.

Probably their idea of the Fountain of Youth.

Against the horizon, I made out the jagged outline of a rocky land. The Isle of Skellerwad appeared surrounded by quite the moat. After seeing the Bland Lands, I wondered how anything—or anyone—could survive on the island. Maybe the fumes drifted away from the inhabitants. For my parents' sake, I hoped so.

"Dusktime is coming," the prince yelled over his shoulder. "Let's get into position at the sand bridge and wait for the tide to go out. Once in Skellerwad, it's imperative we get back before the tide rushes in. It goes out slowly but returns with a vengeance."

We revved to a gallop. I'd always dreamed of riding horseback along the beach, but this little jaunt didn't come close to getting that checked off my bucket list. Gritty, grey dirt engulfed me like swarming gnats. My teeth felt coated with sandpaper.

We slowed to a walk. Each of us now thoroughly coated in grime—an unexpected disguise.

"This is perfect." Brady flashed a white smile across his ashen face. "We'll be camouflaged."

Prince Xander raised a dust-covered eyebrow. "We'll be *what*?"

"Camouflaged," repeated Brady. "That means we'll

blend into the landscape, making it harder for the enemy to see us."

The Prince grinned. "That's a splendid war strategy, my friend. You may've discovered something that will give us an advantage."

Brady winked at me. "Ya *think*?"

"I do. What's your opinion, Lava? Do you see the brilliance?"

Lava cleared his throat. "It does seem clever, Your Majesty." He grinned at Brady and me. "Might even catch on topside."

"Yes, yes, it may. Let's test our theory tonight." He squinted in various directions. "I'd say we've a bit longer until the tide is at its lowest. We've not long to wait."

The sand bridge stretched before us, though water still covered it in many places. The narrow strip bulged up and away, perpendicular to the shores of Skellerwad.

"Tell me, Sadie, how did you like flying on the back of a dragon?" Prince Xander looked amused, like he knew how terrifying it had been.

"Um—"

"She probably doesn't remember," Brady interrupted. "She passed out and missed most of it."

"Brady! I—"

"Passed out?" Xander seemed to relish my shortcoming. "I guess if one's not born with wings"—he glanced over his shoulder to indicate his plumage—"then it may seem unnatural to take flight."

Oh, brother! The birdman is making fun of me? "No, I'd rank being born with feathered appendages much higher on the *unnatural* scale than fear of flying. Fear of flying is quite common among humans."

Lava chuckled. He pressed his spyglass to his eye. "Hate to break up this lovers' quarrel, but I think the tide is almost out. We better move."

"*Lava!*" I saw red.

Xander became all business and testosterone. "Dismount at once. We won't be riding across. Too much risk that our approach will be spotted. When we get close to shore we will lower ourselves and crawl. We've a short window of time to get in and out before the tide returns, cutting us off. Let's move."

My heart careened. Being cut off from the mainland sounded ominous. Would this give us enough time to get Mom and Dad?

The soldier accompanying us—a steely, middle-aged man named Gage—tossed out some feed that would keep our mounts interested in hanging around. There was nothing to tie up a horse in this forsaken place.

We moved amoeba-like across the ridge of sand. Horses or not, how could someone from Skellerwad not spot us? Not counting the island, we travelers were the point of highest elevation for miles.

The closer I came to Skellerwad, the more depressing it looked. Soot-colored dunes morphed into serrated rock formations. Further inland, the shapes of buildings stood silhouetted against the deep-amber sky.

"Ogres have weak eyesight, but we needn't take any chances," Xander said. "We're close enough that we should continue on our hands and knees."

No argument from me. The damp sand kept our movements cushioned in silence. The Gnomes strolled along, shorter than everyone that crawled except Lava.

Fires flecked the horizon to my far right. Civilization seemed distant. Before us, a vacant shoreline boasted random piles of boulders. I followed on Xander's heels when he dashed to the nearest cluster.

"Have you been here before?" I asked the others.

Lava and the Gnomes shook their heads.

Prince Xander nodded. "My father used to take me here for 'stealth storming,' as he called it. He'd bring a few soldiers and me about this time of day. He challenged us to get across the bridge, pick a Windle Weed, and return as fast as possible without getting caught. First one back was rewarded with a lamb roasted in his honor."

"Did you ever win?" Brady rubbed his stomach hungrily.

Xander grinned. "I like lamb."

"Then you know where they're keeping our parents?"

Finally, something straightforward.

His face fell. "Windle Weeds are hard to find, but they grow along the shore. I'm afraid this is the only portion of the island I'm familiar with."

Silly me. Straightforward no longer exists. "Not exactly what I hoped to hear. What's the plan?"

"We need to get close to the main compound—the likely place to find your parents. Then pray we find a way in and out without alerting anyone to our presence." He studied the skyline.

I couldn't resist scoffing at Reiko's earlier words. "Oh, I see. All the strategy planning I missed at the meeting amounts to us *hoping* to find a way inside a place no one has ever been to before?"

Reiko tossed her head and ignored me.

I turned to Xander. "I see why they pay you the big bucks."

"What does that mean?"

"It means *I* could have come up with this lame plan all by myself. In fact"—I turned my glare on Lava—"why did we waste precious time at a pit stop in Goliath-ville when we could've come straight here to grope around in the dark? I do *not* feel good about this."

"Hey, sis, this is our best shot." Brady gave me a stern gaze. "We're here now, and we're with two guys over seven feet tall. To me, *that* is an advantage. Plus, we better move it if we want to make it back before the tide comes in."

I sighed, resigned. "I realize we're out of options. But I assumed we had a clue about what we'd face on this island. It's only our parents' lives hanging in the balance."

Xander put a hand on my shoulder. "Sadie, don't fear. We must have faith that the Maker brought us together for such a time as this."

He looked so emboldened and sincere that I shut up.

Xander glanced at Brady. "Sorry to disappoint you, but I'm only six feet, ten inches tall by your measuring system. I've always been on the short side among my peers."

Brady shrugged. "In our measuring system it's okay to round up to the nearest foot. You're seven feet as far as I'm concerned."

Lava grunted. "Enough chitchat. Let's move. Best I can tell, we need to keep to the left, away from the fires. We find the next cluster of rocks and dash to it, and so on. We'll assess from each vantage point until we find a way to the main compound."

He looked at Xander. "What leads you to believe the Larcen parents are being held in the main compound? Do we know for certain such a place exists?"

"Records of other battles fought by our ancestors," Xander explained. "The compound forms the center of the community, from eating to entertainment to punishment. The dungeons are located there as well. We have a crude map showing the layout of the island."

Lave scowled. "You didn't think it important enough to bring along?"

"Like I said, it's crude." Xander pointed to his temple. "I've got it all right here."

Lava balked. "Yeah, let's hope."

Xander bristled at the sarcasm. "The Nephilim are feared by their enemies and fear no one. Besides our advantage in size, we have exceptional minds able to weigh evidence and make quick decisions. Although I am sorry I cannot offer a more palpable plan, I'm confident I can lead a successful mission. I'm also not too proud to defer to your judgment when necessary. I'd appreciate the same respect."

Lava gave an agreeable nod.

Xander dipped his head. "Lava's instructions were excellent. Let's go."

Duly chastened, we sprinted to the next cove of rocks.

I appreciated Xander's qualifications and his willingness to help, but we were basically improvising.

So much for embracing the moment and anticipating the adventure. What an unproductive point of weakness. *I won't fall for that again.*

CHAPTER TWENTY-NINE

The Ogres' sense of architectural genius came straight from *The Flintstones*. Slabs of rock supporting roofs of rock was the popular theme.

We huddled behind the last outcropping of boulders that stood between us and the village outskirts. Lava hoped to get a read on the best route to the massive complex that dominated the center of town.

I could see the structure from here. My anxiety level rose with each step. I teetered between paralyzing fear and an urgency to rescue my parents.

Lava pressed his spyglass beneath one bushy brow and leaned around the edge of a boulder. "Two Ogres to our immediate right are walking towards the fires. Another dead ahead stepped outside a building—his house maybe. He's lighting a pipe...taking a puff. Now he's walking into town."

The Dwarf scrambled to the other end of the rock for a different vantage point. He grunted *hmmm* and *oh* but said little.

"Well?" Xander risked a peek over the top of the rock.

"Town dump straight ahead." He shoved the telescope into his belt. "Perfect. Coast is clear. Let's go."

Before I could gear up for our next escapade, Brady had me by the hand. We dodged broken pots, the remnants of furniture, and discarded bones. Hopefully the bones of meals past, not the bones of prisoners.

Unless prisoners could double as meals.

It looked like the tail end of town. Desolate. Given a wide berth from society, it was a typical hovel of trash. We slouched behind a broken door, choosing our next move.

I sniffed. "How come it doesn't smell like sulfur?"

"It does," Xander said. "But your nose has grown accustomed to it."

Scary.

"There's a path ahead that goes between some deserted buildings." Xander pointed. "Let's stay close to the walls and work our way towards the complex."

We weaved around the abandoned structures. Even Ogres must have standards about living near a dump. The buildings looked sturdy and useful for something, yet they were vacant.

The landfill receded, and I noticed signs of life. Water in buckets, clothes draped on window openings—holes in the walls, really—and even the odd doll that looked disturbingly human. The inhabitants appeared to have gone out for the evening.

A creepy vacancy.

Reiko scouted ahead. As in Craventhrall, her stature worked to her advantage. Within moments she returned. "Go back. *Now.*"

We scrambled.

Reverberating footfalls snaked through my body.

"I saw somethin', Claude. I did," a deep, gristly voice insisted.

"Well, you seein' a figment of too much grog," an asthmatic voice rasped. "Nuthin' here but what's always here. Which is nuthin'." He laughed at his joke, wheezing and coughing for a full minute.

"Claude, you's thinkin' wrong. Me and grog gets on just fine. I did saw a rat or somethin' over here. Woulda made a fine snack if ya hadn't scared it off with yur coughin'."

"Naw, cain't scare somethin' that ain't here. C'mon,

the chief say we gets to work over dem prisoners s'more tonight, and I don't wanna miss it. Chase yur invisible rat when it's over if ya want."

Their footsteps withdrew. Brady and I looked at each other, wide-eyed. These big lugs could lead us to our parents!

We hung back at a safe distance. Reiko and crew were so adept at tracking that they kept behind the two Ogres but out of eyeshot. The further we crept into town, the more obstacles and potential sightings we dodged. This widened the gap between us and them.

No matter. Every Ogre appeared to be headed in the same direction as our rat chasers. It dawned on me that all of Skellerwad planned to spend the evening at the event involving "'dem prisoners'."

My parents.

How are we going to pull this off in front of a studio audience?

Reiko signaled us to squeeze into the shadows. I backed against a wall next to Brady and watched the Gnome disappear around a corner. Zest took off in the other direction. Time crawled by.

I expelled a long-held breath when Reiko and Zest returned. "Found an ideal spot outside the compound." Reiko jerked her thumb back the way they'd come.

She led us to a narrow alleyway that emptied into the main thoroughfare surrounding the coliseum-type structure. I filed into the confines of the walls behind Xander and Gage—both had to squeeze in sideways. I could see but a slice of the large building from where I stood.

Pressed against the wall and taking shallow breaths, I watched several Ogres pass by less than twenty feet away. I could only glimpse their profiles, but it shot my internal butterflies into frenzy mode. These dudes were gargantuan. If God created man out of dust, He made Ogres out of the rocks of Skellerwad.

They were thick and broad, with pale skin and bristly hair. They matched the Nephilim for height, and then some. Even from our hideout, their body odor could take down rulers and principalities without the use of force.

I hope I get used to their smell like I got used to the sulfur.

Somewhere inside the building, drums pulsated. A chant swelled in cadence to the music, but I couldn't make out the words.

From the direction of the compound, a gravelly voice called, "Move it! Move it! Ya don't wanna miss this. Live humans on display—a rare treat. Let's go! Show's startin' any moment."

Other Ogres rushed past, and the streets emptied. The rhythm of the drums intensified. The crowd's chanting rose like the roar of the Super Bowl.

Reiko chanced a careful look in both directions then gave an all-clear nod. We followed. The Gnome headed in the opposite direction from the Ogres that passed.

The rally cry became discernible. "Hu-man games! Human games!"

Brady grabbed my hand. I had the sudden urge to vomit. The fingers of fear lost their grip. I was angry. I was focused. I had to see this thing through.

Slabs of rock made the coliseum a many-sided polygon rather than a continuous, curving circle. Other large, perpendicular rocks braced the places where two slabs came together. We slipped behind one such structure to confer.

"What's the plan?" I whispered to Lava.

"Find a way inside." He scouted the perimeter.

Duh.

It didn't take long before we found a good-sized gap in the wall. The building had crumbled with age, and Ogres were clearly not so handy in the handyman department. The opening looked doable for everyone except our companions with angelic DNA.

Reiko ventured inside to look around. She emerged with a grin. "This is perfect."

"Excellent." Xander leaned onto his knees and lowered his voice. "Gage and I will continue looking for a breach our size. If none is found, we shall return and whistle through the opening to alert you."

Reiko and Lava nodded their agreement. Mighty, Muscle, and Zest scrambled through first. Lava followed.

Reiko gestured at me. It was my turn. I knelt down, ducked my head, and crawled into the place that—hopefully—held my parents.

CHAPTER THIRTY

A TRUMPET BLAST QUIETED THE INSANE chanting. The volume morphed from full throttle to dead silence in seconds. I was relieved to be in position when everything went quiet.

We stood beneath ancient-looking bleachers. Giant beams of wood creaked and groaned overhead, where hundreds of Ogres gathered, testing the mettle of their seats. If the benches gave way, we were goners. We moved forward, as close as our height allowed. This meant the Gnomes were near the front, while Brady and I stood a few rows back. Lava found middle ground.

Gnarly, filthy feet surrounded me. Between thickset legs, I spied a dirt floor. In the center stood a platform. On the platform sat an imposing, bearded figure. His fine clothes and improved hygiene exuded importance. When silence descended, he stood. With his cape billowing around enormous shoulders, he looked like a walking wall.

"Countrymen! Noble citizens of Skellerwad! Welcome to Day Two of the Human Games!" The Ogre raised his arms, bringing the crowd to its feet.

Day two? My heart sank.

The giant's arms came down, which brought a controlled calmness to the masses. They remained standing.

"Yes! A rare spectacle, a rare treat. Last night we met our resilient little couple. Tonight we bring them back by popular demand. An encore round of the Human Games, especially for you." He cupped his hands around his mouth and yelled, "Bring in the humans!"

For a moment, I couldn't make out a thing. The roar of the crowd made it hard to concentrate. Then two carts pulled by two Ogres lurched into the center of the floor. They stopped in front of the stage. A tarp covered each cart.

Cheers ratcheted up another notch.

I dreaded—and longed—to see what was inside. With sickening anticipation, I couldn't tear my gaze away from the two grimy Ogres as they reached to pull the tarps away.

The bloodthirsty chant of, "Hu-man Games!" began anew. The big thugs played the crowd, building animation. I hung there, suspended. Numb.

The covers fell from the two prisons on wheels. My mother and father lay caged like a couple of animals.

Reality snapped into place. I covered my mouth to muffle a scream. Not that it would have been heard. The frenzied mob grunted and yelled and stomped. *They are the animals.*

My father, who normally buzzed with ideas and life, slumped against the corner of the cage, head drooping, face swollen and bruised. Blood matted his chestnut hair. A rope encircled his neck. A leash.

The massive ankle resting on the bleacher in front of me blocked my mother from view. I shifted to see both cages... and was pummeled by another senseless picture.

My beautiful mother lay crumpled and limp on the bottom of the cart, one arm dangling between the bars. Claw marks raked her forearm. Dried blood smeared her clothing. Dark blonde hair fell in a tangled mess across her eyes and obscured her face. She too wore a leash. A tether.

Tethered parents. Tethered World.

Oh, how I hated that word!

Hopelessness threatened to knock me out. Never had I

been this close to something so harrowing. Never had I felt so impotent. I couldn't bear to watch another moment. The stark reality of my selfish attitude—now exposed like a raw, skinned knee—drenched me in remorse. I buried my face in my hands, sank to my knees, and sobbed.

Sobbed for my parents. Sobbed for my sins.

Though I hadn't articulated the thought—even to myself—a rotten, bitter place had festered inside. It now slunk from the shadows of my soul and revealed its stench. The embers of contempt for my mother's choice of work had fanned into smoldering resentment. I loathed being dragged into her world against my will. Every day spent trapped in this banished realm fed the animosity in my heart.

Now, shame chastised me for my subtle belief that her predicament served her right. A wave of nausea crumpled me further to the ground. *How could I have been so shallow, so self-absorbed?*

The truth made me retch. My narcissistic attitude assaulted me. I had hoped Mom would learn her lesson and walk away from what I had deemed a foolish pursuit.

Oh, God, forgive me!

I didn't have the luxury of muddling through my self-incrimination. My parents needed me clear-headed and ready to act on their behalf. If I didn't compose myself, I'd be no help to them at all. I confessed my smug pride, wiped my runny nose, then stood to face the monsters. They seemed less intimidating after confronting my own demons.

The crowd took their seats. The chaos subsided.

Beside me, Brady didn't seem to notice my meltdown. He stood riveted to the scene. His jaw pulsated. Veins stood out in his neck. His eyes flickered with a fire I'd never seen.

"Well, well," bellowed the goon on the platform. "It looks like our wee, little friends are worn out. Now, now, you two *do* want to come out and play, don't you?"

The crowd roared their laughter.

My father stirred. His head lolled to one side, and he

caught sight of my mother. He jerked upright. "Amy! Amy! Darling, are you all right?" He reached for my mother through the bars of his cage.

I tasted bile. And salty tears.

The Ogres found my father's distress entertaining. Their laughter swelled.

"Oh, Amy! Amy *daaarling,*" the lead Ogre mimicked in a high voice. The crowd ate it up. "All right, enough sniveling, you human coward. It's time to show your fortitude."

The redheaded Ogre nearest my father opened the latch. He reached an iron hand inside the cage and retrieved Dad with a yank on his collar.

"Get your hands off me!" My father twisted and grasped at the bruiser that toyed with him. "Please! No..."

The other Ogre, a bald bulwark, hauled my mother's listless body through the opening of her cage. She roused from her stupor and clawed viciously at him.

It was a sick circus, yet I couldn't bear not to watch. Agony plundered my heart and pleaded with my mind to figure something out. *This has to stop!*

"Please," my father begged. "D-d-do what you want with me. But leave my wife alone. She needs water. Just...please, give her...*no!*"

The bald Ogre clutched my mother by the throat. She dangled like a puppet. Her hands stopped clawing. She latched onto the fat fingers squeezing her neck and tried to pry them away. She gasped and choked and writhed.

I squeezed Brady's arm, desperate. "What do we do?"

He glanced at me, fighting back tears. "What are we *supposed* to do, Sadie? We're a little outnumbered."

"I don't know...pray," I said. "There must be something."

Nearby, Reiko and Lava put their heads together in deep discussion. I hoped they had a plan. I wished I knew what Xander and Gage had worked out. If he'd whistled a signal, I hadn't heard it.

"Feisty little woman, isn't she?" the head Ogre teased. "Careful! Don't squeeze her so hard she passes out again. She's not any fun unconscious."

My father begged for Mom's release. The Ogre holding him clamped an enormous hand over Dad's mouth. The hand curled clear around his head.

The other giant pitched my mother onto her backside. She gasped for breath. He yanked the rope around her neck and brought her to her feet, choking her further.

I wanted to charge this swine and tear him to pieces. Knowing that was impossible, I stood with my fists balled, my breath shallow and ragged.

"Are the contestants ready?" the big oaf bellowed.

The crowd turned their attention to one side of the arena, out of my line of sight. Finally, several Ogres strutted into view, male and female, playing up the crowd like boxers heading into the ring. They wore chainmail and—as if they needed protection—carried ropes, chains, and a wooden wheel.

My parents seemed resigned to their fate. While the crowd fawned over the competitors, my father sidled up next to Mom. He wrapped his arm around her and—it appeared to me—whispered a prayer in her ear.

I breathed a prayer of my own.

"Let the games begin!" shouted the Ogre on the platform. He turned and took his seat, presiding over the event.

The ugliest, most vile-looking woman I've ever seen stepped forward and grabbed my mother's rope. The female Ogre's stringy, blonde hair clung to her Neanderthal head. Sweat trickled down her fleshy face, detouring around the hairy moles—large enough for me to see—that dotted her skin.

"Please…" my father's voice trailed after my mother.

"I…will…not…cooperate!" Mom enunciated each word with resolve. "I will *not*."

The crowd jeered and stomped their approval of my mother's harassment. She spit and screamed and fought like a rabbit in the talons of an eagle.

"You're only making this harder on yourself, Amy *darrrrling*." The announcer continued to taunt them. "If you cooperate, you may actually live through the experience." His droll tone made me want to climb up and yank his tongue from his big, nasty mouth.

My mother's fury subsided. She didn't cooperate, but she stopped raging against the giant.

"Smart human." The female leered down. "If you's a good little girl, you may get somethin' to drink when I'm finished with ya." Amid the shrieks from my father, the Ogress pushed my mother to the ground and hogtied her wrists to her ankles behind her back.

My mother groaned.

I swiped at my wet cheeks. *I'm sorry, Mom. So sorry.*

The Ogress threaded her arm into the circular shape of my mother's body. With no effort she lifted Mom, who screeched from the pain of hanging w th her arms pulled backward. I shuddered to watch her swinging back and forth, gaining momentum. It appeared the female ogre intended to fling my mother through the air to another Ogre that waited with outstretched arms.

They were going to play a game of human ring toss!

I winced and turned my head away when the beastly woman released my mom. Over the din of the crowd, I recognized her pitiful wail and the subsequent yelp when she landed. A quick glance revealed her in the same awful position, but on the forearm of the other Ogre.

The crowd howled. The greasy blonde prepared to catch Mom on her return flight. Not willing to watch the spectacle, I turned my attention to my father.

Big mistake. A beer-bellied Ogre had him stretched prostrate across an enormous wagon wheel. Fatso lashed my dad to the spokes, pulling his arns and legs spread-eagle. The center cog protruded into his spine.

I looked away, unable to tolerate another moment of this insanity. Dropping to my knees, I crawled back through the gap in the wall and collapsed into the dirt with a sob. *I refuse to watch my parents die!*

A hand brushed against my hair and made me jerk my head up.

"Shhh, Princess Sadie, it'll be all right." Xander crouched over me, concern etched on his face.

The insane crowd continued to jeer behind me. I let the tears flow.

"My parents are in there being tortured, and we're *helpless*. How can we possibly rescue them? There's no way to reach them. No way! There're too many Ogres, and they're all the size of a house. I can't—"

"Hey, now! Stop this nonsense," Xander whispered in my ear. "We will *not* give up hope. We've not come this far to stand by and watch your parents die. Now, get up, dry your tears, and help me. I have a plan."

I looked at him, doubtful. "I don't see how you could possibly—"

"*Enough*. Don't argue. Do as I say." Xander had me on my feet and up against the wall before I could form a rebuttal. "We haven't long before the tide moves in. If we don't act soon, we'll *all* be pawns in their games."

He lowered his voice. "Now, listen. Gage is on the roof at this moment, waiting for my signal."

"On the roof?"

"Listen! You need to go back inside and send Reiko and Lava out here. I'll lay out the plan for them. Then you must follow their lead."

"Why can't you tell me the plan? They're *my* parents."

"It's complicated. I only want to explain it once. Trust me, okay?"

I lacked the energy to argue. "Fine. Sure hope it works."

The crescendo of noise and the smell of the brutes struck me again when I crawled inside. I delivered Xander's instructions then resumed my place beside Brady, who seemed oblivious to my absence. He stared ahead.

I followed his gaze, sickened by the sight. Now my mother's wrists were bound together, held by one Ogre. Her ankles were tied and held by another. They swung her in circles like a living jump rope.

Ten yards away, Fatso held the wagon wheel with Dad strapped to it. He rocked the wheel, taking aim, preparing to roll it towards my mother's moving body. The object of the game appeared to be to coordinate his roll with her swing up in the air so Dad would pass beneath her and travel to the Ogress waiting on the other side.

I held my breath and looked down. *Vile, loathsome freaks.*

Cheers and applause hinted that the first attempt had succeeded. I chanced a peek. My dad's upside-down body was suspended a stone's throw away. He looked green from rolling about.

"Fewwwweet! Fewwwweet!" Brady let out a sudden, sharp whistle—a familiar sound when we were looking for one another in a crowd, even in a noisy one.

Dad's eye's sparked. He went from delirious to riveted in an instant. He scanned the crowd. I held my breath, hoping he would see us, wondering if Brady realized the risk he took by alerting him.

The overgrown hag that held my father prepared to roll him back. She rocked the wheel, eyeing Mom's rhythmic oscillations. The instant before Dad rolled away, his eyes found mine. He looked stricken with disbelief and dread.

I felt a quiver of hope and hopelessness culminate with a stab to my heart. *So close. So far. So impossible.*

Dad tumbled towards Mom. The situation went from bad to abysmal.

The rope holding Mom's arms slipped from the grasp of the Ogre. She hurtled to the ground and landed face first in the dirt. My father rolled along the trajectory—and Mom lay strung across his path like a speed bump.

Before I could think it through, I screamed. *"Nooo!"*

The screech of the bloodthirsty crowd drowned me out. They were on their feet, enthralled with the imminent collision.

CHAPTER THIRTY-ONE

The travesty unfolded in slow-motion precision. My father careened dead-on at my mother's ribcage. Thankfully, he could not see the impending disaster.

But she could.

Mom lifted her head, her gaze locked on the wheel headed straight for her midsection. She opened her mouth to scream. I couldn't hear anything beyond my own gut-wrenching shriek.

Like a lightning bolt, something flashed from the rooftop and down into the arena. It was so fleeting, so unexpected... and so perfect. At the last possible instant, two strong arms grasped the rolling torture device and snatched it—and my father—away.

Stunned silence blanketed the stadium. Then shouts of indignation descended as fast as my father disappeared.

I grabbed Brady's arm, exultant.

We didn't savor the victory for long. The Ogre that held my mother's roped ankles yanked her across the ground to himself. He lifted his elephant-sized foot and pressed it against her head. He thumped his chest with his fists and gave a sadistic roar.

Mass confusion swept the audience. Ogres jumped out of the bleachers, bellowing and shaking their fists at the opening in the arena ceiling. Others streamed outside, most likely searching for my father and his rescuer. The view from our hiding place improved with the exodus. So did our chances of being discovered.

Mom screamed under the pressure of the huge foot, but no one—not even the Ogre—noticed. He was too busy staring up like his bewildered buddies. Mom's face turned crimson. Her eyes bulged.

So did mine. *I have to do something.*

A shaft of wood plummeted from above, relieving my desperate thoughts. It harpooned the Ogre between his beady eyes. He fell backward with a thud that shook the ground. His eyes looked up in a lifeless stare.

I gaped. Just like Goliath!

Brady and I hugged each other in triumph.

Elation quickly turned to panic. Mom lay motionless, eyes closed. She had either passed out or...

No! I won't go there. She has to be okay.

The remaining crowd boiled from the stands like angry termites. A thick, wooden beam shattered overhead. Brady and I lunged out of the way. Jumping and stomping and infuriated babble assaulted my ears. A giant-sized temper tantrum.

Clumsy feet stamped around my mother's body in their rush towards the exit. The savages ignored her lying there. Did they assume she was dead?

I held my breath when one big oaf tripped over her body. Mom needed to be moved. *Now.* If not, she might live through two days of torture only to be trampled to death.

Before I could question my impulse, I crawled from under the lowest bleacher. With eyes focused on my goal, I swerved around the filthy feet that came into my line of sight. Agility and instinct took over. My mission propelled me forward.

A minute later I reached my mother. Disbelief washed over me that I had made it this far. I grasped her arm and began to drag her back to the bleachers, thankful the dimwitted Ogres hadn't noticed me... yet. They gawked at the opening in the ceiling while I dodged them below.

Right then Brady swooped in and snatched Mom from

me. "Get under the bleachers and help pull her inside when I get there."

I shot around a tree-trunk leg and dropped to all fours as I neared the lowest bench. An Ogre's foot caught my underside and tripped over me.

Not good!

I rolled under the bleacher, my cover blown.

"More humans! More humans!" The cry carried above the commotion.

I peered out to find Brady lowering Mom to the ground. On his heels, a horde of giants lurched after him.

"Look out, Brady!"

With all my *oomph*, I seized my mother's arm and leg and yanked.

Brady plunged headlong for the bleachers' protection. A colossal hand seized his ankle and hauled him back.

He screamed.

I screamed.

He disappeared into the mob of monsters.

Mom needed a safe place. I grabbed her wrists and dragged her towards the opening in the wall, praying my brother could hold his own.

Brady's voice yelled something unintelligible. It sounded like an all-out fight. He wouldn't go down easily. I plowed ahead, concentrating on what *I* could do with the task before *me*.

I released Mom and squinted through the hole. The coast seemed clear, despite the hubbub in the distance. I bit my lip, debating my next move. A fresh wave of panic throttled me. How would I get anywhere with a limp body that weighed as much as I did?

One thing at a time, Sadie.

A secure place to assess my mother's condition seemed the first, logical step. About twenty feet from the hole a scrubby tree cozied up to a chunk of rock. It would have to do.

I turned and backed out of the gap, my mother in tow. Double checking for stray Ogres, I lugged Mom to the target.

We had no sooner reached it when I heard—and felt—

footsteps clomping our way. I strained to get Mom on the backside of the rock then hunkered down on top of her, hoping to blend in with the landscape.

A gaggle of Ogres came and went. I rolled off Mom, flopped to my back, and took a serious gulp of air. Looking up at the crystal dome of sky, I felt *oh so* trapped. Scaling Mount Thrall was a cakewalk compared to this. Did anyone seriously think we'd make it out of this mess? *Mission: Impossible.*

I squeezed my eyes tight against the burn of hopeless tears.

What's the next thing you can do?

The whispered thought interrupted my pity party. It didn't originate from me.

Okay, God. I'm listening.

The next thing I could do was clear: assess the damage inflicted on Mom. Guilt berated me. Once again, my thoughts revolved around *my* predicament rather than my mother's. I pushed to my knees and looked at her—*really* looked at her—for the first time in... what... nearly a week?

She lay bruised and scabbed and deathly still. Her clothes were tattered and covered in filth. Matted hair surrounded her puffy, pale face. Fresh blood trickled from her nose. One earring had been ripped from her ear, leaving a scabbed, jagged tear. I'd found the other earring at Burgerville.

I slumped onto her chest in a heap of tears. My conscience condemned me again. To think that I had somehow *justified* my mother's kidnapping. How could I be so shallow, so cruel? Her still, limp body accused me that I'd never get the chance to make it right.

Too little, too late.

A million memories welled up. Feelings of failure and remorse twisted inside. It sobered me to recognize my own, stark depravity. I lay there, numb, and listened to the thump of her heart.

A heartbeat?

A heartbeat!

CHAPTER THIRTY-TWO

My muddled world came back into focus. *Mom's alive!* No one knew this—except me. No one could get her to safety—except me. I needed to do the next thing *I* could do, but I had no idea what that might be.

In the distance, shouts and scuffling continued.

I mulled over waiting for someone to find us. This seemed like a safe place. Maybe we could stay out of trouble long enough for…wait!

The tide! We needed to get off this island, not stay put.

Still, how far could I get toting an unconscious body around? I scowled. Where had those three Gnomes run off to? I didn't remember seeing them leave, but that meant little with all the commotion.

Think, think, think.

I studied the landscape for anything that might serve as a makeshift stretcher. From my vantage point, I saw buildings, this lone tree, the big rock, and a few flowering weeds. Nothing else.

Wait. Not just any weeds. Fiendish Flowers!

Thrilled by another divine appointment, I lunged for a stalk. Quickly snapping the flower from the top, I waved the oozing stem beneath my mother's nose.

"Ugh." Her eyes flitted open. She gasped.

"Shhh." I touched my finger to her lips. "You're going to be okay. But we have to be quiet."

She groaned and pushed me away. "Go away. I'm never going to cooperate."

"Mom, it's me, Sadie."

"What?" Her voice came out a scratchy whisper. She stared into my face, confused.

My heart sank. Would she know me after being tortured so badly?

"Oh, Sadie!" She smothered me in the most glorious hug ever. "You're so filthy, I didn't know who you were. How did you—"

"Shhh! We'll talk later. Right now we need to outmaneuver a bunch of Ogres and get you to safety. Can you walk?"

She gingerly moved her legs and arms. "I... I think all my parts are working."

With my help, Mom sat up, trembling. A loud groan escaped when I pulled her upright. She clamped a hand over her mouth. Together, we limped in a circle near the tree, getting a feel for walking together.

"The pain is excruciating, Sadie. Everything hurts. But I don't think anything's broken."

"You're going to have to be tough." I hoped she caught the urgency in my voice. "There's not much time."

"Time?"

"No more talking. Think *stealth*."

I had no idea how to find my way back to the group—if we had a group to find. I did, however, know the location of the alleyway where we'd congregated before sneaking into the arena. I headed in that direction and hoped to see familiar landmarks that would lead us back to the dump.

The noise of the throng receded. Likely because they were chasing members of our party through town. We hobbled to the passageway between buildings.

"How'd you know about this spot?" Mom divided her weight between me and the wall.

"Shhh!" I winced. *That felt wrong.* Bossing my mother became a necessary turnaround in our relationship.

We slid through the alley to the opposite end, using the walls for support. I spied around the corner of the building. Further up the street several Ogres trudged along, but they turned at an intersection and disappeared. The lane looked deserted.

I adjusted my position next to Mom and held up three fingers to signal a countdown. We would scoot to the next set of buildings on *one*.

Three... two...

A hand clamped over my mouth.

"Aghgmffgllf!" I yelled, but it came out muffled.

"Shhh. It's Zest." Her voice hissed in my ear. "Keep quiet."

I nodded. The hand fell away. I turned to see the small warrior clinging to cracks in the mortar, having apparently scaled the wall. She suspended herself above my head and pressed a finger to her lips, looking from my mother to me.

Then she scrambled down. Mom managed an awkward little "happy dance" at the sight of the Gnome. It must have given her a needed adrenaline rush. Her steps lightened.

We followed Zest from buildings to boulders to piles of rubble, navigating through town. At one point, Mom and I leaned against a big pot of water and waited for the all-clear sign from Zest. She'd climbed up a broken wall to assess things from a higher vantage point.

Brady's unmistakable voice caught my attention. I looked at Mom and knew she'd heard it too. I couldn't understand what he said, but he sounded distressed.

Zest waved us over to her perch. When we joined her, she hopped to the ground.

"That was my s-son," Mom stammered. She sagged against the wall. "We need to help him."

Zest looked at me. Helping my brother clearly did not figure into her current strategy.

"We can't leave him," I argued. "An Ogre snatched him in the arena when we were rescuing my mother."

"*What?*" Mom gripped my arm.

Me and my big mouth. Helping Brady suddenly

became non-negotiable.

"I'll take a look and see if there's any way to intervene," Zest whispered. "But there's no room for emotions in a crisis. Only shrewdness. If I feel it's too dangerous, you need to cooperate. Agreed?"

Mom cocked her head, thoughtful. She nodded, but I knew better. You can't get between a mama bear and her cub.

We zigzagged closer to the voices. Brady kept quiet, though we heard an occasional protest—usually along the lines of "put me down and fight like a man!"

At last we spotted the savage crowd surrounding a particular Ogre. With one arm, he held Brady off the ground. My brother dangled by the seat of his pants, twisting and swiping his fists, but to no avail.

The horde didn't see us. They were intent on Brady. We skirted the group and crouched behind a heap of rubble. I peered through several cracks in the debris until I found a clear line of sight.

"He's mine. I caught 'im," bellowed the big oaf. He sounded like a little kid with a frog he couldn't bear to part with.

"Too bad, Brumley. The chief wants 'im. Ya gotta give 'im to us," someone in the crowd shouted back.

"Nuh-uh. You's lyin'. You's gonna eat 'im for supper. If the chief wants 'im, he can come and get 'im."

"Them are words of a traitor, Brumley," snarled one angry Ogre. "Chief hears that, *you's* gonna be supper."

"I can guarantee you I taste nasty," Brady yelled. "But you can't have me without a fair fight. Now put me down, and I'll show you a thing or two."

Brumley looked at Brady and chuckled. "You's a funny little guy. I mights needs t'keep ya around for awhiles before I eat ya. Can play my own Human Games with ya."

The first Ogre stepped closer to Brumley. "Exactly what the chief wants to do with 'im. He wants 'im fer more games." He stuck out his hand. "Now give 'im to me."

"No! Give him to *me*."

That was my mother. She'd managed to claw her way to the top of our hiding place before Zest or I noticed.

The crowd turned around. They saw Mom and gasped. Then they elbowed their way towards her, grumbling and indignant.

I stared up at her, flabbergasted. Not to mention terrified.

"Stop." Mom pushed her palm out at the crowd like a traffic cop. Amazingly, they stopped. "My life for his. I will no longer fight or complain. Let him go. *Please.*"

"Ya thinks we's gonna barter with the likes of you's?" Brumley hollered. "We's can keep this boy and takes you's too. We's not scared of no humans. All's of us can takes on the two's of you's."

"Yeah," the rest of the Ogres chimed in. Half a dozen brutes lumbered towards her.

"Wait! I have a riddle for you."

I gawked. *She's lost touch with reality. Her mind is skewed from the torture.* I had to admit, though, she looked better than I'd seen her during the Human Games. Her spark was back.

Inexplicably, the throng stood there with bated breath. Like puppies waiting for a scrap, they gaped at my mother.

> *"I am two kinds of hair.*
> *One is soft and everywhere.*
> *When you meet two kinds of me*
> *Soon, everywhere I shall be.*
> *What am I?"*

Before my eyes, the Ogres transformed from irate ruffians to pensive individuals. They clustered together, deliberating. Some scratched their heads, confounded. Others rubbed their chins and mulled over phrases.

My brother's captor dropped Brady like a brick. He plopped to the ground and ogled his former abductor. Brumley had clearly engrossed himself in solving the riddle.

This is utterly bizarre.

Mom waved Brady over. He took a few tentative steps. I watched his disbelief morph into elation as he dashed away from the oblivious mob.

Zest gave me an incredulous look. "Let's move out!"

We followed behind, crouching low. Finally, we distanced ourselves enough to take cover and catch our breaths.

"Mom!"

"Brady!"

They grabbed each other in an intense hug.

"Ah!" Mom squirmed. "Watch the ribcage, honey."

"Oops, sorry. Are you—"

"I'm fine. Are *you* okay? Did they hurt you?" Mom thrust Brady to arm's length and inspected him.

"I'm great. But I've got a serious wedgie from being held by the seat of my pants." He yanked at his trousers.

We enjoyed a brief laugh that recharged our spirits.

Zest cleared her throat. "Sorry to interrupt. We need to keep moving. The tide is eminent. Come."

Her sobering words were the reality check we needed.

We had a handful of narrow escapes trying to find the route of least resistance while we crisscrossed town. Without Zest, I doubt we would've made it to the dump. We backtracked so many times, it left me disoriented.

At last I saw the trash heap. We had but a few buildings standing between us and the homestretch. We scurried from the first deserted edifice to the shelter of the second.

Two down, one to go.

Zest shot out from the wall towards the third. She did an about face before we could follow. "They're coming."

Then we heard the ruckus. A torrent of giants headed our way. From the sound of their rumblings about getting tricked, it was the same crowd Mom had outsmarted.

"This isn't good, is it?" I asked Zest.

She looked at my mother. "Know any more riddles?"

CHAPTER THIRTY-THREE

A DISTANT WHISTLE CAUGHT OUR ATTENTION.

"That's Reiko." Zest stiffened and tilted her head. "It's her signal. They're waiting with the horses and Toboggans on this side of the sandbar. She fetched them in order to hasten our escape. Part of Xander's plan since the tide will flood in any time and the Ogres are now well aware of our presence. It's time to duck and run straight through the dump. We're so close, Larcens. Don't lose heart."

Without waiting, Zest bolted for the beach.

"I've got Mom." Brady latched onto her. "*Go!*"

I dashed after Zest, overtaking her with long, easy strides.

"Straight ahead!" she shouted.

We made it to the dump, but the natives were hot on our heels. The debris that had provided camouflage on our way into Skellerwad now became a series of obstacles between us and freedom. We scrambled over small mounds of junk and dodged the bigger pieces.

My side ached, but I pressed on. Risking a peek over my shoulder, I saw swarms of Ogres closing in from every direction.

Brady waved me down. "Sadie!"

Mom had faltered. Brady couldn't manage her on his own.

I ran back to her other side. "C'mon, Mom, stay with

us. We're almost there. You can do this." She slumped onto our shoulders, in and out of consciousness. Her adrenaline had fizzled out. She needed water, pronto. "Hang in there. Please!"

Stumbling under her weight and our lack of coordination left me fighting for breath and low on hope.

Zest ordered us to press on. She scrambled up a pile of junk and waved her scabbard at the cretins to distract them.

Directly ahead I made out the blessed silhouettes of horses and Toboggans. *Almost there.* In the background, Zest taunted the giants. Swords zinged. There's no way one little Gnome can take on a bunch of Ogres.

I glanced back. Zest had company. Xander and Gage had joined the fray. They hovered—gloriously suspended above the angry masses—wings outstretched and billowing, swords alive with movement. My heart soared.

The two Nephilim kept the brutes busy, hoisting themselves out of reach then plunging down to take a swipe. Very cool. While the Ogres swatted at the angel-men, Zest scampered between their feet and slashed their gnarly legs.

Like a bad, slow-motion dream, our efforts to reach the others floundered. The sand made forward progress negligible. Chunks of rock turned into a tedious obstacle course. Rounding a boulder, I had a clear view of four animals, three Gnomes, and one Dwarf. A mental match-up of horses to passengers left me short a couple of steeds—not insurmountable if we doubled up.

Lava ran to assist our struggle with Mom. He grabbed her ankles and laid them across his shoulders, guiding us from the front.

Thank you, thank you, thank you!

We reached the horses and laid her gently on the ground.

"She's dehydrated," I said.

Lava handed me a canteen. I tilted Mom's head back and drizzled water into her mouth, spilling it down her cheek in the process. She came to with a sputter, sat up, then grabbed the canteen and took a lusty drink.

"Thank you." She flopped back onto the sand.

"We need to get you in the saddle, m'lady." Lava leaned onto his haunches beside Mom. "If the tide comes in, you'll not have the strength to swim against it. I need you to mount up straightaway."

I helped Mom sit up, and Brady lifted her to her feet. We faced the clash of Ogres and Nephilim—along with the small but mighty Gnomes—and stood transfixed. The battle raged and boiled in our direction. I caught a whiff of the Ogres' stench.

"M'lady, we must flee." Lava led Cruz by the bridle.

Mom stumbled to her feet. "Yes, sorry."

The Dwarf climbed up first. Brady and I helped Mom into the saddle behind him. "You'll have to take hold of my middle." He patted his sides. "I need ya to stay with me, Amy Larcen. Don't want ya tumblin' backward." He gave me a knowing wink.

"I'm here. I've had water. I'm good to go," she said.

"Excellent." Lava pulled down his hat.

"Wait!" Mom grabbed Lava's shoulders.

He pursed his lips. "What is it, m'lady?"

"Where's Liam? Where's my husband?"

"He's safe on the other side. I'll get ya to him if we can leave *right now*."

"Ready when you are."

Lava turned to Brady and me. "You two, mount together and follow immediately."

They galloped off. Brady and I zipped to the other horse, the one he rode to Skellerwad. He clambered up first.

I had no sooner plopped behind the saddle when an infuriated howl rose above the din. "The humans are getting away!" The mob zeroed in on us. Two giants continued to engage the Nephilim. The rest took colossal strides our way. The Gnomes did their best to skewer the massive men in the feet.

"*Hurry*, Brady."

The horse stamped the ground at the encroaching Ogres. Mighty and Muscle broke free and mounted one Toboggan. Reiko waited for Zest on the other.

Reiko turned to us. "*Go!*"

Brady reined in the snorting steed. "We're not leaving without you."

I wasn't feeling so generous.

Zest disentangled herself and sprinted to where Reiko sat holding out her hand. In one fluid motion, Zest grasped it and flung herself behind her comrade.

"This is no time for chivalry. You must *go!*" Reiko's face turned red with insistence.

Brady had barely managed to turn our horse towards the opposite shore when we heard a resounding rumble. The ground twitched. Our horse spooked. I screamed and clung to Brady.

Reiko charged from behind. "Move it! The tide's coming in!"

Our horse lurched and sidestepped.

"*Arrrgh!*" An Ogre took a last-ditch lunge at us.

Our horse bucked. I clung to Brady. Adrenaline revved another notch.

The uncoordinated oaf lost his balance and tumbled forward, arms outstretched. He swiped at us, missed, and took a face plant in the sand.

The Toboggans sped ahead. Our horse whinnied and found its footing. I looked back at the receding chaos. The thugs stood there, fists and weapons raised, spitting mad. Several pointed towards the impending tide and didn't pursue us.

Xander and Gage brought up the rear, gliding behind and above us. Jaws set. Swords outstretched. Wings undulating. An impressive sight, I must admit.

The horse's strides brought us even with the Toboggans in no time. Each animal spurred the other to greater speeds. A distant sound like thunder, ominous and unrelenting, rumbled.

Then I saw it. And smelled it. A stinking wall of water grew in the distance to my right. It looked capable of bulldozing anything in its path.

I suddenly preferred Ogres.

The shore came into view, specked with dark shapes I assumed were horses and people. My parents! I focused on them and ignored the encroaching tsunami. *Almost there. We're almost there.*

The dark shapes became more distinct. My parents stood side by side, reaching and waving. Lava paced and stopped, paced and stopped.

I felt a mist, then warm-water drops pelted my side. The horse felt it too and gave a resounding neigh. *Oh, God, please help!*

My mother buried her face in my father's chest. Lava stopped pacing. He jumped up and down, silently demanding us to succeed.

About twenty yards from safety the first fingers of water spilled across our path. I squeezed my eyes shut, suspended between faith and despair. I heard the desperate splashing of the horses' hooves.

It could go either way.

The rumbling sensation in my ears and chest told me the water would soon overtake us. I wouldn't allow myself a peek at my parents. I didn't want their anguished faces to be my final vision before drowning.

I cringed and braced myself to be plowed over by a wall of water. Then I felt firm hands grasp beneath my arms and lift me high, out of danger. They pried me from Brady and carried me above the water. I opened my eyes to see Brady being snatched by Gage.

The water overcame our horse. It smacked my legs, hot and stinging. It struck Brady in the face. The liquid avalanche encompassed everything below me. Plummeting waves spewed mist as far as I could see. My world went white—but I felt safe in Xander's arms.

Patches of earth came into view. The water settled. I spotted Mom, anxiously searching the sky. When she saw us and waved, I knew everything would be okay.

Xander and Gage circled once then carefully placed Brady and me on the ground. We ran to Mom and strangled her with a sopping-wet hug.

The next moment I pulled back, alarmed. "Where's Daddy?"

She smiled and nodded towards the watery surge that had calmed to roaring-river status. Dad held the reins of our drenched horse, leading him up the embankment.

"Daddy! Oh, Daddy, we made it."

Dad dropped the reins and ran for me. I rushed into his arms and became sandwiched in a hug with my brother. We were a blubbering mess of laughter and tears.

Mom joined the reunion. I felt as if I might explode from happiness.

Everyone talked at once. I don't think anybody listened. We all needed to speak or we might self-destruct. Soon, we settled down enough to remember we weren't alone.

We unraveled ourselves but kept hold of each other's hands. I looked to where Lava, Xander, and Gage paced along the shore.

Something wasn't right. "Wait. Where're the Gnomes? And the Toboggans?"

I already knew the answer. Pulling away from my parents, I ran to join the others. Their eyes scanned the body of water, faces grim.

Lava shook his head. "I can't believe we made it through the last few days and lost 'em to the water. 'Tisn't right."

I blinked back tears. Dad came and put an arm around my shoulder. I looked at him. "The Gnomes risked *everything* for our family. Repeatedly."

Xander stood nearby. He stared hard at something further down the beach.

I followed his gaze and squinted at a tumultuous spot of water. I rushed to get a better look. Out from the belly of the sea rose a mass of tangled hair and curvy horns. Gripping the horns with all his might sat one of the Gnomes, followed by the other Toboggan and another Gnome.

The Toboggans bounded up the shore towards us. The two exhausted riders tumbled to the ground. I recognized Muscle and Reiko. They choked and spewed into the sand, waterlogged but alive.

I scanned the shore for Mighty and Zest. In the midst of running for my life, I hadn't noticed another day being washed away with the tide. Now, the dusktime light made it difficult to see.

I waded into the water with Brady, searching for our other heroes. A dark object caught my eye. I grappled for it. A small, conical helmet emerged. I held it to my chest and scoured the surface for signs of life.

"Here! Over here!" Brady beckoned us and plunged into the Sulfur Sea. He came up for air then disappeared underwater again. He bobbed to the surface, straightened, and headed for shore holding a petite, lifeless body.

Zest!

I grabbed her from my brother and laid her on the ground. "I'll do CPR."

My mother knelt beside me and helped work off the chain mail from her tiny torso. I alternated between breathing into her mouth and pumping her chest.

The others spread out to comb the water's edge for Mighty. Lava stayed further inland to assist Reiko and Muscle.

I continued to work on Zest but couldn't get a response.

A call in the distance alerted us that Gage had found Mighty. Soon, the other Gnome lay beside Zest. My mother began CPR on him. We worked in silence. The others watched. I had a feeling that CPR was a new concept in the Tethered World.

A cough and sputter from Mighty brought a cheer from the group. He rolled to his side and retched a stomach full of water.

Zest remained unaffected by my efforts. I prayed and talked and worked on her, searching for a spark of life.

Lava placed his hand on my back. "She's not rousin', sweet Sadie. I believe our Zest has perished."

I ignored him. My mind pleaded. *C'mon, Zest. Breathe! We wouldn't have made it without you. Wake up!*

At length, Dad pulled me off her. He cradled my tear-streaked cheeks and looked into my eyes. "You've done all you can, love. I'm sorry. She's gone."

CHAPTER THIRTY-FOUR

Numbly, I watched Lava remove his cape and offer it to my father. "We can bring her back to Vituvia in this."

Dad wrapped the small frame securely in the fabric.

Zest's death was a bittersweet stain on the triumph of our rescue. If not for her brave leadership, my mother and I would not have made it out of Skellerwad. I owed Zest a debt of gratitude but would never have the opportunity to repay it.

Xander fastened Zest's shrouded body to the back of his saddle. Reiko and the other Gnomes evaluated the Toboggans. The creatures were groggy after their underwater excursion, but they came around.

"Let's go, my friends," Xander said. "There's much to do."

I resumed my place with Brady on his horse. Dad rode behind Lava, and Mother sat in front of Gage, supported by his sturdy frame. Neither Mom nor Dad was in any condition to bump along on a horse, but they'd have to tough it out.

I couldn't tear my eyes away from the hump strapped behind Xander's saddle. *I'm sorry, Zest. Farewell.* If we were heading back to Calamus or moving on to Vituvia, I didn't know. At that moment, I didn't care. The stress of Skellerwad had drained me. The hush hanging over our group showed we all shared this sentiment.

The silence beckoned the skeletons of my selfishness to mock me again. They replayed my incriminating attitudes and glazed my conscience with shame. My spirit dwindled to a new low. Each of us had been dragged into this situation—none of us by choice.

How could I blame Mom for this? It's bigger than anyone can fathom.

I hung my head, penitent.

Over the next hour, the steady clomp of hooves pounded down the stress level. Conversation percolated, a diversion I appreciated—though condemnation kept vigil in the back of my mind.

My parents wanted to hear the entire story, from the moment the police knocked on the door to our reunion on the beach. Brady and I took turns filling in the blanks and answering questions. I found it therapeutic to talk about everything in the *past* tense. It meant I survived.

Been there. Done that. Got the T-shirt.

During the course of the story, it came out that Brock and Sophie had journeyed below with us.

"*What?*" Mom's eyes popped wide open. "My son, whom the Trolls want to kill, and my eleven-year-old daughter are here in the Tethered World *without* me?"

"Well, Mom," Brady reminded her. "We would still be *without* you if we didn't come and get you."

"I know." She shrugged. "I appreciate that. It's the principle."

Dad laughed. "It's Mom's job to be overly protective, even from captivity."

"Exactly," she agreed. "I'll have a word with Aunt Jules once we're home."

We continued our tale, giving our impressions of the place. When we shared our horror at finding them tortured in the Human Games, I chose not to divulge my deplorable self-realization. That needed to be handled in private. Besides, I was still sorting through the rubbish.

"You've no idea how utterly hopeless I felt the past few days," Mom lamented. "Being brought out for round two of those horrendous games was more than I could handle."

"I have a *real* good idea about feeling hopeless, actually." *Major understatement.* "This whole experience has been the scariest thing ever. It's beyond any book or fairytale. I seriously can't believe this place exists and you never told us about it. When were you planning to tell us, by the way?"

Oops. I should have probably saved that for later too.

"Sounds like we have a lot to discuss when we get home, Sadie. I promise we'll talk about it."

My account of rescuing Mom and Dad, and her explanation of our secret family history, were two vastly different discussions. I held my tongue instead of pointing out the obvious.

"I'd like to know how you used a riddle, of all things, to get me out of that predicament with the Ogres," Brady said.

Mom giggled. "I'm not an expert on mythological creatures without good reason. It's a well-known fact Ogres love a good riddle."

Lava snorted. "Well-known fact, my *grog.*"

"My research has led me to many bizarre tidbits over the years. Some that I'll never have the chance to test, sadly. This situation presented a unique opportunity. I worked on that riddle when I was locked up, waiting for exactly the right occasion."

"*Hmmph.*" Lava grunted his skepticism. "Well, let's hear your stroke of genius."

Mom repeated her rhyme.

> *"I am two kinds of hair.*
> *One is soft and everywhere.*
> *When you meet two kinds of me*
> *Soon, everywhere, I shall be.*
> *What am I?"*

A reflective silence followed.

"A hare!" Brady poked a finger in the air. "Two kinds of hair. Furry hair versus rabbits, the other name for hares, right? And they multiply everywhere."

Mom applauded. "Bingo!"

"Take note, Brady." Dad used his wise, fatherly tone. "You never know when stray scraps of trivia will save your life."

We shared a good chuckle. Coming full circle, we finally rehashed everyone's perspectives on the escape across the Sulfur Sea. Everything beyond that we had experienced together. The rest was bittersweet.

Reiko rode alongside Brady and me on her Toboggan. I braced myself for a speech about the loss of Zest's life being my responsibility. I wouldn't deny it. Didn't want to. She'd lost her life saving ours. What could I say to make things better?

I looked down at the feisty Gnome. She gave me a warm smile—the first of its kind. "That's quite a story, Sadie Larcen." She saluted me. "An impressive one. You've been through much, and you were brave in the face of many dangers. I'm pleased to say that I underestimated you."

Her quasi-apology took me off guard. I gave her a weak grin and shrugged. "Thanks. And... I'm *deeply* sorry about Zest. She was an amazing warrior. I wish things had turned out differently."

She nodded and trotted past.

I poked Brady. "Did I actually hear words of approval from that stick of dynamite, or did I imagine it?"

"Maybe we both imagined it."

The landscape struck a familiar chord. We skirted a hill, and the gilded city of Calamus sprawled in the distance. Probably the best place to go, considering how tattered and tired we were.

Xander slowed and allowed the group to come within earshot. "When we arrive in Calamus, our doctors shall examine you, Mr. and Mrs. Larcen. If you're well enough to ride on to Vituvia with us, we'll leave straightaway. That is *after* we change into clean garments and take some nourishment, of course."

"Oh, we *will* be going to Vituvia. You can count on that." Mom's tone left no room for debate. "I've not felt this good in days."

"I don't think we have any serious injuries," Dad added. "Nothing food and water won't cure, anyway. The doctor won't be necessary. Going to Vituvia *is*."

Xander twisted in his saddle and looked at my parents. "I can appreciate your desire to stay with your family. But as my guests, I must insist you allow the doctors to examine you. You're *my* responsibility." He spurred his horse ahead, ending the conversation.

Our path widened into a road. The road met up with walls. And the walls contained the splendor of the city of Calamus.

Clean garments and nourishment...here I come!

THE DOCTOR'S EXAM LEFT my mother with a wrapped torso for a fractured rib, bandages on her arms, and stitches in her ear lobe. Dad received stitches for a sizable gash across his shoulder blade and a smaller one on his shin. Numerous bandages decorated his extremities, but nothing appeared broken. I was glad Xander had insisted they get checked.

The rest of us received fresh sets of clothes and a swift scrub down—not in that order. The servants worked us over like a pit crew. What I deemed to be the closure of our adventure, "the end," they treated as preparation for the next big event. At least they permitted us a few hours of beauty sleep before sending us on our way.

I reminded myself that this ordeal didn't end with my parents' rescue. I couldn't mentally check out. Not yet. My parents were *my* major focus, but the safety of the whole realm hung in the balance. I had to see this through. Not my natural inclination, but I was slowly learning "it's not about you, little girl."

Back in the council chamber of our previous powwow, we anticipated a less dramatic reunion with our parents. Platters of roasted turkey legs and chunks of bread awaited us, medieval style, *sans* utensils and plates. We sipped communal goblets of water and swapped them around, much to my discomfort.

Dad stepped inside, a clean—and slightly mummified—version of his former self. We clapped our hands and cheered. He swept his arm towards the hallway. "And may I present my brave and beautiful bride, the lovely Amy Larcen."

Mom entered, slipped her hand into my father's, and curtsied.

Applause and whistles zinged throughout the room. Mom and Dad found their seats. Much to their obvious disappointment, nourishment for them was limited to liquids for now. Servants set down steaming bowls of broth. Mom and Dad seemed to relish their scanty meal like a four-course dinner.

Lava reached for a fourth leg of turkey, but Xander signaled a servant to remove the platter. Lava detoured for a plate of bread and nabbed a chunk before it, too, disappeared.

The prince cleared his throat. "The horses and Toboggans have been refreshed, and so have we. Though we could all use more sleep I believe we should press on to Vituvia, where a battle rages. We must join the fray." Missing the conflict seemed to distress him. The prince had a sense of duty that I couldn't help but admire.

A messenger came in and spoke privately to Xander. He nodded and turned to us. "My mother shall join us."

Queen Estancia had been conspicuously absent since our first meeting in the palace hall. Why did she want to bother with us now? She glided into the room. I stood to pay homage along with the others.

The woman was breathtaking, but not in a way that stirred admiration. More like shock and awe. An impressive ice sculpture had the same effect. Both were big, beautiful, and biting. She peered down her nose at our company then gazed at her princely son with pride. "Well done. You're proving quite a warrior."

Xander bowed his head. "Thank you, my queen. Truly, the valiant effort by everyone made our mission a success."

The queen smiled in a way that said "I doubt that"

then turned her attention to my parents. "Welcome to Calamus. It's an honor to receive the parents of Vituvia's future king, even if he isn't royalty by birth."

Mom met the queen's condescending look with her own fiery gleam. "We appreciate your generosity, Your Highness. We owe you a debt of gratitude in every way. My son, King Brock, of the royal bloodline of the Guardians of the Sword, will surely enjoy good relations with your kingdom for many years to come."

Queen Estancia tilted her head. I couldn't tell if she felt surprised or insulted by my mother's bold response. "I didn't know your family's job—babysitting the Sword, so to speak—came with any claim to royalty."

Insulted.

Before Mom could bare her claws, my father stepped in. "It's true, Your Grace. Amy's lineage is part of a secret, noble bloodline. Because of the delicate nature of keeping the Tethered World from view, the family pedigree is not public knowledge."

"Nor is it Tethered World knowledge, as one would expect such a thing to be." The queen clapped her hands, and footmen appeared. We took our cue and gave our obligatory bows. She strode from the room.

"Charming." Mom's face held no love for the queen of Calamus.

Xander stepped to my parents' side. "Please accept my apologies. Relationships are not my mother's strong suit. She's not a diplomat, but she is a devoted ruler who looks after her subjects with justice. I've learned many exemplary things from her."

Mom softened. "No apologies needed, Your Majesty. It's hard enough to keep a household and homeschool running smoothly. I don't envy your mother's enormous responsibilities."

"You're very gracious." He grinned and turned to our group. "I think we're ready to depart. The horses and Toboggans are being brought to the portico. A small regiment of soldiers shall accompany us. I'll be indisposed at times, conferring with my men, but I shall check on your well-being as often as I'm able."

We followed Xander through the halls, returning to the place where we'd set out to rescue our parents. I marveled that I'd stood right here—minus my parents—less than a day ago. *Mission: accomplished!*

Someone had fashioned a proper casket for Zest. She would ride to Vituvia in dignity for an official burial. The petite box sat securely behind Xander's saddle. Tears pricked my eyes and I turned away.

"The physician insists you ride with someone to help support your ribcage, Lady Amy." Gage stood beside his grey draft horse and offered his hand.

Dad encircled Mom's waist with his bandaged arm. "She can ride on my horse with me."

"You have your own share of wounds to favor." Gage sounded sympathetic. "A long, bumpy ride awaits, which will strain your entire body, both broken and whole. I insist that your wife ride with me."

Dad grimaced. "Fine."

Once situated on our own mounts, we followed Xander through the gate we had used when we headed to Skellerwad. This time, however, we turned in the direction of the river. Soldiers waited for us in the valley, where the River Gambrell separated the Land of the Ancients from the Land of Legend. About fifty men stood at attention beside their horses.

This is a small regiment?

"Mount up." Xander signaled them.

The troops obeyed. They escorted us to a shallow spot at the water's edge. I studied the prince while waiting to cross. Though things started off dicey, my wariness had dissolved, replaced with admiration of Xander's character and skills. No doubt his ego still lurked nearby—but at least he could lay it aside and be serious. I also had a deeper appreciation for the bump beneath his cape. Those wings mesmerized me.

What an extraordinary characteristic.

Xander looked at me. I averted my gaze and hoped to look preoccupied. Awkward.

Once across the river, our caravan followed a trail that meandered through the hills. The narrow path forced us to filter into a line, creating one, enormous trail ride.

It didn't take long for the cadence of horseback to deplete my energy reserves. Though tired, I did not feel an overwhelming need for sleep. I remembered General Muggleridge explaining those in the Tethered World did not require much rest. Their bodies didn't undergo as much stress from the elements. The effect seemed to carry over to humans if they stayed long enough—not counting the stress of running for one's life on a regular basis.

But if the lack of chitchat was any indication, everyone was beat. Mom nodded off and slumped back against Gage. The mountain of a man didn't seem to notice.

The monotony lulled me into occasional numbness. Then like a splash of cool water on a sticky day, the thought of my parents, alive and with me, shook me out of my stupor. I looked at them and smiled out of sheer gratefulness.

Such a miracle!

"You're beautiful when you smile like that." Xander rode up beside me. Lost in my thoughts, I hadn't noticed. My cheeks grew hot.

"Is it that awful for you when we speak?"

I blushed again. "No, it's not awful. That was a nice compliment. Thank you."

"Is there a young man who would be jealous of my attention? If so, then I assure you, I've only honorable intentions."

"No, no, no! There's no one. I'm... shy, I guess."

He chuckled. "You're not shy. You're mellow. You're observant. Those are good qualities."

More blushing.

"After listening to your story, I'm impressed by how you and your siblings rose to the challenges. If I understand your life topside, these experiences are very... different."

I grinned. "Let's just say there's no word in English that comes any closer than *different*, so that'll have to do. It's only by God's grace I'm here and have the guts to face any of this. Don't get the wrong impression of me,

Xander. I'm a chicken. I'm used to a comfortable life in a comfortable home, with normal, teenage plans. Honestly, I can't wait to get back. The closest I ever want to come to this type of adventure again will be reading about it in a book. But I can't go home until we're all reunited and the realm is safe. So for now, I have to do what I have to do."

"You're a *chicken?*"

Out of my whole speech, he's stuck on that? "It's an expression. It means I'm afraid."

He looked perplexed.

I laughed. "We say a lot of things up there that don't make sense down here."

"I've noticed." He smiled. "But Sadie, you don't *act* afraid."

"Being afraid doesn't mean I don't have faith... and courage."

"Obviously not."

"Perhaps you've heard this expression." I cleared my throat. "'Courage is being scared to death, but saddling up anyway.'"

"Sounds like another Topsider phrase. I like it. But how would *I* have heard it?"

"Well, Pilgrim," I drawled. "It was made famous by your friend John Wayne."

CHAPTER THIRTY-FIVE

We gathered for final instructions behind a grove of trees on a bluff near Vituvia. Xander's spies briefed him on what the situation looked like on the battlefield. While the Prince and his scouts conferred, we dismounted and stretched our legs.

"I can't wait to get my hands on my babies." Mom looped her arm through mine. "Brock's going to have to put up with a big, smothering hug whether he wants one or not. And Sophie won't be allowed to leave my sight for a month."

I chuckled. "Good luck with that. She's so pumped about being here she feels guilty. I doubt she'll want to go back to life in boring, old Orchards, Washington, after this."

"I bet," Dad said. "That kid's imagination is the size of a small galaxy."

Xander approached our hodgepodge posse and offered my father a firm handshake. Firm enough to make him wince. "It's an honor, sir, to be a part of securing Vituvia for your son Brock, the future king. I look forward to meeting him after a swift and triumphant victory."

"Thank you, Your Majesty," Dad replied. "I'm grateful for all you've done for me personally, and for all your realm has provided for Vituvia and our family."

"You're most welcome." Xander cleared his throat. "Now, allow me to explain our strategy. Our spies have returned with news of what we face."

"We're winning, right?" Brady looked eager.

Xander seemed pensive. "I can't give you a decisive yes, but I believe it's in our favor. The good news is that the entirety of the battle is here in Vituvia, and doesn't rage in Berganstroud as well. Seems they swept through the mountains only long enough to cause trouble on their way here."

He adjusted his cape, and I glimpsed his silken feathers. "But I'll tell you this: it's bloody. The fighting is intense. So much so that my men could not safely make their way to my father for an official report. We'll deliver your family to the palace in a roundabout way to ensure you're not involved in the fighting. We need everyone safely reunited."

"No way!" Brady smacked a fist against his leg. "Let me join your men. I want to slash up some Trolls."

"*Wrong*." Mom leveled him with a stare. "You're staying where you belong—safe—with your family."

"Aw, c'mon, Mom. You know you've been secretly training me for this. Fencing lessons, karate." He pointed at her. "You had an agenda."

"Those skills are for emergencies only."

"All right, you two." Dad played referee. "Executive-decision time. Brady, don't argue with your mother. You're staying with us."

My brother gritted his teeth and turned away. He knew better than to press the matter.

Xander cleared his throat, breaking the awkward silence. "As it stands, my warrior friend, I have very few soldiers to spare. I'm sending Gage and one other man to lead your family to the palace. I was counting on your skill and bravery to make up for the men I cannot provide."

Brady brightened at Xander's words. "Yes, sir. I'll do it."

"Excellent. A good warrior learns to willingly serve the need of the greater good."

"Your Highness," Lava spoke up. "Am I to take it that the rest of us, the Gnomes and myself, will *not* be escortin' our friends to safety?"

Xander nodded.

"If I may be so bold, I'd prefer to personally ensure my friends make it to the palace. Would ya mind if I went in place of one of yer men?"

Xander paused. "I suppose that would work. Yes. You and Gage as escorts. I don't have a problem with that."

"Thank you, Yer Majesty. This is a job I'd like to see to the end, if ya know what I mean."

Xander nodded and turned to the group. "The time has come. Secure your provisions, make ready your weapons, and mount up."

I walked to Reiko, Muscle, and Mighty with a heavy heart. "Thank you for everything you've done for my family. We're alive and together, thanks to you. I'm so sorry about Zest. She didn't die in vain. I'll never forget her sacrifice."

Reiko gave a hint of a smile. "Merely doing our job, young Larcen. Now it's time to finish this insanity once and for all. Travel safely." She mounted her Toboggan. The others followed suit.

I saluted the Gnomes. "I'll see all of you when this mess is cleaned up. Those Trolls are gonna wish they'd stayed home when you guys hit the battlefield."

They waved and rode off.

Mounting my horse, I watched Xander transfer the miniature casket from his steed to Gage's, strapping it behind the saddle. *How many little boxes would we need by the time this war was over?*

We headed towards a trail through thick trees that covered a lower bluff at Vituvia's back. Xander stood in stoic silence and watched us file by. My heart did a little flutter when he looked at me.

Ugh! Enough of this emotional nonsense.

The trail was wide enough to ride three abreast once we slipped through the narrow opening. The tree-lined hill descended at a steep angle to our left. Gage signaled to keep silent, but the horses made enough noise on their own. Sticks and twigs snapped. Small rocks scuttled down the incline.

We hadn't traveled for long when a different sound startled us. The horses skidded to a halt then reared at the crashing and thudding. I caught my breath.

A sinister Troll blocked our path.

He snatched the bridle of Gage's draft horse. With the flick of his wrist, he twisted the neck of the enormous equine and brought it to the ground. My mother careened over the horse's withers and hit the ground with a crushing *thunk*. The horse fell on Gage, pinning him beneath its weight.

Lava galloped to the front, blade drawn, ready to pounce. The Troll reacted fast. With a guttural yell, he charged the Dwarf. Lava's horse shied to one side and reared.

The rest of us sat frozen, our eyes riveted on the menacing Goliath.

The Troll focused on my vulnerable mother. He advanced towards her with slow, measured steps.

Dad grunted in frustration, trapped between my horse and the trees.

"Back away, you monster!" Brady yelled. He galloped up from behind.

The Troll slammed the horse's muzzle with an iron fist. Brady's horse stumbled into mine, knocked senseless.

The Troll turned back to my mother. He leaned over and swiped a paw at her, when—

Zing!

A dagger-sized sword flew through the air and plunged into the creature's throat. He stumbled and grasped the hilt with leathery fingers. A gurgle erupted from his mouth, along with a spurt of thick, dark blood. He fell backward, dead.

I turned in stunned silence to see our hero. *Reiko?* My jaw dropped. Where did she come from?

She trotted up to the Troll's body and reached down from the back of her Toboggan, yanking her sword free.

I cringed at the fresh gush of blood.

Reiko wiped her sword clean on the shoulder of the

beast and sheathed it.

Lava found his tongue first. "Our dear friend, Reiko, you've saved us yet again. I've never been so glad to see a slain Troll." He chuckled. "Well, that's not quite true. I'm *always* glad to see a slain Troll."

I laughed, releasing my tension. Dad was out of his saddle and next to Mom. He helped her stand, brushing her free from twigs and leaves. Brady's mount came out of its stupor with a vigorous shake of its mane and a stilted neigh.

Gage worked himself free from under the fallen horse. The poor animal struggled to find its footing. Lava dismounted, grabbed the reins, and encouraged the animal to stand.

Reiko smiled. "I convinced Xander that the best person to lead you safely to the palace of the Gnomes would have to be a *Gnome*. He agreed and sent me after you." She shrugged, all business. Then her gaze fell on the wooden casket. It had come loose from Gage's saddle. One end lay shattered where it hit the ground. Reiko turned pale.

Gage snatched up the box and strapped it back in place. With great care, he removed his cape and draped it over the top. Before mounting, the soldier approached Reiko and bent down on one knee.

His eyes glistened. "My friend, today the diminutive has taken down the colossal. Your prowess saved us. I'll never forget what you did, and I'll never underestimate another creature based on appearance alone."

Reiko smiled tenderly at Gage's humility. "I've recently learned the same lesson, soldier. It's an important one for all of us. I'm glad I decided to come along with... with my friends."

Before we could grow emotional, she spurred her Toboggan ahead. We hustled to get situated, but not before she turned and hollered, "What are you waiting for? Let's get your family back together."

CHAPTER THIRTY-SIX

The rest of our travels were blissfully uneventful. Cruz nosed behind Brady's mount. Gage rode ahead of him. With his cape removed to cover Zest's broken casket, I had plenty of opportunities to study the soldier's exposed wings. I found them fascinating.

Reiko kept well ahead of our group, sniffing out danger before we stumbled into it. Two different times I rode past the dead bodies of Trolls, courtesy of the stealthy warrior. I couldn't help but stare at the lifeless lumps of fur when I rode past. Creepy... in a comforting sort of way.

Later, Reiko waited for us to catch up. She led us to a gated barricade that crossed our path and divided the woods. Two guards were stationed at the gateway, clearly prepared to protect it. The undergrowth on either side grew thick with thorny brambles, a natural, razor-wire fence.

Catching sight of Reiko, the soldiers sprang to attention.

"At ease. Open the gate."

They obeyed.

Reiko moved aside and let us ride through before bringing up the rear. "Good work, men," she commended the guards. "You were alert and ready."

We hadn't journeyed far when she instructed us to stop and tie up our horses. "The way down from here is steep—too steep for horses or Toboggans. We'll send someone back later to fetch the animals and bring them around the long way."

Gage helped my mother dismount then removed the casket from his saddle. Using his cape for a sling, he tied it to his back. Reiko led us to a thick rope encircling a tree. "Keep hold of this and let yourselves down slow and easy. We'll descend from smallest person to tallest, spacing ourselves to keep the height discrepancy less of an issue."

We figured out our order of descent. Reiko went first. She leaned into the rope and walked down backward like she did it every day. Well, duh, she probably did.

Lava lowered himself next, matching Reiko's skill. Then it was Mom's turn to go. She struggled to work against the pull of gravity and the pain of her cracked rib. Not a good combination.

"Sweetheart, this isn't a good idea." Dad held his hand out for her to grasp and get her footing.

"I can do this." She eased herself back. "*Ah!*"

Gage reached a long limb towards Mom and plucked her off the rope. He set her down next to Dad. "No, m'lady. I should not have allowed you to try it. I'll help you down."

Dad looked from Gage to Mom. His face battled with pride and acceptance. "Yes. It's for the best."

I went next. *Gulp.* It was steep. Freaky steep. With effort, I concentrated on the rope passing from one white-knuckled hand to the other. *Don't look down. Don't look down.* My arms ached. The rope burned. I strained against gravity and against my sweaty palms.

Brady followed me. Every time I looked up, his backside filled my vision. Great. Lovely view. But it beat looking down.

Dad came next, then Gage and my mother. I could totally see ourselves on the cover of *National Geographic*.

The palace roof waited below. One by one we touched down. Beyond us, the town spread out in tidy, measured streets. Past the town, the fortified wall from which our journey began encircled its protective arms around the city. Beyond that, the war raged, remote and indistinct.

Stationed sentries stood at intervals along the rooftop. Each appeared fixated on the far-off battle. They hadn't noticed our descent.

Reiko wasted no time reprimanding them. "We spent the last five minutes scaling this wall. You never once turned to look for an enemy sneaking up from behind. If I were a Troll, I'd eat you for supper. You *will* be written up, men. Back to work!"

The soldiers cowered, shamefaced. When Reiko finished her diatribe, she brought us to a rope ladder that led to a lower level of rooftops. From there, we crossed to a roof hatch. She pried it open. "Climb down inside."

We descended another ladder and through several attic-type spaces before winding down a primitive staircase that returned us to civilization. Servants and soldiers went about their business. They didn't blink when we spilled out a door and into the hallway.

Reiko flagged down several servants and asked them to tend to our needs.

In no time, we were whisked away in various directions to be cleaned and scrubbed and fed. For me, the highlights of this traumatic journey—besides retrieving my parents in one piece—revolved around food and water and clean clothing. Oh, and nice, fluffy beds, the likes of which I hadn't seen for some time.

Mom and I recuperated in a luxurious room with furniture crafted to human scale. It didn't take long before she cornered our attendants and asked to see Brock and Sophie.

"I'm sorry, Lady Amy." The servants looked at each other and shook their heads. "We don't know their whereabouts. We'll inquire for you. In the meantime, you should get some rest." They pulled the covers back on the four-poster bed and left us alone.

Mom stiffened. "How can I be in the same building as my children and not be able to see them? It isn't right." She lowered herself onto a couch then crossed her arms.

"They're nuts if they think I can rest when I haven't seen my kids. How're we supposed to sleep when there's a war raging? There's too much to think about."

"I don't even feel tired. Too much adrenaline and too much at stake." I walked behind Mom and gave her shoulders a gentle massage.

"Oh, Sadie, that's fantastic."

She'd say that even if she hadn't been kidnapped and tortured. I worked on her neck, lost in thought. I had so much to say but didn't know where to begin.

At length, I asked, "I'm not getting close to any bumps or bruises am I?"

Silence.

"Mom?"

I peered at her face. She was asleep.

With careful movements, I leaned her into the corner of the couch. She snored softly. I covered her with a quilt.

No sleep for me. My thoughts spun, wild and restless. I wanted to check on Brock and Sophie and learn who was winning the battle.

I left Mom snoozing and tracked down Brady and Dad's room. For some reason, the Gnomes separated our family male and female, rather than parents and kids. Maybe it had something to do with their attendants taking care of mixed company.

I rapped on the door and whispered Brady's name. If they were asleep, I didn't want to disturb them.

The door cracked open enough to reveal my brother's face. "Let me guess. Mom's asleep, and you can't sit still."

"How'd you know?"

He pulled the door open to reveal Dad sprawled in a chair, sawing logs.

I grinned. "Mom always says sleep's the best medicine. Let's find Sophie and Brock."

"My thoughts exactly." He stepped out and closed the door.

"Where's Lava? Didn't he come with you?"

"Yeah. He grabbed some food—ike, the biggest

plateful I've ever seen—and said he was off to join his troops on the battlefield."

"What about Gage?"

Brady shrugged. "He stayed behind. I think he wanted to get Zest taken care of."

"I see."

We wandered down the hall and took a few random turns. It didn't take long to lose our bearings. We questioned the Gnomes about Brock and Sophie, but the war seemed everyone's concern. After the fourth or fifth "no," it was time to request someone higher up the food chain.

Someone like Sir Noblin or Revonika.

Success! We were escorted to a set of ornate doors. "They're in a meeting, but I'll let them know you're here."

A moment later, Revonika stuck her head out and beamed. "You're back!" She rushed up, skidding to a stop in front of us, hands clasped. "I'm so pleased to see you've returned. I heard you and your parents had arrived. It's the best news I've had in days!"

Her look turned grim. "Things are tense out there, y'know. Very precarious. We're grateful for the help from Calamus. The good news is we think the tide is turning. The Trolls arrived soon after Queen Judith returned from Berganstroud. It's been ugly these last two days. But since the Nephilim arrived, we've seen success. I'm sorry, but I *must* get back. We can visit more at supper tonight—if we have time to eat."

My brain buzzed, processing Revonika's rapid-fire information. I reached out a hand to stop her chatter. "We're trying to find Sophie and Brock. Can you tell us where they are? Our parents want to see them."

"Brock is with the queen, and...uh..." Her brows furrowed. "I think Sophie's with Brock."

"Okaaay," Brady drawled. "Where's that?"

Revonika swallowed. "On the battlefield. Gotta go!"

She disappeared, leaving me dumbfounded. "The *battlefield*?"

"What on earth are they doing out there?" Brady grabbed his scalp with both hands. "We left them in

Vituvia to stay *safe*. Brock might need to learn to lead troops in battle, but Sophie has no business out there."

"You really think Sophie is going to sit in a castle and play princess when there are giants to slay?" I shook my head. "No way."

"They probably told her to stay out, but she left anyway."

"Ha! No doubt." I threw up my hands. "What now?"

"We can stay here and play it safe or go out there and get dirty. We sure won't waltz through the combat zone and stumble on the two of them chatting. If we go out there, we're involved."

"If the enemy doesn't kill us, Mom will." I laughed. "She'll go ballistic when she wakes up and discovers none of her kids can be found."

"You got that right. So, what's your call?"

A week ago I would've played it safe. Not anymore. I held up my hand for a high-five. "Let's roll."

CHAPTER THIRTY-SEVEN

Finding our way out of the castle proved a battle in itself.

After multiple dead-ends, we resorted to crawling out a window and onto a lower portion of the roof. From there, we hung from the edge and dropped to the ground. G.I. Jane, at your service.

Vituvia felt like a ghost town. A smattering of mothers tended their children in hushed, fretful voices. Elderly Gnomes peered from the windows and watched us pass. Their anxiety was palpable. If these optimistic, jolly people were this tense, it must be for good reason.

We followed the sounds of combat. The clash of metal on metal led us closer to the shouts and cries of war. Maybe this wasn't such a great idea. I grabbed Brady's hand. "Promise me we won't get separated. Stay with me."

He squeezed. "Wouldn't dream of it, sis. Sure you don't want to go back? There's nothing to prove, you know. You've been amazing."

Is he reading my mind? I smiled. "Thanks, but I'm sure. *Scared* but sure."

At last we came to the wall surrounding the town. I hadn't paid much attention to it when we left for Berganstroud. Windows dotted the perimeter, and it appeared to have rooms inside. Quite an immense structure for such petite people.

"Let's find a way to the top of the wall," I said. "Maybe we can get a read on which way to go, instead of marching into who-knows-what."

We took the first opening and found a set of stairs that rose beneath an arched doorway. We climbed the steps, which turned sharply before opening onto the wall. Slowly, we peeked out from the top of the stairwell. Gnomes, evenly spaced along the perimeter, aimed bows and arrows. Cannons boomed. Catapults flung massive stones.

Feeling secure in close proximity to these war machines, we stooped low and scurried between two Gnomes stationed at the parapet. With a start, one of them turned on us, ready to zing an arrow at our throats.

We threw our hands up in surrender.

The Gnome mumbled something about "the nerve of people sneaking about in the middle of a war" and returned to his post. Another Gnome came up from the stairwell. He carried an armload of arrows and made rounds restocking.

Brady and I inched our faces over the barrier for our first glimpse of the battle. Lifeless bodies littered the ground. They lay in stark contrast to the vigorous fighting that percolated the field in hand-to-hand combat. The Nephilim on mighty draft horses faced off against the Trolls. Many of the brutes fought on foot, while others rode large, Griffin-like beasts with heads like eagles.

Great, another creepy creature to get acquainted with.

A cannon ball exploded. Trolls toppled to the ground. Gnomes and Dwarves struggled with Stygians and Leprechauns. Their slender swords glinted then impaled the enemy. Blood spattered friend and foe.

I would never look at Aunt Jules' cute little statues in quite the same way.

"Sophie and Brock are out there, in the middle of *that*?" I shuddered. "How will they survive?"

"I don't know. But I'm not going to sit here and wring my hands. Let's get down there and fight."

"Excuse me." The Gnome who'd delivered the arrows

joined us. "Aren't you the brother and sister of King Brock and Princess Sophie?"

I nodded. "Do you know where they are?"

He looked around as if someone might overhear. Leaning towards us, he said in a loud whisper, "The prophecy is about to be fulfilled."

"Excuse me?" Surely I misunderstood.

"You know. The *prophecy*. Your brother and sister are bound to fulfill it. It's their destiny."

"Sorry, little dude." Brady shook his head. "You need to back up. We've never heard about any prophecy."

The Gnome looked stunned. "Then allow me to do the honors." He motioned us back to the stairwell. "Over here. It's quieter."

We joined him in the narrow passageway.

He sat a few steps above us. "Name's Conley, by the way. No sense remaining strangers, eh?"

"I'm Brady. This is Sadie."

I tensed, wanting to get to the point. "You were saying something about a prophecy?" What's up with mythical creatures and prophecies? Why are there always prophecies?

"Yes. King Clive, great-grandfather to Queen Judith and former ruler of the realm—though only for a brief time—was a great prophet. His prophecies were recorded in his famous book, *The Book of Prophecies*."

"Catchy name," I quipped.

He nodded, clearly missing the sarcasm. "He wrote a prophecy about the Land of Legend being thrown into war. About a wise one and a small one saving the land. We believe your brother and sister are the wise one and the small one."

"*Who* believes that?" I asked.

"Sir Noblin, Queen Judith, and many others."

Brady raised an eyebrow. "How many of these 'prophecies' from King Clive have ever come true?"

Good question, bro.

"This will be the first." The Gnome straightened, proudly.

"Uh-*huh*." I cleared my throat. "What makes you think

he's a prophet if you haven't seen anything he predicted come to pass?"

"Because he predicted the *future*, silly. The future has only now arrived."

He had a point. Still... "What exactly does this prophecy say?"

Conley closed his eyes and recited with dramatic flair:

"When the beasts howl,
The wise one shall come.
When the beasts wander,
The wise one shall protect.
When the beasts rage against the weaker ones,
The wise one shall have strength.
When the beasts consume the small one,
The wise one shall dash them to pieces.
From the small, the wise shall rise,
From the two, the beasts shall retreat.
The hope of the small
will be passed on to all."

When he finished speaking, he gave us a knowing look. "Incredible, isn't it? Surely you can see the importance of this time in our history and the part your family must play."

Puh-leese! I shook my head. "I can't imagine a more vague description. Could be *any* two people, doing what people do to protect their country. No offense, but compared to a Gnome, my sister is a giant. I'd think the *small one* would be your sort of folk, not our sister. And frankly, Clive isn't much of a poet. Only the last two lines rhyme."

Conley scrunched his face. "I didn't say he was a *poet!* He's a *prophet*. Besides, that's a rough translation because Clive didn't speak English. It's obviously talking about your family. What else could it mean?"

"It could mean two *other* people doing what people do to protect their country," Brady repeated.

Conley threw up his hands.

"Look." I tried a calming tone. "It's flattering to think the prophecy may be speaking of our family. I guess we'll know for certain when this is over. What we need to do now is *find* our brother and sister. We haven't seen them in days. Can you help us?"

"That's just it. Your sister has been consumed."

"*What?*" Brady and I shouted.

"You heard me. Consumed. Taken captive," explained Conley.

"That's better than what I was thinking." I shivered. "But it's still bad."

Conley crossed his arms. "Yes. Exactly like the prophecy."

"I don't know." Brady looked skeptical. "Consumed is different than kidnapped."

"It's a figure of speech. Don't you have that where you come from? Hyperbole? Rhetoric?" The Gnome hopped up and down on the step.

"Calm down." Brady pressed his hands towards the Gnome. "What's being done about it? Is Queen Judith negotiating? Is there a rescue plan?"

Conley shook his head. "Not likely. The incident with Sophie happened right before I came with my delivery, not far from where I was working. A scout ran to give a report but I doubt there's been time to respond."

He squinted at us. "Arrows don't grow in gardens, ya know. It's my job to go out on the battlefield and collect the ones that are still in good shape. You see a lot of ugly things out there. Not to mention the danger of trying to avoid getting killed while I do my job."

Brady jumped up. "Look, we can't sit here and yak about this. Sophie needs help. Where can we get weapons? Will you help us find her?"

"And where's Brock?" I stood beside my brother. "You didn't mention him."

"Can't say for sure." Conley stroked his chin. "When he saw what happened to Sophie, he disabled the Styg he was fighting and ran off into the woods."

"Can you get us weapons?" Brady repeated. "And show us where you last saw them?"

"Certainly."

"You've been very helpful, Conley." I patted his

shoulder "We appreciate it."

"Humph. Didn't sound like it a minute ago."

"Sorry. We're a bit...skeptical." I shrugged. "Nothing personal."

He didn't answer but took the stairs down, out of sight. A door creaked open, then shut, then opened again. In a moment he reappeared with human-sized weapons, two swords and two daggers.

"Wow, thanks." Brady took one of each and secured them under his belt.

I did the same.

"Follow me." Conley led us through a narrow path built into the wall. We came to a trapdoor that fed into a long, underground tunnel—built for Gnomes, of course, and painful on my knees. The bodily torture stopped when we ascended a ladder into an enormous, hollowed-out tree.

"Cool!" Brady pressed his eye against a knothole in the wood. There were many such holes lighting up the dark insides of the tree with pinpricks of light, like a starry night.

I put my eye against the nearest hole. More trees. Not helpful. I felt my way to another hole and peeked out. I could make out blurry shapes in the distance, which I took to be people fighting.

"Let's step out and find the closest tree to hide behind," Conley instructed. "From there we'll assess the situation."

A hidden door—part of the trunk—creaked open, exposing an overgrown path through a grove of evergreens. Brady and I crawled out. I dashed one way and hid behind a tree trunk. He dashed to the one beside me. The sound of the battle rang in my ears. *I'm* so *ready for this to be over.*

From between the trees, I spied violent, hand-to-hand combat. Most of it stayed on the battlefield, though some spilled into the edge of the woods. Soldiers from both sides looked weary. The warriors on foot were engaged in slow-motion battles: arduous blows, staggering steps, and labored thrusts. Those on horseback appeared more animated. They charged and grappled with greater fervency.

Most Trolls fought on foot, still head and shoulders taller than Dwarves on horseback. Others rode the creatures I'd spied from the wall. Similar to a legendary Griffin, their bodies were more horse-like than lion-like. Their eagle's heads sported enormous, pointed beaks and melded to wings that, if stretched out, would rival a Cessna airplane.

"What are those animals the Trolls are riding?"

"Hippogriffs. Easier for the big oafs to tame than Griffins—though Griffins were popular in the past."

"Interesting." Something to ask Mom about later.

A commotion came from the denser part of the forest. I shifted around to the other side of my tree trunk and watched. So did Brady. Four Trolls strode into view, wrangling one feisty little girl.

My heart plunged. Sophie was bound and hoisted over the heads of two Trolls. She screamed something incoherent. I stifled a cry. Brady gave me a stern look, much like my father did when I needed to be strong. I bit my lip and tasted blood.

The Trolls carried Sophie through the woods and back towards the battlefield.

How could I stop this?

We tailed the Trolls from a safe distance. The brutes marched into the heart of the mayhem. *It's a good thing Mom and Dad can't see this.*

The combatants closest to Sophie and the Trolls paused to watch the procession. Like a ripple on the water, strife ceased across the battlefield.

The Trolls brought Sophie to a slab of rock that sat like a massive stone stage in the middle of the clearing. On top, a Stygian and a Dwarf disentangled themselves from their skirmish. They scrambled down on opposite sides when they saw the Yetis approach.

One towering Troll bounded onto the rock platform. The two holding Sophie shoved her into his paws. He lifted her writhing body overhead and walked around the huge boulder like a boxer displaying his championship belt in the ring.

Sophie squirmed and screeched.

"Lookie what we have here!" the Troll bellowed. "It might not be the king, but it's the next-best thing."

The enemy went wild.

"Noooo!" Brady sprinted to the rock, sword drawn.

I dropped to my knees beside Conley and covered my face. "I'm going to lose them *both*."

"No, my friend." He squeezed my shoulder. "Don't lose heart. The Maker has the last word. He sent us that prophecy for assurance."

"That prophecy is a load of senseless babble."

Before Conley could react, I heard Brady challenge, "Take me instead if you're man enough to fight. Let her go. She's only a child."

The Troll spun around, nearly dropping Sophie. He reeled backwards and gave a yellow-fanged smile. "Well, well, if it isn't his highness himself. Brave Brock of Vituvia."

Was this a good or bad case of mistaken identity?

Brady stood at the base of the rock. He pumped his fist at the towering beast. "C'mon, Chewbacca! I'm not afraid of you."

The Troll lowered Sophie to chest level and fixated on Brady. He squatted down as if to offer her to my brother, then dropped Sophie on the rock. She cried out in pain.

"Yes, so brave." He stood up, arms crossed. "So brave...and so stupid."

"Brady, behind you!" I screamed.

Two Trolls jumped Brady from the rear. They disarmed him in an instant. Cheers from Dark Dwarves and Trolls erupted across the field.

My impulsive, big mouth attracted attention I didn't need. Two Stygians rushed my way. It was inevitable. I was going down. But I wouldn't go easy. At twice their height, I could inflict damage.

The closest Styg barreled straight for me, ready to plow me over. I slammed my knee into his nose with a satisfying crack. He careened backwards as the other Dwarf reached me. The knee jab had thrown me off balance. The Styg toppled me over. With guttural screams, we wrestled on the ground. I clawed his face, but instead of flesh I only grasped handfuls of his wiry beard.

A glint of steel flashed to my left. Conley moved in. The Dark Dwarf's eyes grew round, and blood gurgled from his mouth. I jerked my head away to avoid the crimson drips. The Styg's grip on my throat loosened. His head bashed into my brow bone.

I winced. "Ugh!"

Before I heaved him away, a Troll towered overhead. His beady, evil eyes drilled mine. A colossal hand descended. It dragged me by my hair, out from under the dead Dwarf.

I screamed and grabbed at his hands. Before I knew which way was up, he pinned me beneath his arm. My face smothered into his matted, brown fur. Protesting further meant a mouthful of hair and no air.

I'm doomed.

"Accept defeat, Vituvia!" the Troll howled from the rock. "Nekronok will soon arrive. Submit to your new authorities, and you will be spared. We will let you live as our slaves."

More cheers.

My captor flung me down on the stone stage like a hunk of meat. I stifled a cry. My head throbbed, a goose egg swelled above my eye, and the length of my spine shot with pain. I lay limp, afraid I might shatter if I moved.

My fears were immediately tested. Someone went straight to work, gagging and tying me up. I found myself face to face with Skoon—that wretched, little Leprechaun! He danced a jig next to my incapacitated body. I glared and screeched against the gag. Fury overwhelmed my pain. *If I make it out alive, you're a goner, ya little demon.*

I squirmed enough to get a view of the horrific scene. Three out of the four Larcen kids sent to save the Tethered World were now bound and tethered.

The enemy chanted, "Nek-ro-nok! Nek-ro-nok!"

Something descended from the dome of the sky. It

careened down to the battlefield. The crowd hushed. The Troll on the rock bowed towards the approaching creature. He spread out his arms as if to offer the bodies of my siblings and me as sacrifices.

A sadistic-looking Troll straddled the back of a flying Hippogriff. The pair circled the rock like a vulture. *Nekronok, I presume.*

The Hippogriff touched down in the space between our shackled bodies. Trolls, Stygs, and Leprechauns kowtowed. The good guys stood in silent defeat.

The eagle head of the giant, flying *thing* loomed above me. Its beak was the size of my arm and capable of a quick lobotomy. He cocked his head, the way birds do, and studied me like I was his first meal in months.

Should I play dead like you're supposed to with a bear?

The bird creature blocked my view of the chief Troll, but I could sense him. Evil slithered from his presence like oozing pus. It drifted down the rock and onto the battlefield.

"We won't be defeated, you big ugly ape. You're going down!" Sophie shouted.

I jerked my head at my sister and tried to yell through my gag but couldn't. *Zip it, sis!* Skoon helped my cause by gagging her.

Tears drizzled my face. I reminded myself of what Conley had said about God having the last word. My faith gauge felt empty.

Nekronok prattled on and on with a victory speech, but my brain numbed. Nothing registered beyond an intense desire to disappear.

Loud shouts from across the battlefield nudged me back to the reality of this nightmare. The ruckus drowned out Nekronok's spiel, and he grew quiet. Even the eagle-monster above riveted his eyes at the commotion. I twisted and contorted to roll over and get a look for myself. Pain ripped through my body.

But my physical pain was nothing compared to the stab of anguish at the sight unfolding before me.

Chebar sat astride Sonnet, the Pegasus. Brock rode in

front of him, hands tied, mouth muzzled. The Yeti's arm encircled my brother in a headlock. "Father! Your Majesty! To make your conquest complete, I offer you King Brock, the now-deposed, future ruler of Vituvia."

CHAPTER THIRTY-EIGHT

"I KNEW THE RUMORS OF YOUR insubordination were false." Nekronok slid off the back of the mutant bird. "No son of mine could be such a traitor. Well done, Chebar. Bravo!"

Chebar nudged Sonnet to the boulder near where I lay.

Coward! Mole! Backstabber! Bitter thoughts flew through my head.

Brock straddled the Pegasus and looked through me. As usual. He seemed calm despite his incarceration. That was *not* usual. Not at all.

"Thank you, Father." Chebar climbed down from Sonnet. "Forgive the pretense of mutiny. I'm grateful that you had faith in me despite appearances." He sprang up onto the rock and faced his father.

"Not a favorite trait to have to exercise, my son. This... *faith*."

They stood a few feet from where I lay. Nekronok gave Chebar an intimidating stare. Chebar held his gaze a moment then stooped to one knee and bowed his head in deference.

Another Troll approached Brock. He plucked him from the horse and shoved him onto the rock platform. My brother rolled towards the feet of Chebar and Nekronok, facing me. His eyes searched mine. Something in his gaze hinted that he understood his predicament as well as I did.

Make that four—out of four—Larcen kids bound, gagged, and out of commission.

Nekronok gave an evil, satisfied chuckle. He yanked Brock to his feet. "Well, well. Looks like there's two of you Brock fellows. No matter, since I own you both." He twitched his head towards Brady. "Bring me that other pitiful little boy, Chebar."

Chebar wrenched Brady upright. My brother struggled to stay erect despite his bindings while Chebar dragged him to Nekronok.

"Ngiarh!" I growled at Chebar through the stuffing in my mouth. Translation: Liar!

A rough yank on my hair forced me to face that deplorable imp, Skoon. He stuffed his fist, and the gag, further into my mouth. "You need to remember who you're talking to, missy. If you're lucky, you—"

Bam! With a well-placed head-butt, I sent the Leprechaun sailing to my feet. The next second I punted him off the rock with a solid *thunk*. It was a beautiful thing.

Nekronok chuckled. "Better watch yourself, Leprechaun. She's five times your size." He turned to my brothers and snatched at their gags. "Have you anything to say before I kill you and take over your kingdom?"

"Never mind." He shoved the cloth back into their mouths so far they coughed and heaved. "I've been waiting a long time for the Flaming Sword of Cherubythe. Why waste any more precious time listening to you?"

Brock glanced at Brady. A strange look passed between them.

Suddenly, Brock's fetters fell to the ground. He yanked the gag from his mouth and pulled out Brady's gag. Brady turned on Chebar—his arms and legs miraculously free—and lunged at the traitor.

Brock descended on Nekronok. With one deft movement, he gave the chief a debilitating karate kick to the gut. The overgrown ape reeled backwards but steadied himself. Brock didn't give up the advantage. He spun, landed a roundhouse kick, and swiped a length of rope from the ground.

Though my right eye had swollen shut beneath a knot on my brow bone, I tore my gaze away from Brock long enough to see that Brady had the upper hand with Chebar. My brother dangled from the Troll's back, choking him in a headlock. The creature gasped for air and faltered.

I braced myself for a rush of Trolls and Stygians. Surely the enemy wouldn't stand by and watch their heroes go down! But a glance across the battleground revealed the Vituvian army engaged with the enemy, clearly revived by this amazing turn of events.

Nekronok mutated to demonized madness. He charged Brock with a bloodcurdling screech. Brock didn't flinch. He sprang up and over Nekronok in an acrobatic feat that looped the piece of rope around the Yeti's neck. He then landed on Nekronok's back with a knee jab to the spine.

The chief Troll reared up and roared. Saliva exploded from his mouth. Brock clung to the rope and wrapped his legs around the big lug's torso. Nekronok staggered. His eyes bulged. Foam frothed from the corners of his lips.

Brock kept a steady grip, but it didn't appear to be enough against such a massive brute. The Troll grappled with my brother's legs and tried to pry them apart. Brock gritted his teeth and grunted, pulling the rope tighter. My good eye bulged when Nekronok squeezed Brock's ankle. I heard a hollow *pop.*

Brock yelped in agony but didn't let up on the rope.

A huge, hairy foot landed beside my head. A Troll rushed past, headed for my brawling brothers. I hoisted my roped legs up and caught him in the shin on his next step. He careened headlong towards Brady. My brother walloped the ape with a kick in the face that sent him tumbling off the rock.

A dark shadow slid across my vision. Nekronok looked up the same time I did. Xander hovered above the beast. His swift, iron fist rammed into the Troll's face.

Nekronok capsized on top of my legs, eyes rolled back. His fangs dripped a mixture of spittle and blood from the blow. Brock released the beast and slid from his back, limping away.

An instant later, Chebar crumpled, unconscious, over his father's body. Brady still had the Troll in a headlock. "Take that, you lying beast!" He shoved the double-crosser in the back and stood.

Between the gag and the weight of the Yetis, I fought for breath. *I've gotta get out from under this pile of primates!*

Two more Trolls scaled the rock and lunged at Brady. Brock whipped Nekronok's sword from its sheath and took aim at the chief's neck. "Stop!"

Xander landed beside Brock, a guardian angel in the flesh.

The Trolls did an about-face and scrammed.

Xander seized the two unconscious Trolls by the scruff of their necks and pitched them aside like a couple of discarded rugs. The twins worked quickly to bind the hands and feet of the monsters.

During the midst of this—inexplicably—the ropes binding my wrists and ankles came loose. The raw ache in my extremities vanished. *What?* I tugged the gag from my mouth and sat up, searching for my accomplice. I saw no one. I flicked my gaze across the rock, focusing with one good eye. Sophie was free too. She looked as perplexed as I felt.

Someone brought the Hippogriff a bucket of feed. It morphed from a wild beast to a domestic freak of nature. It lay down, sphinx-like, and began to eat itself into oblivion.

Though Brock favored his ankle, he and Brady lashed the two Trolls together. With Xander's help they strapped the chief and his son across the Hippogriff's back.

On the battlefield, a few skirmishes continued to boil over. Other conflicts ended with the enemy bound and debilitated—or dead.

The sound of bugles swelled clear and sweet, calming the atmosphere. They broadcast the victory, unfurling their exultant notes like a flag of triumph. A large procession of Nephilim soldiers approached on horseback.

The enemy scattered but found themselves intercepted by victorious Gnomes and Dwarves.

"Make way for the royal procession!"

Xander leapt from the rock to receive the cavalcade. One by one, horses and riders arranged themselves in two rows. They faced one another, forming an aisle in between.

My legs felt unsteady, but I willed them in the direction of my siblings. Sophie, the boys, and I slipped our hands together and watched the entourage arrive. Cheers erupted all around.

And to think that a few moments ago I didn't expect to live through the day.

Once the mounted soldiers took their places, several Toboggans, carrying the governing Gnomes, parked themselves between the horses.

The buglers blasted their instruments again. The allies stood at attention with exultant faces, holding their enemies under submission with ropes or chains. Several Vituvian flags were hoisted in victory.

I glanced at Nekronok and Chebar, wondering if they were aware of their defeat. Nope. They remained unconscious. And they had company.

Several petite people stood on the backs of the flaccid Trolls. They had well-proportioned bodies with pointy, leaf-shaped ears, and were smaller than Gnomes or Leprechauns. They yanked on the matted Yeti fur, laughing and dancing about.

Wow! Another not-so-mythical creature—whatever they are.

The sounds of celebration surged. I turned to see Queen Judith, King Aviel, and Wogsnop riding through the middle of the soldiers. They waved at the Gnomes and Dwarves that pressed between the horses to greet them. The three riders came to a halt in front of our rock.

Xander ordered one of his men to help the queen from her mount and onto the platform. The four of us kneeled. A hush swept through the masses.

"Rise, brave Larcens," Queen Judith commanded. "I applaud yer valor, yer bravery, and yer faith to carry out yer mission and protect the Sword. You've proven yerselves courageous, resourceful, and wise. Vituvia shall be forever in yer debt."

The multitude roared their approval.

The nightmare ends! Finished! Parents—rescued. Sword of Cherubythe—safe. Vituvia—secure. The good guys won. I couldn't stop smiling.

I caught sight of two horses galloping our way. I recognized Gage first, then... Mom and Dad!

My parents rode together. Dad sat in front and Mom behind, one arm around his waist. Her other arm held her ribcage, but her smile hid the pain.

They stopped in front of Xander and dismounted. He helped Mom and Dad onto the platform, where they rushed to the four of us. We were smothered with hugs and kisses and tears of joy. All of my aches and bruises forgotten in the frenzy. It was a big, happy mess of Larcen love, worth every crazy thing I'd gone through. The crowd's jubilation drowned out anything my parents said, but I had a good idea of what they wanted us to know.

I wanted them to know it too. *I love my crazy family!*

When the fervor ebbed, we stood and looked over the battlefield, arms interlaced. My cheeks ached from grinning. Talk about a happy ending!

Queen Judith signaled everyone to quiet down. "The Sword of Cherubythe is safe." Cheers erupted.

"Vituvia is *safe*." More cheers.

"Our enemy is vanquished!" The crowd's delirium sprang off the charts.

The queen didn't seem to mind pausing between sentences. "Yer new king has proven himself on the field of battle. He's fulfilled the long-anticipated prophecy of King Clive. And he's ready to begin his apprenticeship and prepare for his reign when he comes of age."

The throng screamed its approval and broke into a chant. "High King Brock! High King Brock! High King Brock!" Those on stage joined voices, clapping in syncopation.

Brock grinned. Not embarrassed. Not proud.

Just himself...balancing on one leg.

The rally cry calmed. Queen Judith signaled to have Sonnet brought to where we stood. The Pegasus waited with regal composure while Brock hobbled to the edge of the rock and carefully mounted.

Then Sonnet galloped down the aisle of soldiers like a plane on a runway. With wings unfurled, the Pegasus took Brock on a victory flight over the battleground. A torrent of tears soaked my cheeks. He circled near, and I could read the rapture on his face. I smiled and waved both arms. *You rock, little brother!*

The queen continued. Her petite frame belied her commanding voice. "Gnomes of Vituvia, Nephilim of Calamus, Dwarves of Berganstroud, Elves of Willowmist. Tomorrow at this time we will gather for a victory feast. We share this victory because all of us came together, worked together, and fought together for the safety and freedom of the Tethered World. I offer my personal gratitude to every brave warrior on this field. Let each of us give gratitude to our Maker. Long live the peace of this realm!"

Somehow, the crowd found more energy in their vocal cords and gave it up for the queen again. I clapped too, but my enthusiasm waned as my adrenaline took a plunge. I craved a pillow and a blanket more than anything.

"Chain the prisoners together in the valley hollow. General Muggleridge will give ya further instructions," the queen continued. Then she turned to our family. "Larcens, let us depart for the palace. There ye may refresh yerselves and enjoy a proper reunion."

Best proposition I'd heard in eons.

Two Nephilim soldiers trotted their mounts to where we stood. Brady and Sophie swung up behind each of them. Xander whistled, and his brawny draft horse galloped to where he waited. The warrior offered me his hand.

I took it with a smile. A crooked smile that reminded me of my swollen face. My battle scars were beautiful. Hopefully.

The jaunt back to the city sobered me. The splayed bodies of wounded and dead soldiers was a reality check in the midst of the revelry. Freedom had cost them everything. It could've been any one of us Larcens counted among the dead.

I even found it difficult to see the enemy lying lifeless and contorted. To think that such creatures had once roamed Paradise with Adam and Eve. I saw how the Fall had created a rippling effect on everything—everywhere.

It made me ache to the bone.

CHAPTER THIRTY-NINE

The hum of palace activity deflected my thoughts from the battlefield's carnage. The victorious news zinged through the corridors like lightning. Everyone's jovial mood revved up my tired spirit.

Brock needed his ankle checked. The rest of us went to our appointed rooms—girls in one, guys in another—for much-anticipated baths. Getting sudsy and clean invigorated me as well as a nap. I ran puckered fingers through my tangled, dripping hair and relished the feel. Wet equals cleaned.

Though scrubbed, I couldn't wash the day's images from my mind. "I can't stop replaying the predicament we were in. Wish I could shut it off."

Sophie nodded. "Same here." Mom worked a brush through my sister's hair in front of a large, oval mirror.

"Everything flipped around so…miraculously." I swiped Sophie's towel and squeezed the excess water from my locks.

"Yep. A miracle is the only word for it." Mom smiled at our collective reflection. "Each of you was so brave—not that it surprises me. Still, the things you faced… from rescuing us to getting tied up on top of that rock." She shuddered. "I'm terribly glad I didn't see what happened out there. To think of you bound and gagged, strung out on that big rock like human sacrifices—ugh!" She brushed at Sophie's snarls with a vengeance.

"Ouch!" Sophie swatted the brush. "I'm not the enemy."

"Oops. Sorry, love." Mom planted a kiss on her head.

I plopped onto an inviting couch and swung my feet up. With my good eye, I watched Mom work on Sophie. My swollen eye had endured a slab of raw meat and a gooey, herbal balm.

"You should've seen Brock and Brady take down those big apes, Mom." Sophie jumped up, animated. "Crazy stuff! All of their karate training kicked in—literally." She giggled. "And then Xander flew in and helped Brock finish off the chief. He's like a real-life superhero, y'know. He flies and everything. But I still don't understand how those ropes came off our hands and feet. Wasn't that the weirdest thing, Sadie?"

My sister's voice called from a distance. Part of my brain knew the sound waves were directed at me, but the rest of my cranium coasted into dreamland.

"Sadie?"

Did someone say something?

I LIED. THE NAP definitely beat out the bath. But maybe it reigned supreme because I washed away the gunk beforehand.

The sleeping shapes of my mother and sister—along with the sumptuous yet primitive surroundings—reminded me we were safe and together again. A thrill rippled through my body. The way it does when you wake up and realize it's Christmas or the day you're leaving for vacation.

We get to go home.

I closed my eyes and relished this truth, willing the surreal buzz in my brain to take another lap. Nothing awful remained for me to gut out—except maybe the ride home on the back of a dragon. But that was a positive sort of scariness.

Life could finally return to normal.

Normal... did I know what that word meant anymore? Could I pick up where I left off? Could I treat this detour as merely a hiccup in my life as a teenager?

I had no inkling about what repercussions I'd face.

The door to our room creaked open. Joanie shuffled inside with an armful of fine clothing.

"Joanie!" I said in a whisper-shout. "You're here."

Her face split into a wide grin. "Of course I'm 'ere, love. It's time for the party. You know us Dwarves won't miss a chance to eat, drink, and be merry. I begged the good Gnomes to put me to work takin' care of ya."

She winked and dumped her load on a nearby chair. "I heard about the bravery of ye Larcen children." She bowed deeply. "The magnificent Creator gave ya favor. We're so thankful that our land is safe once again."

I smiled. "Me too. I can't take any credit. You never know what you're capable of until you're put to the test."

Joanie nodded. "No doubt, love, no doubt." She looked at the mound of dresses. "Well now, the party starts soon. We need to get ya spiffed up and ready to be presented."

I shook my head, confused. "The party isn't until tomorrow. Why get ready now?"

She chuckled. "It *is* tomorrow, sweetheart. Ye've been sleepin' like the dead. I've come and gone numerous times. None of ya so much as changed positions between visits."

"Seriously?" I couldn't comprehend sleeping that long. *Am I trapped in Brady's body?*

"Seriously."

"Guess we needed it."

"Saving the world is tough work."

"You can say that again."

She looked at me, confused. "Why should I?"

"Oh, not really. It's a Topsider expression. It means you're making a good point."

She nodded. "I see. Now, would ya like to wake yer sister and mother or shall I?"

"Sophie will be thrilled to see your smiling face. You wake her, and I'll wake Mom."

Soon we were taking turns before the mirror, twirling about and practicing our best curtsies. The dresses were grand. Made from piles of silky fabric with intricate embroidery, they were fancier than any prom dress topside. I sensed these gowns were custom made. They fit Mom, Sophie, and me perfectly.

The Gnomes' treatment for my eye had worked wonders. The swelling was more felt from the inside than noticed from the outside—though my skin still swirled with purplish hues.

We followed Joanie through a marbled hallway. My garnet-colored dress made a wonderful swishy sound. I couldn't resist a little spin to watch the skirt billow out. I felt like I'd stepped from the pages of a Jane Austen novel. Now, where was Mr. Darcy?

Joanie called over her shoulder, "I'm takin' ya to the queen's advisory chamber. She wants to meet with the royal families and the dignitaries to discuss tonight's order of events."

We stepped into a well-appointed room stuffed with friends and family. Cleaned up and rested, we looked altogether different from the scruffy adventurers we'd become over the past week. Queen Judith made her way around the gathering, greeting her guests.

Xander's eyes were quick to find me. Mine were quick to look away. I felt that awful, frantic heartbeat again, accompanied by a hot blush. Probably the same color as my dress. Enough! Get a grip.

Rounds of hugs and handshakes took place. I noted that Queen Estancia had condescended to grace us with her presence. She smiled at Queen Judith, but it didn't seem to affect her general air of iciness.

One group settled on comfy cushions that lay strewn across the floor. Others stood. Sort of a casual way to entertain well-dressed dignitaries, but who was I to question the ways of Gnomes?

A space near Brock looked like a good place to plant myself. "Hello there, High King Brock." I squirmed to untwist my dress.

Brock's ankle sported a sturdy splint wrapped with leather cords. It stuck out from his black, linen pants. "I'm not high king. I have to go to school."

"Yes, but you *will* be king one day." I looked at his profile. "I think you'll be a good king, Brock."

He stared straight ahead, but I saw a smile curve his mouth. "Yeah, I know my stuff."

That cracked me up. He did like knowing his stuff lately. "You do. Better than I know mine, I think." The truth of that statement stabbed me with shame, followed by a rush of pride to see my brother come into his own.

Life underground had turned everything upside down.

Sir Noblin stood and cleared his throat. "Ladies and gentlemen, kings and queens, noblemen, friends, and family. What a pleasure it is to have each of you here. Her Majesty, Queen Judith"—he gestured to where she stood—"wishes me to convey the grateful sentiments of all Vituvia to you. Words are inadequate to express our gratitude and joy at the relationship we share with our neighboring countrymen. To live in peace alongside such fine people, to fight for peace beside such valiant warriors is a rich blessing. We're grateful to the Ancient One for providing us with these important relationships and for giving us Gnomes the honor of guarding the powerful Sword of Cherubythe."

I grinned to myself. For someone who felt words were inadequate, Sir Noblin sure used his fair share.

"This battle marked the closest the enemy has come to our precious Sword," Sir Noblin went on. "It also marks the notable advancement of the Trolls in the area of combat and strategy. We can no longer afford to underestimate what they're capable of. However, with the capture of Nekronok, they've agreed to sign a peace treaty that will ensure the safety of our realm—and the Sword—for many generations."

Applause bubbled over. Sir Noblin gave a series of bows. "Yes, friends, yes. It *is* an occasion worth celebrating. That's the plan tonight, I assure you. Let us finish with the formalities here, and then we shall enjoy a splendid evening together." A funny grin lit up his face. "Before that happens, however, it is my pleasure to share a special announcement. A secret."

We looked at each other, eyebrows raised.

"Maybe 'secret weapon' is a better term," he added. "Izzy, please open the door and ask our special guest to join us."

Izzy scampered to the door—it's the best way to describe a small Gnome in fast motion—and pulled it wide to reveal… nothing.

Then a bulky figure stepped into the doorframe. A collective gasp filled the room.

Chebar faced us, a sly grin on his leathery lips.

CHAPTER FORTY

King Aviel shot up, indignant. "What's the meaning of this? Why is this vermin not chained in the dungeon and left to rot?"

Queen Judith stepped between the Nephilim king and the Troll. "There's no need to lock up a friend, dear Aviel. Allow—"

"*King* Aviel." Estancia stepped beside her husband.

The king ignored his wife. "A *friend*?"

"Yes." Queen Judith laced her fingers together. "Allow me to explain, Your Highness—*es*, and see if you don't agree."

King Aviel stepped back and crossed his arms, jaw flexed.

Queen Estancia moved into the gap. Aviel plucked her back to his side before she could speak her mind. The queen gave him an angry look but held her tongue.

Sir Noblin wrung his hands. He looked from the king to Chebar, then at the rest of us. "Chebar, our new friend, was our secret weapon. *He* came up with the plan to pretend to deliver King Brock to Nekronok as a show of allegiance. *He* thought to fake Brock's fetters, allowing Brock to take on Nekronok. And it was Chebar's quick thinking—when he stood behind Sir Brady—to work the ropes free and whisper in his ear to follow Brock's lead.

Thanks to Chebar, our Sword and our royal household are safe. There's peace in our land once again."

Silence descended. Mouths hung open. I glanced at Brady. A smirk lingered on his cut and bruised face. He looked pleased with himself for keeping the 'secret weapon' a secret.

Queen Judith stepped to Chebar and looped her arm through his. "Chebar *is* our friend. He took care of me at the Eldritch, and his plan took care of the realm."

A smattering of applause punctured the silence. It gained momentum as we stood. King Aviel and Queen Estancia did not join in the revelry but looked less agitated.

Chebar grinned and offered a stiff bow. Then he held up his hands and signaled for quiet. "Thank you for making me feel welcome." He turned to King Aviel. "I understand your hesitancy, Your Grace. If the tables were turned, I would harbor the same reservations."

The King gave a curt nod.

How rude! *We* could *all* be rotting in a dungeon right now if it weren't for this hairy hero.

"Working against my Father was not my first choice, nor an easy one," Chebar admitted. "But he made a series of harmful decisions for our Troll community—or Bigfoot community if you prefer." He winked at Mom. "Decisions that would adversely affect our peaceable neighbors. Something had to be done. I felt compelled to do it."

Sir Noblin cleared his throat. "Chebar's brilliant plan put him back into Nekronok's trust. Better yet, the chief has no idea of Chebar's collaboration with us. We now have a friend—as the saying goes—in high places. Someone on the inside who believes in Vituvia's duty to guard the Sword. Chebar stands with us in peace.

"A treaty has been signed, allowing Nekronok and Chebar safe passage back to Craventhrall in exchange for their binding cooperation. The agreement states that the ancient boundaries remain firm, and the Trolls will cease any military efforts to the contrary. They have, furthermore, agreed to occasional visits from a committee of Dwarves, Gnomes, and Nephilim to assure ourselves they're keeping the pact. We'll also form a council, which will include members of each community—including Trolls—to work through situations that arise. Are there any questions?"

Chebar would return to Craventhrall a clever champion, which kept suspicion off him. A win-win situation. Brilliant!

We took turns thanking Chebar for his brave efforts and wished him well. He would remain incarcerated with Nekronok until they left Vituvia—and conspicuously absent from the celebration. The fewer who knew of Chebar's role, the better. Once arrangements were finalized, the Dwarves would escort the two Trolls back to Craventhrall.

And then we shall all live happily ever after.

THE PARTY WAS IN full swing by the t me I joined the festivities on the palace lawn. Meadow Faeries frolicked about like luminescent spheres. A Dwarf band rocked the house with their flare for folksy jigs. Groups of people and creatures danced and chatted, enjoying refreshments that lavished a long line of tables.

The surreal spectacle heightened my senses. Everything swirled with enchantment, including my imagination. A sentry blew his bugle. The musicians and participants ground to a halt, and expectant faces turned our way.

The trumpeter lowered his instrument. A Dwarf stepped beside him and bellowed out introductions. "Presenting, their royal majesties...King Aviel and Queen Estancia of Calamus. Prince Alexander of Calamus."

Applause and cheers swelled.

"Chief Wogsnop of Berganstroud."

The Dwarves chanted, "Wog-snop! Wog-snop! Wog-snop!"

"Queen Judith of Vituvia."

Wild celebration exploded. The queen stepped forward with regal poise, every bit the equal of Estancia. The band struck up a tune, and the applause settled into rhythmic clapping. Our spry, Great-aunt Judith took to the music, hefting her layered skirt high enough to give room for skilled footwork.

Did she really need to retire? I couldn't keep up with her.

Queen Judith pranced her way to where Brock stood. He clapped stiffly but looked transfixed by the variety of life that throbbed everywhere. He snapped into focus when the Queen took his hand and pulled him out on an impromptu dance floor cleared just for them.

The bystanders' cheers rose to new heights, and I joined in the revelry. "Way to go, Brock! You're the man with the moves." *What I wouldn't give for a camera right now!*

Despite his rigid stance and splinted ankle, Brock kept tempo and pulled off a few lopsided steps. When the song wound down, he stretched out, holding our aunt at arm's length. The queen spun inward towards her partner, and he supported her in an enthusiastic dip. The finale!

The onlookers cheered their approval. Most of them, anyway. Xander's parents merely observed—no doubt too dignified for the audacious display before them.

The revelry subsided, and introductions resumed. The Dwarf raised his arms and signaled for calm. "It's apparent everyone is well-acquainted with the *newest* member of the Vituvian monarchy. Presenting His Highness Brock Larcen, Vituvian king in training."

The crowd cranked up the volume again, showering my brother with admiration. He smiled and stood there in his awkward way. I wanted him to bow and acknowledge the fanfare. To this menagerie of people, however, it seemed Brock could do no wrong. They loved him. He fit.

I flushed. Why did I always project my expectations on everyone else? *I've got serious soul searching ahead of me.*

"Let's welcome the king's parents, Sir Liam Larcen and

her Ladyship, Amy Larcen. Also, Brock's siblings—Sir Brady, Lady Sadie, and Lady Sophie." We stepped forward. I gave the crowd my best curtsy and felt more awkward than Brock looked a moment before.

When we took our seats, servants paraded over with a sumptuous spread of food. Queen Judith didn't appear interested in playing hostess, though. She pushed back her chair and joined the throng of dancers.

I grinned. Aunt Judith would prefer to dance in much the same way Brock would rather watch *Spy-bots—* endlessly.

Joanie bustled back and forth, fussing over us. "Comfortable? Thirsty? Wait 'til you taste *this*." At one point, she set a covered platter in front of my siblings and me. "A special treat for the Larcen clan." With a flourish, she removed the silver, domed lid.

I jumped in my seat and gave a yelp.

Four little creatures smiled up at us. They hugged their knees, squished in their hiding place. I recognized them as the same mischievous critters that had danced on top of Chebar and Nekronok when they lay shackled to the back of the Hippogriff.

"Surprise!" They hopped to their feet and performed a zippy jig that ended with a bow. Then they giggled and— *poof*—disappeared!

I flinched. "What was that about?"

"Yeah! Who were they?" Sophie bounced in her seat.

"They're Elves from the Woods of Willowmist," Joanie explained. "They wanted to thank ya in their own sweet way. They're a wee bit shy. But they're also the reason ya found yerselves free from the ropes on top of that great rock yesterday. The Elves invisibly came and untied yer bonds."

"How cool!" Sophie oozed amazement.

"Yes, we'd like to thank them," I said.

They reappeared.

I blinked. "Thank you!"

"Yes," Sophie added. "We're so grateful. You're all very brave. Becoming invisible is an awesome superpower."

They blushed and chuckled. Then they bounded off the table and into the crowd, where many more of the little Elves scampered about. They danced and played tag around the feet of larger partygoers.

Guests took turns performing while we ate—magic tricks from the Elves, trained animal stunts from the Gnomes, and a Dwarf skit that included a hilarious imitation of John Wayne. My personal favorite came from a deep-voiced Nephilim warrior, who sang a song equivalent to an African spiritual. It reverberated through the gathering and cast a mellow tone.

When the band resumed, they kept to the subdued tempo. Couples swayed in time to waltzes and other complicated steps that involved switching partners. Queen Judith stayed out there mixing it up. She was clearly the pizazz of the party and everyone's favorite partner.

I ate more than my share then worked off some calories dancing with Dad. He looked remarkably better than the day before but still moved with care. Next, I enjoyed Brock's version of slow dancing—holding me at arm's length in proper dance posture while stiffly rocking back and forth, favoring his ankle. With no eye contact or hint in body language, he caught me off guard more than once with a spin or a dip.

"Whoa!" I shouted. Before I recovered, we were back to his robotic rocking. "C'mon, Brock. Loosen up a little. Feel the music."

Brock gave it a shot but couldn't find the groove. I laughed.

A towering presence infringed on our partnership. My laughter trailed off when I saw the looming figure.

"May I?" Xander wanted to cut in.

Brock would have none of it. He tightened his grip and shook his head. "No, no, no."

I looked at Xander with round, innocent eyes and shrugged. Brock and I twirled off into the crowd.

When the number ended, Mom popped in to take my place as Brock's partner. Before I took two steps, Xander snatched me up. "My turn, Princess." He winked.

My first instinct was to tense up and act indifferent, but we'd been through too much together to play coy. "Very well." I took his hand. My other hand reached for his shoulder but settled for his bicep. His enormity made me self-conscious and terribly aware of my vulnerability—and equally aware of his rock-hard muscle beneath my hand.

Man of Steel. *This one doesn't need a cape to fly!*

My feet barely brushed the ground in his arms. I felt like a little girl again, twirled around by my father.

I blushed. *Xander is definitely not Dad.*

When the song finished, he pulled me away from the celebration and eased me onto a bench. He dropped to one knee, facing me.

I gulped. Oh no. At home this usually means—

"Sadie." His voice was unsteady. "I know we're from two different worlds." His silver-blue eyes appeared soft and sincere in the dusktime light. "And I know there's nothing either of us can do about it at this point."

I felt my face flare—a neon sign advertising my inner turmoil. My heart threatened to detonate. There was no way I'd risk opening my mouth to speak. I pressed my lips together, to be safe.

He took my hands in his. "I want you to know that I've never met a girl like you. You're brave and funny, and yet so... soft. I find myself wanting to protect you one minute and compete with you the next. It's strange and wonderful to feel this way. I hope you'll come back to our world and allow me to be amazed by you again."

I laughed, which melted my tension. "Of *course* you've never met a girl like me. All the girls you know are eight feet tall with their own jet packs attached to their backs."

"Jet pack?"

"It's a modern, motorized version of wings," I explained. "I appreciate your flattering words, and I can say the same: I've never met anyone like you, either. You give the expression 'tall, dark, and handsome' a whole new twist."

"Handsome?" Xander straightened his back and swelled his chest like a male bird.

"Don't get all puffed up and proud." I grinned, hoping he'd sense my teasing. "I'm trying to explain that it's no wonder we're amazed by each other. It's because we're so *different*."

"Yes."

"And…since we *are* from such different places and on unrelated paths, it wouldn't be realistic to consider anything beyond our mutual…um…amazement."

"True. But you will come back, right?"

I squeezed his hands and hoped the truth wouldn't be too stinging. "I've no idea if I'll return. It's been a wild, astonishing journey, Xander. I appreciate all you and your people did for my family. You risked so much. You were truly heroic. However…" I paused. "To be honest, I don't want to come back here if it can be helped."

Poor guy looked like I'd just shot his puppy. "*What? Why not?*"

"It's been rough." I shrugged. "I'm not like Sophie or Brady. I'm not a fan of danger or anything too out of the ordinary. I'm content to pick up where I left off Topside and pretend this never happened."

He dropped my hands. "You want to act like you never met me?"

Oops. I'm an idiot. "I'm sorry, Xander. I don't mean that the way it sounds. The fact is, I'll never forget *you*, Xander. I doubt I'll forget *anything* about this place. It's opposite in every way from where I live. That's just it. It's so different, it feels like a dream. When I'm home, this'll all seem like an alternate reality. A place contrived in my imagination."

"I think I understand what you're saying. If I traveled topside, I'd probably have the same perspective."

I nodded. He's catching on.

"Take me with you, Sadie. So I can understand."

Scratch that. "No way. You'd never blend in. The people in my world would either turn you into a superhero or lock you in a laboratory and dissect you feather by feather."

He chuckled. "I have no idea what you just said— which probably means I should stay put. Guess I'd be so far out of my element I'd want to rush back home. Like you, right?"

I smiled. "Exactly."

He clasped my hands and leaned into my cheek. My breath caught. "I'll never forget you, Princess Sadie. I shall petition the Creator to bring you back someday."

With that, Xander stood and walked away. I fought back pesky tears and watched him meld into the crowd.

There's no future here, and no sense crying.

My gaze lingered over the scene before me. This menagerie of "myths" danced and celebrated as real as my family. More than that... a *secret part* of my family. A whole world intertwined with my ancestry, and—whether I liked it or not—with my life now.

I turned and left the merriment, headed to my room. Sleep would muzzle my thoughts and usher in the great day of our return topside. *My* world.

It couldn't come fast enough.

CHAPTER FORTY-ONE

HOME. THE WORD SENT A BUZZ through my sleepy body like a shot of caffeine. Nate and Nicole. Ollie and Mindy-loo. My own room. My cell phone. My friends. College plans. Normal life within my grasp.

Anticipation launched me out of bed. On a nearby chair lay the welcome sight of my jeans, cleaned and mended. My first glimpse of normal. Joy! I pulled on the familiar, comfy clothes and felt closer to home already.

I wondered how Odyssey would know we needed a ride. Would the fog cover materialize? If not, maybe we'd have to camp inside Beacon Rock for a day or two. I could live with that. At least I'd be on *my* side of the earth's crust.

Excited by the prospect of being home within the day, I turned to wake my mom and sister. The thrill of the upcoming journey would be sweeter if I could share it. Mom snuggled next to Sophie in the four-poster bed. Sophie still wore her dress from the feast.

I placed a hand on Mom's shoulder. Her eyes flitted open. A contented smile sprawled across her mouth. "Good morning, sweetheart." She sighed. "Today's the day, isn't it?"

"Yes!" I squealed and leaned over to peck her cheek. "I'm so happy. I had to wake you guys up to be happy *with* me."

Mom laughed and stretched. "Just think. By tonight, all of us will be together again—even Nicole and Nate and Aunt Jules. We should order a big pizza and three gallons of ice cream to celebrate."

"Definitely."

"Sophie, my sweet." Mom leaned over my sister and stroked her hair. "Time to wake, sleepyhead. Today we go home."

Sophie's eyelids cracked open. She looked at Mom then turned to me. "We're going home?"

I grinned and nodded.

Sophie scrunched up her eyes and curled into her pillow. She let out a ragged sob.

"Sophie, why are you crying?" Mom laid a hand on her back.

"I don't want to go home! I love it here. I want to stay with the Gnomes. Why can't I stay? I could look out for Brock."

Mom and I exchanged looks of alarm. We wouldn't *all* be together. How could I forget? Brock was staying here.

Mom rubbed Sophie's back. "Honey, it's noble of you to want to stay with Brock. You're the sort to love the adventure of this place. But Nate and Nicole need their big sister. We want you with us. Heading home without Brock is painful enough. I could never leave you *both* behind."

Sophie didn't reply, but her crying lost its edge.

Mom slipped out of the covers and began to dress.

I plopped down next to Sophie and brushed a lock of hair from her face. "It's hard to think of leaving Brock, but he's doing things here that he could never do at home. He's connecting with the Gnomes and thinking through things. Remember when Chebar carried Brock through the battlefield and flung him on the rock? He landed right beside me. He looked at me in a way he never has before, Soph. I didn't understand it at the time. But looking back, I can see he was engaged in the plan."

"What do you mean?" The pillow muffled Sophie's

voice.

"Chebar needed Brock to be part of the deception—the double-crossing of Nekronok—and he played it perfectly. You know how miraculous that is? He *pretended* to be tied up. He waited until the right moment to shake the cords loose from his wrists. He took down the leader of the Trolls with well-placed blows and fast thinking. It's incredible. Brock was meant for this. He's going to be fine."

Sophie rolled over and looked at me through wet lashes. "Brock doesn't *ever* pretend, Sadie. That's one of those abstract things he doesn't do."

I nodded. "But he did."

She showed some teeth. "Yeah, he did."

"I think God wanted to challenge my preconceived notions. With Brock. With Mom and Dad. He's shown up in ways I never expected. Even when I didn't expect Him at all. He can be trusted to watch over Brock while we're apart."

"True." She grinned. "What's one more miracle?"

I laughed. "Exactly. Let's get up, get you changed, and have some breakfast."

"All right. I hope Joanie's still here. I like her biscuits."

We finished readying ourselves about the time a servant came to escort us to breakfast. We soon stood outside the doors of the Great Hall, meeting up with Dad and Brady.

"Where's Brock?" Mom glanced around.

"They've got him all set up for the summer," Dad said. "He slept in his own room last night. Mr. Independent."

Mom gave a wistful smile. "Hmmm, who would have thunk it?"

Dad planted a kiss on a pale bruise that stained Mom's cheek. "It's one incredible thing after another with this family."

I loved seeing them being *them* again. Their P.D.A. used to embarrass me, but not now. *A little bit of normal, right here.*

A trumpet blast sounded behind the doors. The sentries standing on either side pulled them open. An entourage of Gnomes and Dwarves stood to greet us. The queen and Brock had already found their seats. Judith gestured us to join them.

Quite the farewell breakfast. Wogsnop, Lava, and Joanie stood on one side of Brock and Queen Judith. Sir Noblin, Revonika, General Muggleridge, and Colonel Smarlow waited on the other side.

Sophie and I didn't get Joanie's biscuits for breakfast. Instead, we were thrilled to share a meal with her. The best of everything about our adventure had joined us at the table. Our family—alive and well—and all of our new friends. What a stellar way to conclude our visit.

Everyone's here... except for Xander. I smacked that thought down before it could take up residence. I was glad the Nephilim went home. These were the friends from our escapades who really mattered.

Liar.

Sir Noblin cleared his throat. "If I may interrupt your meal a moment? For the sake of making preparations, would the Larcen family prefer to travel to the Woods of Willowmist on horseback? Or would you like the Meadow Faeries to transport you in the same manner they brought you here?"

"The Faeries!" Sophie's hand shot into the air.

"Who are the Faeries, and what are they going to do with us?" Mom arched a questioning brow.

I started to explain, but Sophie cut me off. "Don't tell Mom and Dad. Let them be surprised."

"Maybe I don't *want* to travel by Faerie." Mom crossed her arms.

"Mom, you're supposed to be the expert on all these legend-things. Why wouldn't you want to experience the stuff first-hand?"

"Sophie has a point, Amy." Dad leaned back in his chair, clearly amused. "You're in danger of being demoted from 'expert' to 'chicken,' at least around the house."

"That would be tragic. Faeries it is."

"Excellent." Sir Noblin smiled. "We shall finish breakfast and see you off shortly."

My lungs constricted. We'd leave so soon? Mixed emotions bombarded me. I wanted to get back to life as I knew it, yet I didn't feel quite ready to say goodbye. I glanced around at the sea of faces. Each had whittled his or her way into my heart.

The announcement subdued the atmosphere. We lingered over breakfast, stretching out our last bit of fellowship together. Afterward, I followed Joanie back to the room with Mom and Sophie. We washed up and took turns letting the Dwarf brush our hair and make it beautiful. The chitchat slowed. Those last few minutes felt fragile. I spoke little, hoping to sear each detail into my memory.

When Joanie finished, she handed me a satchel of food and supplies. "This here is for yer journey back. I've heard how long and tedious those tunnels are. Ye may need some nourishment."

I looped the bag over my shoulder. "Thank you. For *everything*." We embraced. "You were like a mother to Sophie and me when we weren't sure we'd see ours ever again. We'll miss you terribly." I grabbed her and shed a few more tears. Sophie joined our bittersweet farewell.

Mom walked over and placed her hands on the little woman's shoulders. "Joanie, you've no idea how much it means to know you were there for my girls. I've no doubt God sent you as an answer to my prayers from captivity. I can't properly express my gratitude. Know that we will never forget your lovingkindness."

Joanie hugged my mother, long and hard. Though physically different, they were kindred spirits.

WITH AN ACHING HEART but eager feet, I followed the others back to the council room—the place where I'd first laid eyes on my Gnome friends.

Dad and the twins were already there. Tears flowed when Brady gave Brock a ferocious hug. This parting would be most difficult on Brady. He was Brock's self-appointed shadow. Brady protected him; coached and cheered him; and often interpreted Brock's behavior for the rest of us. The two were inseparable.

Until now. Brady would leave part of himself in Vituvia.

Me too. Part of me would always be connected to this place. Literally tethered here—like it or not.

We shared a tearful time all around. Loving on Brock. Hugging Queen Judith, Lava, and Revonika. Shaking hands and thanking the others—Sir Noblin and Izzy, General Muggleridge, Smarlow, and Wogsnop. An extra hug for Joanie.

I swallowed and wiped my face. The hardest part was now behind me. Then I turned to find Reiko, Mighty, and Muscle standing back, watching the commotion. *Wrong.*

Tears surged again. Reiko had been so vital during this whole, dizzy mess. Without this Gnome's logic and warrior skills, our journey might have turned out much differently—and not in a good way. One or more of us may have died.

Wait. One of us did die.

"Oh, Reiko...I..." Words escaped me. I knelt to embrace the petite warrior, crying harder than I'd cried all morning. I blubbered in her ear, "I'm heartbroken over Zest. I'm sorry you lost her." I encircled Muscle and Mighty with one of my arms and included them in my penitence. "I'm sorry your sister died trying to save us. I'm sorry for complaining. Thank you for all you sacrificed."

I pulled away to look into their eyes. I wanted them to see that I meant every word. To my surprise, each of them was as red-faced and tear-streaked as myself.

"Apology accepted, dear friend." Reiko smiled up at me. "Please accept mine. I was often harsh, and I misjudged your character. You proved yourself brave and resilient in tremendously difficult circumstances. I'm proud to know you."

From the corner of my eye, I caught sight of my parents embracing Brock in an emotional goodbye. I gave Reiko a final squeeze and rushed to join them, despondent at the thought of leaving my little brother behind.

Sir Noblin cleared his throat. "This way, please."

It was time.

We slowly disentangled from Brock. My arms and feet felt like lead. I trudged behind the others to the open space where we'd first landed in Vituvia. My head spun when I remembered that our arrival here had taken place one short week ago—give or take. In many ways, I felt as if I'd been a part of this place for a lifetime.

In some ways, I have.

I grabbed Dad and Sophie by the hand and looked out at my family and friends—all shapes and sizes—and waited.

"Beam me up, Scotty!" Brady joked.

We chuckled. Humor, a welcome antidote for our heaviness. We were so weighted down, the Faeries probably couldn't carry us across the room.

A subtle breeze lifted my bangs—the first sign of our tiny traveling companions. Gossamer flecks appeared and quickly swelled in number. My eyes could follow their movements at first. Then their speed increased, and I felt encircled with light and laughter. My hair and clothing whipped around in intense *Wizard-of-Oz* fashion. I huddled close, knowing what would happen next.

Mom let out a little squeal and giggled like she does on roller coasters.

Looking past the blur of Faeries, I noticed an engaged smile on Brock's face. He didn't look through us. He looked *at* us. His gaze traveled across our group like he wanted to memorize the significance of this moment.

Our eyes met. I smiled at him.

And he winked.

A Sneak Peek at Book Two in
The Tethered World Chronicles
Coming October 1, 2016

The Flaming Sword

CHAPTER ONE

"IS SHE DEAD?" SHOCK SHIMMIED UP my spine at the sight of Great-aunt Jules crumpled in my mother's arms. I couldn't tear my gaze from her glaring black eye, the size and color of a plum.

"Sadie!" Mom shot me a scornful look and shifted from under the weight of our Irish aunt. Not hard to do, since she was smaller than my eleven-year-old sister, Sophie. "Why do you always imagine the worst? Run and get a wet washcloth for her face."

My breath came in shallow spurts. I dashed to the guest bath and scrounged a cloth from the cupboard, turning the tap full blast. Maybe it would drown my growing alarm. It takes a certain strain of vicious behavior to attack an elderly woman in such a way.

And I've got my reasons for imagining "the worst." With vindictive force I wrung out the washcloth and darted back to Mom.

"Sophie! Brady! Come downstairs," Mom shouted. "*Now.*"

Mom snatched the washcloth and pressed it against Aunt Jules' forehead. With her other hand, she stroked the crimson curls around auntie's face, speaking in hushed tones. If not for the unnatural angle of Aunt Jules's limp body, she might have been sleeping peacefully.

I knelt beside Mom. "What's this?" I reached for a piece of paper auntie clutched to her chest.

"Don't touch it." Mom's tone made my fingers recoil. "Someone broke into her house. They left a note."

My mind reeled. Her tidy, beach bungalow was in a safe, gated neighborhood where everyone looked out for each other. My uneasiness swelled.

Footsteps bounded down the stairs. Brady and Sophie stumbled into each other at the sight of our aunt.

"Oh, no!" Sophie's hands flew to her face. "Is she dead?"

"For Pete's sake," Mom shook her head. "What's with you kids? No. Aunt Jules fainted. It happens."

"When did she get here?" Brady crossed to the couch. His lanky, fifteen-years-and-growing body towered over Mom and patient. "Is she sick?" He crouched beside me.

Mom ignored his question. "Carry Aunt Jules upstairs to Brock's bed. She's hurt…and who knows what else. Prop her feet on a pillow."

Aunt Jules moaned when Brady scooped her up.

"Sophie, get an ice pack and a glass of water," Mom ordered. "And Sadie"—she gave me a serious look—"Call your dad. Tell him 'code: curator.'"

"Code? We have *codes* now? I thought all of our bizarre, family secrets were finally out in the open." I was treading on thin ice. But the last six weeks had uncovered a host of skeletons from our family's creepy closet. Living specters that had rocked my world.

"Not…now." Mom looked ready to snap.

With a huff, I turned to find the phone. I used speed dial to call my dad at the Camas School of Cosmetology, the cosmetology college he owned. His occupation was only one of the numerous quirky things about my family. It helped that I was homeschooled—yeah, that qualified as quirky too—so we didn't constantly have to explain things like this to multitudes of people.

"Camas School of Cosmetology. This is Dinah. How may I direct your call?"

"Dinah? Hey, it's Sadie. I need to talk to my dad."

"Sorry, Sadie. Your dad hasn't come in yet. Did you try his cell?"

"What? Are you sure?" I leaned against the wall. "He left like two hours ago. I didn't try his cell. He keeps it silent at work."

"Hmm. Lemme double check. I'm usually the first person to see him, but maybe he snuck past. Hold on."

I held on and walked into the kitchen, dodging Sophie and her icepack and water. "Oh, my goodness."

My two-year-old brother, Nate, sat in his booster seat, covered in oatmeal. In all the uproar, the poor kid had been left to mind his manners strapped to his chair. Cradling the phone on my shoulder, I grabbed a bunch of paper towels and mopped the gummy stuff from his face.

"Sadie? No sign of your dad. Sorry."

"Okay, thanks for checking. I'll try his cell." The oatmeal had migrated to my fingers. I leaned over the table and let the phone plop from the crook of my shoulder.

Nate clapped his sticky hands together, making slimy, suction noises between his fingers. "Mushy. Mushy." He smiled at the goo. The pale-colored oatmeal contrasted with his chocolaty Ethiopian skin. I envied my adopted brother's year-round tan.

"Yep. It's mushy, little man. Hang on." I crossed to the sink for more wet towels and caught sight of my youngest sister outside on the tire swing. "Hey, Nicole," I called through the open kitchen window. "I need your help. Come 'ere."

She slid open the patio door and peeked inside. A pink, plastic tiara nestled lopsided in her honey hair.

"Would you finish cleaning up Nate? I have to do something for Mom."

"Sure." Nicole took the paper towels and zeroed in on the moving mound of muck. At only seven years old she tackled most of Nate's needs with the skill of a seasoned babysitter.

I picked up the phone and headed to the privacy of the living room. Something about using code words made me feel like I better keep the convo under the radar. While Dad's cell rang, I wandered to the front window and pondered the cryptic meaning of my mother's words. *Curator? Isn't that an old person in charge of a museum or something?*

"You've reached the voicemail of Liam Larcen..."

I caught sight of my haphazard reflection in the window. I didn't want to dwell on the pimple on my chin, the cowlick in my brown locks, or the smudged mascara I forgot to wash off the night before. Instead, I focused my attention past the mess that was me and peered outside while I waited for the voicemail beep.

Is it kosher to leave code words in a voicemail?

Aunt Jules' old VW Beetle was parked crooked in our driveway and blocked both of our family vehicles. She obviously parked it in a hurry.

Wait.

"Oh my!" I smacked the phone on the windowsill and booked it upstairs. "Mom! Mom!" Nausea swirled in my gut. I whipped around the corner and skidded to a stop in my brothers' bedroom. Everyone —that was conscious— jerked their heads in my direction.

I took a deep breath, then another, dreading what I had to say.

Mom paused in the middle of placing a blanket over Aunt Jules. "Sadie, please. Spare us the dramatics."

I slowly exhaled. "Dad's car is still in the driveway. He never went to work."

The blanket slipped from Mom's hands. "What?"

"His car. It's there. In the driveway." The words impregnated the room with sinister implications. My mind flashed back to earlier this summer, when both my parents went missing.

Mom shook her head. "No. He kissed me goodbye. I

watched him walk out the door."

Sophie shoved the icepack at Brady and brushed past me.

"Sophie!" Mom's eyes flashed. "No, ma'am. Get back here."

Sophie shuffled back in the room, arms crossed and chin set.

Mom raised a warning finger. "*No one* goes outside."

"Amy?" Aunt Jules' eyes were still closed. "What's going on?"

Mom clasped her hand over Aunt Jules's clenched fist. Unconscious or not, Auntie kept a stranglehold on her scrap of paper. "Someone broke into your house, remember?"

Aunt Jules's mouth pressed into a frown, an uncommon sight for the cheerful woman. She blinked. The swollen bruise twitched. Her gaze settled on Mom. "I know what happened t' *me*, pet. Did somethin' happen to Liam?"

Mom bit her lip. She appeared to weigh the wisdom of sharing bad news on top of bad news. "Uh, not sure. He left for work a couple of hours ago, but his car's still here."

"Ya think it's related to what happened to me?" Aunt Jules tried to roll onto her side. Her emerald eyes winced with the effort.

Mom gently pushed her back to the pillow. "That remains to be seen. I still don't know what happened. You barely made it into the house, mumbling about a break in, when you passed out." She handed Aunt Jules the icepack. "Here, use this on your eye. When you're feeling better, we'll talk."

Aunt Jules shoved the pack away. "Won't be needin' that. Nothin's wrong with me that a steamin' cup o' tea won't fix. It's painfully clear we've got loads of talkin' to do."

"Um..." Sophie looked at us like we'd been struck with amnesia. "Dad's *missing*. Shouldn't we call the police?"

"It's true, your father's not here." Mom swallowed. "But...that doesn't mean he's missing. I mean, not in *that* way. It's doubtful." Her voice grew quiet. "Not after what happened before."

"Family meetin', doodlebugs. Soon as the kettle whistles." Aunt Jules worked her legs out of the blankets.

"Nonsense." Mom barred her way. "You've had a terrible scare. You're hurt. Now lie down and ice your eye...please. We'll bring you the tea."

"Amy Ann Larcen! If I say I'm fine, then I'm *fine*." The spunky little redhead swung her legs off the bed and stood. "I won't be lyin' here when earth-shatterin' events are takin' place right under our noses. You've no idea how serious this is."

Sophie, Brady, and I exchanged troubled glances.

Mom looked resigned to Aunt Jules' insistence but grabbed the icepack. "Fine. But you're going to keep this on your eye. You've got a terrible *periorbital hematoma*, and it needs attention."

"Poppycock!" Aunt Jules straightened her twisted, velour sweat suit. "Don't throw that highfalutin medical talk at me, *nurse* Amy. Nobody dies from a black eye. If ya don't mind, I'd like to speak to ya about *this*"—she waved the scrunched paper at us—"or somebody else is likely to go missin' while I'm lyin' here like a helpless lump o' sugar."

"Yes, let's talk about that." Mom looked like everyone was teetering on her last available nerve. "Before we do anything else, would you mind explaining what kind of burglar beats up their victim and leaves a note?"

"It wasn't a burglary." Aunt Jules shook her flaming curls. "Nothin' valuable is missin'. These intruders weren't thieves, chipmunk. Leastways, they weren't today because they didn't find what they came for. Which is why they left this for me." She indicated the note and sat back down on the edge of the bed.

Mom looked puzzled. "Okay..."

"Ya think me brain is addled, don't ya?" She leveled her gaze at Mom. "Listen, sweet pea. There's somethin' stirrin'. And it has to do with me late husband."

Mom shifted her weight and looked impatient. "I'm not following you. What could the intruders possibly want in regards to Uncle Daniel? He's been dead for over thirty years."

I shifted closer to my brother and sister. Their expressions a mixture of confusion and skepticism—just like my brain.

One lone tear slipped down Aunt Jules's cheek. "Thirty-eight years, actually." She stroked the crinkled letter repeatedly across her lap. Her head shook slowly. "This note. I wouldn't believe a word of it, but..." Another tear dripped.

"But *what*?" I burst out.

"But I'd know this handwritin' anywhere. I know who penned these here words like I know the wrinkles on me own face."

Mom lowered herself onto the bed and placed a gentle hand on top of our aunt's nervous fingers. "*Whose* handwriting?"

Aunt Jules let out a ragged sigh. "The date, see?" She pointed. "This note was written last week. But I'd swear by the dragon's lair that the handwrit n' belongs to me dear husband, Daniel."

The Flaming Sword releases October 1, 2016

ACKNOWLEDGMENTS

ELEPHANTS ARE PREGNANT FOR TWENTY-TWO MONTHS. *The Tethered World* took six years to birth. I'm not sure what kind of creature that makes me, but finally it's . . . a book! And it didn't arrive by stork or by zookeeper. It came because many people believed, prayed, worked, and cheered me along. For each individual, I'm beyond grateful.

Thank you, Billy, for your unwavering faith in the gifts God has given me. This story wouldn't exist without you. A dozen years and two laptops later, dreams are becoming reality and it's so much sweeter because you're willing to dream alongside me. I love you, Superman!

Thank you McKenzie, Garrett, Delaney, and Olivia for letting me read adventures to you from the Greats, and for listening to some rather dull stories of my own along the way. You guys have all patiently waited to read *The Tethered World* because—y'know—I've been a mean mother and made you wait until there was a real book to hold. Hope you recognize a bit of your own childhood within its pages. In the process of writing this tale, you've gone from being little kids to young adults. I'm sad that we won't be sitting around the table and reading this together after dinner. Time waits for no author to become published, I'm afraid.

There's no love quite like a mother's. I'm blessed to still be on the receiving end of that fierce, my-daughter-can-do-anything kind of love from my mom (aka Joanie). Thank you for always being there, Mom. I love you back!

Behind every debut author is a seasoned mentor showing the novice the ropes. Susan Marlow, you've been my mentor and friend since I reviewed your story, *Trouble with Treasure,* six years ago. Thank you, Smarlow, for taking me under your wing, for persevering through my rough, *rough* draft of *The Tethered World,* and for holding my hand while I hobbled along the path to publication. Your editorial prowess is second to none and I continue to learn from your attention to detail. The Lord has used your wisdom, encouragement, and friendship in boundless ways.

Many sets of eyes and hands have helped to whip this novel into shape. The team at Mountain Brook Ink was providentially brought into my life and has been such a pleasure to work with. Miralee Ferrell, your professionalism and enthusiasm are contagious, and I hope to be worthy of your continued faith. Lynnette Bonner, your cover design absolutely nailed the feel of my story, and I'm so glad you and Miralee ignored my creative crisis. Nikki Wright, I'm glad I didn't have to face the scary road of publicity on my own. Thank you for your help in that endeavor.

A good content editor is worth her weight in iced lattes (those are *very* valuable to me). Judy Vandiver, you've gone above and beyond—and back again—and it's been a joy to work with you and get to know you. I'm quite sure it's not coincidence that so many things in my tale reflect many things in your own life.

Carol Robb, your keen eye and desire for "more" helped enrich the story on many levels. I'm grateful for the time we spent working together.

To my sisters in the Manet Writer's group, I'm incredibly thankful for each of you. Your encouragement, love, and laughter, your talents and insight...all add up to a great joy and delight in my life. I know my adventure is only the first to be published among the many worthy tales told around coffee and finger foods.

Friends and family from SWCC, TAFA, Redeemer, Fort Worth, Mississippi, and beyond... your lives have had a beautiful impact on my own. I love you all. I wanted to share this experience with you by adopting your name (not your likeness!) in one way or another wherever I could. My *nod* to our relationship and what you mean to me. If you cannot find yourself in this story, remember there are two more to be told. Or, you might have a name I can't quite contrive :-)

I would also like to give a shout-out to my cousin, William Love, for mapping the Tethered World for me. Your artistic gifts have helped to bring the adventure to life even though I've been there in my imagination for many years. I love it!

Above all, and extending beyond my capacity for words, is my gratefulness to a loving and merciful God Who has allowed me to fulfill a lifelong dream. He owes me no such thing. He's given me everything in Christ. I lack nothing, even if I never write again. But He *does* give in such abundance and *does* allow more than I deserve. As such, He has given me this great, joyful opportunity.

All glory to Him!

ABOUT THE AUTHOR

HEATHER FITZGERALD grew up in Orchards, Washington (considered part of Vancouver). She loved creative writing and loathed math. In third grade she began her first book, *Rubber Bands and Mashed Bananas*, pounding it out on an old-fashioned typewriter. With no typing skills or knowledge of white-out, Heather eventually gave up.

Though she married and settled down in Texas, "write a book" remained on her bucket list. Family life included homeschooling four children, one with autism. A favorite pastime was reading adventures with the kids. After they read through The Chronicles of Narnia, Heather's desire to write became too powerful to ignore.

She began to blog and work on story ideas. When author Susan K. Marlow read Heather's review of her book, *Trouble with Treasure*, she contacted Heather and asked, "Are you a writer?" By God's grace, Susan saw something in Heather's writing and began to mentor her.

Heather joined North Texas Christian Writers and attended writing workshops. A prompt from Susan sparked Heather's original ideas for *The Tethered World*. This book is the result of six years of writing and a gazillion edits (with equal parts coffee). Though the novel is YA Fantasy, Heather prefers to call it Family Fantasy. She hopes families will read it aloud and enjoy the adventure together.

The Tethered World
Discussion Questions

1. Sadie felt embarrassed by her parents' occupations. Was there ever a time when you felt that way about someone in your own family (their personality or occupation)? How did you deal with it? Did you learn to appreciate that person's unique personality or occupation, or was it always a struggle?

2. Sadie preferred reading about adventures over experiencing them. Brady and Sophie, on the other hand, were excited to face the unknown. Like Sadie, have you been forced out of your comfort zone and into situations beyond your control? How did you handle those circumstances? Did you find yourself focused on your own discomfort or did you learn to embrace the challenge, and maybe even enjoy it? If you're more like Brady and Sophie, explain how you approach new challenges, even when they may be scary or intimidating.

3. Sadie found herself making faulty judgements based on her fears and/or how she perceived others. From the dragon, to the Toboggans, to Reiko, Sadie often let her fears or preferences hold her back. Can you give an example of how you have misjudged a person (or Gnome) from a first impression? Do you think your reaction to such encounters can cause others to misjudge you in return?

4. Of course, discernment is wise and valuable. There were times that Sadie questioned whether Chebar could be trusted, or if she could tell a good Dwarf from a bad one. Since villains don't wear name tags—and often disguise

themselves as the good guys—how can you wisely interact with others without being paranoid or prejudiced?

5. Sadie and Sophie had very different personalities. Compare and contrast the sisters and how they worked through their conflicts. How did they learned to help each other in spite of their differences? How have personality clashes affected you, for better or for worse?

6. In the end, Sadie realized that God's faithfulness brought her family through very challenging circumstances. She admitted that He was there, often when she wasn't aware of it. Discuss the times in your life when God brought you through overwhelming situations. Were you mindful of His guidance all along, or did you look back and see how He carried you, even when you felt hopeless and alone? Do such times help you face new challenges with a greater awareness of His hand on your life?

More Ways to Tether Yourself to The Tethered World

Learn more about the characters
and creatures of The Tethered World:

www.heatherllfitzgerald.com

When you visit,
Sign up for Heather's newsletter
and be the first to learn about the release of
Book Two, *The Flaming Sword.*

Search for "Heather L.L. FitzGerald" on Facebook.

Follow The Tethered World on
Instagram: Tetheredworld

Tag your quirky and mysterious photos with
#tetheredworld hashtag too!

Twitter: WriteFitz

Follow Sadie Larcen on Pinterest:
www.pinterest.com/sadielarcen

Follow Amy Larcen's Bigfoot Blog:
www.landoflegend.net

I would love to hear from you,
however you like to stay connected!

Cast of Characters

(in order of appearance)

Sadie Larcen: bookish, sixteen-year old girl; prefers reading about adventures over experiencing them; fears roller coasters and failure; resides with her family in Orchards, Washington.

Lt. Garrett & Deputy McKenzie (aka Unibrow & Barbie): officers from the Clark County Sheriff's Department that alert Sadie to her family's van being abandoned

Amy Larcen: Sadie's mother; leading expert on Bigfoot; blogs about all things myth and legend, particularly Bigfoot; visit her blog at www.landoflegend.net

Liam Larcen: Sadie's father; cosmetologist; kidnapped with his wife, Amy.

Brock Larcen: age fifteen; autistic twin to Brady; excellent memory and excels at karate; prefers a schedule and the number seventeen.

Brady Larcen: protective twin to Brock; easygoing and bighearted; Sadie's right-hand man in the Tethered World.

Nate Larcen (aka Nate the Great): adorable, adopted brother from Ethiopia; almost three years old.

Sophie Larcen: clever and adventurous eleven-year-old sister; pretends to live in medieval times.

Nicole Larcen: sweet, seven-year-old sister; a big help with her baby brother.

Great-aunt Julie (aka Jules): fun-loving Irish aunt and twin sister to Judith; sculpts garden gnomes; reveals the Larcen family history to Sadie and her siblings; resides in Cannon Beach, Oregon.

Dragon: winged reptile the size of a small bus; powerful neck and tail; phosphorescent skin; resides topside; alternates lairs between Beacon Rock and Haystack Rock.
- Odyssey: transports the Larcens to Beacon Rock

Leprechauns: stand approximately two feet tall; well-proportioned bodies; male leprechauns born with a beard; affinity for moss, mushrooms, and gold; reside in the Hallows of Nimmickdell.
- *Skoon*: leads the Larcens through the belly of Beacon Rock and into the Woods of Willowmist

Meadow Faeries: resemble butterflies with tiny arms and legs, carried by gossamer wings; transport the Larcens to Vituvia in their faery cyclone; reside on plant stems in the meadow between the Woods of Willowmist and Vituvia.

Gnomes: approximately eighteen inches tall; stout bodies; pointy hat adds another eight inches; small but deadly; will protect the Sword of Cherubythe at all costs; reside in Vituvia
- Sir Noblin: Premier Advisor to the Queen
- Revonika: Noblin's assistant; in charge of public relations
- General Muggleridge: military advisor
- Colonel Smarlow: Chief of Covert Reconnaissance
- Reiko: head of Special Forces
- Mighty, Muscle, and Zest: siblings part of Stealth Gnomish Warfare and Clandestine Operations (SGWCO)

Dwarves: half as tall and twice as wide as the average Topsider; fond of facial hair and pipes; reside in the Berganstroud Mountains.
- Chief Wogsnop: leader of the Dwarves of Berganstroud; head of the Berganstroud army
- Glavashian (aka Lava): soldier in the Berganstroud army; has a special connection to Sadie
- Joanie: motherly nurse/housekeeper; cares for Sadie and Sophie

Sleeping Serpents: snakes that spawn in Brodger Creek; three to six feet in length.

Clovenboars (aka Toboggans): curvy horns, fangs, and dreadlocks; about the size of a panther; the Gnomes' transportation; able to see invisible Leprechauns; native to the wilds of the Tethered World and in the paddocks of Berganstroud and Vituvia.

Dark Dwarves (aka Stygians): same build as Dwarves; pale, grayish skin; patchy hair and beard; allied with the Trolls; reside in the dens beyond Berganstroud.

Trolls (aka Bigfoot, Yeti, Sasquatch): hairy, broad-shouldered creatures; ape-like faces; XXL foot size; reside at The Eldritch at Mount Thrall.
  - *Chebar*: sixth son of Chief Nekronok
  - *Nekronok*: chief Troll; prefers to be addressed as "Worshipful Master"; wants control of the The Flaming Sword of Cherubythe

Queen Judith (aka Queen of Vituvia): energetic twin to Jules; retiring soon; savant; resides in Vituvia.

Nephilim: Traditionally considered half angelic, half human; average height eight feet; well proportioned; wings a recessive trait, mostly seen in the royal family; see Genesis 6:4; reside in Calamus.

Prince Alexander (aka Xander): first-born son of the royal family; assists the Larcens in rescuing their parents; commands the Nephilim army; infatuated with Sadie.

King Aviel and Queen Estancia: rulers of Calamus; assist Vituvia in their war with the Trolls.

Gage: seasoned soldier and Xander's right-hand man.

Ogres: large and thick-bodied; average seven to eight feet tall; lumbering, and not well spoken; sweat profusely; enjoy torturing humans before using them for

stew meat; love a good riddle; reside on the Isle of Skellerwad in the Sulfur Sea.
- Announcer: unnamed Ogre during the Human Games
- Brumley: captures Brady

Hippogriffs: winged creatures with the head, breast, and talons of an eagle, and the back legs and rump of a horse; offspring of a mare and a Griffin; easier to tame than their legendary counterpart; ridden by Trolls in the war against Vituvia; reside in the wild and in Craventhrall.

Elves of Willowmist: slender, petite creatures with pointy noses and ears; shy but playful; can turn invisible; reside in the Woods of Willowmist.